THE DARK BELOW

I0823681

ALSO BY SHERRY RANKIN

The Killing Plains

THE DARK BELOW

SHERRY RANKIN

This is a work of fiction. Names, characters, organizations, places, events, and incidents either are products of the author's imagination or are used fictitiously. Any resemblance to actual persons, living or dead, or actual events is purely coincidental.

Text copyright © 2026 by Sherry Rankin
All rights reserved.

No part of this book may be reproduced, or stored in a retrieval system, or transmitted in any form or by any means, electronic, mechanical, photocopying, recording, or otherwise, without express written permission of the publisher.

Published by Thomas & Mercer, Seattle
www.apub.com

Amazon, the Amazon logo, and Thomas & Mercer are trademarks of Amazon.com, Inc., or its affiliates.

EU Product Safety Contact:
Amazon Media EU S. à r.l.
38, avenue John F. Kennedy, L-1855 Luxembourg
amazonpublishing-gpsr@amazon.com

ISBN-13: 9781662521171
eISBN: 9781662521188

Cover design by Will Speed
Cover image: © Bob Pool © Nature Peaceful © vvvita / Shutterstock

Printed in the United States of America

For Deb, Steven, Shelly, and Al, with love and thanks

We grow accustomed to the Dark—
When Light is put away—

—Emily Dickinson

Prologue

Cody Puckett sat still in his saddle on the lip of a shallow arroyo, gazing across the darkened scrubland. He'd been riding the range, keeping watch since nightfall, and his insides felt hollow and cold. The microwave burrito he'd eaten for supper had worn off hours ago. Where the hell was Chase?

He'd promised to be back at the ranch by one to take his turn on guard duty, but he was probably drunk again, passed out in an alley somewhere. The Navy was supposed to have made a man out of him. But as far as Cody could tell, Chase was still the same irresponsible jackass he'd been in high school. Cody had been a little kid, back then. But he remembered a lot.

Cody sighed and rubbed his burning eyes. It was nearly three a.m. The November moon, smoky and yellow, was already sinking behind the rim of the Callahan Divide, which reared up like a line of broken teeth, black against the stars. He pulled out his phone, shielding the glow with his hand. No missed messages—just his own long string of increasingly furious, profanity-ridden texts.

He reread them and winced. Chase might be a screw-up, but he was Stan Loudermilk's son—and Cody owed Stan a lot.

He shoved the phone back into his pocket, and shivered. A chill wind was rising, edged with frost. The stars looked sharp and hard. In the distance, a pack of coyotes broke into a chorus of staccato yips and howls. The Appaloosa gelding nickered uneasily.

Time to move.

Cody turned the horse and picked his way along the arroyo's edge until the clatter beneath the gelding's hooves told him he'd reached the old military service road. The base had been decommissioned for fifty years, and the blacktop was so cracked and weed-choked that it was almost invisible. East, it led to the ranch's fence line, where a cattle guard opened onto Route 137. West, it ran to the abandoned missile silo—a place Cody avoided, though Chase had always found it strangely fascinating, as if it held some dark secret he already half knew but still needed to hear. Could that be where he was hiding? He went there, sometimes, to be alone—or to sober up.

Cody sat still, fingering the reins. In the distance came a faint metallic groan. Gooseflesh rose on his arms. Against his thigh, he could feel the rifle in its leather scabbard, solid and reassuring. The horse tossed its head and nickered again.

Cody clicked his tongue and nudged the gelding into a brisk trot, heading west.

After a mile, he reached the silo and stopped. All was quiet. Strange that there was so little above ground to mark the massive structure below. The flat disc of the silo pad lay gray and empty in the moonlight.

Cody sat still. Nothing moved but the night breeze through the switchgrass. Then, he heard it again—the creak of heavy iron. It came from the access port a few yards off—an angled structure that jutted from the desert floor like a cement outhouse.

He dismounted, tossed the reins over a cedar bush, unholstered his rifle, and walked toward the port. In the silence, his boots crunched loudly on the caliche.

Rounding the corner, he stopped. Chase's pickup was parked under the big mesquite on the far side. He must be down in the silo.

But something was off. The port's heavy steel door and outer metal grille stood ajar. They were never left open—not even when someone was inside. Preventing unauthorized access was Stan's strictest rule. They'd had problems with vandalism before—local teenagers, drunk and goofing around. But it was dangerous.

Too many ways to get hurt in the silo. Last thing we need is a lawsuit, Stan always said.

A gust of wind caught the grille. It creaked again.

Cody took out his phone. No use trying Chase—no reception underground. He pulled up Stan's number, then hesitated. Stan would want to know if Cody had checked inside. And what could he say to that? *I'd rather stab myself in the eye with a rusty ice pick than go down there alone at night*? He could already hear the sigh. "Fine, I'll be there in ten," Stan would say—but he'd be thinking something else.

Cody switched on the flashlight app and checked the pickup. The keys dangled from the ignition. Chase's Stetson sat on the dash. Cody placed a palm on the hood. Cold.

Gripping the rifle in one hand and his phone in the other, he approached the port. The Maglite Stan kept on a hook behind the door was missing. The phone's weak beam illuminated only the first few steps of the access shaft—a winding five-story staircase that plunged into the earth.

Back in the '70s, when they'd decommissioned the place, the Air Force had stripped it bare—lights included. Chase the Prodigal had returned home last fall with a plan to turn the silo into a money-making venture. He and Stan had started renovations. They had work lamps down in the launch control room and in the main missile chamber. But not on the stairs.

Cody stood on the top step, sweating despite the chill. *If Chase freaking Loudermilk can do it, so can you.*

His fingers felt clammy on the rifle's stock. He swallowed. Then, with a deep breath, he stepped through the doorway and into the dark below.

Chapter 1

No one was speaking.

Teddy Drummond noticed the silence and came out of her reverie with a start. Eighteen pairs of eyes were fixed expectantly on her. She'd been staring at a desk by the window—a desk that should have been occupied, but wasn't. Its vacancy made her uneasy, like the first low rumble of thunder on a sunny afternoon. Not that it was unusual for undergraduates to cut a lecture now and then. But this absence worried her.

Teddy blinked and looked around. What had she missed? A plump, pink-skinned boy was standing near the back of the classroom, holding his phone. He cleared his throat.

"Professor Drummond?"

"I'm sorry, David—what's the question?"

"What do I do if the subject keeps telling me to go fuck myself?" He gestured toward the only other student not seated—a wiry girl in a Cowboys sweatshirt, also holding a phone.

Giggles from the students. The girl in the sweatshirt popped her gum and grinned.

Teddy pulled herself together. "In police work, hostage negotiation's about trust. You're there to make sure everyone gets out safe—including the offender. You've got to make *her* believe that."

"Yeah, but how?"

"Keep her talking. If she's talking, she's not shooting. Go ahead—try it again."

David looked unsure but raised the phone to his ear. The girl gave him a provoking wink. *She's gonna eat him alive*, Teddy thought. *And so will the criminals.* He wasn't really cop material, but telling people that never worked. They had to learn the hard way. It was an exasperating process to watch.

Her eyes drifted back to Chase Loudermilk's empty desk. She'd been frustrated with him lately, too—but for different reasons. He'd enrolled in her Intro to Criminal Justice class in the new year, and it hadn't taken long to see he was something special. Sharp, observant, good with people—eager for a law enforcement career. A former Navy diver. Nice guy, though with a hint of vulnerability in his eyes that suggested he'd been through a lot. He seemed to Teddy like someone dropped into the wrong life and fumbling for a way out. He reminded her of her younger brother, Curtis, in the year or two before his death—tentative, uncertain, wearing hope like a layer of raw, new skin.

Chase was one of those students you couldn't help being drawn to, no matter how impartial you tried to be. It wasn't often someone with his potential landed at a dusty little community college in the middle of West Texas.

But this semester was another story. Teddy had hardly recognized him when he'd walked into the classroom in September—disheveled, withdrawn, disengaged. He'd spent the first two months of term staring out the window, or hunched over his desk, scribbling in a sketchpad—when he showed up at all.

After four years, Teddy was starting to realize teaching could be as exasperating as police work.

"Bang!"

She snapped back to the girl in the Cowboys sweatshirt, who was aiming a finger gun at David. She blew imaginary smoke from the barrel and holstered it with a flourish.

"She shot me," David said. "What now?"

Before Teddy could respond, a short, dark-haired girl raised her hand. "Can I ask a question, Dr. Drummond?"

"I'm not a doctor," Teddy said automatically. "What's the question?"

The girl licked her lips, nervous but steady. "I heard you shot a guy during a hostage situation once. What went wrong?"

A hush fell. Students shifted uncomfortably—some curious, others embarrassed.

Teddy felt the familiar, clutching knot in her gut. *What went wrong*. It was a question she carried like a scar—numb and faded, but painful underneath. One she'd long since learned not to touch.

Her gaze flicked to the clock above the door. Almost three.

"You can't control everything," she said. "Ultimately, the perpetrator's a free agent." She knew she sounded defensive. She closed the textbook and reached for her bag. "We'll pick up here Wednesday."

As the students filed out, a slender boy in a tracksuit approached.

"Professor, me and my project partner were supposed to meet this morning, but he stood me up. He's not in class, either."

"Who's your partner?"

"He sits there."

The boy pointed to Chase Loudermilk's desk. Light from the window sliced across the laminate. The chair was pushed back, like a question left hanging.

Teddy slung her bag over her shoulder. "I'll reach out to him."

Emerging from the classroom, she was mildly surprised to find Donald Waddell, the chair of the Political Science Department, waiting in the hallway. A podgy, balding career academic, he'd offered her the adjunct gig at a particularly low moment in her life, when she'd been on administrative leave, pending investigation. The pay was less than she'd made as a detective, but Waddell had sold her on the regular hours and lower stress.

And he'd brushed off her lack of an advanced degree. "In a Criminal Justice program like ours, real-world experience is priceless."

Quitting the force had been a relief, and Teddy had hoped the career change might save her floundering marriage. It hadn't. But maybe nothing could have.

"Happy Monday," Waddell said. "How was class?"

Teddy glanced around. No students nearby. "I'm not the right person to teach hostage negotiation, Don."

Waddell waved the concern away. "They've heard things—they're curious. Teachable moment."

"It's not something I want to talk about." She turned to go.

He fell into step beside her. "There's a detective here to see you."

Teddy stopped. "Who? Why?"

"Raina Bragg. She's in your office."

Teddy blinked. The name landed like a weight in her chest—familiar but almost forgotten. Her fingers tightened on the strap of her bag. "Thanks for the heads-up."

Heart pounding, she ducked into the ladies' room to shake him off and gather herself. It was empty. She dropped her bag by the sink, turned on the tap, and gulped cold water.

Straightening, she brushed back a few strands of mouse-brown hair and met her gaze in the mirror. "It's only Raina," she whispered. "You've known her all your life."

Her reflection frowned back. Did she always look like that? There was a kind of guarded tautness in the high-cheekboned face, a wary caution in the hazel eyes that hinted at years of watchfulness, a habit of reserving judgment. Once a cop, always a cop.

What did Raina see when she looked at her? Did she ever reach for the phone and stop herself, the way Teddy sometimes did?

Teddy tossed the paper towels into the trash can and picked up her bag, heading for the stairs.

Chapter 2

As an adjunct professor with little seniority, Teddy had been assigned the smallest space in the Political Science Department that could be called an "office." It had a bleak institutional look that she hadn't bothered to alleviate, though Maureen, the department's administrative coordinator, had tacked up a few promotional posters "to give it a pop of color." The office held a desk, a bookcase, and two straight-backed chairs. One was already occupied when Teddy walked in.

Raina Bragg stood and adjusted her gray blazer. She was in her early forties, sturdy and tough-looking, with close-cropped, silvery hair and faint acne scars on her cheekbones. A detective's badge hung on a chain around her neck—a badge she was proud of, Teddy knew.

Raina's expression was unreadable. She pushed up her heavy-framed glasses and nodded. "Hi, Teddy."

"Hi, Raina. Been a while."

Silence. The women studied each other. Stone Creek was a small town, but they'd worked hard to keep out of each other's way for the past five years. Raina looked worn, the skin around her lips and eyes more puckered than Teddy remembered.

She's thinking the same about me, Teddy thought. They were the same age, after all—and the intervening years had been tough on both of them. Now they were staring at one another across an unbridgeable divide.

"Close the door," Raina said.

Teddy complied, tossing her book bag in the corner. She sat behind the desk. "How've you been?"

Raina remained standing. "This wasn't my idea, so let's skip the chitchat."

Teddy brushed a few eraser crumbs off the desk. "Did the Health Department file another complaint against my dad?"

"This isn't about Milton. The county can bulldoze his rat's nest and slap you with elder abuse charges, for all I care."

Teddy felt a quick flash of the old resentment. She'd only done what any cop would've, under the circumstances.

"What do you want, Raina?"

Raina stared over Teddy's head at a promo poster of students tossing a frisbee. She looked both sullen and nervous. "The Chief sent me. We need some help."

"Funny way of asking."

"Are you going to help, or not?"

"Depends. What's going on?" Teddy gestured to the opposite chair.

Raina hesitated, then sat. "Chase Loudermilk's a student of yours?"

A sudden twinge of anxiety constricted Teddy's throat. She knew by Raina's expression that it showed. "Yeah. Why?"

"What can you tell me about him?"

"I don't know him that well—personally, I mean. He just started the program in January. But he's the kind of student you remember. A veteran, mid-twenties. More mature than most college kids. Best in the class, actually. He seemed to know what he wanted. But something changed over the summer. This semester, he's been different."

"How so?"

"Depressed, maybe. I smelled alcohol on him in class a few times. At this rate, it'll be a miracle if he passes Police Systems and Practices."

"Did you ask him what's wrong?"

"Yeah, of course. He wouldn't say. I figured it was a breakup, or maybe trouble at home. He's been living with his folks while he goes to school. That can't be easy." Teddy frowned, running her thumbnail along the edge of the desk. "I thought he was doing better, though."

"Better, how?"

"He came to see me a few weeks back. More like himself—asked if I'd give him a second chance, let him turn in some missed work. Said he'd been dealing with personal stuff, but he was getting help."

"From who—a therapist?"

"Didn't say. But that's what I figured."

"You believed him?"

"For the last three weeks, he's done great. Then today he bails on his project partner and skips class." Teddy shifted uneasily. "Why? Is he in trouble?"

Raina was watching her closely. "You could say that. He's dead."

Teddy stared. Something twisted inside, a wave of nausea rising. She swallowed and forced herself to focus. "When? How?"

"He was found this morning just after six, inside a derelict missile silo on his family's ranch. Dewayne Forrester found him—machinist at the John Deere plant."

"Yeah, I know Dewayne. What was he doing out there so early?"

"Scuba lessons. Silo's full of groundwater. The Air Force pulled the sump pumps fifty years ago when they decommissioned it. Chase was a Navy diver. He's been giving lessons to help pay for school. Dewayne showed up at five-fifty to get a dive in before work. Said Chase always met him topside to help carry gear. His truck was there, but no Chase. The silo door was open, which was odd. So he went in and found him—on the dive platform."

Raina pulled out her phone and handed it over. Teddy flipped through the photos. Most were dim and grainy. A young man in jeans and a blood-soaked Patagonia jacket lay on his back on wooden planking. His right hand clutched a pistol. The mouth and jaw were mangled and bloody, but she recognized the eyes, the dark-blond hair. A fan-shaped plume of blood and tissue extended from the upper left side of his head.

Teddy had a sudden, sharp memory—her father's voice on the phone, tinny and slurred. "Curt's dead. You need to come home."

Her chest tightened. She took a long, slow breath. She'd seen dead bodies many times, but it was different when you knew the person well—and when they were so young. What a damned waste.

Teddy handed back the phone. "Suicide?"

"Looks like it. It's his own pistol—a .500 Smith & Wesson Magnum. Gift from his grandfather. Huge gun. He shot upward, through the mouth. His dad says it's the only handgun he ever used, and he never loaned it to anybody. Kept it in a lockbox in his closet. Plus, he left a note."

Raina swiped through more photos, then passed the phone back. The screen showed a close-up of a crumpled sheet of notebook paper. Block capitals, heavy and uneven. The bottom had been torn away. Teddy enlarged the image.

I CAN'T LIVE WITH MYSELF ANYMORE
PLEASE HELP, WHAT I DID
IS UNFORGIVABLE, MATTHEW, CHA—

"That was next to him," Raina said. "Most of his name's missing, but his mother swears it's his handwriting. You agree?"

"I wouldn't know. Student assignments are all word-processed, nowadays. But it sounds like him. He had terrible punctuation."

Teddy stared at the screen. The handwriting looked young, unformed—like it had all the time in the world to settle into itself. A depressing thought.

She shook it off. "Who's Matthew?"

"No idea. Chase's phone and laptop are missing, so we haven't been able to check his contacts. We were hoping you'd know."

"He never talked much about his personal life—not to me. What do his folks say?"

Raina shrugged. "Haven't really questioned them yet. They were too upset this morning. The Chief asked them about the note and the gun. His wife was Inez Loudermilk's sister, you know."

"Is that why you're here? Wally's getting pressure from the family?"

"Ever met them? Inez is super religious. She's insisting Chase didn't kill himself. It's clearly suicide, but the Chief wants to keep her happy." Raina hesitated. "You said Chase was depressed?"

Teddy leaned back. "Yeah, but it's strange." She opened her laptop and scrolled through emails. "He wrote last Thursday, asking for reference letters."

She turned the screen, and Raina scanned it. "He was transferring?"

Teddy nodded. "At the end of term. Didn't seem to care where, as long as it was far away. If he was suicidal, why bother?"

"People aren't always logical when they're spiraling."

"Maybe." Teddy stared at the screen. "Let's see those pictures again."

Raina's eyes narrowed, but she handed over the phone. Teddy scrolled rapidly.

"What are you looking for?" Raina asked.

Teddy stopped on a close-up. "I knew something didn't sit right."

Raina snatched the phone back. "What? What is it?"

"Gun suicides usually go through the temple or mouth, right?"

"He did shoot himself in the mouth."

Teddy shook her head, staring down at the mangled wet void—all that remained of Chase Loudermilk's lower face. "His mouth was closed. The bullet went through his teeth." She tapped the screen. "Ever seen that?"

Raina frowned. "Makes no difference. It's instant lights out, as long as you hit the brain."

Teddy gazed at the photo and tried to imagine Chase's last moments. Would anyone—no matter how desperate—press the muzzle of a gun to their own clenched teeth and pull the trigger? Raina was right—closed mouth or open, it didn't matter, really. And yet there was something so repellent in the thought . . .

Teddy looked up. "It's weird, don't you think?"

"His hands could've been shaking. Maybe it went off early."

"He was ex-military, used to high-pressure situations."

Raina scowled. "What are you saying—that it's staged? Someone killed him?"

Teddy thought of Chase in class last week, leaning over his notes—focused and alive.

"It's unusual, that's all. If I were you, I'd dig deeper."

Raina rolled her eyes. "The oracle has spoken." She pocketed the phone.

"Don't get defensive," Teddy said. "It's just—when you rush the call, you miss things."

"The JP thinks it's suicide. So don't tell me how to do my job." Raina pushed back her chair and stood up.

"Come on, Raina. You asked."

"About his state of mind—not manner of death. You're not a detective anymore." She buttoned her blazer. "I've got what I needed. Thanks."

She slung her purse over her shoulder and left without saying goodbye.

Teddy sat motionless, staring at the wall. They'd once been inseparable—maids of honor at each other's weddings, academy roommates, rookies together on the Stone Creek force. Raina had always been a good cop. Conscientious. Detailed. But she lacked detachment—the ability to stand back from things, to reserve judgment—which had hampered her career. It had been Teddy who'd been promoted to detective after Will Potts retired. Raina only got the badge after Teddy quit.

Was Raina up for the challenge of an investigation like this?

Teddy tapped her pencil on the laptop's keyboard. Then she checked the time. Four o'clock. Julia and Henry would be finished with choir and football practice soon.

She texted Alan: *Can U pick up kids? Something came up.*

Then, shrugging on her jacket and grabbing her purse, she walked out, slamming the door behind her.

Chapter 3

Teddy made the twenty-mile drive north up Route 137 with Tim McGraw blaring from the radio. She hated country music and usually drove in silence. It was her time to think. But today, silence was the last thing she wanted. The gray-green blur of the scrubland rushed by as she fixed her eyes on the yellow centerline, willing herself not to remember that sweltering June afternoon five years ago.

"Don't go there, don't go there," she whispered to the rhythm of the road.

Avoidance—not the healthiest coping strategy, the shrink used to insist. But thinking about things was worse. The events of that day haunted her, the *what-ifs* following her like swarms of biting flies.

What if she'd never made detective? Someone else would've caught the call that day. It wasn't the kind of thing that happened often in Stone Creek. Most complaints were routine—domestic altercations, bar fights, DUIs. In fact, towns this size usually didn't have detectives. Major investigations, when they arose, got bumped to the sheriff's office or to the Rangers.

But Stone Creek, on the northern rim of the Concho Valley, was close enough to San Angelo to inherit its problems and justify having a detective on the municipal payroll. Meth had hit the region hard. Fatal overdoses. Vehicular manslaughter. And lately, a string of horse thefts—still a felony in Texas.

But nothing had prepared her for that terrible day.

Strange how so much could hinge on a single afternoon, Teddy thought. Days passed, quiet and unremarkable—until one came along that began like any other but exploded like a hydrogen bomb, splitting so many people's lives into a *before* and an *after*. That's why the *what-if* game was useless. Everything that happened was stacked on top of countless decisions, like the teetering junk piles in her father's house—each one random and incidental and utterly far-reaching. Some she'd never talk about. Not to Alan. Not to Berna. Not even to herself.

What if she'd never become a cop? She hadn't meant to. When she'd left home at eighteen, the plan had been college, then law school, then anywhere—as long as it was far away. But her family was a black hole, impossible to escape.

If she hadn't quit school when her brother Curtis died, she might be a successful attorney by now. But her father would probably be dead. And after Danny went to prison, her nephew Shane would've ended up in foster care.

Then again, maybe Curtis wouldn't have killed himself if she'd stayed. Or if they'd had a decent childhood. If their mother hadn't left. If their father hadn't been such a screw-up.

If, if, if. She could chase the *ifs* forever. But there was nothing to point to—nothing to blame. Just billions of choices that had somehow coalesced with the remorselessness of gravity to put Detective Teddy Drummond at that house on Boxhill Drive on June 17, 2020 . . .

In the aftermath, Raina had blamed Teddy. That hurt—but Teddy understood. Pain and rage couldn't be felt in a vacuum—they had to land somewhere. Like water vapor looking for a surface on which to condense.

Over the years, Teddy had sent her cards, texts, voicemails. All met with stony silence. Nothing could bridge the divide between them now.

She'd done the right thing—the only thing she could, under the circumstances. At least, that's what she told the voice that woke her at three a.m. whispering, *You could've tried harder. You could've done more.*

It didn't matter. No answer could satisfy that voice. A thing could be right and at the same time horribly wrong.

"Don't go there!" she said aloud, startling herself.

The scrubland reeled by, and Tim McGraw wailed. Teddy rolled down the windows and let the cool November air rush in, whipping her hair wildly around her face. She breathed deep, then shut the window, smoothed her hair, and cranked the music louder.

After twenty miles, she spotted yellow police tape stretched across a gate on the west side of the road. A utility cruiser sat on the shoulder, a young officer hunched on the running board, tapping his phone. When he saw her, he thrust it in his pocket and leapt to his feet.

Teddy rolled down the window. "That how you stand guard, Ortega? Playing Call of Duty?"

Ortega, a fresh-faced kid barely out of high school, reddened. "Candy Crush. You're the first car in twenty minutes." He swallowed. "Gonna tell the Chief?"

"I don't work for him anymore. Let me through, and we'll call it even."

"Can't. Chief's orders. Official business only."

"This *is* official. Detective Bragg consulted me this morning."

Ortega blinked. Everyone in the department knew about the bad blood. "Maybe I should check." He reached for his radio.

"Suit yourself. I'd hate to accidentally mention the Candy Crush thing."

He froze, thumb on the button. "Aw, c'mon, Ted."

"Relax, Ryan, I'm joking," Teddy said. "Get the tape—I'll tell the Chief I bullied you into it."

Still doubtful, Ortega held up the police tape. Teddy drove beneath it, tires grumbling on the cattleguard, and followed a dirt track a mile through empty scrubland to a broad, crumbling roadway. In the brush stood a rusted, bullet-pocked sign:

DEADHORSE MISSILE SILO
AIR FORCE RESTRICTED AREA:
AUTHORIZED PERSONNEL ONLY

The weeds hissed beneath the truck's chassis as she followed the abandoned service road. It was a pretty area, she thought—open scrubland scored with dry creek beds and dotted with yucca and prickly pear. A long rim of ragged bluffs skirted the horizon to the southwest. Closer and to the east ran Deadhorse Mesa, its flanks dark with thickets of juniper and sapodilla.

Strange how few signs of military occupancy remained on land that had once been home to a major Air Force installation. No derelict barracks or Quonset huts—only this broken roadway, half swallowed by the desert, like the set of some postapocalyptic Western.

After two miles, Teddy spotted a cluster of vehicles ahead—Stone Creek police SUVs, a sheriff's van, and Chief Ramirez's dusty gold Suburban. Uniformed officers were milling around, a few smoking. She recognized most of them. They turned to watch as she pulled up and got out.

When Raina had mentioned a missile silo, Teddy had visualized something tall, like the grain elevator west of town. But she saw only a paved disc sixty feet wide, like a helipad, and beyond the sheriff's van, a concrete hut, its heavy metal grate and door standing open.

As Teddy approached, Raina came out of the hut, a flashlight in her hand. She froze when she saw Teddy. "What the hell are you doing here?"

Before Teddy could reply, Chief Wally Ramirez emerged behind Raina, nearly knocking her sideways. He was a tall, broad-shouldered man in his early sixties with coarse, grizzled hair and a leathery face. He gave Teddy a curt nod as he switched off the Maglite.

"Wait here, Bragg," he said.

Raina stopped him. Teddy couldn't hear the words, just Raina's fierce whispers and the Chief's low, even replies. Finally, he shook his head, put his hands on her shoulders, and steered her aside. She threw up her hands and stalked away through the grass.

Ramirez started toward Teddy but paused when he spotted a trio of patrolmen nearby. "Are you jackasses smoking? This could be a crime scene."

"Thought it was a suicide, Chief," said the shortest of the three, a sulky-looking officer Teddy didn't know. He had thinning dark hair and a petulant mouth, like a prematurely balding Elvis.

"Shut up, Fiske. Are you a medical examiner? Till there's a death certificate, we treat it as suspicious. That's protocol. And y'all better not be throwing them butts on the ground. If I gotta pay a crime lab to sort out your hillbilly DNA from real evidence, it's coming out of your paychecks." He snatched the cigarette from Fiske's mouth, stubbed it out on his Maglite, and jammed it into the man's breast pocket.

Teddy hadn't seen Ramirez in a few months. As he approached, she was surprised at how rough he looked. His eyes were red-veined and sunken. He needed a haircut.

She opened her mouth, but he cut her off, hooking a hand under her elbow and leading her out of earshot.

"Why are you here, Drummond?"

"You sent Raina to ask for my help."

Ramirez crossed his arms. "You know damn well that wasn't an invitation to join the case. I just wanted some background."

"If that's all you wanted, you'd've sent someone else. You knew Raina'd get me fired up. Guess what—it worked."

Teddy glanced past him. Raina had apparently walked off the edge of her fury and was glaring in their direction, hands on hips.

"I sent Bragg because she knows what she's doing," Ramirez snapped. "Didn't want your opinions filtered through one of *those* ding-a-lings." He jerked a thumb at the loitering officers. "Last thing we need is a public blowup between you two. This is Bragg's case. You're not a cop anymore."

"You know I'm qualified. It's not like you fired me—I quit. And I've got a current PI license."

"No one's hired a PI. Go home. We'll talk later."

Teddy started to argue, but stopped when her phone rang. She checked the caller ID. Her daughter Julia, fifteen and a sophomore in high school. Teddy's heart sank. Had Alan missed her message about picking up the kids?

But no. Julia and Henry were home doing chores in the barn. Something was wrong, though.

"Fancy won't eat, Mom. She's pawing the ground. I'm scared it's colic."

Teddy groaned. Horses were exasperating, always getting something wrong with them. "Too easy to spook, and too many guts," Berna Robles, the local vet, liked to say.

Teddy didn't much enjoy riding, but she'd ended up with several horses over the years. Other things, too. Stone Creek had no Animal Services Department, and police were always being called out to investigate and sometimes confiscate neglected and abused animals. Teddy, with her old department ties, inherited many; and Berna channeled even more her way in exchange for free vet care.

She rehomed those she could. The rest stayed. Currently, her hobby farm was home to one horse, seven goats, three pigs, a dozen dogs, countless feral cats, and a blind donkey named Sebastian.

"You're a *sucker*," was Alan's opinion. Teddy's zoo, as he called it, had been a point of friction between them. It drained money and made vacations impossible.

"We never have fun anymore," he used to say.

Teddy sighed into the phone. "With this cool weather, she's probably not drinking enough. Walk her, see if she'll take water."

"Can you please come home?"

Teddy glanced at Ramirez. He was showing signs of impatience. "I'm in the middle of something, Jules. Be home soon as I can."

"Then I'm calling Berna."

"Don't. She's not supposed to do large animals anymore. If you need help, find Shane—he's either at the greenhouse or at Grandpa's. Call me if Fancy's worse."

She hung up. Ramirez was scowling toward the cruisers.

Teddy cleared her throat. "Look, Chief, I know you care about this case. Chase was your nephew, right?"

"By marriage. What's that got to do with anything?"

Teddy lowered her voice. "I'm thinking this might not be a suicide."

That got his attention. "Why?"

Teddy told him about Chase's transfer plans and her suspicions regarding the fatal shot. "Could be nothing. Raina's photos aren't great. I thought if I saw the scene . . ." She paused. "C'mon, Chief—half an hour. Chase was my student. I want to help."

Ramirez ran his knuckles along his jaw. He looked back at Raina, then sighed. "What the hell. You're here. A walk-through won't hurt. Maybe you'll catch something we missed."

"Evidence techs been through?"

"They're in there now. When they're done, we can move the body. But if the ME rules it suicide, it's case closed."

"Doesn't feel right to you either, huh?"

Ramirez hesitated. "Just covering my bases, Drummond. Once the scene's turned back over to the family, that's it."

"Where is the scene? I don't see any silo."

"We're standing on it. C'mon, I'll take you down."

Chapter 4

Teddy followed Ramirez toward the concrete hut. Raina waited nearby, arms crossed. She had put on mirrored sunglasses, hiding her expression.

Teddy let the Chief do the talking, not that he ever said much. After his wife's first cancer diagnosis, all he'd told the station was, "I'll be out a few days. Potts is in charge." Two years later, the eulogy he gave at her funeral was the first time Teddy had heard him publicly reference Eula's illness.

Now, he said simply, "Teddy's gonna take a look. Lead the way, Bragg."

Raina hesitated, then turned without a word. A few broken cinderblocks and empty five-gallon paint buckets were piled against the wall of the hut. One of the cinderblocks had been co-opted as a doorstop, keeping the steel grate and door from blowing closed in the brisk autumn wind.

As Raina stepped forward, Teddy stopped her. "Talk me through it first. Is this the only entrance?"

Raina said nothing. Teddy turned to Ramirez, who nodded.

"Stan keeps it locked, but Dewayne Forrester found it open this morning." He pointed to a battered white pickup beneath a mistletoe-strangled mesquite. "That's Chase's. Tailgate was down, windows up. Key's in the ignition, hat's on the dash. It was like that when Forrester arrived."

"Locked?"

"Nope."

"Know what time Chase got here?"

Ramirez glanced at Raina, who scowled behind her glasses.

"Told his folks he had Bible study, then bowling with some friends. Said he'd be home before one, but never showed."

"Should be easy to verify," Teddy said.

Raina's scowl deepened. "His dad says he sometimes sleeps in the silo—especially when he's been drinking."

"So he could've come back any time?" Teddy looked around. "No CCTV?"

"Only at the main gate," Ramirez said. "Nothing's on that footage. He probably used the east gate, like you did."

"Any cameras in the silo?"

"No. Not much of anything down there."

Teddy walked toward the white pickup. The others followed, Raina muttering something under her breath.

At the truck, Teddy peered through the window.

"Did Forrester notice whether the engine was hot or cold?" she asked.

"No, but it was cold by the time I got here around seven," Raina said. "Chase's body was already stiff. He'd been dead for hours."

Teddy looked in the truck bed—a couple beer bottles, a blue tarp, a few mesquite twigs, and a globe of mistletoe, freshly snapped at the stem. She glanced up. The lowest branches of the mesquite tree hung six feet above the bed.

"Wonder what broke off this mistletoe? Nothing on the truck's tall enough to hit it."

"Maybe it came from somewhere else," Raina said. "Could've been riding around for days."

"It's not wilted. And why's the tailgate down?" Teddy scanned the area. "If Chase was hauling something, where is it?"

"Enough with the Sherlock Holmes routine." Raina turned to the Chief. "We going down, or not?"

Ramirez ignored the question. "We missed that about the mistletoe, Bragg. Make sure the techs bag it with the rest."

They walked to the concrete hut, and Teddy looked through the doorway. A steep flight of stairs plunged into darkness.

"Glove up, everyone." Ramirez produced a packet of blue nitrile gloves from his pocket.

Raina snapped on a pair, pulled her flashlight from her belt, and ducked inside.

Ramirez unholstered his Maglite. "Follow me. Fair warning—it's cramped in there."

There was no handrail, though drilled holes in the wall showed where one had once hung. The military had stripped the place bare. Teddy had always had a problem with tight spaces. The Chief knew that. He also knew why, and had never given her grief about it on her performance reviews, though he'd required her to seek professional help when it interfered with her job. A few sessions with a counselor in San Angelo had helped, but hadn't cured the phobia.

The stairwell was narrow, encased in concrete. Descending behind Ramirez, Teddy worked to control her breathing as she groped along the wall. Raina was twenty-five steps ahead, a dark silhouette against the Chief's flashlight beam. Periodically, the stairs leveled out and turned sharply, passing through massive steel blast doors a foot thick and curved on one side, standing open on rusty hinges the size of fire hydrants. The air grew colder, with an earthy, mildewed smell. Hollow echoes magnified their footsteps.

Fifty feet down, they caught up with Raina in a small vestibule. A dark passage opened at the far end. But on the left, bright light was spilling through a doorway.

Teddy followed the others through it, and blinked.

After the gloomy, claustrophobic stairwell, the room in which they now stood seemed dazzlingly bright and spacious. It was a large, circular chamber, freshly painted white and shaped like a hollow donut. In the center, a massive steel column towered from floor to ceiling. The place was lit by a pair of halogen work lamps near the door.

"This is the silo?" Teddy asked. "It's smaller than I imagined."

Ramirez shook his head. "Launch control room, back in the day. Chase was using it as a staging area for dives."

The room was sparsely furnished—a card table, two metal folding chairs, and a ratty sofa with wooden arms and orange plaid upholstery. Vintage seventies, by the look of it. A rolled-up sleeping bag rested on one end; a stack of faded beach towels on the other.

Wire shelving along the wall held a microwave, a mini-fridge, and bins of supplies. A wetsuit, fins, and other diving equipment were piled in a heap against the wall.

"Quite a set-up," Teddy murmured. "You said Chase slept here sometimes? Looks like he practically lived here."

Her eyes landed on the card table. A camo-colored backpack sat beneath it.

"That's his," she said.

Raina nodded. "His laptop and phone aren't there. They weren't in his truck, either."

"What about the house?"

"Checked his room this morning. Nothing."

"He might've left his laptop somewhere," Teddy said. "But a kid his age doesn't go anywhere without his phone."

"He could've ditched it. Maybe didn't want his folks going through it after he died."

"Can I look in the backpack?"

Raina frowned. "I checked it. Just a notebook, doodles, a couple textbooks."

"Fresh eyes can't hurt, Bragg," Ramirez said.

Raina's jaw tightened, but she shrugged.

Teddy knelt and unzipped the pack. Inside, she found a notebook, an accounting textbook, and *Criminal Investigation* by C. P. Gilchrist. She held it up. "This is for my class."

She flipped through it. A pink rectangle fluttered out—a 3x5 notecard, folded in half. Teddy opened it. Handwritten in heavy block capitals were the words "ONE TRUE THING."

"I guess we missed that," Raina said, leaning in. "What's it mean?"

"Beats me." Teddy stood up.

Raina pulled up something on her phone and angled the screen toward Teddy. "Chase's suicide note."

They compared it to the notecard.

"Handwriting doesn't match," Raina said.

Ramirez cleared his throat. "Ever seen that card in class? Was Chase using it as a bookmark or something?"

"Maybe. Can't say that I noticed." Teddy pulled out her phone and snapped a picture.

"Let's bag it," Ramirez said. "Might get prints."

Teddy handed the notecard to Raina and knelt again. She pulled out the notebook. It was college-ruled, with the lines printed in pale blue ink.

"Suicide note's on the same kind of paper, but we can't prove it came from that pad," Raina said.

Teddy leafed slowly through it, studying its contents.

Twenty years ago, during her brief stint in college, she'd spent each class writing frantically in notebooks like it, trying to keep up. These days, most students took notes on their laptops or tablets, if at all. A lot of them didn't bother, since many professors posted their lectures online.

So she wasn't surprised to find in it only doodles and sketches—horses, birds, West Texas landscapes.

Chase had been a skilled artist. She'd seen him scribbling in class but had no idea he'd had this kind of talent.

Among the drawings, she recognized the outline of Deadhorse Mesa. Another depicted a sheer white cliff with water lapping at its base. At the top, among a stand of dark pines, human figures were visible. Others floated in the water below.

Teddy frowned thoughtfully at the drawing. Nowhere near Stone Creek looked like that. West Texas bedrock was red, not white. Was this an actual place? Something from a dream? On impulse, she snapped a picture and turned the page.

When she reached the end, she closed the notebook and stood. "That Chase's gear?" she asked, nodding at the dive equipment by the wall.

Ramirez looked to Raina, who nodded. "I assume. It's labeled 'C. L.'"

"Wonder if Chase usually kept it here?"

"I'll find out."

Teddy felt a brief, nostalgic pang. The back-and-forth was like old times. They'd been a good team, once. She snapped a few more pictures around the control room, then gestured to the work lights. "Were those on when you got here?"

Raina nodded. "We haven't touched them. Dewayne told us he didn't either."

"Are they always left on?"

"Stan says no," Ramirez said.

"Hmm. So where's the body?"

"Main missile chamber. This way."

Chapter 5

Teddy followed the others out of the launch control room. Raina and Ramirez switched on their lights and turned left into a dark passage, even narrower than before, with Raina leading. As they made their way down more flights of stairs, the sense of claustrophobic oppression grew. The weight of the earth above them pressed down like a giant hand—as if gravity itself were increasing with each step. Teddy tried to focus on the flashlight beams that jumped and juddered along the walls—but her vision blurred, and she felt light-headed.

"You okay, Drummond?"

Ramirez was a few steps below, looking up at her, and Teddy realized suddenly that her breaths were coming in ragged gasps that echoed off the concrete.

She stopped. "It's a little narrow."

"You should've stuck with that therapist." Ramirez climbed back toward her. "Close your eyes. Hold onto me. We'll be through the worst of it soon."

"I'm okay—" she started.

"Dammit, Drummond, just do it."

Teddy sighed, put her hands on his shoulders, and closed her eyes. Step down. Step down. Step down. Their footfalls reverberated in the stairwell. She could hear the creak of Ramirez's leather belt.

Even Raina's tread sounded sharp and close, though she was thirty feet ahead.

"Here's a landing," Ramirez said. "Left turn. Right turn. Now more stairs." He was narrating their progress, trying to keep her grounded.

The humidity had risen, though the temperature had dropped. Teddy's shirt clung to her damp skin. After more steps, the passageway leveled out.

Ramirez stopped. "Okay."

Teddy opened her eyes.

Ahead stood a gaping steel door, its frame as massive as some prehistoric dolmen. Above it, a rusty sign read: "DANGER: AUTHORIZED PERSONNEL ONLY."

She followed the others over the threshold and into a tunnel even narrower than the stairwell. It was circular and made of corrugated metal streaked with rust. The air was dank and cold. Water droplets clung to the ceiling. One struck Teddy's cheek; another slid coldly down the back of her neck. She shivered and walked faster.

At the end of the tunnel, a faint light glowed. An icy breeze struck her face. The echoes intensified in the still air. She sensed open space ahead.

"Easy. Watch your step." Ramirez caught her arm as she pushed forward.

Teddy stopped. Her breath smoked in the frigid air. "Damn."

They were standing on a metal ledge, like a small railed balcony, high on the wall of an immense vertical shaft some sixty feet across. Far above, nearly hidden in shadow, a pair of colossal steel doors stretched across the ceiling. A city bus could have dropped between them. Teddy looked over the railing. Water glimmered far below, its mirrored surface black as ink in the dim light. Drops plinked and echoed in the cavernous space, rippling the shadows that danced along the curved concrete walls.

To Teddy's right, a gap in the railing opened onto a narrow flight of steel steps descending to a wooden platform that floated on the water. On the platform, a single halogen work lamp cast a stark circle of light. Two figures in disposable white coveralls were moving carefully around something sprawled on the planking.

Teddy looked away. "This place is unbelievable."

"You're only seeing a quarter of it," Ramirez said. "That water's a hundred and forty feet deep. Only spot in Texas that meets the specs for deep-water dive certification—unless you drive to the Gulf."

"That's how Chase got the idea to offer lessons?"

Ramirez nodded. "I helped him and Stan build that platform last spring."

"How does a private rancher come to own something like this?"

"Military built dozens of these silos in the sixties, after the Cuban Missile Crisis," Ramirez said. "Most were decommissioned and the land sold off years ago."

"Are they all full of water?"

Ramirez shrugged. "The ones in West Texas are. Water table's pretty high."

Teddy had seen photos as a kid—black-and-white images of the installations in their prime. But nothing could capture the terrifying reality of this place. She tried to imagine the silo without the water—a massive missile filling the empty space, towering eight stories into the shadows above, aimed squarely at the Soviet Union and loaded with a warhead hundreds of times more powerful than the bomb that destroyed Hiroshima.

At the same time, she knew, on the other side of the planet, some other missile had waited out the Cold War in some other silo with its sights trained on West Texas.

The world could've ended before I was born, she thought. The idea made her dizzy.

Forcing her mind back to the present, Teddy stared down at the two white-suited figures bent over the body of Chase Loudermilk. This silo, designed for death, was both a terrible and a strangely fitting place to die.

Aloud, she asked, "What do people do with these places—besides give scuba lessons?"

"Mostly nothing," Ramirez said. "It's the ranchland that's valuable. The silos are a nuisance—they attract kids and thrill-seekers. Lawsuits waiting to happen. But you can't demolish them. It'd cost millions. Most folks just lock 'em up and ignore 'em."

"I've heard of some being turned into doomsday bunkers," Raina said, speaking for the first time since they left the control room.

Teddy squinted into the gloom. "Can we go down? I'd like to look at the scene."

Raina shrugged. "We've come this far."

Ramirez holstered his Maglite. "Careful. That water's freezing."

Teddy followed them down the steep metal stairs, which were more like a ladder, she thought—the prefabricated accordion type. They were slick with condensation and swayed beneath her feet. Her fingers cramped with the effort of clutching the rails.

As they stepped onto the dive platform, the techs looked up and nodded. Behind them, Teddy glimpsed Chase Loudermilk's blue-jean-clad legs and his ratty black Chuck Taylors, with doodles on the rubber toes and frayed, knotted laces. He'd worn them often to class. A heavy sadness settled on her shoulders.

She knew how to put aside emotion during an investigation, but she hadn't often dealt with the deaths of people she knew well. In her mind, she saw Chase at his classroom desk, hunched over his notebook, dark-blond hair falling over his face. She pushed the image away.

"You have a tendency to run from pain and fill up the space with work," the San Angelo shrink had told her once.

No shit, lady. Who doesn't? Teddy remembered thinking. But what she'd said was, "I think I'm done with therapy for a while."

"How's it going, boys?" Ramirez called to the techs.

One was kneeling beside a case, stowing an expensive-looking camera. "Almost finished. Five minutes, and the scene's yours."

Teddy looked around. The platform was maybe fifteen feet square. On one side, a small inflatable dinghy floated, moored to a cinderblock perched on the edge. Near it, a metal dive ladder descended into the dark water, every rung visible in sharp detail. She was surprised. The water was actually crystal clear, though at first glance its surface appeared as black and impenetrable as polished obsidian.

She tried to imagine Chase—whose freckles and unkempt hair had made him look like a teenager—climbing down that ladder in fins and a wetsuit, heavy air tanks on his back, regulator in his mouth. What would it be like to step off the bottom rung and sink one hundred and forty feet into icy darkness—to feel the crushing weight of water as the abyss swallowed you whole? What kind of person did that—or wanted to?

Teddy shuddered and looked back up the narrow stairs. "How are you getting him out? You can't fit a stretcher down that, can you?"

Ramirez rubbed his neck. "Sheriff's sending one of them basket stretchers, like they use for canyon rescues."

"Hope we can get it done today," Raina said. "Sooner the ME has the body, the better."

They waited as the crime scene techs packed their gear.

"We'll check the truck next," the taller one said, peeling off his mask.

Ramirez nodded. "Bag everything—including the twigs and mistletoe."

When they were gone, Teddy followed Ramirez and Raina across the platform. Although she'd seen pictures, she wasn't prepared for the sight of Chase Loudermilk's body. He lay on his back two feet from the water, his eyes wide and staring. His mouth was a red, wet wound. Congealed blood had matted his hair and pooled on the decking, turning the wood black. The techs had wrapped both his hands in paper bags to preserve any evidence. They'd also collected the teeth and bone fragments she'd seen in Raina's photos.

Teddy stood for a long moment, staring down at her former student. She remembered him in her office, twisting the strap of his backpack. *Sorry I've been such a screw-up. I'm gonna do better—I swear. I'm getting help . . .*

It was impossible to look at him now without remembering that other time—that other body—five years ago. There'd been no time to think, to weigh consequences—just training and muscle memory.

The recollection left a bitter, coppery taste in her mouth. She blinked, forcing the image away. Guilt had a flavor of its own. "He looks surprised."

"Sudden deaths always do," Raina said. "Even suicides."

"Why is that?"

"Death's always a surprise, I guess." There was an edge in her voice, sharp and familiar.

Teddy avoided her eyes. "I'm glad Dewayne found him. Thank God his family didn't have to see this." She winced. "Sorry, Chief. I forgot he's your wife's nephew."

Ramirez stared at the body, his expression unreadable. "At least Stan and Inez won't need to ID him."

"How'd they take the news?"

"Like you'd expect." Ramirez sounded slightly defensive. "They were in shock. We kept it brief. Asked a few basics, took a look at his room. I told them we'd talk again soon."

"Any chance I could sit in?"

Raina's eyes darted to Ramirez, but she said nothing.

"We'll cross that bridge," he said slowly.

Teddy nodded. She scanned the platform. "Where's the gun?"

"Bagged it. Note, too," Raina said. "Didn't want them getting knocked into the water. The sheriff doesn't have deep-water divers. We'd have to call in the Rangers."

"You might want to call them in, anyway."

"Why?"

"Chase's phone and laptop are missing, right? If you were down here and needed to hide something, what would *you* do?"

Raina and Ramirez both turned and stared at the black, still surface of the water.

"Oh, shit," Raina said.

"You think—" Ramirez began, but a clatter on the steel stairs cut him off.

All three turned. A young officer was descending toward the platform. Teddy recognized her—Bertie Loomis. She'd been hired shortly before Teddy left the force.

"Chief, hey Chief—" Loomis called.

"Stop there, Loomis. Stay off the platform," Ramirez said. "What's up?"

"Phone call—for Drummond."

"Who is it?" Teddy asked.

"Your ex. Says it's urgent."

Teddy sighed. Alan's idea of "urgent" rarely matched hers. Probably couldn't find Henry's orthodontic wax or something. When he'd pitched the idea that they should both continue living in the house while they paid off Henry's medical bills, she'd warned him he'd need to pull his weight. And to his credit, he seemed to be trying—though his girlfriend took up a lot of the slack at times, Teddy had noticed.

Still, he'd gone to a lot of trouble to track her down. Had something happened to one of the kids? Alan was a good dad, but he had a tendency to panic in a crisis.

She nodded to Loomis and tucked a strand of hair behind her ear. "I'll come."

Ramirez handed her his Maglite. "Hope everything's okay."

Chapter 6

The long climb back through the silo's dank, narrow passages felt less suffocating than the descent. Teddy focused on Loomis's heels in front of her and tried not to scroll through her inner database of disaster scenarios. But it was hard not to.

Stay in the moment. Don't react till you know what you're dealing with, the shrink used to say. But she wasn't a cop. Police work burned away the denial most people wore like armor. Cops saw enough to know bad things could happen to anyone.

Teddy allowed the fear to propel her up and up. Eventually, the bright rectangle of the access port appeared above them like a beacon in the darkness.

Emerging into the sunlight, Teddy squinted against the sudden glare. Compared with the silo's icy chill, the autumn air felt warm. The county crime-scene techs were combing through Chase's truck, while several Stone Creek officers loitered by their vehicles, chatting. Teddy shook her head. If she'd still been a detective, she would have ordered them to begin a grid search.

At her truck, she checked her phone. A dozen missed calls and texts—from Alan and Julia. And one from Berna Robles, the vet.

Shit. The horse.

When Julia had called earlier, the mare hadn't sounded that bad. But colic could turn critical fast.

Teddy hit speed dial. Alan answered on the first ring.

"Where the hell have you been?" His voice was high with panic.

"Long story." She climbed in and started the engine. "What's going on?"

In the background, she could hear Julia's sobs, the frenzied whinny of a horse, men shouting.

"Fancy started rolling and thrashing," Alan said. "Shane couldn't get her up. Julia's terrified, having a meltdown. Berna's here now, with some guy. But they're not having much luck."

As Teddy shifted the pickup into second gear, she heard a muffled murmur. Then Alan again: "Here's Berna."

Berna Robles had been the only large-animal vet in Stone Creek for three decades. She and Teddy had bonded over their mutual concern for neglected animals. She was immensely experienced and utterly unflappable. If anyone could get a handle on the situation, she could.

"What's the story?" Teddy asked.

"Horse is down," Berna said. "If she keeps rolling, she'll twist."

Teddy groaned. An intestinal twist was the most severe type of colic—often fatal. "Think she's twisted already?"

"A rectal's the only way to find out," Berna said. "But Rick can't do one while she's thrashing."

"Rick's the new guy?"

Berna was sixty-two, with osteoporosis. "Just my luck," she'd told Teddy when she got the diagnosis. "Black women don't usually get this—it's supposed to be one of the perks."

Her doctor had warned her off farm calls. But Berna wasn't ready to retire. A widow whose only child had died at fifteen, she coped by keeping busy. Eventually, she'd agreed to limit herself to clinic work and had finally hired a large-animal vet, though Teddy hadn't met him yet.

"He started last week," Berna said. "Don't worry, Rick knows his stuff. But that horse has to get up, or we're looking at a very bad outcome."

Teddy was approaching the perimeter fence that skirted Route 137. She honked the horn until Ryan Ortega appeared and raised the police tape.

"I'll be home in twenty," she told Berna as she clattered over the cattle guard. "We'll get her up somehow."

Back on asphalt, Teddy floored the accelerator, turning the scrubland into a wheeling gray-green blur.

◆ ◆ ◆

Teddy's hobby farm sat two miles west of town on fifteen acres of cleared scrubland dotted with shinneries of live oak and mesquite. The property also housed Drummond Nursery and Lawn Design—Alan's landscaping business.

Several vehicles were parked in the tall grass beside the barn when Teddy turned up the long, crushed-gravel drive bordering the south pasture. She recognized all but one—a dusty blue Ford F-150. A man she'd never seen before was kneeling in the truck bed, rummaging in a toolbox. One of Teddy's farm dogs—a black-and-white shepherd mix named Skunk—had jumped up beside him and was nosing at his back. But as Teddy parked and climbed out of her pickup, the dog leapt down and ran to greet her.

The man looked up. He was in his mid-thirties, stocky and powerful-looking, with dark hair and a bony, sullen face. His coveralls were streaked with dirt and manure. He looked sweaty and tired. He nodded and wiped his forehead with his sleeve.

Teddy nodded back and scanned the barnyard. Alan was waving from the paddock fence. His thinning blond hair was mussed, and the look on his round, pink, normally cheerful face told her things hadn't improved.

Not that Alan's emotions were a particularly reliable gauge. He tended to freeze up when other people got upset—especially the kids. That was why he preferred plants to animals, she thought. You didn't have to work to make plants like you. And Alan needed to be liked. He was the quintessential "good cop" in their parenting partnership—a fact Teddy often resented.

As she approached, he turned, and she realized Julia was in his arms, sobbing into his shirt.

Berna Robles was leaning on the fence nearby. She was a tall, angular woman with sharp cheekbones and dark, deep-set eyes. Her silver-gray dreadlocks were pulled back into a long ponytail, and she wore patched blue coveralls and rubber boots.

"It's about time," Alan said when Teddy reached him. He gestured at their daughter and mouthed, "What do we do?"

Teddy laid a hand on Julia's shoulder. "I'm here, Jules. We're going to take care of Fancy."

Julia looked up. Her pretty, heart-shaped face was streaked with black lines of mascara. Damp strands of auburn hair clung to her forehead. "This is your fault, Mom—you told me not to call Berna. We waited too long."

Teddy's response was cut off by a shrill scream and loud clatter from inside the paddock. Skunk barked, while Julia sobbed and buried her face again in Alan's shirt.

Teddy turned. Fancy, a chestnut mare with a darker mane and tail, lay near the barn. In her agonized thrashing, she'd gotten wedged against the wall. As she kicked and struggled, her hooves scrabbled on the wood. She couldn't turn over or get her legs under her. She was covered in foamy sweat. Panic showed in the whites of her rolling eyes.

Teddy looked at Alan. "Where's Shane? You said he was helping."

"He got too close—took a hard kick," Alan said. "Cracked a couple ribs, I think. Wouldn't go to the ER. He's walking it off somewhere." Alan gestured vaguely toward the outbuildings behind the barn. "He'll be back."

"What about Frankie? I saw his car." Frankie Aguilar, like Shane, had worked for Alan's landscaping business since high school.

"He's doing deliveries."

Teddy kissed Julia's head. "I'm going to fix this, Jules."

She moved down the fence to Berna. "Has the new guy done the rectal yet?"

Berna shook her head. "Mare hasn't been up long enough. Rick's grabbing some rope. Gotta get her on her feet. A down horse is a dead horse." She kicked at a small stone in the dirt. "Pissing me off, having to watch and not help."

Teddy slipped her arm through Berna's and drew her down the fence line. "If Fancy has a twist, then what?"

Berna lowered her voice. "She'd need surgery. But even if we got her into the trailer, I'm not sure she'd make it to the equine hospital in San Angelo."

"What are you saying?"

"She's twenty-eight, Ted. That's old. She's in a lot of pain. If we can't get her up soon, the kindest thing is to put her down."

"I'm not doing that," Teddy said. "Julia's had enough trauma for one year."

"I brought what we'd need. Just in case."

"I'm not doing that."

Teddy turned and nearly collided with the dark-haired man she'd seen earlier. He had a coil of rope over each shoulder.

He wiped his hand on his coveralls before extending it. "Rick Castillo."

Teddy was in no mood for social niceties. "What's the plan, Rick?"

Rick ran a thumb over his chin and glanced at Berna, who said, "Rick, this is Teddy, the owner."

"What's the plan?" Teddy said again.

"Gotta get her away from the wall. Ain't a one-person job, though. Where's that guy Shane?" Rick looked around.

"I'll help." Berna set a foot on the lowest fence rail.

"No you won't," Teddy said. "You'll break a hip. I'll do it."

Telling Skunk to stay, she climbed the fence and followed Castillo across the paddock, stopping several yards from the horse. Fancy looked spent now. Her eyes were glazed, half closed. Her legs were still crumpled awkwardly against the wall.

"She won't last much longer, will she?" Teddy asked.

"Not like that."

"What—" Teddy began, but turned at the sound of footsteps.

Julia stood behind her. Her face was pale and tear-streaked, but her jaw was set.

"I'm helping."

"It's dangerous, Jules."

"She's my horse."

Teddy glanced at Rick, who shrugged. "Your call."

Teddy sighed. "Stay right by me, Julia. Understand?"

Julia nodded. "What do we do?"

Rick slipped a coil of rope off his shoulder, looped one end into a lasso, and handed it to Teddy. He did the same with the second rope.

"Stay back." He stepped toward the mare and stood twirling the lasso, as if he were waiting for some cue. The horse didn't move.

Rick clicked his tongue. "C'mon mare, let's go. Let's go, mare."

When Fancy didn't respond, he put two fingers in his mouth and let out a piercing whistle.

The horse kicked out feebly. The lasso arced through the air and slipped over the foreleg closest to the wall. Rick backed away, tightening the knot.

"Hold this." He passed the rope to Teddy. "Keep it taut. Gimme that other one."

Panicked by the rope, Fancy jerked and flailed. Teddy nearly lost her grip. Julia rushed in, and together they managed to keep the lasso from slipping off.

The mare kept kicking, and it took Rick several tries to snag the far hind leg.

"Okay," he said. "On three, we back up and pull like hell. Got it?"

Teddy nodded.

"One, two, *three*."

Teddy and Julia both wrapped the rope over their shoulders and tugged. The momentum flipped the mare away from the barn and onto her sternum. Fancy scrabbled, then found her footing and pulled herself up.

Julia started forward, but Rick grabbed her arm. "Watch it! She may go down again."

Whipping a hypodermic from his coveralls pocket, he pulled off the needle cap with his teeth and moved quickly to the horse's head. Before Teddy could react, he had found the jugular with his thumb and plunged the syringe into Fancy's neck. She whinnied and reared, pawing the air as he scrambled away.

"What the hell did you give her?" Julia demanded.

"Tranquilizer."

"Was that necessary?" Teddy asked. "She can barely stand as it is."

"Won't knock her out," Rick said, recapping the syringe. "Just calm her enough I can do a physical."

Julia glanced anxiously at the mare. "To check for a twist?"

Rick nodded.

"What happens if she's got one?"

"Let's not borrow trouble, Jules," Teddy said.

Julia ignored her. "What happens if she's got a twist?"

Rick scratched his forehead. "Depends. If it's bad, best thing's to put her out of her misery."

Julia stared, and her eyes hardened. She turned and walked away.

Teddy threw up her hands. "You don't have kids, do you?"

Rick shrugged. He pulled a bandana from his back pocket and wiped his face. "C'mon, let's back off. Give the meds time to work."

Chapter 7

The sun was sinking behind the darkening tree line as they crossed the paddock. Teddy's nephew Shane was leaning on the fence. His threadbare Wranglers and brown canvas jacket were streaked with dirt, and he held his right arm tightly against his side, breathing hard.

"You look beat," Teddy said. "How do you feel?"

He rubbed his eyes. "Like I been shot with a twelve-gauge."

She patted his shoulder. A few yards away, Alan was gesturing urgently.

"I want to see those ribs in a minute," she told Shane.

She climbed the fence and walked over to Alan.

"What happened?" he asked. "Julia just stormed off fit to kill." He waved toward the barn. "Did I do something?"

"Not everything's about you, Alan. The new vet told her Fancy's chances aren't great." Teddy glanced around. "Where's Henry—at Miguel's?"

Alan stared darkly at Rick, but said, "It was intense out here. Lyric took him inside to play video games."

Teddy felt a sudden rush of annoyance. *What's she doing here at this time of day? We had a deal,* she wanted to say. But this wasn't the moment.

She counted to three. "We need to have another talk about boundaries," she said instead.

Recently, she'd been making a greater effort—verbally, at least—ever since Julia had said: "You're such a cliché, Mom. Women shouldn't trash other women. You and Dad are divorced. Dad's happy. Deal with it."

That had stung. Particularly since, as clichés went, nothing beat a middle-aged man dating a yoga instructor half his age. But Teddy had managed not to point that out.

Alan didn't seem to appreciate her restraint. "Boundaries? You're the one who went AWOL this afternoon. It was your turn to pick up the kids, *and* to cook. I was at a job site. But one text from you and I'm supposed to drop everything." He shoved his hands in his pockets. "You're a teacher now—I shouldn't have to call Dispatch to find out where you are. I thought we were past all that."

"We are. But—"

"Forget the excuses. I'm going to go find Julia."

Teddy sighed. "Don't smother her, Alan. Give her space."

"It's not smothering—it's parenting." He shook his head. "Another argument I'm sick of. Julia's a kid. She needs us."

"She's fifteen. How's she going to learn to handle her own problems if you're always rushing to the rescue like she's a toddler with a boo-boo?"

"Not everyone wants as much emotional space as you, Ted." He moved toward the barn.

Teddy watched him go. "For God's sake," she muttered, turning away.

Berna and Rick stood a few yards off, watching Fancy. The mare was still on her feet but her head sagged, and her lower lip had begun to droop.

"Won't be long now," Berna said as Teddy approached.

Teddy nodded. "I'll check on Shane."

Her nephew was still leaning on the fence, now smoking a cigarette. Shane Spivey was a short, wiry twenty-seven-year-old with sandy brown hair and a narrow face. He was more like a son than a nephew. Teddy and Alan had raised him after her older brother Danny went to prison. Shane was a good kid, though his life hadn't been easy, and he'd struggled off and on with drugs. Lately, though, he'd been doing well.

Teddy laid a hand on his shoulder. "Let's see the damage."

He winced as she reached for his shirt. "Ow! Careful." He peeled off his jacket and tossed it over the fence rail, then lifted his t-shirt. A shallow, crescent-shaped cut and a bruise the size of a dessert plate bloomed along his right side.

Teddy leaned closer. "Perfect hoofprint." She pressed it gingerly. "Is it hard to breathe?"

Shane flinched. "*Damn*, Aunt Teddy." He pulled down his shirt.

"You need X-rays."

"Doctors don't do nothin' for cracked ribs."

"Your lung could be punctured. You shouldn't smoke."

"Lungs are fine."

"We should clean and wrap it, at least. I'm not sending you back to Grandpa's like that. You'll catch tetanus in that junkyard of his."

Shane started to argue, but Rick Castillo walked up.

"Mare's good to go. I'll need someone to hold her head. Even sedated, she ain't gonna like it." From his pocket, he produced a plastic glove the length of a tennis racket.

"I will." Shane set his boot on the bottom fence rail.

"No you don't." Teddy pulled him back. "Go ice those ribs, or you won't be able to move tomorrow."

He turned away, grumbling, and Teddy followed Rick into the paddock.

The procedure went surprisingly smoothly. Fancy stood still, her head drooping almost to the ground, while Rick worked.

"She have a twist?" Berna called from the fence.

"Nope. Impaction." Rick stripped off the glove. "Reckon she's dehydrated."

"How do we fix that?" Teddy asked.

"Tube her. Best do it now, before the sedation wears off. Can you get me a bucket of warm water?"

"I'll grab the gear," Berna said, heading for the van.

The sun had set, and the sky was a deep periwinkle, though no stars were yet visible. Teddy entered the barn and nearly collided with Julia, who was on her way out. Her face was tear-streaked, but she looked calm.

"You okay?" Teddy asked.

"I'm fine."

"Where's your dad?"

"Lyric called. Henry's starving. Dad went up to the house so they could figure out dinner."

Great—one more ball she'd dropped. Teddy felt a flicker of anxiety. She'd meant to stop by the store for more mac and cheese.

It was getting harder to find things Henry would eat. Since the bike accident that shattered his jaw over a year ago, he'd become self-conscious about his appearance—and nervous, even fearful, about chewing.

"How's Fancy?" Julia asked. "Is she—?"

"Good news. The new vet says tubing her should do the trick."

Tears started in Julia's eyes. "Thank God."

While Julia ran to the tack room for a bucket of water, Teddy switched on the pole light and went back to the paddock.

Berna had returned with a long plastic tube and a gallon jug, which Rick was opening. When he saw Teddy, he set it down.

"Listen, your kid can't help this time. Too dangerous. No telling how the mare'll react."

When Julia arrived with the water bucket, Rick picked up the jug and poured in some clear, viscous liquid.

"Mineral oil," he said. "Loosens things up." He looked at Teddy. "Grab the lead rope, will ya?"

Teddy nodded. "Stand back, Jules."

"No way." There was a look in Julia's eye that Teddy knew well. She'd been stubborn from birth.

"You don't want Fancy associating you with something this unpleasant," Berna said, taking Julia's arm. "Let's watch from the fence."

Julia hesitated, then allowed herself to be led across the paddock.

Teddy had never seen a horse tubed before. She held the lead rope while Rick tried to slide the tube into the mare's nostril. Even sedated, Fancy tossed her head, pawing and snorting. Her nose began to gush blood, and with each snort, they were drenched in a gory mist.

"C'mon, you bastard," Rick muttered, pausing to wipe his eyes.

Teddy could hear Julia's anxious voice from the fence line. "Should they stop, Berna? She's losing a lot of blood."

"The tube's irritating a nasal membrane," Berna said. "It'll quit."

After several more tries, Rick managed to insert the tube and pump the oily water into the horse's stomach.

When he had finished, he removed and coiled the tube. His shoulders sagged. He was dripping with water, oil, and blood. In the glare of the pole lamp, he looked comically bedraggled. *I probably do, too,* Teddy thought.

The sedation was wearing off, and Fancy had picked up her head a little. Blood still dripped from her nose.

Julia hurried forward and stood beside the mare.

“Keep a close eye on her for a couple hours,” Rick said, picking up the jug of mineral oil. “Walk her, get her guts moving.” He looked at Teddy. “Wouldn’t leave any horses out overnight—Sid Steffke had one stolen yesterday. Fourth in the county since June, Berna says.” He slung the tube over his shoulder. “Call if the mare starts rolling again. Berna’s got my number.” He nodded goodnight and walked away.

Suddenly, Teddy felt bone-tired. What a day. She wanted to rest. She wanted to check on Henry. She wanted a beer and a three-hour bath.

As she returned the bucket to the tack room, her mind strayed to the Loudermilks, and she felt chastened. Teddy knew grief. She’d lost her mother, lost Curtis. But losing a child—that was different.

How must it feel to sit in a quiet house with your son lying in that cold, dark pit, underground but not buried—while strangers took photos and measurements, as if he were some scientific specimen?

Teddy switched off the tack room light and headed back to the paddock, watching for a few minutes as Julia walked Fancy in slow circles.

When she was confident the mare would be okay, Teddy said, “I’m going to clean up a little. Then I’ll come take over so you can eat.”

“I’m not hungry,” Julia said without stopping.

“Okay, so you can do your homework, then.”

“Just go away, Mom.”

“Jules—”

“It’s a little late to go all parental now.”

“What’s that supposed to mean?”

“Fancy could’ve died. I called you like twenty times this afternoon. If you taught class and came home like you were supposed to, you would’ve been here when everything went to hell.”

Teddy took a breath. "I'm sorry, Jules. I'm sorry this happened."

"Oh my God, Mom. *Seriously?* What next—you're gonna tell me mistakes were made?"

Despite the coolness of the evening, Teddy felt suddenly hot. Her temples pounded. She grabbed the mare's halter. "Jules, look at me. You've had a bad scare, so you're pissed. I get that. But I've had a pretty horrible day myself. I'm going to clean up and check on Henry. I'll be back in an hour. If you need help sooner, call me or Dad."

She let go of the halter and walked away, the dog trailing at her heels.

The sky was black and spangled with stars. Teddy found Berna packing equipment into her van.

"Whoa," the vet said when she saw Teddy's face. "You look fit to be tied."

"I'm so sick of being the bad guy in this family. I quit my job, take a part-time teaching gig to be more present, but I'm the neglectful parent? Meanwhile, Alan has his gal pal practically living with us, but the kids think he's a freaking saint."

"Hurricane Julia strikes again?"

"Cat Five. She held it together while we were working on the horse."

"It's always the storm surge after that gets ya." Berna grinned.

"She's so moody lately. Secretive. What am I doing wrong?"

"Nothing. Julia's just like you. That's the problem. Y'all are both stubborn as army mules. Give it time. In ten years, you'll be best friends."

"You didn't have this with Grayson, did you?"

"Lord, no. We were opposites. Got along great. But if he'd lived, we'd probably be clashing now. That's my point."

Teddy squeezed her eyes shut and pinched the bridge of her nose. "I can't think about it anymore." She looked up. "Where's Rick? I didn't get a chance to thank him."

"Hal Grobiner called," Berna said. "He's got a steer choking—on apples, probably. Same story every fall. Lets his herd graze that orchard of his, then acts surprised when they choke. Rick went to handle it."

"What do you think of him?"

"Dumb as a sock full of soup."

Teddy laughed. "Not Hal—Rick. Do you like having another vet around?"

Berna shut the van door and stretched her back. "Rick's fine. But I'm bored out of my skull, stuck in the clinic all day treating hairballs and infected anal glands. I miss farm calls."

"You made it out for this one."

"Alan was practically hyperventilating on the phone. Where were you, anyway?"

Teddy hesitated, glancing toward the paddock. "Word'll be out tomorrow, so I'll tell you. But I don't want Jules overhearing. Grab your bag—one of the barn cats has some sick kittens. We can talk while you take a look."

Chapter 8

The barn—a metal prefab with stalls, tack room, and hay loft—had garage-style doors at either end. Inside, the air was warmer, filled with the scents of hay and manure and the quiet shuffle of animals in their stalls. Bales of straw were stacked in an open area at the west end. Behind these, in a makeshift nest, a litter of week-old kittens lay curled asleep.

Setting down her black vet case and lowering herself onto a bale, Berna picked up a kitten, which squealed in protest. "Snotty noses and raspy breathing, eh?" She pressed her stethoscope to its chest. "Some kind of rhinovirus." She flipped open her case and grabbed an otoscope. "So, where were you this afternoon? Your phone was off."

"Not off—out of range." While Berna worked, Teddy gave a quick summary of the afternoon's events, though she mentioned nothing about a possible murder.

Berna shook her head. "Oh, jeez. Chase Loudermilk? He was never the same after Grayson died."

"Were they friends?"

"Camp friends, I guess you'd say." She picked up another kitten and set it on her knee. "Ever met his folks? They go to my church. Inez is sweet. Real religious. She homeschooled her kids—was a little overprotective, maybe. So Chase didn't have a lot of buddies around here. But he was at the quarry when Grayson fell."

The kitten was mewling, trying to crawl away. Berna raised a finger in a "hang on" gesture and resumed the exam.

Teddy watched. For years, Berna would go quiet at the mention of her son's name. A decade later, she was talking calmly about the accident.

I guess time really does heal all wounds, Teddy thought. Aloud, she said, "Shane was there. He had a rough time, too." She remembered how withdrawn he'd been after camp that summer. He'd dropped out of school halfway through his senior year. She'd found pot in his room several times. When he was arrested with harder drugs, they'd had to ask him to move out.

"It was traumatic for all those boys. Survivor's guilt."

The kitten shrieked, and the mother cat—a lean calico—shot through the open barn door and leapt onto a nearby bale with an angry hiss.

Berna returned the kitten to the nest and stroked the calico's back as it licked its brood. "No worries, Mama—I didn't hurt them."

Teddy stooped for a better look. "They okay?"

"Lungs aren't too bad. I think we caught it early." Berna pulled out a bottle and syringes. "I'll give them all a shot of antibiotics. Hand me one, will ya? That mama cat knows you. If I reach in, she'll tear me a new one."

The kittens had started nursing, kneading their mother's belly with tiny forepaws. Teddy pulled one away and gave it to Berna.

"How'd Chase seem to you? Ever run into him at church?"

"He just started coming a month ago. Seemed okay." Berna injected the kitten. "Inez said he'd had a wobble, was trying to get back on track. Figured she meant booze—he's had problems before."

"I think something happened over the summer that messed him up." Teddy took the kitten back and passed her another. "His folks mention anything?"

Berna shook her head. "Have you asked them?"

"I'm not a cop anymore. It's Raina's case. You should've seen her today, Berna. She could hardly look at me."

"Give her time, Ted."

"It's been five years."

"If the tables were turned, would five years be enough for you?" Berna held up her hand. "Some breaks don't heal right. You can't expect them to. You and Raina won't ever be the same. Nobody's fault—just how it is."

They finished treating the kittens, then stopped to pet Sebastian, the blind donkey, before heading outside.

At the van, Berna put away her case. "Gets dark so early now."

Teddy looked up. The waxing moon was rising. It cast a diffuse yellow light over the ridgeline. "I'd invite you to dinner, but there's nothing in the house. I'm not exactly crushing it as a working mom. And now I have to go face Alan's adorable girlfriend looking like the bride of Freddy Krueger." She gestured to her blood-soaked shirt.

"You don't have to put up with it. You could ask him to move out."

"Can't afford to till we pay down some debt."

"How long?"

"Couple years—if Henry doesn't need more surgery."

Berna looked at her. "Could be worse, Ted. At least Henry's alive."

Teddy flushed. "I'm sorry, Berna. I shouldn't bitch to you of all people."

Berna waved. "I don't mind now. Gets easier as time goes by." She glanced toward the paddock. "Mare should be fine. Rick did good work."

"Text me his number when you get home? He said to call if she gets worse."

"Will do." Berna climbed into the van. "Later, Mrs. Krueger."

The shepherd had wandered up as they talked. Teddy scratched his ear as she watched Berna's taillights vanish behind the cedars near the road. She gave the dog a final pat and turned toward the house.

◆ ◆ ◆

The Drummond Place, as everyone in town called it, was a long, low ranch nestled among live oaks between Teddy's barn and Alan's greenhouse. Its cedar-shingled walls and deep front porch gave it a settled, comfortable look. A few years ago, they'd built a guest suite onto the garage—no kitchen, but a bedroom, sitting room, bathroom, and its own exterior door. It had been meant for Alan's mother after his father died. But she'd surprised everyone by moving to Fort Worth to marry an elderly widower she'd met through her sister.

Alan had moved into it after the divorce. It didn't connect to the main house; to get from one to the other required going through the garage. But neither door was ever locked. The kids moved freely back and forth—and, to Teddy's annoyance, so did Alan.

He'd been bringing Lyric around for weeks before Teddy caught on. She'd woken earlier than usual one morning and spotted a bright yellow VW Beetle parked behind the juniper bush near the guest suite's outer door. That had not been a good day.

The Beetle was there now—indiscreetly parked in the middle of the driveway behind Alan's work van. Teddy went through the open garage and paused at the laundry room door. She looked down. Her most comfortable teaching shoes were caked in mud, manure, and blood. She muttered a curse and kicked them off.

Inside, she stepped over a pile of mucky work boots. A small mirror hung above the washer. Teddy checked her reflection, and wished she hadn't. Her face was streaked with grime, her hair stiff with dried blood.

In the hallway, the air smelled of cooked onions and garlic. She heard the muted clink of dishes and the murmur of voices. Alan and Lyric. As she debated a detour through the dining room, a shaggy gray mutt the size of a baby hippo galumphed through the door and launched himself at her, whining eagerly and whapping the wall with his heavy tail.

"Shhh, Jabba—down!" Teddy whispered. Too late. Two other dogs—a one-eyed chihuahua and a terrier mix—let out a volley of barks and came running.

"Teddy, that you?" Alan called.

Teddy sighed. "Yep, it's me." She scratched Jabba's ears before shoving him down. "Thanks a lot, you big dumb ox."

She greeted the smaller dogs, then went into the kitchen. Alan was pulling bowls from a cupboard. Lyric, in one of Teddy's aprons, was stirring a large pot on the stove. She was wearing pink cross-trainers, spandex leggings, and a tie-dyed halter top. A long blond ponytail hung down her back. They both turned, and their eyes widened.

"Are you okay?" Alan set down the bowls with a clatter. "Do you need to go to the ER?"

"I'm fine. Fancy had a nosebleed." Teddy pushed a clump of stiff hair out of her eyes. "What's going on? You cooked?"

"Lyric did."

"Cowboy stew," Lyric said cheerfully. "My grandma's recipe. Figured it's something Henry can eat. Be ready as soon as the corn muffins are done. Fifteen minutes."

"Terrific." Teddy left the kitchen.

In the family room, Shane was asleep in the recliner, an ice pack wedged against his ribs. Henry sat on the floor in front of the sofa—a skinny, freckled nine-year-old with brooding eyes in a face still puffy from his latest surgery. He wore a hooded sweatshirt, the hood pulled up despite the warmth of the room, and was cutting cardboard with a pair of children's scissors. Craft supplies lay strewn around him. A sheet of bright green posterboard on the coffee table was covered in strange shapes and symbols.

Teddy stooped to examine it. "Hey bud. That's looking great."

Henry glanced up. His cheeks were flushed and sweaty. "You have blood on you."

"I was helping the vet."

"How come Lyric picked me up? I thought you were gonna."

Teddy felt her shoulders tense. "Lyric did? Not Dad?"

"He couldn't get there in time," Henry said. "Where were you?"

"Something came up at work."

Not a lie, exactly—but not the whole truth. An image flashed in her mind—Chase Loudermilk's body sprawled on the dive platform, surrounded by water black as ink. How natural it felt to reach for the stockpile of half-truths she used to throw out like chaff to shield her family from the worst parts of police work. Henry had only been five when she'd resigned. He couldn't possibly remember what it had been like. But he was staring at her doubtfully.

She nodded at the posterboard. "Decided what to call the new game?"

"Bug Battle Arena. Fire ants versus black widows. It's almost finished, Mom. Wanna play?"

"I need to clean up and help Julia with Fancy. Tomorrow after school?"

"Promise?"

"Promise."

"I'm gonna find some red rocks and some black ones, and paint bugs on them for game pieces."

"Great idea." Teddy felt his forehead. "You're too warm, bud. We talked about no hoods in the house, remember?"

"Dad said it's okay. Just not at the table."

Teddy sighed. She was too tired to play bad cop tonight. "We know what you look like. You don't have to hide."

Henry fingered a hoodie string. "I just like wearing it." He resumed cutting the cardboard.

Teddy watched him for a moment, then kissed the top of his head. "All right, bud. I'm going to take a shower."

She moved toward the hallway.

"Is Fancy okay?"

Teddy turned back. He was watching her, a flicker of anxiety in his eyes.

She smiled. "She's okay. The vet fixed her."

In her bedroom, she shut the door and stripped off her filthy clothes. She craved a long soak but wanted to get back to the barn. Turning on the shower, she soaped up and stood beneath the hot spray until the water streaming off of her hair and body ran clear. When she got out, the bathroom was so thick with steam that she grabbed her towel and went into the bedroom to dry off.

In her robe, she was rummaging in the closet for jeans and a sweatshirt when her phone buzzed on the nightstand.

She picked it up. A text from Julia: *Fancy's ok, I'm ok. Don't need help.*

Teddy sat on the edge of the bed and typed: *I'll keep u company. B there in 5.*

The reply came instantly: *I want 2 b alone.*

"For God's sake," Teddy muttered, dropping the phone onto the quilt.

What now? Her instincts said give Julia space. But what if her instincts were wrong? She'd grown up with wretched role models and had never trusted herself when it came to parenting. She'd admitted to the therapist once that she hadn't really wanted kids. She'd been scared of screwing them up.

The therapist had shaken her head. "The fact that you worry about being a good parent means you probably are one."

At the time, Teddy had found that reassuring. It wasn't much help now.

Down the hall, she heard Alan's voice. "Go wash up for dinner, Henry."

Dinner. Her stomach growled. If she wasn't going to the barn, she should go to the table—try to be sociable. Encourage Henry to eat. But the shower had sapped her last reserves. The thought of cowboy stew and small talk with Alan and Lyric made her want to crawl beneath the blankets for a week.

Teddy pictured Henry clutching his hood-strings. She'd go to dinner. Leaning back against the headboard, she closed her eyes. Five seconds to gather herself. Then she'd get dressed. Walk to the door. Be a mom who showed up.

Chapter 9

A soft knock woke Teddy up. She'd been dreaming. At first, the old nightmare—of being trapped in a cramped space in smothering darkness. Angry voices. Crashing sounds. But this time, new details: the *plink* of dripping water, the groan of the earth's weight above. A muted *tap, tap, tap* from somewhere nearby. She'd tried to scream, but dark water had filled her mouth—warm, metallic. Like blood . . .

She sat up, breathing hard. She was still in her robe. Her hair had dried.

She checked her phone. Ten twenty. She had a missed call from the Chief. Also a text—*Call me if u get this b4 11.*

The knock sounded again.

"Ted? You up?"

"Yeah, come in."

The door opened, and Alan entered carrying a Lone Star beer and a steaming bowl. "Thought you'd be hungry."

"Shit—I was getting dressed for dinner. Guess I crashed. Is Henry—"

"He's fine. He's asleep."

Alan set the bowl and bottle on the nightstand, then shoved his hands in his pockets.

"How about Julia?" Teddy asked. "She didn't—"

"I took her some food. She wants to stay with Fancy a little longer. I gave her till eleven."

"It's a school night."

"She's too worried to sleep, anyway. Gotta pick your battles."

"I guess."

"Lyric's gone home—if you're wondering. Early yoga class."

Teddy reached for the bowl and sniffed its contents. "How'd Henry do with this?"

"So-so. I made him eat six bites, but it took him twenty-five minutes. Finally told him if he drank the broth, he could have ice cream."

"He's getting worse. Should we call a counselor?"

"If we treat him like he's broken, he'll think he is. Once the palate expander's out and the swelling goes down, he'll bounce back."

"You've got to catch phobias early, or they can really mess you up," Teddy said. "Which reminds me—I think we should get him a new bike for Christmas, before that turns into a phobia, too."

"So he can jump over another ditch and break something else?"

"We can't bubble-wrap him, Alan."

Alan flopped into the armchair by the window. "Ted, it's late. Let's talk about it tomorrow."

"Yeah, okay." She picked up the spoon and took a tentative bite. "Damn, this is good. How'd someone that young learn to cook like this?"

"Lyric's twenty-nine. She was even married once."

"And now she lives with her parents—when she's not here."

"She's starting chiropractic school next fall. She's saving up."

"How'd y'all meet? You never told me."

"She came into the greenhouse to get a rosebush for Mother's Day. She was wearing a Dallas Stars t-shirt."

"You found the only other hockey fan in West Texas, huh?"

Alan grinned. "Yeah. Of all the gin joints in all the towns . . ." His face sobered. "Lyric's nice, Ted. You'd like her if you gave her a chance."

"Right. Henry said she picked him up after football."

"I was on a job when you texted. What was I supposed to do?"

Teddy took a sip of beer. "Yeah, sorry." She explained what had happened at the silo. "Chase was my student. I wanted to help." Her throat tightened.

"You really cared about him, huh?"

Teddy stared out the window. She thought of Chase bent over his notebook in class. His line drawings had been so delicate, so at odds with what she would have expected from a rancher's son hardened by military service. Again, she saw his lifeless form—skin chalk-white in the glare of the work lamp. The ragged wound where the mouth should've been.

Was he still there, alone in the dark?

She pushed the thought away. "Something was going on with him. Wish I'd asked more questions."

"He reminds you of Curtis, doesn't he?"

"A little. I should've tried harder to help. I want to help now, if I can."

"So you're back to police work? I thought you liked teaching."

Teddy shrugged. "It's fine. But I feel a little irrelevant. Like I've fallen out of my life."

"You're quitting?"

"I didn't say that."

"Is this about fixing things with Raina? Because if—"

"That's not it." Teddy turned the bottle in her hands. "Something's wrong with this case, Alan. I can feel it. Chase needs me."

"Our kids need you, too." Alan rose and headed for the door. He looked tired. "Night, Ted."

"Night."

When he was gone, Teddy rubbed her eyes and picked up her phone. Ten forty-three. She wavered for five minutes, wrestling with herself. Finally, she dialed.

Ramirez answered on the first ring. "Drummond—figured you were in bed." His voice sounded a little loose, as if he'd had a couple drinks.

"I am. Where are you? The silo?"

"Nope. We got the body out—it's on its way to the morgue."

"Did y'all interview the Loudermilks?" Teddy slid off the bed and rummaged in a dresser drawer for pajamas.

"They were in no fit state. I told Stan someone would come by first thing."

"Let me know how it goes." Teddy shut the drawer with her hip.

A pause. Ramirez cleared his throat. "Here's the thing, Drummond. Inez insists Chase didn't kill himself. But I reckon the ME's gonna rule this a suicide. JP's leaning that way. If that happens, my hands are tied. Can't burn resources on something that ain't a crime—especially with me being family."

Teddy tossed the pajamas onto the bed. "What are you saying?"

Another pause. "You still think this was murder?"

"I never said that, Chief. But I think it merits investigation."

"I agree."

"You do?"

"Yes." She heard the clink of ice cubes, and he swallowed. "It's tricky, Ted. This is Raina's case."

"She thinks it's suicide."

"Raina's a solid detective. Whatever happened, she'll figure it out. Thing is, if I have to shut this down, Bragg's off it. I'd like to have someone else who's already up to speed—someone outside the department who could keep going."

"Is that legal?"

"You're a licensed PI. Stan and Inez could hire you."

Teddy went to the window and pulled back the curtain. "You're asking me to run a parallel investigation? Raina's not going to like that."

"I'm asking you to consult. Ride along on interviews, help gather evidence. Just till the ME's report comes in. Right now, it's a police matter. But you'll be current, just in case."

Teddy looked out at the moon. "It's been a tough couple years for the kids."

"How 'bout going with Raina to talk to the Loudermilks in the morning? See what you think. We'll go from there."

"She's okay with that?"

"She'll come around."

Teddy stared out the window. A cloud crossed the moon, and its edges glowed silver. She wanted to know what had happened to Chase. But also, joining an active investigation would feel like stepping back into her own skin—after four years of wearing someone else's.

She let the curtain fall. "Okay. I'll go. No promises after that."

Tuesday dawned, cool and bright. The cloudless sky had a dull, steely sheen that suggested rain later on. Teddy awoke to a text—*Loudermilk Ranch, 9 a.m.* It was from Raina, not Ramirez. Hopefully, a positive sign.

She checked that the kids were up, then stumbled to the kitchen to make oatmeal. Outside, Alan's work van was gone. Tuesdays were delivery days. To Teddy's relief, Julia was in a better mood than she had been the previous evening. She'd woken early and found Fancy contentedly munching hay in her stall.

When Julia headed out the door, the goodbye kiss she gave Teddy was perfunctory but not grudging.

"I'm riding my bike to school," she said. "I work at Petal Pushers till nine tonight—Ruby needs help with inventory."

While Henry got washed and dressed, Teddy hurried through morning chores, then packed his lunch and hustled him into her truck. As they pulled out, Frankie Aguilar sped past on his way to work at the greenhouse. He was a couple years younger than Shane, with curly black hair and a wide grin. He waved cheerfully as he passed.

Teddy dropped Henry at Stone Creek Elementary, then checked the time. Eight o'clock. Too early for the Loudermilk ranch. She headed west on Colonel Priddy Avenue and stopped at the Skinny's, a grimy gas station and convenience store on the edge of town. Teddy usually avoided it. Frankie Aguilar's sister worked there. She was sweet, but Teddy tended to shy away from anything that reminded her of what had happened on Boxhill Drive. This morning, however, she didn't have time to get across town to the supermarket.

Inside, she spotted the dark, glossy head behind the counter. Jasmine was stocking the cigarette rack. Teddy loaded a half-gallon of milk, several cans of mandarin orange slices, a four-pack of toilet paper, and some squashed-looking cheese Danishes into a basket, and carried them to the register.

Jasmine's face lit up. She was a petite twenty-two-year-old, with long, straight hair and enormous dark eyes. "Mrs. D—how you been?"

She seemed so genuinely pleased to see her that Teddy felt ashamed. To the Aguilars, Teddy was a hero. Somehow, their gratitude stung more than Raina's cold anger. Teddy steeled herself for a casual chat. When she left the store, she felt exhausted and relieved.

Five minutes later, she pulled into the weed-choked driveway of a squalid little wood-framed house on Route 137, just north of town. It had once been a goat farm. But the goats were long gone, and the land had reverted to scrub.

Teddy killed the engine and, carrying the groceries, navigated through piles of discarded appliances, scrap metal, and other debris. A dozen feral cats basking on the steps darted beneath the house as she approached.

The porch was half rotten. Johnson grass grew through the gaps. A new-looking security camera hung from the eaves. She picked her way past moldering burlap sacks of empty Miller Lite cans and opened the front door without bothering to knock.

"Dad, it's me."

No answer. The blinds were drawn and the house dark. Teddy wrinkled her nose at the sharp, fetid stink—a combination of cat urine and rancid garbage. Stacks of yellowing newspapers and dismembered machine parts crowded the room.

She threaded through the mess to the kitchen. The air was murky with smoke. Milton Spivey sat at the table, the only usable piece of furniture in the house, besides his bed. He was a gaunt, sinewy man in his early seventies, with sallow skin and wispy white hair that stuck out in all directions like a dandelion gone to seed. He wore faded overalls and a plaid shirt, one sleeve pinned over the stump of the arm he'd lost in Vietnam. A cigarette smoldered in an ashtray beside an open can of Miller Lite. He was eating mandarin orange slices straight from the tin with a pickle fork.

He looked up with pale, bleary eyes. "What happened to you last night? Thought you was comin' by."

"We had a horse go down."

"What was I s'posed to do for supper? Ain't nothin'." He waved his fork around the kitchen.

"Give me a break, Dad—everything I bring rots in the fridge. You live on orange slices and booze." Teddy set the bags on the table. "Here's some milk and pastries, if Shane wants any." She glanced out the window. Her nephew's truck was parked beside the tiny, mildew-streaked camper behind the house. He was normally at the greenhouse by seven. His ribs must be pretty sore.

Milton dropped his fork and surveyed the groceries. "Didn't bring no Miller Lite. Told you I'm about out."

"And I told *you* I'm not buying you beer."

She opened the refrigerator to put the milk away. The handle was sticky. A line of ants crawled up the door. She washed her hands and dried them with a paper towel. When she tossed it into the overflowing garbage pail, a crumpled letter on county letterhead caught her eye.

She pulled it out. "Dad, what's this?"

Milton drained his beer. "Health Department thinks they can bully a veteran."

Teddy scanned the letter. "This says you have thirty days to clean up before they take you to court." She checked the date. "It's from a week ago."

Milton picked up his cigarette. "People need to mind their own goddamn business."

"This place is a health hazard, Dad. It stinks."

"It's them rats—they die in the walls." He flicked ash into the tray. "What can they do, sue me? I ain't got nothin'."

"They can send in a crew with a roll-off dumpster and gut the place. That what you want?" A dull pain was pulsing behind Teddy's eyes. She looked at her watch. "I've got to go, Dad. We'll talk about this later." She folded the letter and tucked it in her back pocket as she left.

Chapter 10

Driving north on Route 137, Teddy rolled down her windows and let the cool morning air flood the cab. At the Loudermilk ranch, she went past the gate she'd used the day before and made her way around to the main entrance. It was marked with an archway, orange with rust, that bore a metal sign—a wrought-iron cursive "L" above a crescent of rebar—beside the words "THE ROCKING L RANCH."

She checked the dashboard clock. 8:45. Raina's patrol SUV was already parked in a stand of mesquite saplings beyond the gate.

Teddy pulled alongside. "You're early, too."

"I wanted to catch you," Raina said. "We should go in together. Leave your truck here." Her tone was flat. Mirrored sunglasses hid her expression.

Teddy complied. But when she climbed into the SUV, Raina didn't start the engine.

Teddy waited.

Finally, Raina said, "Let's get a few things straight. One, this is my case. You think you're a better detective than me. You're not. I'm not your sidekick. I don't need Edwina the Magnificent riding to the rescue. So, you follow my lead. Got it?"

"Got it. What else?"

"We're not friends. We're not partners. I don't want to hear about your piddly-ass problems. And you don't ask about mine. We do the job, then go our separate ways."

"Fine by me."

"Good. Let's go."

The Loudermilk ranch house sat two miles southwest of the gate, nestled near the foot of Deadhorse Mesa. It was an old-fashioned place built of rough-hewn limestone with a porch on three sides. An expensive-looking gravel bike leaned against the porch rail—out of place in the rural setting.

Raina pulled up near the garage. As Teddy stepped out, a pale flash caught her eye. She looked up.

A rider on a buckskin Appaloosa was halfway up the mesa's western flank, looking down at them. The slope was still in shadow, and the rider wore a large white Stetson that hid his face, but the slim build and loose posture suggested a teenage boy.

"Raina," Teddy whispered, nodding toward the horseman.

When the rider noticed them looking, he continued up the slope. The faint clatter of hooves on stone reached them a moment later.

"Who's that?" Teddy asked. "Do the Loudermilks have another kid?"

"A daughter," Raina said. "Married. Lives in New Mexico."

As they approached the porch, the front door opened and a tall, slender man in his late thirties emerged. Teddy recognized him—Mark McKissick, junior pastor at Calvary Baptist in Stone Creek. She'd met him several times at Berna's house. He was a longtime friend of the vet and also chaplain at the community college, where she'd occasionally encountered him.

McKissick wasn't looking very pastoral at the moment. His wavy brown hair was damp with sweat, and dust had settled in the fine lines around his eyes. He wore jeans and a green cycling jersey.

Teddy glanced again at the gravel bike by the porch rail, wondering why he hadn't driven.

McKissick trotted down the steps. He shook Raina's hand, then Teddy's, and caught her eyeing the bike.

"My little Prius bottoms out on these ranch roads," he said. "Inez is inside. She asked me to stay with her today—is that okay? Or should I go?" When Raina hesitated, he added, "I saw Chase Sunday evening. He was at our campus Bible study."

Raina and Teddy exchanged a glance.

"You can stay," Raina said. "But we'll want a separate interview later."

"Of course."

"You said Inez is here. Where's Stan?" Teddy asked.

"At his forge, I think. Want me to get him?"

Raina shook her head. "We'll find him later."

Teddy knew what she was thinking—Stan and Inez would be more candid if they didn't have to worry about protecting each other's feelings.

They followed McKissick up the steps and through the door. The place was homely and unpretentious, but immaculate. Vacuum tracks stood out on the living room carpet. The maple coffee table gleamed.

McKissick paused, frowning. "She was here a minute ago."

Raina and Teddy followed him down a short hallway into the kitchen, where the odors of coffee and fried bacon still hung in the air. A tall, angular woman in a gray dress and a blue gingham apron stood at the sink, elbow-deep in suds, with a skillet in one hand and a steel-wool scrubber in the other. She was gazing blankly out the window at the mesa behind the house.

"Inez, the police are here," Mark said.

Inez Loudermilk jumped but didn't turn around. She began scouring the skillet so vigorously that bubbles arced through the air. When Teddy had seen her in town, Inez had always looked neat and disciplined, with shoulders back and head held high. Now, she was hunched over the sink, her normally tight coil of iron-gray hair frazzled and half undone.

Mark laid a hand on her shoulder. "Come sit down, Inez."

"I need to keep busy," she said stiffly. "Jen and her family are coming in tonight." She dropped the pan and started scrubbing the countertop in small, furious circles, as if trying to eradicate something only she could see.

"We'd like to talk to you about Chase, Mrs. Loudermilk," Raina said.

Inez bit her lip but continued working.

"He was one of my students," Teddy added. "I want to know what happened."

At this, Inez dropped the dishrag back in the sink and turned. Soapy water dripped from her hands onto the braided rug. She thrust her head forward. Her eyes looked both vacant and fierce, as if they were staring through Teddy to something far away.

"You want to know what happened?" Inez said. "Someone killed my boy."

"If that's the case, we need to act fast," Raina said. "Is there somewhere we can talk?"

Mark handed Inez a dishtowel. "Let's go into the living room."

Inez fidgeted, twisting the towel in her hands. "I always watch the sun come up over the mesa."

She nodded toward a piece of framed needlework on the wall. It read, "'Weeping endureth for a night, but joy cometh in the morning.' Psalm 30:5."

Mark glanced at Teddy and Raina. "Let's sit out back, then. I'm sure the detectives won't mind."

Raina nodded the go-ahead. Mark slipped his hand under Inez's arm, but she pulled away and headed for the back door.

They emerged onto a patio shaded by a large pecan tree, its leaves turning a rusty yellow-brown. A weathered picnic table sat beneath it, along with several deckchairs and a large doghouse. A chicken coop stood nearby, and beyond that, a vegetable garden—mostly bare now, except for a few dried corn stalks and a row of purple kale. A hundred yards behind the house, a pole barn sat at the foot of the mesa. Puffs of black smoke were rising from a shed beside it.

Inez, still clutching the dishtowel, lowered herself stiffly into a chair facing the bluff. Teddy and Raina sat close to her, and Mark perched on the picnic table. A gray-muzzled Labrador clambered stiffly out of the doghouse and lumbered across the patio before flopping down beside Inez, who broke the silence.

"Why didn't Wally come? Chase was his nephew."

"That's why he didn't," Raina said. "It's protocol."

Inez's lips tightened. She said nothing.

"You said Chase was murdered, Mrs. Loudermilk. What makes you think that?" Teddy asked.

"Chase would never harm himself. Never." Inez fastened her intense gaze on Teddy. "Self-destruction's a blasphemy."

Teddy glanced questioningly at Mark, who looked slightly uncomfortable.

"There's a verse in the New Testament—'Every sin and blasphemy can be forgiven except blasphemy against the Holy Spirit,'" he said. "But it doesn't specifically mention suicide."

"What greater blasphemy could there be?" Inez demanded. "It's the one sin you can't repent of. 'Our bodies are the temple of the Holy Spirit.' Chase didn't come through two tours in Afghanistan just to harm himself here."

"Veterans often do, though," Raina said gently. "Mental health issues aren't moral failings."

"You think he killed himself," Inez said bitterly.

“We have to ask questions,” Raina said. “Why do you think he wrote that note?” She pulled out her phone and thumbed through the photos. “‘I can’t live with myself anymore please help, what I did is unforgivable, Matthew, Cha—’” she read aloud. “You said yesterday it’s his handwriting.”

Inez had been twisting the dishtowel around her fingers. Now she stood and began to pace. “I know my boy. He hadn’t given up. He was going to school, starting a business. He and Stan were fixing up that silo, getting furniture for it at garage sales. Would he go to all that trouble and then end his life? I don’t know why he wrote that.” She waved the dishtowel toward Raina’s phone. “But I know this—people don’t ask for help in suicide notes.”

“Do you—” Raina began.

“I can’t stand here doing nothing—I can’t.” Inez flung the towel over her chair, grabbed a wire basket by the door, and walked away.

Mark stood. “She’ll talk better if her hands are busy.”

Raina got up. “Whatever works.”

With the Labrador trotting behind, Teddy and Raina followed Mark across the lawn, catching up with Inez at the chicken coop. In the run beside it, a half-dozen hens were clucking and scratching in the dirt.

A long, hinged lid covered a row of nesting boxes on one side of the coop. Inez had propped it up with her shoulder and was pulling out eggs, examining each before placing it carefully in the basket. The dog sat beside her, staring up as if expecting a treat.

“Let me hold that for you,” Mark said, reaching for the lid.

Teddy and Raina took up positions on either side of Inez. Teddy watched her closely. Grief took many forms, but Inez’s behavior felt odd—uneasy and evasive.

“We’ve got a few more questions, Mrs. Loudermilk,” Raina said. “We won’t keep you long.”

Inez didn't look up. "All this talk. My boy's in the morgue, and whoever killed him is out there." She waved a large brown egg in the air.

"It's frustrating, I know," Teddy said. "But if someone murdered Chase, this is how we catch them."

Inez said nothing.

"The Chief asked you this yesterday," Raina said. "But now that you've had more time to think—do you have any idea who 'Matthew' might be? The one Chase mentioned in that note?"

Inez shook her head. "Matt Barnett's the only one I can think of."

"The dentist over on Elm?" Teddy asked.

"He goes to our church, but I can't think why Chase would write to him. We use Dr. Canaddy." She reached into another box, gently nudging aside a white hen and removing a speckled egg.

"Did you ever notice Chase talking to Barnett?" Teddy asked McKissick.

The pastor shook his head. "Just polite hellos."

"Did he maybe have a friend on campus named Matthew?"

"Not that I'm aware," McKissick said. "But I didn't know Chase that well. He only started coming to Bible study a few weeks ago."

"I'll ask around. Maybe one of my students knows." Teddy stepped closer to Inez. "Chase didn't strike me as suicidal, either. But I did notice a change this semester. His schoolwork fell apart. Did something happen over the summer?"

Inez bit her lip and rubbed an egg clean with her apron. "Stan and me noticed it, too. We had a horse stolen in August, but I doubt that was it. Summer's always been hard for Chase, you know, since Grayson Robles died."

Raina looked skeptical. "That was ten years ago."

Inez pulled a pair of white eggs from the last box. "I know. But every summer, Chase goes into a funk. This year, he never snapped out of it. Came home drunk a few times—after being sober for so long. I was worried sick."

"What about Stan? How'd he feel?" Raina asked.

The question startled Inez. She fumbled the eggs, and one fell with a soft slap. The dog jumped up and began licking the golden goo from the dirt.

Inez flushed and smoothed her apron.

"What was the question?"

"Was Stan worried about Chase?" Teddy asked sharply.

Inez looked east, toward the bluff. A nimbus of yellow light had begun to glow above its rim. The sun would clear the top any minute. Finally, she said, "Stan sometimes gets angry when he's worried. But I thought it helped."

Teddy and Raina exchanged a look. "Thought what helped, Mrs. Loudermilk?" Raina asked.

Inez kept her eyes on the bluff top. "There was an argument a few weeks back. They both said . . . things," she murmured. "But Chase started doing better, after that. Stan knew the right way with him. Sometimes, Chase needed tough love."

"When was this blowup?" Teddy asked. "Three or four weeks ago?"

Inez tore her eyes from the mesa's summit and looked at her. "How'd you know?"

"He came to my office around then, apologized for slacking off. Said he'd been going through something, but he was getting help. Do you know what kind of help?"

"Maybe Bible study. He started attending about that time," McKissick offered. He'd closed the nesting box lid and was scratching the dog's ears. "He was there Sunday. Seemed in good spirits. After the study, he and some of the other kids went bowling."

"I don't think that's what he meant," Inez said. "He told me he was seeing a counselor."

"Who?" Raina asked.

But Inez didn't know. Neither did McKissick.

Teddy started to ask another question, but Inez suddenly pointed. "There!"

They all turned. The sun had erupted over the rim of Deadhorse Mesa, bathing everything in dazzling light. Shadows sprang across the ground behind them. From the pecan tree, a mockingbird sent out a complicated trill, then flew off in a rustle of leaves and whir of white and gray.

Several pecans rattled to the ground, along with a few sickle-shaped leaves. One landed in Inez's hair and stuck, fluttering like a yellow feather. Her eyes were shut, her face tilted toward the light. When she opened them, she smiled.

"There," she said again. "It'll be all right now."

Chapter 11

Inez walked back toward the house with the basket of eggs over her arm, leaving the others staring at each other.

Mark broke the silence. "She's sensitive. The doctor gave her something for anxiety last night. If she seems a little off, that's probably the reason."

"There's no rulebook for how to handle losing a child," Raina said. "Even if you know how it happened, and why." She looked at Teddy, who stared back, unblinking. If she flinched at every dig, she might as well quit the investigation now.

"Let's talk to Stan," Teddy said.

"I'll take you to the forge," McKissick offered.

Raina lifted a hand. "Inez needs you. Just point us in the right direction."

McKissick looked slightly disappointed. "Sure. That path, toward the barn."

"What'd you make of Inez?" Raina asked as they picked their way through the tall grass.

"She's right—people don't ask for help in suicide notes," Teddy said. "But the unforgivable sin stuff seems a little out there."

"Here's what bothers me—she said suicide's the only unforgivable sin. But in that note, Chase says what he *did* was unforgivable. Past tense. So he can't mean suicide." Raina stopped. "Something doesn't add up."

Teddy slapped a late-season mosquito off her wrist. "To me, the weirdest thing about that note is the sign-off. People who kill themselves leave notes to their loved ones. Nobody knows who this 'Matthew' is."

"We should talk to the kids he bowled with Sunday. And I want to visit the lanes—check video footage."

"Let's find his therapist, too, if we can," Teddy added. But Raina was already walking away.

The pole barn sat at the foot of the mesa, ringed by thickets of juniper and skunkbush. As they neared, they heard the clang of iron from the shed beside the barn. Its roll-up door stood open. Tools and scrap metal littered the dirt floor. Rows of chisels, punches, and files hung on a pegboard above a worktable crowded with unfamiliar metal objects. Against the rear wall loomed a drill press the size of a vending machine, and next to it, a brick forge ventilated out the roof with a stovepipe. The place had a pleasant smell, metallic and earthy—a blend of charcoal, oil, and oxidized iron.

Stan Loudermilk stood at an anvil bolted to a large tree stump, shaping a glowing hunk of metal with a pair of long-handled tongs and a blacksmith's hammer. Although the Loudermilks kept to themselves, and Stan came into town less often than his wife did, Teddy had seen him a few times. He was in his early sixties, brawny and barrel-chested, with a leathery face and thick gray hair. He wore a plaid shirt flapping open over a brown t-shirt and charcoal-smudged jeans.

Stan glanced up, saw them watching, and scowled. He turned without a word and plunged the glowing metal into a nearby water drum. A loud hiss and a cloud of steam erupted.

"Hi Stan," Raina said. "This a bad time?"

"No. Just felt like pounding somethin'." He pulled the cooled metal out of the water and dropped it in the dirt, along with the tongs and hammer. Stripping off his gloves, he came around the anvil. "Heard from the medical examiner?"

"Not yet."

Stan ran his palm roughly through his hair. "What d'you want, then?"

"The more we know about Chase's state of mind in recent days, the better," Raina said.

"Don't see why it matters. He shot himself. Nothin' you can do now." His voice was bitter and a little unsteady.

"Inez thinks someone killed him," Teddy said.

Stan picked up a thermos near the anvil's base. "When Inez can't handle reality, she makes up her own. No harm in it—it's just her way." He unscrewed the lid, and Teddy smelled coffee.

"What if she's right?" she asked.

He paused, thermos raised. "She ain't. Chase wrote that note. Gun was his, too."

He seemed more angry than sad. Maybe he was one of those people whose strong emotions always morphed into anger, no matter how they started. Teddy had a tendency that way herself, she'd discovered back in her therapy days.

She pushed the thought aside. "When's the last time you saw that gun?"

"Month ago, maybe." He drank, then wiped his mouth on his sleeve.

"Could Chase have loaned it to anyone?" Raina asked.

"No way. It was his prize possession. My old man gave him that pistol when he turned fourteen. He kept it in a lockbox in his bedroom, because of the grandkids."

"Where'd he keep the key?"

"On his keychain, I reckon. Never asked."

"Anyone else have access?"

"Not that I know of."

Teddy cleared her throat. "Any idea why Chase would hurt himself?"

Stan scuffed his boot in the dirt. "Wish I knew."

"Inez said you and Chase had a blowup a few weeks back. Around that time, he told me he wanted to transfer schools."

Stan screwed the lid back on the thermos. "What are you getting at?"

"Can you tell us what you argued about?"

"About his boozing and slacking off. I gave him an ultimatum—straighten up or go back to Galveston. Told him there's faster ways to die than drinking himself to death."

Raina looked slightly shocked. "That's what you said?"

"You don't have to sound so interested. That ain't why he did this."

"How do you know?"

"Because he *did* straighten up. For the last month, he was doing good. Inez and me thought he was back on track."

"But you're still sure it was a suicide?" Teddy asked. "Doesn't it seem possible—"

Stan held up a hand. "Look, I know what you're doing. I heard Inez on the phone with Wally last night, pushing him to make this into something it ain't. But that don't mean I gotta go along with it." He set down the thermos and dusted his hands. "Chase was doing better. Something must've happened Sunday to set him off. Don't matter what, 'cause he's gone. Now, show some respect. Let us grieve in peace." He turned his back and moved to the long table against the wall.

Raina and Teddy exchanged looks.

Raina stepped closer. "I know it's uncomfortable, Stan. But we have to investigate every unattended unnatural death—even suicides."

Stan said nothing. He rummaged through a pile of scrap, picked up a thin, flat iron bar about a foot long, and set it in the forge.

"You said something must've happened Sunday," Teddy said. "Can you walk us through that day?"

Stan flipped a switch. A fan kicked on, and the coals inside the forge flared white. After a while, he pulled out the glowing bar and carried it to the anvil.

Teddy tried again. "When was the last time you saw Chase?"

"Sunday afternoon around two, I reckon." Stan picked up the hammer and notched the bar in the middle, then began tapping along its length. "We went to church, came home, had lunch."

"All three of you?" Raina asked.

"All four. Chase and Inez and me, plus Cody."

"Cody?"

"Cody Puckett. His dad was an Army buddy of mine—first Gulf War. Vernon died a few years back. Cirrhosis. Cody didn't have no mother, so we fostered him. Works here now."

"How old is he?" Raina asked.

"Nineteen. Big help around this place."

Teddy thought of the tensions that had sometimes arisen from her own insistence on taking in Shane. Had Inez and Chase resented Cody? Was that why he'd been fostered, not adopted?

"Does he wear a white hat and ride a buckskin Appaloosa?" she asked.

Stan looked up. "You seen him?"

"I think so."

"We'll need to talk to him," Raina said. "What happened after lunch?"

Stan bent over the anvil again. "Inez went to lie down. Cody come out to check the horses. I asked Chase if he wanted to head to the silo—we was working on wiring the place, putting in a chemical toilet. But he said he had some reading to do. He planned to hit the campus library for a few hours, then go to some Bible study. I told him be back by one a.m. He said he would."

Teddy was surprised. "Chase had a curfew? He was twenty-five."

Stan had knocked the metal bar into a C-curve, but it was cooling. He walked it back to the forge. "Nah, not a curfew. We been riding night patrol. Had a horse stolen a few months back. Cody was covering dusk to one, and Chase was supposed to take over till five."

"What do you think happened?"

Stan took his time. "Like I said, I reckon something happened in town that upset him. If he came home drunk, maybe he went to the silo to think. I told him I'd kick him out next time he screwed up. Maybe he figured life ain't worth it." His throat worked. He pulled the bar from the forge and laid it over the horn, hammering with swift, hard strokes.

"You don't think he came back to the house?" Raina asked.

"No. I'd have heard. I'm a light sleeper."

They watched Stan work. Teddy realized suddenly that he was making a horseshoe.

"You're sure he couldn't have gotten in the house before he went to the silo?" she asked.

"I'm sure."

She took a step closer. "Then how'd he get the gun? You said it was in his bedroom."

Stan lowered his hammer. "I dunno. Earlier, I reckon."

"Could he have been carrying it for protection? Did he ever mention any trouble?"

Stan looked disconcerted. He dropped the hammer and pulled out a pack of Marlboros. "Never said nothing to me. Chase didn't have a lot of connections here. He ain't lived here for years."

Raina shuffled impatiently. "This is all guesswork. The simplest explanation's that he slipped in the house for his gun Sunday night, and you just didn't hear."

Stan's hands shook as he lit a cigarette. "That ain't what happened."

"You don't know that."

Stan slapped the anvil. "I *do* know, goddammit."

"How?"

"Because he couldn't." Stan took a long drag and exhaled the smoke away from them. "Inez is alone at the house a lot, and she gets nervous. So I installed some one-sided deadbolts couple years back. Can't open them from the outside. I was up late Sunday. When Chase missed his time and wasn't answering his phone, I got mad."

"You locked him out?" Teddy asked.

Stan flicked the ash off his cigarette and glared at the ground. After a beat, he nodded.

There was a heavy silence. "Why didn't you tell us this yesterday when Wally and me spoke with you?" Raina asked finally.

Stan looked up, his eyes red-rimmed and furious. "Because I felt bad," he snapped. "Still do. What if he tried to get in? What if me locking him out pushed him over the edge? I didn't want Inez knowing." He stubbed out the cigarette on the anvil. "Chase must've had his gun with him—in his truck, maybe. Might've been target shooting last week. He did that, sometimes. But I'll tell ya this—if that Magnum killed him, it was his doing. He didn't let nobody else use that gun."

"Who had access to the silo?" Raina asked.

"Just me and Chase. Had a key cut for him when we started fixing it up." Stan slumped, staring at the gray metal cooling on the anvil. "He loved that place. Always did. He was real excited about starting that dive business. I thought he might want to do it full-time, but he was set on being a cop."

"You didn't approve?" Teddy asked.

"I didn't care, long as he was happy."

Teddy was wondering whether it would pay to push Stan further when she heard the sudden thudding of hooves on turf. She turned in time to see a buckskin Appaloosa vanishing into the barn.

She looked at Raina, who nodded. "That's all for now, Stan. We'll have more questions later. If that's Cody, we'd like to talk to him."

Stan nodded, glassy-eyed. He dropped the horseshoe into the dirt. "C'mon, I'll introduce ya."

Chapter 12

They followed Stan around the corner and into the pole barn—a tin-roofed structure of unpainted wood, weathered and gray, with a pitched gable and sloping wings supported by heavy posts.

Teddy took stock of her surroundings. The place was as cluttered as Stan's workshop. One side of it was open, housing tractors and other farm vehicles. Rusted machine parts and rotting tires were stacked against the walls, along with portable steel gate panels, a battered cattle ramp, and a manure-smeared squeeze chute.

A row of stalls ran beneath the hayloft on the other side. At the far end of the breezeway, a tired-looking horse stood with its head down in front of a stall. The teenager in the white Stetson was unbuckling the cinch. He flung the saddle and blanket over a sawhorse, then reached to remove the bridle.

Stan raised a finger and thumb to his mouth and whistled. "Cody, come on over here."

Cody spun around. He was tall and lanky, wearing dusty boots and faded Wranglers. His denim work shirt was too large and hung loosely on his shoulders.

He removed his hat. His face, sunburned beneath a mop of unruly auburn hair, had a pinched, anxious look.

He gnawed his upper lip and took a few tentative steps forward. "Who's this?"

"Police. They want to talk to you," Stan said.

Cody froze.

"You're not in trouble," Raina added quickly. "Just a few questions about Sunday night."

Cody's mouth opened, then closed. He half turned, hesitated—then clapped his Stetson on his head, grabbed a handful of mane, and vaulted onto the horse's bare back. He slapped the reins against its neck and the animal leapt forward, racing out the eastern door.

Raina threw up her hands. "Seriously?"

"Damn stupid kid," Stan muttered, kicking up a spray of dirt and straw.

Teddy jogged to the door. Fresh hoofprints pocked the ground, heading south.

She ran back. "Let's get to the truck."

"You won't catch him in no truck," Stan said. "Not out here."

"Forget it," Raina said. "I wanted his take on Chase's state of mind, but we can talk to him later."

Teddy lowered her voice. "Maybe this kid knows something. He ran for a reason."

"Probably just has a joint in his pocket or something. I'm not wasting hours tracking him."

"Suit yourself." Teddy turned to Stan. "How do I catch him?"

Stan's eyes narrowed. He glanced at Raina, then back at Teddy. "Cody don't know nothin', but I'll take ya. Sooner y'all wrap this up, the better." He waved for her to follow and vanished behind a backhoe.

Teddy started after him, but Raina grabbed her arm. "You said you'd follow my lead. This is my investigation."

"Then investigate," Teddy said, pulling free. "You're assuming Chase killed himself. Maybe he didn't. If Cody knows something, we need to find out now." She moved off, but Raina shouldered past her.

"Fine, we'll do this. But if you ever undermine me in public again, you're off this case."

A number of replies came to mind, but Teddy managed to keep them to herself. She'd already won—letting Raina have the last word cost her nothing but the cheap thrill of snapping back. All that mattered was getting to the truth.

They found Stan in the open bay on the barn's south side, where two four-wheelers were parked, one yellow and one army green.

Stan was already on the green one. "Key's in the ignition." His engine roared, and he tore out of the barn, leaving a haze of blue smoke and acrid exhaust.

Raina threw her leg over the saddle of the yellow ATV and turned the key. Teddy hesitated, then clambered onto the seat behind her as the vehicle lurched ahead. Stan had already vanished into a thicket of mesquite, but a cloud of red dust hung above his path, making him easy to follow.

The trail, which ran along the western foot of the mesa, was well traveled. Horse manure and cow patties dotted the ground, along with dozens of overlapping tire tracks. Mesquite branches met above their heads, and Teddy had the sensation of riding through a dense yellow-green tunnel, tight and airless. The thick dust made it difficult to breathe.

After a mile or so, Deadhorse Mesa came to a sudden end on their left, and they shot out of the mesquite into open country. The land before them, a vast expanse of jumbled stone and thick, low scrub, sloped gradually away to the south. The sun shimmered beneath the ragged skirts of a heavy cloudbank. Somewhere to the east lay the missile silo, and Teddy thought she could make out a strip of pale gray that might be the military service road.

The scrubland was crisscrossed with narrow cow trails and broader tracks left by ranch vehicles. On one of these, a glint of chrome and a distant dust cloud were all that could be seen of Stan's ATV, now far ahead. There was no sign of the Appaloosa.

Raina revved the engine, and they raced down the slope. The trail was narrower here. As they tore through the dense, shoulder-high scrub, Teddy's teeth chattered with the vibration, and stiff branches of saltbush and yucca whipped her arms and legs. A thorny stem struck her cheek. She touched the place; her fingertips came away bloody.

After a mile or two, the scrub thinned, giving way to a broad plain of mixed grasses scored by deep gullies. Navigating through mats of buffalo grass and sagewort, they finally caught up with Stan at the brink of a deep ravine. He had stopped and was standing on the seat of his ATV, shading his eyes and gazing southeast.

"Where is he?" Raina asked.

Stan jumped down. "Went into the gulch and up the other side. See the hoofmarks?" He pointed to a narrow path that snaked into the arroyo. "No way down on these four-wheelers."

Teddy shaded her eyes and scanned the plain. No sign of Cody or the horse. The land dropped off steeply to the south, blocking the view.

"What do we do?" she asked.

"We go back," Raina said. "We've wasted enough time on this snipe hunt."

Stan climbed back on his ATV. "Cody ain't got nothin' with him, not even a bedroll. He's gotta come home. When he does, I'll bring him in."

"Does he live with you?" Teddy asked.

"He's in a cabin on the property." Stan gestured back up the trail.

"Can you show us?"

"I reckon so."

The sun had vanished behind the cloudbank and a stiff wind whistled through the scrub as Teddy and Raina followed Stan back to the homestead and parked the four-wheelers in the barn.

Teddy checked her phone. Almost eleven. She had a missed text from a number she didn't recognize: *Hi it's Rick Castillo. Berna gave me yr #. How's the mare?*

Still little off feed, but better, she typed.

She stuffed the phone in her pocket and hurried after the others, who had exited the barn on a dirt path that led past the blacksmith's shed.

Her phone buzzed.

I'll swing by tonite, check her again.

Teddy pursed her lips. It seemed a shame for him to come out just to confirm Fancy was fine. Besides, she knew she'd be tired by evening and in no mood to make small talk.

She wrote, *I think she's ok*, then hesitated. If Fancy took a downturn and Julia found out Teddy had refused the vet's offer, she'd never forgive her.

She deleted the message and instead typed, *Thx. 6 p.m.?*

Castillo responded immediately with a thumbs up.

She caught up with the others a hundred yards north of the barn, where a long, low structure sat among a grove of shaggy junipers. When Stan had mentioned a cabin, Teddy had pictured a pioneer-style log construction. But this was a modern, prefab building shaped like a shipping container, with a low porch tacked on the side.

Stan led them up the steps and reached for the doorknob.

"Hang on." Raina peered through the window. "No probable cause—nothing in plain sight. We can't go in."

"Why not?" Stan wiped dust out of his eyes with the tail of his shirt. "What are you looking for?"

Teddy leaned on the porch rail. "Cody could've been leading us away from here for a reason. Might be something he doesn't want us to find."

"Look," Stan said slowly, "Cody didn't do nothin' to Chase. But my wife's hanging by a thread, and the sooner y'all wrap this up, the better. If looking around this cabin will help, you got my permission."

"We'd still need a warrant," Raina said.

"Why? I own the place. Cody sleeps in here, but he don't pay rent."

"He's still got a reasonable expectation of privacy."

Stan scratched his cheek. "No he don't. I use this place to store supplies that can't be kept in the barn. Everyone's in and out of it all the time. Cody knew that when he started sleeping out here. He don't even have a key. He just wanted someplace he could blast his godawful music without Inez fussin' about it."

Teddy turned to Raina. "What do you think?"

Raina hunched her shoulders. "Probably okay, if he doesn't have exclusive control. Not that it really matters. None of this will end up in court." She looked at Stan. "Wait out here."

They stepped inside. Teddy wrinkled her nose. "Smells like chemicals and dirty socks."

The cabin had one room. It had been built to serve as living quarters, with a kitchenette on one end. But the walls had been lined with metal shelves stacked with tubs of powdered cattle supplements, mineral blocks, and jugs of dewormer. Two refrigerators stood side by side, one labeled "Cattle RX."

At the far end of the cabin, a living space had been cleared, with a futon bed, a bookcase, and a shabby recliner. The sleeping bag Cody had been using as a comforter lay in a heap on the floor, amid a pile of boots, dirty laundry, and pieces of disassembled electronics.

Raina pulled nitrile gloves from her pocket and handed Teddy a pair. "I'll take the kitchen—you start over there. Just a quick pass, flag anything that looks wrong."

Teddy picked her way through the clutter to the futon and examined the bedding, but she found nothing more interesting than a pair of dirty tube socks. A nightstand held a lamp, loose playing cards, and a tin of Skoal.

Then she noticed the corkboard above the bed. A photo was pinned in the center—a red-haired boy of six or seven beside a sinewy bald man in cargo shorts and a Marine Corps t-shirt. Everything else on the board appeared to be hand-drawn sketches very different from those they'd found in Chase's backpack—the grim reaper on a motorcycle; a screaming skull; a hand clutching a dripping knife.

Teddy pulled out her phone and snapped a picture.

She looked beneath the mattress and under the bed, then glanced around. Raina had finished with the kitchen and was now scanning the ranch supplies, moving Teddy's way.

Teddy checked the recliner. On a tray table beside it lay a jumble of cheeseburger wrappers from Sonic, a few crushed Sprite cans, and several charcoal pencils. A box of Cocoa Puffs sat on the floor underneath. She picked it up and flipped open the tab. At first glance, she saw nothing but the usual opaque bag, half full of cereal. Then something metallic caught her eye. She reached between the box and the inner bag and pulled out a small spiral-bound sketchpad.

She looked up. "Hey, check it out."

Raina, now at the bookcase leafing through tattered paperbacks, stood and came over. Teddy angled the sketchpad so she could see. It was filled with drawings like those on the corkboard—morbid, well executed, and ghastly.

When she turned to the last page, she froze.

Raina sucked air through her teeth. "Holy shit."

The final sketch depicted a man on his back—a ragged wound where his chin and mouth should have been.

"Cody saw the body," Teddy said.

"When? Nobody's been down there but cops since Dewayne found him." Raina paused. "I guess it's possible Dewayne described it to him."

Teddy shook her head. "It's too exact." She tilted the notepad toward the window. "He's even got the doodles on Chase's shoes."

"He'd seen those shoes before."

"Yeah, but would you think to include a detail like that unless you were an eyewitness? I wouldn't."

"If Cody found the body first, why didn't he call it in?" Raina asked.

"Good question."

"This wasn't in a locked drawer or anything?"

"Cocoa Puffs box."

"Good." Raina snapped a photo of the sketch, then pulled an evidence bag from her pocket and handed it to Teddy. "We can take that with us. Come on. Let's see what Stan can tell us."

Chapter 13

When they emerged from the cabin, Stan was sitting on a bench by the door, his head in his hands. He looked up.

"Find anything?"

Raina sat beside him. "Stan, how many years has Cody lived with y'all?"

Stan rubbed the back of his neck. "Vern died in 2013. Cody was seven, I believe. He's been here ever since." He shifted. "Why?"

"How old was Chase then?"

"Thirteen or so."

Teddy leaned against the door. "Did him and Cody get along?"

Stan's eyes narrowed. "Sure."

"No friction? Cody fit in okay?"

"Oh." Stan leaned back and scratched his cheek. "For the most part. A few bumps in the road."

Teddy nodded. "Was he ever jealous of Chase?"

"Why would he be?"

"Chase was your natural son. Cody might've envied that."

"They weren't around each other that long."

"How come?" Raina asked.

"Chase went into the military academy when he was seventeen. Navy after that. We hardly saw him till he moved home last year." Stan folded his arms and looked from Raina to Teddy. "You can't read too much into Cody running off. He's just a kid." He noticed the sketchbook in Teddy's hand. "What's that?"

Teddy started to respond, but Raina cut in. "There's a drawing we want to ask Cody about."

To Teddy's surprise, suspicion faded from Stan's face. He chuckled. "The kid draws some crazy stuff. Wants to do comics or something. But trust me—he wouldn't hurt a fly."

"When you see him, let us know. We need to talk to him."

Teddy and Raina walked back to the house. Entering through the patio door, they found Mark McKissick in the kitchen, slicing a picnic ham and tucking the meat into zippered bags.

"People have been dropping off food all morning. They want to help, but they don't know how." McKissick smiled faintly, nodding toward the table, which was crowded with foil-covered dishes. "It'll take weeks to eat all this. Thought I'd freeze some, save Inez the trouble."

"Where is she?" Teddy asked.

"Lying down. Even with the meds, she had a rough night. Figured I'd stay till y'all got back, in case you needed me." He gestured to a pitcher on the counter. "Want some tea?"

"No thanks," Raina said. "We'd like to look around Chase's room."

Mark nodded. "Inez said you would." He set down the knife and wiped his hands. "I'll show you the way."

"No need. But stick around. We may have questions."

Raina, who'd seen Chase's bedroom the day before, led the way down a long, gloomy hall. Compared with Cody's messy cabin, Chase's room was spartan. The bed was made with military precision; the nightstand, desk, and dresser were bare.

The austerity surprised Teddy. It didn't fit someone who doodled on his class notes and his shoes.

"Did Inez get in here and tidy up?" she asked.

"No. Looked like this yesterday."

The room didn't take long to search. Teddy checked the closet. On the top shelf, beside a stack of winter blankets, she located a small metal lockbox, unlocked. Inside was a full carton of hollow-point Smith & Wesson cartridges.

She took a few pictures, returned the box, and checked the closet floor—shoes, boots, deployment bag, guitar case. She moved the hamper aside. Behind it sat a blue gift bag. Teddy picked it up and stepped out for a better look. Inside was a flat, tissue-wrapped object.

"Hey, check this out," she said.

Raina was sitting at the desk, rummaging through drawers. "What is it?"

"I don't know. Okay to look?"

"Inez said we could."

Teddy carried the gift bag over and slid the contents onto the desk. She pulled away the tissue. Inside was a framed pencil sketch—a close-up of a woman's braceleted arm.

Raina sat back. "Where'd you find that?"

"Closet."

"Is there a card?"

Teddy fished in the bag and found an unsealed envelope containing a rectangle of white cardstock. A message was scrawled on the back.

She read it, then passed it to Raina. "Not signed or dated, and not addressed to anyone."

"'Thanks for all your help,'" Raina read aloud. She pulled out her phone and thumbed through the photos. "Handwriting matches the suicide note."

Teddy picked up the sketch. The arm looked smooth and young. On the wrist was a charm bracelet of the type worn by teenage girls. The fad was a little dated now—though according to Julia, it was making a comeback—but it had been huge when Teddy was a kid. Raina had had one in fifth grade. Teddy had coveted it. That Christmas, she'd gotten her own—a gift from her mother. She hadn't thought about that bracelet in years. It was a painful memory now. Her mother had run off with a truck driver two weeks later, and Teddy had always wondered if she'd already planned to leave when she wrapped it and put it under the tree.

Only three charms were visible in the sketch—a honeybee, ballet slippers, and a bird.

"Chase must've drawn this," Teddy said. "The style's similar to the sketches in his backpack. Wonder who it was for."

"Inez said he was engaged for a while, back in Galveston. His fiancée broke it off. Maybe it was for her?"

"I don't know." Teddy glanced at the bag and note. "Doesn't have a 'girlfriend' kind of vibe."

Raina took photos, then repacked the bag. "Put it back. Stan and Inez might want it."

Teddy nodded. "Find anything in the desk?"

"Not much. A Bible, school supplies, some AA literature. This might be something, though." Raina opened a drawer and held up a yellow sticky note. "Same handwriting as the suicide note."

Teddy took it in her gloved fingers. "A phone number. What twenty-five-year-old writes numbers on paper anymore?" She did a quick search on her phone. "Galveston area code."

"I took a picture," Raina said. "We'll call it later."

She put the note back, and they returned to the living room. Mark McKissick had finished in the kitchen and was on the sofa flipping through a photo album.

He looked up. "Relics from happier times. Stan's never caught the digital-camera wave."

Teddy glanced down at the page that lay open on his lap. One photo showed a group of young boys playing flag football. In another, they were shirtless and laughing, paddling canoes on a still, dark lake. Sheer limestone cliffs rose behind them, topped with pines.

"There's no cliffs like that around here," she said.

"It's down in the Hill Country. That summer camp where all the local kids used to go."

"Oh right—Shane loved that place. It was defunct by the time Julia got old enough."

McKissick turned the page. Another image—twenty or thirty boys in front of a log cabin, grinning at the camera. Shane, maybe twelve or thirteen, stood near the back beside an eleven-year-old Frankie Aguilar, much shorter then, balancing on tiptoe to see over the shoulders in front of him.

Two boys in the front row held up a hand-painted sign—"Camp Wildwood, 2011." The one on the left was stocky, dark-haired, with caramel-colored skin and sensitive, intelligent eyes. The one on the right was taller, thin and pale, his dark-blond hair damp and plastered to his forehead. Teddy recognized them both. She spoke without thinking.

"God, that one's depressing."

McKissick nodded.

Raina leaned in. "You knew both of them?"

"I met Grayson after I moved here in 2012." Mark tapped on the image of the dark-haired boy. "Him and Berna were members at Calvary Baptist. But the Loudermilks went somewhere else, then. I didn't meet Chase till last year."

"You said Chase hadn't been coming to the Bible study very long," Teddy said. "Any idea why he started?"

Mark sighed and closed the album. "Something upset him this summer."

"What was it?"

He hesitated, got up, peered down the hallway. Then he walked to the far end of the living room. Teddy and Raina followed.

"He wouldn't tell me," McKissick said in a low voice. "But it started him drinking again."

"Think it could've been about his engagement falling through?" Raina asked.

"I didn't get that impression. I've talked to lots of kids going through breakups. This felt different. He said he might end his life—but he never mentioned a girl."

Teddy and Raina exchanged a look.

"He said that?" Teddy asked.

"Not directly. Things like 'I can't take it anymore,' or 'I'm scared I'll do something drastic.' I wish I'd pressed him, but—"

Raina threw up her hands. "Why are you just now telling us this?"

Mark looked sheepish. "Inez was with us earlier. I didn't have the heart."

On top of a nearby bookcase stood a Texas-shaped wooden plaque etched with the words "God's Country." Mark picked it up and turned it in his hands. "I thought he was talking about drinking himself to death. There's no AA chapter in town. He joined the Bible study for support."

Teddy thought of Chase in her classroom, sequestering himself by the window. Silent. Withdrawn. Nothing like the gregarious student he'd been last spring.

"He was older than most college kids," she said. "Did he fit in?"

"He was quiet, at first. But he was coming out of his shell. I took it as a good sign when he wanted to go bowling with everyone after the study Sunday night."

"You didn't go?"

Mark smiled. "Too tired. Sunday's a day of rest for everyone but the pastor. I went home."

Raina pulled out a notepad and handed it to McKissick. "I'd like the names of everyone who attended."

"No problem."

As McKissick wrote, Teddy wandered around the room, studying the photographs—one of a young woman in a wedding gown; another of Chase, looking strange with a buzz cut, standing stiffly in his Navy dress blues before a US flag.

A ceramic frame on the TV cabinet labeled "Christmas 2014" held a snapshot of the family—minus Stan, no doubt the photographer. In the center, a teenage Chase was playing tug-of-war with a black Labrador puppy in front of the Christmas tree. Everyone else looked on, laughing—except for a small auburn-haired boy in Ninja Turtle pajamas who was huddled in a corner of the couch. His eyes were fixed on Chase with an odd expression, both wistful and sullen. The only photo of Cody Puckett in the room.

Teddy rejoined the others. Mark McKissick had returned the notebook, and Raina was scanning the list of names. She asked if all of them had gone bowling.

Mark wasn't sure but said it would be easy to find out. "Just check Instagram and Facebook."

As they were leaving, Teddy paused. "Did you know Chase was planning to transfer schools?"

McKissick hesitated before nodding. "He asked me for a character reference. Told me not to tell anyone."

◆ ◆ ◆

Back in the police SUV, Teddy and Raina bumped slowly northeast along the gravel track toward the main ranch gate. Neither spoke.

As they were rounding the northern shoulder of Deadhorse Mesa, Teddy broke the silence.

"What do you think?"

Raina didn't respond. Her jaw was tight, and she stared out the window, one finger tapping the wheel in a nervous, uneven rhythm.

Teddy cleared her throat. "Something bothering you?"

Raina said nothing.

After half a minute, Teddy unbuckled her seatbelt and turned toward her. "Stop the goddamn car, will you?"

Raina braked hard, and a plume of red dust rose around them. "What the hell?"

"Are you gonna keep freezing me out every time I open my mouth?"

Raina looked over. In her mirrored sunglasses, Teddy saw her own face—defensive and furious.

"Oh, for God's sake. Not everything's about you."

"Then what?"

"None of your business."

"Is it because I pushed to go after Cody? It worked, didn't it? If we—"

Raina laughed bitterly. "You think that's why I'm upset?"

"Look, the Chief asked me to be here. I didn't force my way in."

"Has it occurred to you that this is hard for me? No, of course it hasn't. Talking to the Loudermilks, seeing what they're going through—it feels shitty." Raina turned and stared out at the scrubland.

After a moment, Teddy sat back. "I'm sorry."

The air inside the SUV seemed to thrum with the pressure of everything unspoken between them. Teddy's ears rang. She rolled down the window. The dark cloudbank she'd noticed earlier had slid off to the east. The day had grown sunny and warm, but the air was cool beneath the mesa's shadow.

The seconds ticked past. It seemed impossible to speak, and impossible to keep silent. She groped for a safer topic.

"What do you think about the case?"

"Clear suicide. McKissick's information settles it." Raina reached for the gear shift. "And for the record—you did force your way in. You showed up at the silo yesterday, doing your 'Edwina the Indispensable' act for Ramirez, reminding him how much better you are than me. And it worked. So spare me the self-righteous, misunderstood bullshit. Let's just do our jobs."

Chapter 14

The Stone Creek police station stood on Colonel Priddy Avenue, the main road through town. It looked like something from a Western set—whitewashed brick, a keystone facade, and two picture windows flanking a frosted glass door. Until twenty years ago, the building had been a retail establishment, and above the door, the words "Mudrey's Hardware" were still faintly visible.

Teddy, who'd followed Raina back in her own truck, parked behind her in the station lot and went inside. It was lunchtime, and the place was fairly empty. The receptionist, a plump, balding young man with a cheerful face and thick West Texas drawl, was on the phone. His right eyebrow rose slightly at the sight of Teddy and Raina together, but he greeted Teddy with a nod.

On the reception counter sat a large bowl of Dum-Dums for kids who came in with their parents. The receptionist had been sucking on a lollipop but had taken it out of his mouth to answer the phone and was holding it in one hand.

"Is the Chief in, Brendall?" Raina mouthed.

Brendall gestured with the lollipop toward the rear of the building.

Raina secured Cody's sketchbook in the evidence locker. Then they made their way to Ramirez's office. His door was open. He was at his desk, reading something on his computer.

He looked up. "Y'all coming from the Rocking L?"

Raina nodded and started to sit down, but Ramirez shook his head.

"It's almost one. Let's go over to Ridgell's—my treat. We'll talk there." He stood and grabbed his hat.

The day was growing humid, and the sky was a deep hazy blue. A few ragged clouds were drifting in from the southwest as they walked the two blocks in silence. Ridgell's BBQ was not much to look at. It was a squat cinderblock shack on a side street lined with seedy businesses and weed-choked lots. Nearby, a dozen picnic tables sat on a concrete patio beneath a tin roof.

The patio was crowded. Teddy noticed a few customers watching them as they approached. By nightfall, news that she and Raina had eaten lunch together would be everywhere. Small-town life had its drawbacks.

They ordered their food and, a few minutes later, were carrying Styrofoam containers of brisket and cups of iced tea around the shack. A muddy red stream called the Little Branch ran behind Ridgell's, with a few picnic tables along its trash-cluttered banks.

"We'll have more privacy back here," Ramirez said, heading for a table beneath a large mesquite.

They brushed away leaves and dried mesquite pods and sat down.

"I guess you're wondering how it went with Inez and Stan," Raina said, pulling her plastic fork from its cellophane wrapper.

"Hold up—you'll give us indigestion. Ten minutes won't make or break us." Ramirez sounded tired. His eyes were bleary and a little bloodshot. He looked like he'd slept badly. He tucked a paper towel into his collar, opened his container, and squirted barbecue sauce onto slices of steaming brisket.

They ate in silence, listening to the gurgle of the creek behind them. A half-starved, pregnant calico crept from the brush and lay in a patch of sun-dappled knotgrass, watching them hopefully but keeping her distance. Teddy ate quickly and tossed a few scraps to the cat while she waited for Raina and Ramirez to finish.

When he'd swallowed the last of his meal, Ramirez wiped his hands and took a long drink of tea.

"Okay. Tell me."

Raina recounted the morning's events, with Teddy occasionally chiming in. Ramirez listened closely. He was keenly interested in the notebook they'd found in Cody Puckett's cabin. Raina handed him her phone with the photo she'd taken. He took his readers out of his breast pocket and studied the screen.

"This kid Cody ran when he saw y'all?"

Teddy nodded. "He's hiding something."

"Stan doesn't think so," Raina said.

"We didn't show Stan that sketch."

Ramirez clicked his tongue. "If Cody found the body, why didn't he call 911?"

"Maybe he panicked, afraid he'd get blamed."

Ramirez enlarged the photo with a calloused thumb and forefinger. "Dewayne Forrester called 911 just after six a.m., right? But our guys didn't get there till—what, six thirty? Maybe Cody showed up in that window, and Dewayne let him go inside for a look."

"It's possible," Raina said. "I'll find out."

"What do you think, Drummond?" Ramirez asked.

The calico, emboldened by the handouts, had jumped on the table. Teddy set her gently on the ground.

"The simplest explanation's usually right. Either Cody found the body before anyone else and for some reason didn't call the cops—or he killed Chase."

"If it's a murder," Raina said.

"Yeah. If."

Raina waved away the idea. "He'd have to be terminally stupid to kill Chase and then draw the crime scene."

"A lot of killers are terminally stupid," Teddy said.

Ramirez removed his readers and chewed on one of the temple tips. "Does Cody have a motive?"

"Maybe. We won't know till we talk to him."

"Cody didn't kill Chase," Raina said. "There's no way he could've got the gun."

"Could Chase have loaned it to him?" Ramirez asked.

"Stan nixed that." A yellowed mesquite frond fluttered onto the table, and Raina brushed it away. "Besides, Chase told McKissick he might end things."

"McKissick thought he was talking about drinking," Teddy said.

"Murder doesn't fit the facts. Suicide does. Simple as that."

"Depends which facts you're looking at."

Raina's eyes narrowed. "The gun was in a locked case. Chase's handwriting's on the note. He talked about ending it." She ticked off the list on her fingers. "I'm not spinning a conspiracy theory, here."

"You're cherry-picking. Where's the bullet casing? Where's Chase's phone? People don't ditch their phones before dying unless they've got something to hide. Or someone else does."

Raina's nostrils flared slightly, and Teddy felt it—the brittle edge beneath the argument. Something personal.

"That's speculative," Raina snapped.

Ramirez raised a hand. "Neither theory's a perfect fit. No point debating yet. We're just getting started."

The breeze had picked up and swung around to the west. Dark, brisket-scented smoke from Ridgell's billowed in their direction.

Teddy coughed into her sleeve. "What about Chase's phone? Are the Rangers sending a dive team?"

"We're waiting on the ME's report," Ramirez said. "Rangers won't come if it ain't a homicide."

Raina fanned the air with a napkin. "When's the autopsy?"

"Tomorrow. Body went to Lubbock this morning. I told them it's time-sensitive, but we probably won't hear anything till Thursday, at the earliest." He wiped his eyes with a folded handkerchief. "Let's get out of here before we suffocate."

As they stood, Teddy's phone vibrated. A text from Alan: *On a job in San Angelo till 5. U R picking Henry up after practice @ 4:30?*

Teddy looked up. Ramirez and Raina had gathered the trash and were waiting.

"Go on. I'll be right behind you," she said.

They moved off. Teddy gave Alan's text a thumbs up.

As she was sliding the phone back into her pocket, it buzzed again: *U promised 2 play his bug game today. Don't forget.*

Her thumb hovered over the middle-finger emoji, but she thought better of it and put the phone away.

They walked south along Culpepper Road. No one spoke. As they passed a small frame house with rotting jack-o'-lanterns on the porch, Teddy broke the silence.

"Let me ask you something, Chief."

Ramirez turned. "What is it?"

The wind blew hair into Teddy's eyes. She brushed it behind her ear. "Inez mentioned a blowup between Stan and Chase a few weeks ago—said Chase sometimes needed 'tough love.' Sounded like there's some backstory there."

Ramirez sucked his teeth. "When Chase was in high school, things were rocky. He started acting out after that Robles boy died at camp. Stan got fed up and sent him to the military academy in Harlingen. Eula always said Stan blamed himself for Chase's drinking. Felt guilty for sending him away."

"Wonder why he came back?" Raina said.

"He was doing pretty good in Galveston. Got himself clean, got a good job. But Inez said he wanted a fresh start after his engagement fell through." Ramirez paused. "Maybe he needed closure with Stan, too. I got the impression he wanted to patch things up."

Teddy said nothing and avoided looking at Raina. Closure. Forgiveness. Were they ever really possible? Some things, once broken, were irreparable. Or maybe they only seemed that way because neither side knew what to do.

◆ ◆ ◆

Back at the station, Ramirez headed for his office.

Raina looked at Teddy. "Let's try that number we found in Chase's bedroom."

As the department's only detective, Raina had a small office of her own. It had once been Teddy's, and it felt strange to see someone else's name on the nameplate. Inside, Raina shut the door. She'd taken more care with the space than Teddy had. A potted fig tree stood in the corner, and a jade plant hung in a macramé sling by the window. The desk had been moved; square indentations still marked the thin carpet where it used to stand.

Family photos were pinned to the corkboard—the Braggs at the beach on South Padre Island; Raina and her husband, Anthony, dancing somewhere under palm trees and twinkle lights; Calvin, their youngest, in his football uniform. On the desk sat an 8x10 studio portrait of Raina and Anthony on a garden bench, with Terrence and Calvin standing behind them, grinning. Terrence looked fifteen or sixteen in the photograph—so full of life. Hard to reconcile with the version that showed up in Teddy's dreams, uninvited and ageless.

Raina noticed her staring. "I don't want you looking at that." She grabbed the photo and shoved it into a drawer, then sat down.

Teddy flushed. She wanted to say something—anything—that might bridge the distance between them. But there were no words for that kind of history.

Instead, she dropped into the chair opposite Raina and asked the first question that came to mind. "What did you think of the Chief's story?" Better to focus on facts, something she could manage.

Raina opened a bottle of water that was on the desk and took a drink. "Makes sense. But I don't see how it gets us anywhere."

"The Chief said Chase left Galveston because his engagement fell through. What if that's not the only reason?"

"What do you mean?"

"He wouldn't write his fiancée's phone number on a Post-it, would he?"

Raina pulled out her phone and opened the photo of the sticky note. She picked up the desk phone, punched the number for an outside line, and dialed.

"Put it on speaker," Teddy said.

Raina hit a button, and the ringtone echoed in the small room. They waited—four rings.

Then a mechanical click, and a recorded voice: "Hi, this is Matt. Leave a message."

Chapter 15

Teddy and Raina stared at each other. Both jumped when the voicemail *beep* crackled over the speaker.

Raina leaned in. "This is Detective Raina Bragg with the Stone Creek Police Department. It's urgent that I speak with you." She left a callback number and hung up.

"Think he's the Matthew we're looking for?" Teddy asked.

"Can't be a coincidence."

Teddy ran her hands along the arms of her chair. "If that was a suicide note, why didn't Chase include Matthew's last name?"

"Suicide notes are never formal."

"Yeah, but think about it. Stan and Inez don't know this guy. If Chase wanted him to get the note, you'd think he'd give more info."

Raina pursed her lips. "He may not have been thinking clearly. We'll know more when the guy calls back." She glanced at the wall clock. "How much time do you have?"

"I've got to pick up Henry at four thirty."

"Let's split up. I'll hit the John Deere plant—find out if Dewayne Forrester saw Cody at the silo yesterday. You check the bowling alley. Maybe they've got footage from Sunday night."

They made their way past the kitchen and through the windowless squad room, where a pair of officers sat at army surplus desks typing up reports. In the lobby, Caleb Brendall was sucking another lollipop and playing Yahtzee on his phone.

"I'm expecting a call from a guy named Matthew, last name unknown. I gave him this number." Raina nodded toward the desk phone at Brendall's elbow. "Let me know the second he calls."

Brendall saluted her with his sucker, grinning.

"Save some of those for the kids," Raina said. "Your tongue's purple, for God's sake."

Outside, they were heading for their vehicles when a shout stopped them. Brendall was waving from the station door.

"Chief says wait!"

Teddy and Raina exchanged a look and started back. Before they reached the door, Ramirez emerged, his phone in one hand and his Stetson in the other.

"We're at the station now," he said into the phone. "Pull around back." He hung up and dropped the phone in his breast pocket. "Bragg, Drummond—follow me." He put on his hat and started toward the rear of the building.

"What's going on?" Raina called as they hurried after him.

"Stan's two minutes out," Ramirez said. "He's got Cody Puckett."

On the south side of the building was a metal door that led directly to the booking desk and the station's two small holding cells.

As they rounded the corner, a muddy blue pickup turned into the lot. Stan Loudermilk stopped in the loading zone and got out, leaving the truck running. Through the windshield, Teddy could see a second figure in the passenger seat—the auburn-haired boy who'd run from them that morning. He was glowering at his lap.

Raina went to the truck and jerked open the passenger door. "You gonna cooperate, or do I have to cuff you?"

Cody shot her a sulky look. "Cuff me for what? I ain't done nothin'."

"You've hampered a police investigation, for starters. Let's go."

Cody climbed out. Raina took him by the elbow.

"Put him in the interview room," Ramirez said.

"I don't have to talk to nobody," Cody mumbled. "I got rights."

"If you're trying to look innocent, you're not off to a great start," Raina said as she pushed him through the door.

Ramirez turned to Stan. "Where was he?"

Stan Loudermilk looked like he'd aged twenty years in one day. His hair was mussed, his eyes bloodshot. His whole body sagged.

"Caught him trying to slip back into his cabin."

"When?"

"Forty-five minutes ago, I reckon."

"He must've come back just after we left," Teddy said.

Stan nodded.

"Let's go inside, Stan," Ramirez said. "Bragg and Drummond may want to talk to you after they speak to Cody."

Stan stared at the brickwork of the station's wall. "Gotta run an errand first."

"Come on, Stan, you don't need to be running errands today, of all days."

Stan met his eyes. "It's the funeral home, Wally. Gotta discuss arrangements. Inez ain't up to it."

Ramirez laid a hand on his brother-in-law's shoulder. "Want company? I can get away in an hour."

"Rather get it over with." Stan cleared his throat. "Any idea when—?"

"When you can bring Chase home? End of the week, I hope."

Stan nodded and turned to go, then stopped. "One thing—Cody can't come back to the ranch."

"Why not?" Teddy asked.

"Inez won't have it." He rubbed a calloused hand roughly over his face. "My fault. I told her y'all took some suspicious drawings out of his cabin. She put two and two together and got five, thinks Cody mighta hurt our boy. She never really took to him."

He reached into the pickup's bed and pulled out a duffel bag. "I packed him a few things. Cody's dead broke—don't even have a vehicle. If you'll take him over to the Econo Lodge on 137 when you're done, I'll cover it. Maybe Inez'll soften up in a day or two."

Stan blinked. His face was slack.

"Don't worry about it, Stan," Ramirez said, taking the bag. "We'll help him figure something out."

"Does Cody know we found his notepad?" Teddy asked.

Stan shook his head. "I didn't say nothin', and Inez never spoke to him."

After Stan drove away, Ramirez turned on Teddy. "Y'all should've known better than to tell him about that drawing."

"We didn't give details," Teddy said, a little defensively. "He saw us carrying out the sketchbook. We had to say something."

They went inside, past the booking desk, and turned down a narrow hall to the interview room. Raina was standing outside, staring at her phone. She looked up, blinking fast. Her eyes were red.

"You okay?" Teddy asked.

Raina didn't answer. "Be right back—I need to make a call." She gestured to the door. "He's not under arrest, but I read him his rights. Go on in, try to establish a rapport."

Raina turned and walked off.

Teddy looked at the Chief. "Is she all right?"

Ramirez rubbed the back of his neck. "What do you mean?"

Teddy studied his face. Had he really not noticed?

Ramirez had always been a solid police chief. Not perfect—he could be overbearing, at times, and had a tendency to patronize female officers. But he was fair and decisive. However, in the four years since Teddy resigned, he'd changed. He seemed duller, more distant. Since his wife died, he'd been living alone. Maybe he was still struggling to cope with the loss.

"Never mind," she said, moving to the interview room door.

"Just get him talking," Ramirez called after her. "Put him at ease."

◆ ◆ ◆

The interview room was dreary by design—a cramped gray space just big enough for three chairs and a metal table bolted to the wall. Teddy went in and closed the door. Cody Puckett was wedged in the corner behind the table, his head in the crook of his arm and his white Stetson pulled down over his face. He looked asleep, though his knees bounced nervously.

Teddy laid a hand on his shoulder. He raised his head and pushed back his hat.

"Reckon I dozed off." He stretched and yawned theatrically.

"Want something to drink?"

"Nah, I'm good. Wouldn't mind a spit-cup, though." He pulled a tin of Skoal from his pocket.

Teddy stepped out and returned with a Styrofoam cup.

Cody took it and removed his hat. "Where's the other cop—the pissed-off one?"

"If you mean Detective Bragg, she'll be back in a minute." Teddy sat across from him. "I'm Teddy Drummond. I'm assisting with the case."

Cody looked startled. His eyes widened, then narrowed. "*You're* Teddy Drummond? I thought—I mean, you don't look like—" He blinked, then opened the tin and wedged a pinch of tobacco under his lip.

Like what? Teddy wondered. She said nothing.

Cody shut the tin and looked up. "What am I here for? Am I under arrest?"

"We need a statement."

"Didn't have to drag me here like a criminal."

"We tried to talk this morning. You ran off."

"I don't like cops. Don't mean I did nothin'."

"No one's saying you did," Teddy said. "Tell me about Sunday night. Stan says you were on patrol."

Cody nodded. "Chase was s'posed to take over at one, but he blew it off." He shifted. "Leastways, that's what I thought then."

The door swung open. Raina slipped inside, carrying a mug and a yellow legal pad. Her mascara had been redone, but her eyes were still faintly red. She sat beside Teddy and nodded for her to continue.

Teddy turned back to Cody. "Go ahead. What did you think when Chase didn't show? Were you worried?"

"Hell, no. I was pissed. Figured he was drunk in an alley somewhere, left me holding the bag again."

"It happened before?"

"Plenty. Earlier in the fall. Stan gave him hell a few weeks back, and he straightened up. But he was bound to mess up again."

"Did you try calling?"

"Texted a few times. Got nothin'."

"When did you start texting?" Raina asked.

"Around one thirty, I reckon."

"Can we check your phone?"

Cody's eyes narrowed. "Why?"

"Those texts would help us nail down a timeline," Teddy said.

He hesitated. "Guesso." He pulled out his phone and frowned. "I forgot—I deleted them."

Raina reached across the table and snatched it.

"Hey, what the hell?"

"You said we could check." Raina scrolled through the apps. "You just happened to erase all your messages the day after Chase died?"

"Storage was low. What's the big deal?" Cody licked his lips. "It was a suicide, right?"

"Mind if I borrow this a few minutes so our techs can take a look?"

Cody tipped his chair back and leaned against the wall. "Go ahead." His voice was casual, but a flicker of worry played in his eyes.

Raina stood and left the room.

Cody dropped the chair with a thump and reached for the cup. "What's her problem?"

Teddy looked at him, considering how to respond.

When she'd been the department's sole detective, Teddy had always asked Raina to assist with interrogations. Raina had been the empathetic one, the good cop, a perfect counterbalance to Teddy's more confrontational style. Teddy had sometimes fantasized about healing the rift between them, stepping back into their friendship as into a pair of favorite jeans. But that was impossible. Raina was different now. They both were.

She shook her head to clear it. "We're trying to get the facts straight. It's all routine."

Cody spat into the cup. "Don't think the other lady got the memo."

"It's just you and me now. Go on. You texted Chase, and he didn't answer. What then?"

"I rode the range till dawn."

"You didn't think about calling Stan, telling him Chase was missing?"

"Hell no."

"Why not? Afraid you'd get Chase in trouble?"

Cody laughed sourly. "Chase needed to get in trouble."

"Then why not call Stan?"

"Stan had the late shift the night before. He needed the sleep."

Teddy thought of the Christmas photo in the Loudermilks' living room—teenage Chase at the center; little Cody huddled in a corner, staring at the older boy with dark, resentful eyes.

"That the only reason?" she asked.

Cody scratched his temple. "I dunno. Reckon I didn't want Stan to think I couldn't handle things."

"You value his opinion?"

"He's been good to me."

"What about Inez? Has she been good to you, too?"

Cody's face darkened slightly. "She don't like me much. Never has."

"Why not?"

"You'd have to ask her." He gnawed at a cuticle on his thumb.

"She ever hit you?"

"Nah, nothin' like that. She just don't like me. I was livin' in the house till last year. After Chase come home, Inez wanted me out."

"Out of the house?"

"Out of the way. Stan wanted me to help him and Chase with the silo, but Inez pitched a fit."

"Maybe she thought they needed father-son time, after so long apart."

"Maybe." Cody pushed his hat aside and leaned in. "Everyone thought Chase turned his life around, but he wasn't fooling me. That guy was about as useful as a soup sandwich." He shot her a look—half guilty, half defiant. "Just 'cause he's dead don't change how I feel." He paused. "You won't tell Stan, will ya?"

"No."

The door opened. Raina came back in.

"Where's my phone?" Cody demanded. "You said you only needed it a few minutes."

"You'll get it back before you go." She sat down and gave Teddy a look—she'd been watching from the CCTV. She nodded for Teddy to continue.

"Okay, Cody, let's wrap this up. You rode the ranch all Sunday night. See or hear anything unusual?"

He hunched his shoulders. "Nothin' till the sirens came."

"You didn't go in the silo?"

"Never went near it."

Raina shifted. "You sure?"

"That place creeps the hell outta me."

Raina glanced at Teddy, then pulled out her phone and slid it across the table. "Care to explain this?"

Cody stared at the photo of the sketch from the cereal box. After a moment, he looked up.

"I drew it. So what?" His mouth sounded dry.

"The only time you could've been down there to see that was before the body was discovered. Which means you just lied."

Cody looked back at the phone screen.

A sharp knock sounded at the door. Ramirez stuck his head in. "Bragg, Drummond—a word."

They pushed back their chairs. Raina snatched her phone, and they hurried into the corridor.

"What's up?" Teddy asked.

Ramirez led them down the hall until they were out of earshot. He stopped near the empty booking desk. Beneath his leathery tan, he looked pale, and he was sweating.

"Just heard from Morley Taggert—the ME up in Lubbock." He wiped his face with his sleeve. "Chase's death was a homicide. No doubt about it."

Chapter 16

A yellowjacket had gotten into the station—probably when they'd brought Cody through the rear door. It buzzed past Raina's head, then skimmed so close to Teddy's cheek that she could feel the minute air current against the tiny hairs on her skin.

She waved it off. "You said the autopsy was tomorrow."

"It is." Ramirez hooked his thumbs in his belt.

"Then how do they know—" Raina began.

The Chief held up a finger. "They tested Chase's hands. No gunshot residue. He didn't shoot himself."

Raina fidgeted with her wedding ring. "Was it the gun we found?"

"Don't know yet. Taggert said it ain't a contact wound. Gun was probably fired from a few inches away."

"Did he give you time of death?" Teddy asked.

Ramirez pulled a small blue sticky note from his pocket. "'Likely between ten p.m. and midnight Sunday.' That's a quote."

"Chase was home in time for his shift," Raina murmured. "Why'd he go to the silo? Did he take someone—or meet someone?"

"His phone might tell us, if we can find it," Teddy said.

"And get anything off it," Raina added. "Won't be easy if it's in that water."

Ramirez nodded. "Soon as I got off the horn with Taggert, I called the Rangers. Their dive team's on that reservoir case near San Angelo. Once they finish, they'll let me know." He lowered his voice. "How's it going with Puckett? Think he's our guy?"

"Strong person of interest," Raina said.

"Any evidence?"

"Only circumstantial," Teddy said.

"But there's a lot of it. He hated Chase. Had plenty of opportunity. Deleted his texts. Plus, he went total deer-in-the-headlights when I showed him that sketch."

The Chief looked at Teddy. "What do you think?"

Teddy shifted. Everything Raina had said was true—but something felt off. "Hard to say. He's hiding something. He's scared. But not of prison. Something else."

"Think y'all can get it out of him?"

Teddy waited for Raina to answer. She didn't.

"We've been playing a little good-cop, bad-cop," Teddy said finally. "Seems to be working."

Ramirez tapped his thumbnail against his teeth. "Dial up the heat, see what happens. But don't overdo it. Don't want him lawyering up."

He turned to go, but Raina stopped him.

"Hang on, Chief." She hesitated, pressing her lips together. "You said Teddy was here in case this got ruled a suicide. You said if it was murder, you'd send her home."

Teddy felt a hot flush creep up her neck. *No good deed.* She thought of the things still on her plate—like prepping for tomorrow's class, figuring out what to say to students about a classmate's violent death. Chase hadn't been close to anyone, as far as she knew. But death hit the young hard.

She also had to pick up Henry. Play Bug Battle Arena. And on top of everything else, Rick Castillo was coming by tonight to check on Fancy. Did Raina really suppose she'd let herself be dragged into this case because she had nothing better to do?

Teddy opened her mouth, but stopped herself at a glance from Ramirez.

He looked at Raina and rubbed his thumb under his jaw. "Now's not the time, Bragg."

"I want to know—is it my case or not?"

"Sure it's your case. But this Puckett kid's our only suspect. Sounds like Drummond's got a rapport. Y'all finish up with him, and I'm sure she'll be happy to step away."

He turned to Teddy for confirmation. She wanted to say *screw this* and walk out. But she thought of Chase's body on the platform, of Inez scrubbing her grief into clean countertops.

She sighed. This wasn't about her.

"Whatever you need," she said.

Raina squared her shoulders. "Just making sure we're clear on the plan," she snapped, and walked away.

Teddy caught up at the interview room door. In their absence, Cody had regained his composure. He was tilted back in his chair, feet on the table, trying to look self-assured. *Trying too hard*, Teddy thought. Her eyes drifted to his boots—and something caught her attention.

Before she could get a closer look, Raina pushed his legs off the table. "If I were you, I'd drop the shit attitude," she said as they sat down. "You could be in a lot of trouble."

Cody sat up straight and adjusted the legs of his jeans. "Trouble for what? Drawing a picture?"

"You lied about seeing the victim."

Cody's brow knotted. "Victim? Chase offed himself."

Raina shook her head. "That hasn't been determined."

"But—he left a note."

"Homicide's a strong possibility."

Cody turned to Teddy. "Is she for real?"

Teddy nodded. "Does that surprise you?"

"Well, yeah." He rubbed the back of his neck. "Figured he finally done it."

"Finally?"

Cody stared at the tabletop. "Chase—he used to get depressed. Crawl into bed for days, sometimes."

"Is that why he drank?"

"I dunno if he drank 'cause he was down, or if he was down 'cause he drank. Maybe neither. When he come home last year, his folks thought he changed." He snorted.

"You didn't?" Raina asked.

"Guys like him don't change. I wasn't one bit surprised he took the easy way out."

"Except maybe he didn't," Teddy said. "Can you think of anyone who'd want to hurt him?"

"Maybe in Galveston. He did drugs sometimes. Mighta had somebody after him."

"He ever mention names?"

"Nah."

"What about here?"

"He wasn't around here long enough to make enemies." Cody shifted. A vein pulsed in his temple.

"You're lying," Raina said.

"No I ain't."

Teddy scooted her chair in. "Cody, come on. Right now, you're our main suspect. So if there's someone else, you should tell us."

He ran his hands along the chair arms. "Nobody was after him, far as I know."

"You didn't like him," Raina said sharply.

"Don't mean I killed him."

Teddy leaned forward, palms flat on the table. "Stonewalling's not your best move."

He looked at her uneasily. "What d'you mean?"

"Maybe you and Chase argued. Maybe he went for you, and you defended yourself. Whatever happened, it's best to get your side of the story on record."

Now Cody looked seriously alarmed. "I didn't kill him—I swear. I didn't go near the silo."

Raina pulled out her phone and thrust it toward him. "This sketch says you did. How'd you know what the body looked like if you weren't there?"

"I—I heard Stan and Inez talking."

"No way. Details are too precise. You were in that silo because you killed him."

"That ain't true." Cody's hands clenched. His knuckles went white. "Do I need a lawyer?"

Raina drew in a breath, but Teddy cut in.

"That's your call. If you killed Chase, yes. But if you didn't—if there's some simple explanation—tell us so we can cross you off the list."

Cody ran his tongue over his teeth. "I didn't kill Chase. Didn't see him that night, alive or dead. That's the truth."

Teddy leaned back. "It's not, though. You know it, and we know it."

Cody crossed his arms. "You weren't there—you can't prove nothin'."

"Can anyone back up your story?" Raina asked.

"My horse and a couple coyotes. I was alone all night, for chrissakes."

"Let me see your right boot," Teddy said.

Cody and Raina both stared at her. Cody's eyes narrowed. "Why?"

"Humor me. Put it back on the table."

Raina moved her mug and notepad aside.

Cody hesitated.

"Look," Teddy said. "If you didn't kill Chase, you've got nothing to worry about. Right?"

His eyes flicked down, then up. He wanted to check his boot—Teddy could tell. After a pause, he shrugged and swung his leg onto the table.

Both women leaned in. After a beat, Raina inhaled sharply. She'd seen it.

"Were you wearing these Sunday night?" she asked.

"Sure. They're all I got." He started to lower his foot, but Raina grabbed his cuff.

"Hang on." She snapped a photo.

"What is it?" Cody demanded.

He wrenched his leg back, propping his ankle over his left knee and twisting the boot toward his face. "I don't see nothin'."

"There's blood," Teddy said.

"Where?"

Raina's pen was lying on the table. Teddy picked it up and pointed. "Right there, that speck on the outsole."

Cody stared at the red-brown spot the size of an apple seed. He blanched, freckles darkening across the bridge of his nose.

"We was castratin' bull calves a couple months ago," he said suddenly. "That's probably what it's from."

Teddy studied him. "I grew up on a goat farm, Cody. No way any rancher was cutting calves in September—too much risk of maggots."

Cody's eyes darted between her and Raina. "Jackrabbits, then. I forgot—I shot a couple last Monday."

Raina took the pen from Teddy and jotted something down. "That's your story?"

"It's the truth. Ask Stan. Hell, ask Inez. I gave 'em to her. She cooked them up that night." He licked his lips, which were puckered and dry. "Am I under arrest?"

Raina looked up from her notepad. "Not yet."

"I can leave, then?" Cody started to rise.

Teddy raised a hand. "Bad idea."

"You sound thirsty," Raina said. "Want some water?" She got up.

Half out of his chair, Cody hesitated, then sat back down. "Yeah."

When the door closed behind Raina, Teddy leaned across the table. "Make this easy on yourself. Tell me what really happened."

Cody's face was sullen. He crossed his arms. "I did shoot rabbits. If you don't believe me, I reckon I need a lawyer."

"You can have one any time. But here's the thing—you're not walking out with that boot—we're sending it for testing."

Cody opened his mouth, but Teddy shook her head, stopping him. "Hear me out. I believe you didn't kill Chase. But I do think you went into that silo. I'm not sure why you won't admit it. But if that blood comes back as Chase's, you're screwed. Nobody'll believe anything you say, after that."

Cody's forehead glistened with sweat. From across the table, Teddy caught a sour whiff of fear. His hands flopped into his lap.

"I don't know what to do, I don't know what to do," he mumbled.

"Then tell me the truth."

Cody was fighting tears. His sniffles and the ticking wall clock were loud in the silence.

Teddy waited. After a moment, she could hear Raina's footsteps returning from the kitchen.

She got up. "Be right back," she said and slipped into the hall.

Raina was just reaching for the door. A plastic water bottle was in her hand.

Teddy put a finger to her lips. She shut the door gently, and they moved a few feet away.

"What's up?" Raina asked.

"He's about to come across with it, I think."

"Great. Let's close the deal."

She started toward the room, but Teddy touched her arm. "Let me keep going solo."

Raina pulled away. "Are you kidding?"

Teddy blinked. "No. What's the problem?"

"What's the problem? You really don't see it, do you?"

"See what? I think we'll get more out of him that way."

"I told you this morning—I'm not playing sidekick on the Teddy Drummond Show. I did that for thirty-five years, and I'm done. I'm the detective, not your damn gofer."

"What are you talking about?"

"This shit's been going on since second grade. You're not pushing me aside again."

Teddy's temples throbbed. "Nobody's pushing you aside—you left the room."

"To get the kid some water." Raina waved the bottle in Teddy's face. "I was trying to distract him from leaving—and it worked."

Teddy pushed her hand angrily away. "Yeah, it worked. That's how good-cop, bad-cop runs—bad cop scares the suspect, good cop gets the confession."

"And you assumed I'm the bad cop because I want you off this case?"

"I assumed you're the bad cop because you were acting like the fucking bad cop."

Raina drew in a breath. Held it. Let it go. "You're trying to show Wally you're indispensable. But this is my case. Deal with it—or get lost." She pointed down the hall toward the rear exit.

Teddy kept her voice even. "Raina, I'm not trying to edge you out. I've got enough on my plate without this. So let's just go back in and find out what the kid knows. Okay?"

Raina's arms were crossed, her expression unreadable. Several seconds passed. Finally, she dropped her arms.

"Fine," she said, and turned away.

Chapter 17

Still pulsating with anger, Teddy followed Raina up the corridor. She wasn't sure how long she'd been gone. A lot could change in a short time. Cody had been on the verge of cracking; she hoped he hadn't regrouped.

When they opened the door, he was still hunched over, sniffling into the crook of his arm.

Raina slid the water bottle across the table. "Here you go."

Cody looked up. His cheeks were pale and tear-streaked.

"Thanks." He wiped his eyes with his sleeve.

Teddy nudged a box of tissues toward him, but Cody ignored it. He grabbed the water and guzzled half.

"Ready to tell us what happened?" Teddy asked.

Cody capped the bottle. "My old man used to say *prisons are full of suckers who didn't lawyer up*."

"We're not trying to trick you," Raina said.

"You're allowed to lie to me, though, right?"

Teddy leaned in. "That blood on your boot means we've got to focus on you till we can rule you out. If we can't, this could go to court. You don't want that."

Cody stared at her. "You'll tell Stan and Inez I had nothin' to do with it?"

"If that's the truth."

He yanked a tissue from the box and sat for several minutes, absently pulling it apart and piling the shreds on the tabletop. Finally, he wadded them into a tight ball and tossed it into the trash.

"I told you the truth, mostly. But I didn't tell everything. Here's what happened."

He spoke haltingly—stopping, starting, doubling back—but slowly the narrative unfolded. He'd been riding the range Sunday night like he said. The weather was chilly, and as the hours crawled by, he got increasingly annoyed that Chase hadn't shown up. He texted him several times, each message nastier than the last.

"After a while, I was cussin' him out," Cody said. "Just venting, you know? Thought he was out partying while I was freezing my ass off."

He was riding along the old military access road when he heard a noise from the direction of the silo. Thinking Chase might be sleeping one off inside, he went to check. The silo door was open. Chase's truck was parked nearby.

Raina looked up from her notepad. "What time was this?"

"Little after three, I reckon."

"Had the truck been there long?"

Cody shrugged. "Hood was cold."

"That's when you went in the silo?"

Cody nodded, rubbing his knuckles on his jeans. "I hate that place. Especially at night. I swear it's haunted."

He'd checked the control room first. It was empty, but the lights were on, and Chase's backpack was by the table.

"Then I went down to the launch chamber."

"Chase was already dead?" Teddy asked.

Cody swallowed. "Yeah."

"Did you check for a pulse?"

"Stayed on the balcony. Wasn't no point tryin' CPR—you could tell."

"What then?"

Cody hesitated. The room was silent except for the scratching of Raina's pen.

"I just stood there. Then I freaked. You know that feeling when you're a kid, and you think a monster's about to grab you from under the bed? I had to get out. So I ran."

Teddy understood. The silo had unsettled her, too. His story tracked—for the most part.

"What about the blood on your boot?"

"I'm comin' to that." Cody pulled out his Skoal tin and wedged in a fresh plug. "I got outside and jumped on my horse. Wanted out of there."

Raina's pen stopped. "You didn't think to report finding a body?"

"Course I did." He tossed the tin onto the table. "I headed for the house to get Stan. But after a couple miles, I turned around."

"Why?" Raina asked.

Cody squirmed. Teddy thought she knew the answer. "Because of those texts you sent?"

Cody flushed a mottled crimson. "Stan's the only one who ever gave a shit about me. I was scared he'd—"

"Kick you out?"

"Nah." He dragged his palms down his face. "Chase was depressed, ready to off himself. And here I was, cussin' at him, callin' him names. If Stan saw that, he—he wouldn't like me no more." Cody stared hard at the tabletop. "Sounds stupid, I know."

Teddy leaned back. "Not at all."

The scratching of Raina's pen faltered briefly, then resumed. After a moment, she said, "So you went back in. To do what—erase the texts from Chase's phone?"

Cody shook his head. "It was password-protected. I was just gonna toss it in the water. Figured that was easiest."

This time, he'd forced himself all the way down to the dive platform.

"How did it look?" Teddy asked quickly.

"Like I drew it. I didn't touch nothin'—just stepped in a little blood, I guess." He looked up. "Tried not to, but it was everywhere."

He'd checked Chase's pockets, then the platform, then the control room. The phone was gone.

"What about his laptop?" Raina asked.

"Didn't see that, neither. Checked the backpack—and the truck."

"You get in the bed of the pickup?" Teddy asked.

"Just looked over the side."

"Then what?"

Cody hunched his shoulders. "Nothin'. I left. Rode the ranch till I heard the sirens."

Raina flipped back a page in her notes. "If the phone was gone and you weren't worried about those texts, why not call 911?"

"I shoulda. But I was freaked out. Just wanted to get away." He drained the last of his water and crushed the bottle in his fist.

Teddy glanced at Raina, who cleared her throat. "You went down to the platform and looked around. You didn't disturb the body or take anything?"

Cody shook his head.

"Think carefully," Teddy said. "It's important."

"I didn't, I swear. I—" He stopped. His face changed. "Oh, damn."

Raina lowered the notepad. "What?"

"I did take one thing."

Silence. Cody's face had gone pale.

"Look at me," Teddy said. "What was it?"

Cody met her eyes. He dug something out of his jeans pocket and placed it on the tabletop with a soft metallic clatter.

Teddy looked at Raina, who pulled a pair of latex gloves from her pocket, put them on, and picked it up. A thin gold chain with three charms—a honeybee, ballet slippers, and a bird. Some of the links were stained a dark brown.

Teddy sat back, staring.

Raina drew a sharp breath. "Where was this, exactly?"

Cody shuffled his feet. "On the platform next to Chase."

"Ever seen it before?"

He shook his head.

Raina laid it across her gloved palm, then compared it to the photo she'd taken of the drawing in Chase's closet. She turned her phone to show Teddy.

"Why'd you take this?" Raina demanded. "You've watched enough CSI shows to know better."

Cody blushed. "There's this girl—a really nice girl. We been seein' each other a while." He glanced nervously at Teddy. "I thought maybe . . ."

Teddy almost laughed. "You thought you'd give her a bracelet you found beside a corpse?"

"I could never afford somethin' like that," he mumbled. "Wasn't gonna tell her where I got it."

He picked at a fingernail, his cheeks blazing. Raina looked skeptical, but Teddy believed him. It wasn't the sort of lie a nineteen-year-old boy told on himself.

"What was it doing down there?" Raina asked.

Cody looked up. "I dunno."

"You must've wondered."

"Figured one of Chase's dive students dropped it."

"Any women taking lessons from him?"

Cody threw out his hands. "I dunno."

Raina held up the bracelet, swinging it gently. "Did Chase have a girlfriend, somebody he might've planned to give this to?"

"Never said so, but that don't prove nothin'. He wouldn't tell me. We weren't buddies."

"Anything else we need to know?" Teddy asked.

Cody hesitated, then shook his head. But Teddy had the strong impression he was holding something back.

Eventually, Raina stood. "Give me your boots."

Grumbling, Cody kicked them off, and Raina picked them up.

"We'll take a break." She gestured for Teddy to follow.

"Hey, what about me?" Cody asked. "I gotta take a leak."

"Hang tight. I'll send someone in."

Before they reached the door, there was a sharp knock. A hollow-chested young man with an acne-scarred face stood in the hallway, holding Cody's phone.

"Got it downloaded. Should have everything tomorrow." He handed it to Raina.

"Thanks, Bobby."

Bobby nodded and headed off. Raina turned and tossed the phone on the table. "Here ya go."

Cody picked it up. "Can I leave? I'm not under arrest, am I?"

"I don't know. I'm going to ask my boss."

Teddy saw a flicker of alarm in his eyes. "You believe me—right?"

"Our motto's *trust but verify*," Raina said.

"But if you checked my phone—?"

"We downloaded it. Now our tech's going through metadata, recovering deleted files—call logs, texts, search history. All that. If it corroborates your story, I'll be inclined to believe you."

Cody looked sick. "There might be some stuff—"

"We're not here to judge your browser history," Teddy said. "We only care about material relevant to this case."

Cody swallowed noisily but said nothing.

“This door’s going to be locked,” Raina said. “But someone’ll be here in a minute to take you to the bathroom.”

Teddy and Raina stepped out. At a supply closet, they grabbed evidence bags, then headed to Raina’s office. After so long in the windowless interview room, Teddy looked outside and was startled to see how low the sun had fallen. She glanced at the wall clock. Three fifty. It would take her ten minutes to get to Henry’s school. She pulled out her phone and set a reminder for half an hour.

Raina was snapping photographs of the bracelet and boots and sliding them into bags. When she finished, she dropped into her desk chair and peeled off her gloves.

“What do you think?” She held up the clear plastic envelope containing the bracelet. “Why was this by the body?”

Teddy leaned against the file cabinet. “Chase never talked to me about the dive business. I don’t know who his clients were.”

“Might not be a client’s. Could’ve been a girlfriend’s.” Raina tossed the bag on the desk.

Teddy picked it up. “Except girls don’t wear charm bracelets as much anymore.”

“Maybe it’s the killer’s.”

“Or maybe it has nothing to do with the murder.” Teddy lay the plastic bag on her palm and traced the small gold shapes with her finger. Someone had picked out these charms. They meant something to somebody. Her mind flashed to the bracelets she and Raina had as kids. She wondered if Raina was thinking of them, too.

“You’d think finding out it’s a homicide would simplify things.” Raina rubbed her temples. “It’s a shame Cody got to that bracelet first. Not much point checking for prints now.”

Teddy pushed away from the file cabinet. “Let’s go update the Chief.” She caught Raina’s quick frown. “Then I’ll get out of your hair, I promise.”

Raina nodded tersely and pressed a button on her desk phone. "Brendall, get some slip-ons for the kid in the interview room and walk him to the bathroom, will you? He's not under arrest, but he's detained for now. So keep an eye on him."

She stood and left the room. Teddy started after her, still carrying the bracelet. It would be good to ask Stan about it, if he was in the building. But almost immediately, she changed her mind and tossed it back on the desk. Raina could show him the photograph, if she wanted to. No father should have to hold a piece of evidence covered in his own child's blood.

Chapter 18

The door to the Chief's office was closed, which was unusual. Raina knocked quietly. After a pause, Ramirez opened it and stepped back.

Stan Loudermilk sat in front of the desk, clutching a coffee cup. He looked shellshocked—probably from his visit to the funeral home. Teddy recognized the look. When Curtis died, Milton had gone on a two-week bender, leaving Teddy—just twenty—to plan the funeral alone. Years later, she'd helped Berna make the arrangements for Grayson.

She remembered the surrealism of walking through a showroom of caskets, as shiny and polished as new cars at a dealership, while a funeral director described their features in hushed, respectful tones—*this one is impermeable, with an inner-spring mattress lined in watered satin.*

What would it be like to choose one for your own child? Teddy couldn't imagine, and didn't want to try.

Stan's unshaven face was sallow and haggard. He smelled faintly of alcohol. Had his coffee been doctored? It was against policy, but everyone knew Ramirez had kept a flask in his desk since Eula died.

The Chief looked nearly as worn as Stan. He waved Teddy and Raina into seats and dropped heavily into his chair.

"I was telling Stan what the ME said about the manner of death."

Teddy was surprised. The ME hadn't released the death certificate—or even performed the autopsy. The call to Ramirez had been strictly confidential.

Beside her, Raina shifted. "Think that was a good idea, Chief?"

A pointless question, now. Ramirez didn't answer.

After an awkward silence, Raina turned to Stan. "This must be a shock. I'm sorry."

Stan turned the cup in his hands. "It'll make Inez feel better. She's been sayin' it all along." He cleared his throat. "Tell me this—did Cody Puckett kill my boy?"

"His story needs to be verified," Raina said cautiously. "We're holding him overnight, but we're not arresting him yet."

Stan grunted. His bleary eyes shifted to Teddy. "What do *you* think?"

Teddy's palms were damp. She wiped them on her knees. "We're still gathering evidence."

"Don't gimme that official bullshit. What does your gut say?"

She hesitated. She wasn't sure. Cody's story tracked, but he hadn't told them everything. He'd clearly disliked Chase, and he'd looked panicked when Raina mentioned recovering deleted phone data. Was he just worried about irate text messages and a sketchy browser history? Or something worse?

Stan was leaning forward, waiting for her answer. His bloodshot eyes were keen and focused. He looked cold sober. Teddy sympathized with his need to know. But West Texas had a long history of vigilante justice, and grieving fathers weren't known for restraint.

She glanced at Raina, who was scowling, then at the Chief, whose head moved in an almost imperceptible shake. *No.*

Teddy sighed. "Too soon to tell, Stan."

His shoulders fell. The energy left his face.

Raina turned toward him. "We think Chase knew his killer. Anyone he'd invite down there late at night?"

Stan rubbed his jaw. "He used to hang around that Aguilar boy sometimes—years ago, I mean."

"Frankie?"

"Yeah. Shane Spivey, too."

Teddy sat back. "My nephew?"

"They all used to go to that camp down near Ingram when they was kids—you remember. But I ain't heard Chase mention either of 'em since he come back. Mostly been staying on the property, when he ain't at school."

"Was he dating anyone?"

"Not since his fiancée left him, far as I know."

Raina pulled up a photo on her phone. "This bracelet was found in the silo. Ever seen it?"

Stan took the phone, squinting at the screen. "Don't look familiar. Ask Inez—she's the noticing type." He seemed about to say more when a knock stopped him.

The office door opened before Ramirez could answer. Brendall poked his head in. For once, there was no lollipop in his mouth.

"We're in the middle of something," Ramirez said.

"Sorry, Chief, it's urgent." Brendall's eyes landed on Raina. "Got a sec?"

Ramirez slapped the desk. "For God's sake, Brendall, just say it."

Brendall gripped the doorframe. "It's the kid—he ain't in the interview room." He looked at Raina. "I went to take him to the john like you asked. But he's gone."

The silence that followed was broken by the shrill, electronic arpeggio of Teddy's phone alarm. She fumbled to shut it off. Chairs screeched—everyone was moving.

"What the hell happened, Brendall?" Raina snapped as they hurried down the hall. "That door was locked."

They reached the interview room and froze.

"Shit," Raina whispered.

Above the table, a ceiling tile had been pushed aside, leaving a dark rectangular opening through which Teddy glimpsed an air-conditioning duct and some thick orange wires.

"He shinnied over to the breakroom, went out the window there," Brendall was saying.

Teddy shook her head. This was the problem with living in a small municipality with chronically underfunded public services. The town council had dragged its feet for years about building a proper police station. Now, there'd be an outcry about the sloppiness of the Stone Creek force, especially after word of Chase's homicide leaked. But with the station housed in a refurbished hardware shop, this sort of thing was bound to happen.

"What do you want us to do, Chief?" Raina asked.

Ramirez was staring up at the ceiling hole, rubbing the back of his head. "People don't run unless they got a reason. I want him back—we got grounds for an arrest." He glanced at the wall clock. "Where would he go, Stan? Who does he hang with?"

Stan blew air through his lips. "Nobody. He barrel-races at the rodeo, but otherwise he don't go nowhere."

"Sure about that?" Teddy asked. "He mentioned he was seeing some girl."

Stan's eyebrows rose. "News to me. He's on foot and he ain't got no money. Won't get far."

"Brendall, tell Bobby to fast-track that phone," Raina said. "Maybe Cody's got friends you don't know about, Stan."

"If I was him, I'd hitchhike," Teddy said grimly.

Raina looked at Ramirez. "Only three roads out of Stone Creek. If we find security footage, we might see which way he went."

Ramirez nodded. "There's three of us. We each take a road."

He turned for confirmation to Teddy, who checked the time and winced. She was already late. "I need to pick up Henry."

Raina pulled out her phone. "Bertie Loomis can help. I'll find out where she is."

Ramirez shook his head. His earlier weariness was gone; he was all business now. "No time. The kid could be miles away in half an hour." He looked at Teddy. "Can Alan get your boy?"

Teddy glanced at her phone. Alan's last message blinked back at her: *U promised 2 play his bug game today. Don't forget.*

She thought of Henry in his hoodie last night, hunched over the bright green game board. "It's almost finished, Mom. Wanna play?"

In a few years, he wouldn't want to play games with his mom anymore. Such a silly, simple thing. But important.

So was Chase.

Once a case got under her skin, Teddy couldn't leave it alone. She'd told herself this time would be different. She wasn't a cop anymore—she wouldn't get reeled in.

But the hook was already set.

She glanced at Stan. He was watching her, an unreadable expression on his face. *You still have your son.* Was that what he was thinking?

She hesitated, then nodded to Ramirez. "I'll figure something out. I'll take 137 north."

"I want to help, too," Stan said darkly.

Ramirez grabbed his arm. "You've been drinking. You're not driving nowhere."

"Try and stop me, Wally."

"Don't make me lock you up. Call a friend to take you home. You should be with Inez today."

As she headed for her truck, Teddy found that a cool front had blown through. Gusts of wind scattered yellow hackberry leaves across the parking lot. She shivered. The sky overhead was clear, but a steel-gray cloudbank, towering and ominous, was advancing from the northwest.

As she pulled out of the lot, she called Alan. An emergency had come up—could he pick up Henry? "Tell him I'll be home in an hour. I'll play with him then."

"You've gotta be kidding. Football practice ended ten minutes ago." Alan's voice was tight with frustration. He and Shane were on a job in San Angelo. They wouldn't be home till dark. The line went silent. Teddy could hear his angry breathing.

Then, in the background, Shane's voice, muffled and distant, yelled, "Woah, watch it with that live oak, you dickheads! Hey, Uncle Alan—"

The line rustled, and Alan shouted something back. "Look, Ted, I gotta go. Want me to ask Lyric if she can get him?"

Teddy's left eyelid twitched. *Lyric.* She made herself exhale. "No, thanks. I'll manage." No way in hell was she letting Lyric pick Henry up two days in a row.

It was four fifty when she reached the field across from the school. The Pop Warner coach, a balding, red-faced thirty-year-old who ran the local pharmacy, was packing footballs into a mesh bag by the bleachers as a handful of boys waited for their rides.

They were absorbed in some sort of impromptu game that involved throwing pebbles through the chain-link fence, but Henry sat alone on the curb with his hoodie up and his gear piled beside him, scuffing his sneakers in the dirt. Teddy felt the familiar twinge in her chest. *Dammit, dammit, dammit.* She threw the truck into park.

"You okay, bud?" she asked, coming around the front bumper.

Henry cinched the hood tighter and grabbed his backpack and helmet. "You're late."

"Sorry. Got held up." Teddy picked up the rest of his gear and followed him toward the truck. "Why are you sitting by yourself? You didn't want to play with the others?"

"I'm just tired." Henry opened the truck door and climbed inside.

Teddy slid behind the wheel and looked at him. His face was turned toward the window. Henry had always been a quiet kid, but since his accident and surgeries, he'd shut down even more.

"You okay?" she asked again.

"I wanna quit football, Mom."

"Did something happen?"

Henry hunched his shoulders. "It's no fun, now. I just sit on the bench and watch. When can I play again?"

"Probably a year, the doctor said. But it's good to stay connected with the team. Want me to talk to your coach? Maybe he could give you a job to do."

"No. I wanna go home."

Teddy sighed and turned the ignition. "We've got a couple errands to run, first. Then I want to play Bug Battle Arena."

Henry looked at her. He seemed surprised that she'd remembered. "Dibs on fire ants. You can be black widows."

"Perfect," Teddy said.

◆ ◆ ◆

Teddy threaded her way back to Colonel Priddy Avenue and turned north onto Route 137, stopping after a few blocks at the Skinny's parking lot. She pulled up beside the first pump, gassed up the truck, then parked in front of the ice machine.

"I've gotta go inside for a couple minutes," she said.

"Can you get me a Snapple? Kiwi strawberry?"

Teddy gave him a thumbs up. "Lock the doors."

As she entered the convenience store, the door chime rang, but no one responded. The place had been robbed once, years ago—the elderly clerk left tied up in the manager's office. Looking around the empty store, Teddy felt uneasy.

She entered the hallway marked "Employees Only" and pushed through a swinging door. Jasmine Aguilar was behind the office desk. Frankie stood over her in his green coveralls blazoned with the "Drummond Nursery and Lawn Design" logo. They were speaking in low, urgent tones.

"I told you what would happen if you didn't lay off," Jasmine whispered. "You pushed too hard."

"Gimme a break, Jazz. That's got nothin' to do—"

Jasmine, partly facing the door, saw Teddy enter and cleared her throat. Frankie stepped quickly away.

Teddy glanced from one to the other. "Y'all all right?"

"Mrs. D!" Jasmine looked relieved. "Didn't think I'd see you again today."

"Sorry to barge in. Couldn't find anybody out front." She turned to Frankie. "Thought you were working till six."

Frankie rubbed his eye with a dirty thumb. "Been making deliveries. Better get back to it." He shot a look at his sister, then ducked out.

Jasmine stood and smoothed her hair. "What can I do for you, Mrs. D?"

"I need to see your security footage from the last hour—anything showing the road."

Jasmine stared blankly. "But you're—"

"I'm assisting the police. Wally Ramirez sent me."

Jasmine didn't move.

"It's urgent, and I've got Henry in the truck." Teddy pulled out her phone. "I can have the Chief call your boss directly."

Jasmine shook her head. "That's okay, I trust you."

She tapped a few buttons on the keyboard of an ancient-looking PC. Teddy walked around and leaned over her shoulder.

A grid of grayscale images filled the screen—live shots of the store's interior, plus exterior views of the doors and fuel pumps. Beyond the pumps, Route 137 was clearly visible.

"Show me those pumps from four thirty on," Teddy said.

Jasmine typed quickly. Together, they watched a sped-up recording—cars zipping in and out, customers pumping gas with comic velocity. Then, in the background, a figure flashing from right to left.

"*There*. Replay that."

They watched it again in real time. At four fifty-six, Cody Puckett appeared, walking north on 137. Though in sock feet, he moved quickly, with long, sloping strides, shoulders hunched and head down. His face was half hidden beneath the white Stetson. A car sped past. He didn't look up.

At least he's not hitchhiking, Teddy thought.

Passing the store, Cody pulled out his phone. He was raising it to his ear when he vanished off the screen.

His movements were deliberate—weighted with finality and purpose. He looked like someone with a plan. Where was he going?

Teddy straightened and stretched her back, still staring at the screen. She'd already logged the timestamp, the stride, the posture—all the details years of training had taught her to notice. But she was still missing something. Not the facts themselves, but the way they sat together. Like a question she hadn't yet figured out how to ask.

Chapter 19

She was out the door of the Skinny's and halfway to her truck before a glimpse of Henry's head through the window made her stop.

"Damn."

She ran back in, grabbed a strawberry kiwi Snapple from the cooler, and paid quickly. Less than a minute later, she was behind the wheel, turning left onto Route 137.

Henry popped open the bottle. "Our house is the other way."

"I need to check something first."

"Check what?"

"Tell me if you spot anyone walking on the road or in the fields."

Teddy passed her father's house at seventy and continued another five miles before giving up and turning around. Cody wouldn't have made it this far on foot—not in his socks.

Driving back, she turned on her headlights. Sunset was still a half-hour off, but the sky was growing dark. The cloudbank had advanced. Lightning flickered at its edges. Approaching her father's place again, Teddy eased into the weedy drive.

"Why are we stopping at Grandpa's?" Henry asked as Teddy parked beneath a scraggly hackberry tree in the yard. "It smells in there."

"You can wait in the truck." Teddy gave him her phone. "Here, play a game. I won't be long."

Picking her way up the rotting porch steps, she went inside. Her father was at the kitchen table. He wore a pair of cracked reading glasses. A screwdriver was in his hand; a black, baseball-sized object sat on the table in front of him. Beer cans littered the tabletop.

Teddy waved a housefly off her cheek. "What are you doing, Dad?"

Milton looked up, his eyes yellow and rheumy. "Going through this stuff Shane brought me." His voice was slurred. He gestured with the screwdriver at a box on the floor.

Teddy glanced inside. A tangle of plastic, metal, and wire. "More junk?" She needed to have a heart-to-heart with Shane. "You're supposed to be getting rid of stuff, not collecting more."

"This ain't junk." Milton held up the object. "Got legitimate resale value."

"When's the last time you sold anything?" Teddy asked. "What is that, anyway?"

"'Lectric gate lock. Shane got it at a job site."

"Dad, the Health Department—"

Milton dropped the screwdriver and stood. "Come here to bitch at me? Or was there somethin' else?" He wobbled to the refrigerator and grabbed a beer. Teddy glimpsed the half-gallon of milk she'd brought that morning, still unopened.

"Actually, I was wondering if that camera on the porch works."

Milton shuffled back to the table, popped the beer tab, and drank.

"My stuff's junk unless you need it, huh?"

"Is it working or not?" Teddy rubbed her eyes.

Milton wiped a dribble of beer from his chin and belched softly. "Sure, it's workin'."

Teddy waited, but he said nothing more. "Well? Can I see the footage?"

He tipped back the can again. "For the right price."

"Oh, for God's sake—what do you want?"

His eyes glittered. He was enjoying this. He'd always been a bully. Old age hadn't changed that—just forced him to adjust tactics.

"An apology would be nice."

"Dad, stop jerking me around. If you're gonna play games, I'll go up the road and ask the Masseys."

Milton shrugged and picked up the screwdriver.

Teddy threw up her hands. "Fine, I'm sorry—you're a brilliant entrepreneur. They'll make documentaries about you. Now, show me the footage, or you can get someone else to be your grocery delivery service."

Milton grinned and pushed away from the table.

Teddy followed him down another hall into his bedroom. The bed was unmade, the sheets dingy and yellowed. A chest freezer the size of a sarcophagus hummed against one wall, the lid piled with laundry and junk.

Milton rummaged beneath a pile of bleach-stained towels and pulled out a tablet. "Here. Check it yourself if you're in such an all-fired hurry." He handed it over and left the room.

Teddy leaned against the freezer and tapped the screen. It was cracked and had a cluster of dead pixels in one corner, but it worked. She found the right app and pulled up the feed from the porch camera—the blacktop of Route 137 in the foreground, and beyond that, a vista of empty scrubland stretching to the hazy outline of the Callahan Divide.

She fast-forwarded through the footage from five p.m. A few cars, some pickups, a couple semis. At eight past, Shep Massey rode by on horseback, checking his fence line across the highway. At five eleven, someone on a bicycle zipped through the frame, heading south toward town. Teddy replayed it in slow motion. Mark McKissick. Probably returning from the Loudermilk ranch.

No sign of Cody. She ran it twice to make sure.

Teddy exhaled and looked up at the bug-filled light fixture. Cody might've turned off on one of the side roads between here and the Skinny's—but most of them looped back to town. And he hadn't looked like someone circling back.

More likely, he'd arranged a pickup. She thought of the call he'd made outside the Skinny's. Maybe he'd been ringing someone for help.

She ran the footage again, studying the vehicles that passed. No license plates were legible, and most drivers were alone. But at five eighteen, a dark pickup with a dented right fender passed, heading north. A passenger sat in the front seat, face obscured by the brim of a white Stetson.

The shoulders looked a little too broad to be Cody's, but she wasn't sure. She zoomed in, but the image pixelated and blurred.

Her scrutiny of the footage was interrupted by a series of sharp horn blasts. She put down the tablet and hurried outside.

Henry had opened the truck door and was leaning out, waving the phone. "It's Frankie—he says it's important."

Teddy climbed behind the wheel and took the call. "What is it?"

Frankie sounded worried. "I'm back at the greenhouse. Some guy's at the barn—says something's wrong with Julia's horse."

"Shit," Teddy muttered, hanging up.

"You're not supposed to cuss in front of me," Henry said.

"Sorry."

Teddy checked her messages. One from Rick Castillo: *At yr barn. U said 6, rite?* Then: *Mare not good.*

She looked at the dashboard clock. Six eleven. *B there in 10*, she typed.

"Fasten your seatbelt, bud. We gotta go."

The wind was rising as Teddy pulled up the drive. The live oaks by the house were tossing stiffly, their dark, shiny leaves flashing with the movement. Rick's blue pickup sat by the barn. Teddy parked beside it, hitting the brakes a little too hard and throwing them against their seatbelts.

"Go to the house," she said.

Henry peered at the dark porch. "Nobody's home. I wanna stay with you."

Teddy shook her head. If something was seriously wrong with Fancy, she didn't want him there. Keeping animals could be great for kids—but there were some things a nine-year-old shouldn't see. Henry's year had been tough enough.

"You'll be fine. Let the dogs out and get started on homework."

"What about Bug Battle Arena?"

"I'll play when I'm done."

"No you won't." He didn't sound angry. Just matter-of-fact.

"I'll be up soon. Promise. Call if you need anything."

They climbed out. Henry, still grumbling, shouldered his backpack and headed for the house.

Teddy watched until he was safely inside. Then she went into the barn. Skunk, the shepherd mix, was pacing and whining in the breezeway. When he saw her, he ran up and circled her legs, barking.

Teddy gave him a quick rub and made her way to Fancy's stall.

As soon as she entered, Teddy knew it was bad. She'd expected to find the mare agitated, or possibly thrashing on the ground. Instead, Fancy lay flat on her side, stiff-limbed and shaking. Her flanks were slick with foamy sweat, her belly distended.

Rick Castillo was kneeling beside her with a stethoscope pressed to her ribs. His shaggy dark hair hung down, obscuring his face. Teddy's feet rustled in the straw. He looked up.

"Stay back in case she starts rolling." He stood and came toward her.

"Is it colic again?"

Rick pulled the stethoscope from his ears. "Yeah, but her gut's twisted now. Ain't something I can fix."

"Oh no." Teddy's pulse quickened. She ran both hands through her hair. "What about surgery? Berna mentioned an equine hospital in San—"

He shook his head. "She's going into shock. Even if you got her in a trailer, she'd never survive the trip."

"Can we tube her again? That helped last night."

"Last night she didn't have a torsion."

He was watching her closely now, his expression steady and grave. Giving her time to catch up.

Teddy's thoughts stuttered. "You're saying put her *down*?"

"She's in a lot of pain." Rick looked back at the mare. "See how bloated she is? Guts are fixin' to rupture, if they haven't already."

Teddy pressed her knuckles against her eyes. After a moment, she dropped her hands and stared at the horse. Fancy's eyes were glazed beneath half-closed lids. Her tongue lolled in the dirt. Each breath was a terrible rasping wheeze.

Teddy turned away, pulling out her phone. "I want Berna's opinion. I need to tell Julia I did everything I could."

Rick nodded. "I get it."

Teddy stepped into the breezeway and dialed. Berna answered on the second ring and listened while Teddy explained.

"I was afraid of this," she said. "I'm closing up now—be there in a few."

Teddy thanked her and hung up.

She tried Julia's cell, but it went to voicemail. Teddy left a message telling her to call. Then she dialed the flower shop.

"Petal Pushers, this is Ruby. How can I help you?"

Ruby Franks, the owner, was in her seventies—a shrewd old hippie who'd come from Oregon years ago. Julia adored her.

"Hi Ruby, sorry to interrupt. Can I speak with Julia? It's urgent."

For a moment, Ruby didn't answer. Then: "She's not there? She left on her bike twenty minutes ago. She was having bad cramps, wanted to go home."

Teddy checked the time. Six thirty-eight. Petal Pushers was ten minutes away by bike, even for someone not feeling well. Then she remembered that, when she'd made her shopping list last week, she'd asked Julia if she needed pads. *Not till next month—just finished*, Julia had said.

Teddy thanked Ruby and hung up. She tried Julia's three closest friends. None said they'd seen her. Teddy thought they were telling the truth, but she wasn't sure. No one could lie like a teenage girl, given the right motivation. Still, a thread of unease coiled in her chest. Julia wasn't normally this evasive.

Teddy tried her again, still with no luck.

Where r u? Call me now. Urgent.

Her thumbs hovered over the keyboard. She almost added *Fancy down*—but decided against it. She didn't want to scare her. Not yet.

She hit send and leaned against the tack room door, eyes shut. When she opened them, Rick was standing in front of Fancy's stall, watching her.

"Daughter won't answer?"

Teddy exhaled. "She would if I told her Fancy was dying—but I don't want to say that in a text."

"You never put one of those tracking apps on her phone?"

"No. But I will after this." The fight it would spark with Julia would be brutal—but necessary if she was going to lie and sneak around. She'd been more distant than usual. Moodier, too. Something was going on.

Teddy brushed back a strand of hair. "Look, I know a decision needs to be made. But Julia'd never forgive me if—"

Rick raised a hand. "I gave the mare something to take the edge off. Won't last long, but it'll buy us some time."

Teddy nodded. "Thanks." Skunk was whining, pawing her leg. She scratched his ear. "God, I'm dreading this. Julia loves that horse."

"Putting them down's never easy."

"She's going to hate me."

"A torsion's no one's fault."

Teddy blew out a breath. "Maybe not. But it's more satisfying to blame someone, isn't it?"

Rick leaned against the opposite wall. "Daughters, huh? I hear ya."

"You've got kids?"

"One. She's twelve."

Teddy's eyes dropped to his left hand, then quickly away. No ring, but that didn't mean much for a large-animal vet. She knew from Berna that preg-checking cows and replacing uterine prolapses weren't jewelry-friendly jobs.

She looked up. Rick had seen the glance.

"She lives in Port Arthur, with my ex. I don't get to see her much." He scratched the back of his neck, like he wasn't sure what else to say.

Teddy wondered what had brought him to West Texas, so far from his family. Probably a sad story. She started to ask—but didn't. Not the right moment.

From the stall came a high-pitched, breathy whinny. Rick's brow furrowed.

"Ain't my business, but—would your daughter maybe answer the phone for her dad?"

Teddy blinked. She pulled out her phone, checked the time, and dialed Alan. When he picked up, she heard his van's radio and the noise of the highway in the background. She explained the situation, and Alan didn't waste time asking questions.

He and Shane were ten minutes from home. "I'll try Julia and get back to you."

Teddy paced the breezeway, chewing a fingernail. Thunder rumbled in the distance. Ducking into the tack room, she splashed water on her face at the utility sink, then stood, phone in hand, checking the screen every few seconds.

After five minutes, Alan called back. "Straight to voicemail. Same as you."

Another thunderclap, louder this time.

"She's on her bike, Alan," Teddy said. "There's a storm coming. I'm stuck here."

"Shane and me'll drive around, check Dairy Queen, Ridgell's, that shinnery west of town where the kids hang out. Let me know if she turns up." She heard him swallow. "Hey Ted, don't worry. I'm sure she's fine."

Teddy hung up. More than half an hour had passed since Julia left the flower shop. Where the hell was she? A cold knot settled beneath Teddy's ribs; her lungs felt tight and breathless.

She looked around. Rick was back in the stall, stethoscope in his ears, listening to the mare's belly.

"How's she doing?" Teddy asked.

"Drugs are working, for now. But they won't last much longer." He stood up and joined her in the breezeway. "No luck with Julia, huh?"

"No." Teddy fiddled with the brass latch on the tack room door, opening and closing it. When she registered what she was doing, she shoved her hands in her pockets. "God, what a day."

"Berna said you're a detective?"

"Used to be. Now I teach." Teddy paused. "She probably also told you I'm helping with the Loudermilk case?"

Rick nodded. "Stressful?"

"You could say that. It's—" She hesitated, then went on recklessly. "It's bringing up a lot. The detective I'm working with—we used to be friends. Now she hates me."

"What happened—can I ask?"

A curry comb was hanging near Teddy's shoulder. She took it off the hook and began pulling hair from the tines, just to give her hands something to do. She'd never talked about it—not to Alan, or the therapist. Not even to Berna. Now here she was—standing in a barn with a man she'd known less than twenty-four hours, choking on the weight of all that had gone unsaid. The past few days had weakened her defenses, and this crisis with Fancy—so close on the heels of everything else—had tipped her past whatever line she'd been holding. The words slipped out before she knew she was saying them.

"I killed her son. Five years ago. Hostage situation. He had his ex-girlfriend and her brother at gunpoint. He shot first. Not at me—at one of the hostages. I didn't have a choice." Her voice took on a defensive edge. "And before you ask why I didn't just shoot his gun arm—I couldn't. It's too risky. If I'd missed—"

"I wasn't going to ask that," Rick said. "Your friend hasn't forgiven you?"

"How could she? How could anybody?"

Rick was quiet for a moment. "Damn. That's a hell of a thing to carry."

"Terrence was a great kid—the last kid in the world you'd expect to do something like that." Teddy turned the comb in her hands. "I still don't understand it."

"Great kids carry everyone's expectations. That pressure can get real heavy, real fast."

"Raina thinks I could've talked him down if I'd just tried harder."

"What do you think?"

“I . . . don’t know. I try not to think. I tell myself she’s wrong—and most of the time, I believe it. In the daytime, anyway.” Teddy hung up the comb, brushed loose hairs from her sleeve, crossed and uncrossed her arms. Nothing felt comfortable. “No matter how I think about it, I’m either letting myself off the hook or beating myself up. Drives me crazy.”

Thunder rolled overhead. Rain began to patter on the metal roof.

A low, wheezing groan came from Fancy’s stall. Rick ducked inside.

Teddy followed, but stopped when her phone chimed with a text from Henry: *It’s creepy here by myself. R u coming soon?*

In a bit.

I’m STARVING. Can I have ice cream?

Teddy hesitated, trying to remember what was in the fridge. *Have something healthy. Apple sauce.*

Henry responded with a green vomiting-face emoji.

Teddy checked the time. Nearly seven. No word from Alan.

The sky was dark, the air thick. Her ears popped with the approaching storm. It was close now.

She looked in the stall. Rick was on his knees, palpating the mare’s belly. No point asking how she was doing. His expression told the story.

Something flashed in Teddy’s peripheral vision. She turned. Headlights swept across the open breezeway door. The rain was briefly illuminated against the blackness, silver needles slashing to the ground.

“Berna’s here,” Teddy said.

Rick looked up. “Good.”

Teddy stepped outside and groaned. “Are you kidding me?”

A yellow VW Beetle had pulled up nearby. Lyric got out. She was wearing slacks and a silk top instead of her usual spandex.

"Alan's not here yet," Teddy said.

Lyric nodded. "I just talked to him. He told me what's going on."

Of course he did. "Then you know why I don't have time to chitchat." Teddy knew she was being rude, but she was too worried and exhausted to care. "Go on up to the house, if you want. Henry's there." She turned.

"Teddy, wait."

"What?"

"Want me to figure out dinner—so you can deal with this, I mean?"

Teddy's eyes narrowed. Maybe this was a strategic play—some move in a relational chess game. Or maybe she was sincere, and Teddy was just being suspicious.

She ran a palm over her face. "Okay, yeah. That'd be great."

A gust of wind scattered leaves across the yard. It was fully dark now, and the rain was picking up—cold, needling drops that crept down her collar. Hopefully Julia was somewhere warm and dry—upset about something maybe, and hiding out. Not pedaling through rain-slick streets while distracted drivers tore past—

No. It was no good thinking like that. Dwelling on catastrophic scenarios was paralyzing—an occupational hazard of both police work and motherhood. She needed to stay focused on the moment.

Teddy watched the VW's taillights recede up the drive. Then she pulled her jacket tighter and headed back to the barn.

Chapter 20

The sky was black. Lightning flickered in the west. Rain was hammering the barn's metal roof by the time Berna's work van pulled into the drive and parked by the paddock. Teddy watched from the breezeway as her friend jumped out and ran to the door, one hand holding the hood of her waterproof and the other clutching her veterinary kit.

She peeled off her jacket and brushed back her silvery dreadlocks. "Any change?"

"Not for the good." Teddy's throat tightened.

Berna laid a hand on her shoulder, then headed for the stall.

The exam didn't take long. Within five minutes, she stepped back into the breezeway with Rick behind her. Berna was shaking her head.

"Sorry, Ted. I think Fancy's ruptured already. Cold extremities, and her mucus membranes are almost black. Even surgery wouldn't save her now."

Teddy pressed the heels of her hands into her eyes. "I was afraid of that."

She checked her phone again. Still nothing from Julia or Alan.

Her thoughts felt scattered. She gripped the phone until her palm ached. What now? Where to start? Everything felt urgent. Chase had been murdered, Cody was in the wind. And now Julia was missing, maybe still out there in the storm. With so many simultaneous crises, it was hard to find the bandwidth even to think, let alone make a decision of this magnitude.

Berna's voice was quiet. "What do you want us to do?"

Teddy shoved the phone into her pocket. Fancy's condition—that was the emergency in front of her. It had to be resolved.

She exhaled and cleared her throat. "Can the pain be controlled a little longer? Julia's going to want to say goodbye."

Berna and Rick exchanged a look. A bright flash lit the breezeway, followed a few seconds later by muted thunder.

Rick scratched his jaw. His dark eyes were on Teddy's. "Mare's heart rate's sky-high."

"Meaning—?"

"Meaning she's in a lot of pain," Berna said.

Teddy stood still, listening to the clatter of rain on the roof. Her shoulders were tight. The pulse in her neck throbbed. Not trusting herself to speak, she closed her eyes and nodded.

Rick turned and ducked back into the stall. Berna slipped her arm through Teddy's and led her to the end of the breezeway. They stared into the darkness, watching the storm. Berna made small talk to distract her until Rick returned, carrying his vet kit.

His shoulders sagged. "It's done." His eyes met Teddy's. "You made the right call."

"Doesn't feel that way."

"Never does," Berna said and gave her arm a quick squeeze.

"I hope Julia understands." Teddy wiped her eyes with the back of her wrist.

"Sorry it worked out like this," Rick said. "Call if you need anything. Seriously." His voice was quiet, but the offer felt real. He gave a brief nod and ran for his truck as lightning flared and thunder boomed overhead.

"I better get home, too, before the roads wash out," Berna said.

She was turning to go when a pair of headlights sliced suddenly through the darkness.

Expecting Alan, Teddy was startled when the lights cut off and Raina appeared, carrying a large black umbrella. She ducked into the breezeway.

"What's going on?" Teddy asked, her stomach tightening. Raina hadn't been here in five years. Whatever it was, it had to be bad.

Raina shook off the rain and closed the umbrella. She looked at the vet. "Hey, Berna. I need to speak with Teddy, if you don't mind."

"I was just going," Berna said. She gave Teddy a quick hug, pulled up her hood, and hurried out.

Teddy turned to Raina. "What is it? Did you find Cody?"

"Not yet." Raina pulled out her phone. "It's about Julia."

The ground seemed to tilt under Teddy's feet, as if she'd stepped off a curb she hadn't seen. She steadied herself against the wall. "Oh God. Is she okay?"

Raina's brow furrowed. "She's not here? I need to talk to her."

Teddy's immediate sense of relief was followed by the familiar static of irritation. "Get in line."

"What's that supposed to mean?"

"She's out there somewhere, on her bike." Teddy waved into the downpour. "She's not answering her phone. Alan and Shane are looking—" She stopped, registering Raina's words. "You need to talk to her about what?"

"Bobby Castle recovered the stuff Cody erased from his phone. He's still going through it. Turns out Cody and Julia are friends. Really *good* friends."

Teddy stared at her. "What the hell are you talking about?"

Raina held out her phone. Teddy snatched it and scrolled through a long string of downloaded texts. The conversation was with someone Cody had entered in his contacts list as "Sweet

Cheeks." A number of photos left no doubt about the identity of the correspondent.

Teddy stared down at a selfie of Julia in cutoffs and a bra, sprawled on the fuzzy pink beanbag chair in her bedroom. On the floor beside her lay Hoppity, the stuffed kangaroo she'd slept with since she was two.

Teddy's stomach churned. Her mouth went dry. She knew what she was looking at, but somehow it didn't compute. She could see the threadbare spot on the tip of the kangaroo's left ear. Julia used to suck it as a toddler to send herself to sleep.

It took her a moment to realize Raina was speaking. "Looks like they met at the Concho Valley Rodeo a few months back. The relationship moved fast, obviously."

Teddy tore her gaze from the screen. No wonder Julia had been so moody and secretive lately. What was Alan going to say? She concentrated on the sound of the rain, the musky odors of hay and manure—anything to stay focused.

Her head throbbed. Outside, a brilliant flash split the sky; the tree line across the drive leapt forward, sharp and distinct against the scudding clouds. She squeezed her eyes shut and saw a coppery negative of the image behind closed lids. Julia was out there somewhere—maybe alone, but maybe not.

Teddy looked at Raina. "Cody's nineteen—he's an adult. Julia's a child. If he laid a finger on her—"

Raina held up a hand. "Let's find them first—assuming they're together."

Teddy exhaled slowly. "The Skinny's security footage caught Cody heading north on 137 just before five. He was on the phone."

"Calling Julia to meet?"

"Maybe. But Ruby said Julia didn't leave Petal Pushers till six fifteen." Teddy handed back the phone. "Cody never made it past my dad's—not on foot, anyway. I checked his camera feed."

"That's what—a mile past the Skinny's?"

"Two, give or take."

Raina slipped the phone into her pocket. "Just for the record—you didn't know about Julia and Cody's relationship?"

Teddy stared at her. "Are you seriously asking me that?"

"I have to."

"Think I'd interrogate Cody with you all afternoon and not mention it?"

Raina said nothing. She was still waiting for an answer.

Teddy threw up her hands. "No, Raina. Jesus. I had no idea."

After a pause, Raina nodded. "Okay."

Teddy's phone rang. "It's Alan." She raised it to her ear. "Did you find her?"

"I was checking to see if she's home," he said. He sounded tired and worried. "Any news?"

Teddy told him about putting down Fancy but left out the rest. He didn't need to hear about this latest with Cody while navigating wet roads in the dark.

"We'll keep looking," he said.

"I will, too. We'll cover more ground."

"You should stay there in case she comes home. It'd be bad if she walked into the barn and found Fancy like that."

Teddy hesitated. Her instinct was to get in the truck and drive. But Alan was right. Someone had to be there. She flexed her neck and heard it pop. "Yeah, okay. Keep me posted."

She hung up and stood gripping the phone.

"No sign?" Raina asked.

Teddy shook her head and explained.

"He's right. You stay." Raina reached for her umbrella. "I'll help look. She doesn't have a car, and neither does Cody. Only so many places they could be."

"Thanks," Teddy said. "Really. I mean it."

"It's for the case, not for you." Raina turned away.

Finally alone, Teddy checked the time. Almost seven forty. Over an hour had passed since she'd gotten home. It felt longer. She walked down the breezeway to Fancy's stall. The mare lay on her side, the sweat still drying on her flanks. Finally at peace. Someone—probably Rick—had removed her halter and hung it on a nail above the hay rack.

Teddy knelt beside her. "You were a good girl," she whispered, stroking the firm, glossy neck. "Such a good girl." Grief settled in, heavy and familiar. Julia should have been here—should've been the one to say goodbye. Fancy had been her friend for most of her life.

Skunk had followed Teddy into the stall. He licked her cheek and whined. She pressed her face into his fur, trying to settle her nerves. She was still sitting there twenty minutes later, when her phone rang.

It was Julia.

Teddy answered before the second ring. "Jules, where are you?"

Julia was nearly incoherent. Through her sobs and the sound of the rain, Teddy made out two words.

"You're at the *Buffalo Wallow*?" What the hell was she doing there? "Did something happen?"

The reply was incomprehensible, a garbled torrent of language and tears.

"Jules, Jules—it's okay. Don't move, sweetie, I'm coming."

The rain beat down as Teddy ran across the muddy drive and jumped into her truck. She sped up Little Branch Road, dictating texts as she drove—first to Raina and then to Alan: *J AT WALLOW. URGENT.*

The streets were deserted. The asphalt on Colonel Priddy shone like an oil slick, and most of the side roads had become rivers. Teddy ran both traffic lights and flew past Donovan's Feed and Seed at the eastern edge of town.

Clear of buildings now, she could see Stone Creek running parallel to the road on her right. It was swollen and dark, choked with fallen limbs. Two miles out of town, the creek broadened into a muddy red pool known locally as the Buffalo Wallow.

The saucer-shaped depression had been formed a century and a half earlier by the great herds that migrated through the Callahan Divide. Long after the buffalo vanished from the plains, the locals diverted the creek to fix a flooding problem, inundating the wallow and turning it into a wide place in the stream the size of a small pond.

As Teddy approached the spot, her headlights caught a metallic gleam on the shoulder of the road. She slammed the brakes and rummaged in the console for her flashlight.

It was still raining, but the worst had passed. Thunder rolled more faintly overhead. She crossed the road. Julia's bike lay on its side, front wheel spinning in the wind. Teddy shouted her name, but got no reply.

She swept the flashlight over the fields, then down the bank into the Wallow. The water was high and moving fast, clogged with debris at the far end where the stream narrowed and shot through a cement culvert.

A faint cry rose over the wind. Teddy froze, then shone the light across the water. Someone was standing neck-deep in the middle of the Wallow.

"Jules!"

Julia half turned. Her face was pale and stricken. She was clinging to something that was being pulled toward the culvert.

Why wasn't she trying to get to shore? She was a strong swimmer.

Teddy's first impulse was to charge down the bank, but the Wallow's shoreline had been reinforced with football-sized stones, now slick with rain. If she twisted her ankle, there'd be two people to rescue.

She cupped her hands. "Jules, let go—swim toward me!"

Julia shook her head and shouted something Teddy couldn't make out.

She pulled out her phone and dialed 911. Stone Creek's emergency crews were tied up on calls, the dispatcher told her. San Angelo could send help, but it would take longer.

Teddy hung up. Where the hell were Raina and Alan? She checked the time. Only seven minutes had passed since she'd arrived.

She stepped closer to the edge. "Jules, please—come this way."

Julia shook her head and shouted again, pointing toward the culvert. Teddy narrowed the beam. The culvert was jammed with limbs and brush. Anyone pulled inside would be pinned by the current and would drown.

"Dammit." Teddy started down the embankment—then froze at the wail of a siren and a blaze of blinding light.

A police SUV skidded to a stop. The door slammed, and Raina appeared, squinting into the glare of Teddy's flashlight.

Teddy started to explain, but Raina had already taken in the scene. She stripped off her jacket and tossed one end to Teddy. "Use this—I'll anchor you."

Teddy handed her the flashlight and phone. Using the jacket like a rope, she picked her way across the slick stones. Then she waded into the Wallow. Her boots slid on the muddy bottom. The water was frigid. The current tugged at her legs, but it wasn't overpowering.

As she drew closer, she saw what Julia was holding. Not a log or a tree branch—something half submerged, swathed in fabric.

"Let go, Jules. It's okay—I've got you."

But Julia shook her head. “He’ll f-float away,” she said through chattering teeth.

Teddy looked again. Socks. Hair. The dull gleam of a belt buckle. The head lolled in the current, and a face surfaced, bloated and pale, but unmistakable.

Cody Puckett.

Chapter 21

Although the rain was tapering off, the water was still rising, the current stronger now. Teddy cast a nervous glance at the black mouth of the culvert.

"We have to help him, Mom—I think he's alive." Julia's face was strained and white, her voice raspy with shouting. She was insistent, but not panicked. Resolved.

When had she gotten so level-headed? Teddy shelved the question—and the flicker of pride that came with it—as soon as it registered. Something to unpack later.

But Julia was wrong. Cody wasn't alive. Even in the dim light, Teddy knew. His skin had the puckered, spongy look she'd seen on bodies pulled from water. He'd been dead a couple hours, at least.

As she checked for a pulse, her mind raced. How had he ended up at the Wallow? The Skinny's cameras had shown him heading in the opposite direction. Had he come here alone? Was this an accident? Suicide? And most urgently, to Teddy's mind—what was Julia's role in all of this?

"Mom, we need to *do* something." Julia was clutching Teddy's arm with stiff, icy fingers. Were her lips turning blue?

Teddy forced herself to focus. It was too late for Cody—but Julia needed to get out of the water, fast. "Let's bring him to shore."

She waded around the body. Together, they managed to tow it across the Wallow and out of the water.

"Hurry, Mom—do CPR." Julia's voice was thin, shaking with cold.

"I can't on these rocks, Jules."

"Then let's carry him to the road!"

"I'm sorry, honey. It's too late. Let's get you to the truck. You need to warm up." Teddy reached for her, but Julia flinched away.

"You haven't even tried. You have to do something. Help him!"

She suddenly sounded very young. It had been years since she'd shown this kind of implicit faith in the grown-ups' ability to fix things—*a sign of her desperation*, Teddy thought. A Hail Mary appeal when all else had failed. But this wasn't a case of a skinned knee or broken toy. Julia was a level-headed kid. Farm life had taught her about death. On some level, she had to know. She just needed time. Anything Teddy might say would only work as an irritant. So much of parenting a teenager was knowing when to shut up.

The storm was sliding to the east, and the rain had stopped. A chill wind seethed through the cottonwoods along the creek, drying the stones lining the Wallow's bank. Teddy looked up. Raina was picking her way toward them.

She aimed her flashlight at the dead man's face.

"Don't." Teddy pushed her hand aside. "Stay with him till the emergency crew gets here, will you? I need to get Julia home."

Raina looked at Julia and nodded. She pulled Teddy's flashlight and phone from her pocket and gave them back.

"Come on, Jules," Teddy said, helping her up. Julia's clothes clung to her skin. She'd lost one of her flats, and blood oozed from a cut on her foot. "Careful, baby. Watch your step."

The rocks were less slippery now. Julia said nothing. Her earlier frantic energy was gone. Her body shook, and her teeth chattered.

Teddy cursed herself for not carrying an emergency blanket in the truck.

A stone tilted beneath Julia's foot.

"Watch it," Teddy said.

As they scrambled up the bank, she was struck by a sudden, dizzying relief. If she'd arrived a few minutes later—if the storm had knocked out phone service—how differently things might've gone. Julia might be lying dead on the rocks beside Cody. Teddy had seen young bodies pulled out of worse places. She knew what it was like to arrive too late to help. Too late for anything but grief, second guesses, body bags.

Not this time. This time, they'd been just in time—at least for Julia. Not every parent was so lucky. She wondered if Raina was thinking the same.

They crested the slope just as a green work van pulled up. Alan and Shane jumped out. In the headlights, Shane looked young and scared. Alan's hair was mussed. He'd been raking his fingers through it, a habit when he was worried.

Shane was staring wide-eyed at the body. Alan hurried to them. Julia collapsed into his arms, sobbing. She'd always gone to Alan for comfort—Teddy felt the old pinch of that, quick and familiar. But right now, she was just glad Julia felt safe. She reached up and brushed a strand of damp hair off her daughter's face.

"What happened?" Alan mouthed.

Teddy waved the question away. "Get her out of the wet. I'll be right back."

As she turned, Julia grabbed her sleeve.

"Mom, somebody did this to him," she said. "Cody told me he saw someone on the road—someone he knew. That's gotta be who killed him. You have to find them—you have to."

Teddy gripped her shoulders, feeling the delicate bones through the soaked fabric. "What do you mean? Did he say that tonight? What time—"

"Come on, Ted, she's in no shape for the inquisition," Alan said.

"Yeah, okay." Teddy held out her hand. "Let me see your phone."

Julia frowned. "Why?"

"Because somebody's dead. If you're right, it'll help me catch who did it."

Julia sniffled and pulled her phone from her pocket. "It's waterlogged."

"Maybe the data can be salvaged."

Julia was still shivering. Alan rubbed her arms. "Come on, baby, let's get you in the van."

Teddy touched his sleeve. "Don't leave yet. The EMTs should check her out."

She turned and made her way back to the water's edge. The storm had rumbled off. A few stars blinked through the shreds of swift-moving cloud, and the moon was rising, hazy and yellow, out of the receding squall line.

Raina had put on latex gloves and was kneeling beside the body. She looked up when Teddy approached. Her face was unreadable. Teddy used to know what she was thinking. Not anymore.

Something had shifted, though. Not between the two of them—but inside Teddy. Telling Rick about Terrence had knocked something loose. She felt it, like ground settling after rain.

No time to sort out what it meant—or where it might lead. If Julia was right, this was a crime scene. She needed to focus.

Raina was already speaking. "Cody didn't drown." She pulled back his shirt collar and aimed her flashlight. Its batteries were beginning to fail, but even in the dim light, it was impossible to miss the vivid indentation across the dead boy's throat.

Teddy's flashlight was brighter; she directed it at the wound. It was narrow, biting deep beneath the jawline. Tiny scratches scored the skin around the purple welt.

"He was strangled," Raina said.

"Fought, too. Those are fingernail marks," Teddy added.

"Happened not long after he left the station. His face is already stiffening."

The low rumble of engines and a flicker of red lights broke the moment. A fire truck pulled up—a red diesel pickup with equipment compartments built into the back. The Chief's dusty gold Suburban was right behind it.

"It's about time," Raina muttered.

"You called the Chief?"

"Got his voicemail—left a message."

Before Ramirez had unbuckled his seatbelt, two firemen jumped from the truck and hurried across the rocks with a backboard. One was Kenny Nagle, whose mother, Maureen, worked in the Political Science Department.

Kenny knelt beside the body. "Let's get him off these rocks."

Raina raised a hand. "He's dead. Don't touch him."

Kenny protested, then backed off when Teddy said, "Rigor's already setting in. We need to preserve the scene."

As the firemen retreated, Ramirez picked his way over.

"Ambulance is five minutes out. What's the story?" His breath carried a whiff of alcohol, dulled by cherry menthol. A cough drop—probably to mask the booze. Did he drink every night, now? Teddy wondered.

They explained what had happened. Ramirez listened, staring down at his boots.

"Who called it in?" he asked.

"Julia. She and Cody had a thing," Teddy said. Better he hear it from her.

His eyebrows rose. He looked at Alan's van, as if just now noticing it. "You should've told me this afternoon."

"She just found out," Raina said. She explained about the discoveries on Cody's phone.

Ramirez threw up his hands. "Why the hell wasn't I notified?"

"I tried calling you." The edge in Raina's voice was unmistakable.

Ramirez turned back to Teddy. "How'd she find him? They arrange to meet here?"

"Don't know. She said he called—told her he saw someone he knew."

"What time?" Raina asked.

"No idea. I'm not even sure it was tonight. I checked her phone, but it's fried."

They all three glanced toward the van. Julia was watching them through the passenger window, her face ashen.

"We need to find out," Raina muttered, starting up the bank.

Teddy caught her arm—a little harder than she meant to. "She's in no fit state tonight. I'll bring her in tomorrow for a formal interview."

"First thing," Ramirez said, unwrapping a cough drop. "Is this a dump site? Or was Puckett killed here?" He gestured toward the Wallow, then popped the lozenge in his mouth.

Before either woman could answer, they heard the wail of an approaching siren. The fire truck had gone, but an ambulance was pulling up. "Concho Valley Regional" was stenciled on the side. Two EMTs climbed out, and Alan waved them over.

"I'll talk to them," Ramirez said. "Y'all check the shoreline, see if anything turns up." He moved off.

While Raina retrieved evidence bags and more gloves from her SUV, Teddy remained by Cody's body, watching the quiet shuffle of her family near the ambulance. Shane was in the van. Alan hovered nearby as the EMTs assessed Julia. When Alan saw her looking, he motioned for her to join them.

She climbed the bank. Julia sat at the rear of the ambulance, hunched under a foil blanket, her face turned away. Alan met Teddy at the road.

"They're saying she's in good shape, considering," he said.

Teddy felt a rush of relief. "Thank God."

"When they're done, I'm taking her home."

"Good. Listen—just keep her away from the barn. Say I fed the animals. And don't tell her about Fancy, okay? I need to break that news myself. I'll be home in a few minutes."

Alan crossed his arms. He looked unconvinced, but he nodded.

Teddy's eyes drifted to Julia, now standing and talking to the EMTs. She looked small. Alone.

I should go home, Teddy thought suddenly. *She needs me*.

But the scene still needed working. And Raina couldn't do it on her own.

Strange how quickly it came back—that feeling of being pulled in two directions.

Teddy said goodbye to Alan and turned back, hating how easy it was.

The work always won. It had to. Until they found who did this, nobody's kids were safe.

She walked back to Raina, who handed her gloves and bags.

"I'll send a team tomorrow for a full daylight sweep," Raina said. "For now, grab anything that seems fresh or out of place. I'll head toward the culvert. You go the other way."

The basin of the Wallow was dark. Water lapped and eddied against the stones as Teddy moved along the bank, panning her flashlight and stooping to peer into crevices. She found cigarette butts, crumpled beer cans, shards of broken glass, and lengths of discarded fishing line, some still tipped with hooks. Most of the litter had been there a while—the typical detritus of a West Texas riverbank. The Wallow was a popular fishing hole, but not during a storm.

Maybe that was the point, Teddy thought. Whoever had strangled Cody had to be a local—someone who knew there'd be no witnesses on a night like this.

“Hey, I found something,” Raina shouted.

Teddy straightened, rubbing her lower back. Raina was at the far end of the Wallow. The slope was steeper there as it rose to meet the dirt track that crossed the culvert, and the stones lining the shore had sloughed into a heap near the water. Raina stood on top of the pile, peering at something in the rocks.

Teddy edged toward her. “What’d you find?” A rock shifted beneath her foot, and she threw out her arms for balance.

Raina had her phone out and was snapping pictures. She picked up an object and dropped it into an evidence bag.

“Pack of Marlboros. Soaked, but looks fresh. Stay there—I’ll come to you.”

While she waited, Teddy glanced up the bank. Alan was helping Julia into the van. The EMTs were talking with Ramirez near the ambulance.

The van’s engine started. It made a clumsy three-point turn on the narrow road.

Teddy turned back as Raina called again.

“Hey, shine your light over here—my flashlight’s dead.”

She had climbed down from the rock pile and was picking her way toward Teddy along the water’s edge. The pale disc of her dying flashlight bobbed in the darkness.

Teddy moved to help. For a second, it felt like they were partners—like the last five years hadn’t happened. She aimed her Maglite at Raina’s feet and held it steady as Raina ducked under the limbs of an overhanging cottonwood. The footing there was treacherous—the rocks slick with algae and the shadows inky black. Raina’s boot slid sideways. She wobbled but caught herself.

Teddy started forward. “Wait—that’s not safe. I’ll give you a hand.”

“I’m fine.”

A lot had changed. But not everything. Raina had always been stubborn. So was Teddy.

"Stop, you're gonna fall."

Raina ignored her and kept coming.

Teddy had almost reached the tree when a gust of wind shook the branches, sending down an icy spray that dimpled the surface of the water beneath it. Raina flinched and slipped.

"Watch out!" Teddy shouted.

Too late. Raina's foot twisted and she pitched forward, arms flailing. Her flashlight flew into the Wallow, and she hit the rocks hard on her knees and elbows, falling onto her side with a groan.

Teddy rushed forward, but Ramirez and the EMTs got there first. Raina's arms were scraped and bleeding. Her ankle had started to swell. The EMTs locked arms and carried her back to the road, where they examined her leg. It should be x-rayed, they said.

Raina waved them off, saying she'd be fine with an ice pack and a couple ibuprofen. But when the Chief insisted, she agreed to ride with the ambulance to San Angelo. She called Anthony to meet her there.

Ramirez stayed to wait for the Justice of the Peace, who had to examine the scene before Cody's body could be removed. The paramedics had pronounced him at nine fifty, though he'd clearly been dead for hours.

"I'd wait with you, but I need to check on Julia," Teddy told the Chief.

"I'll be fine unless a bunch of rubberneckers show up," he said. "Called Loomis—she's coming for backup."

Julia's bike still lay where she'd left it. Ramirez helped Teddy load it into her truck. Her flashlight was fading now. She switched it off and opened the driver's door.

As she started to climb in, Ramirez's phone rang. He answered, frowned, and waved for her to wait.

When he hung up, he rubbed his eyes. "Goddammit, Stan."

"What happened?" Teddy asked.

"That was Inez. Stan ain't home yet, and he ain't answering his phone." Ramirez made a low, frustrated noise. "Wherever he is, he better have an alibi." He gestured toward Cody's tarp-covered body.

"No kidding," Teddy said.

Stan, with his Marlboros. Stan, who'd asked if Cody killed Chase. Cody would've trusted him. Let his guard down.

Ramirez spoke again. "Go on home, see about Julia. I'll send some guys to look for Stan. Let you know when we find him."

Teddy nodded and slid behind the wheel. She hadn't thought of her kids in nearly an hour. She'd known this would happen. Alan probably had, too.

This is why I retired, she thought grimly. *It's not even my job. What the hell am I doing?*

No point beating herself up now. Julia was waiting. Time to go home.

Chapter 22

It was nearly eleven by the time Teddy turned onto Little Branch Road. Her clothes were stiff and uncomfortable; the wet socks chafed inside her boots, and a blister had started to form on her heel. She'd never felt so tired.

As she turned into the drive, a car was pulling out. Lyric's yellow VW. Its high beams flashed in greeting as it passed. Teddy felt a twinge of shame. Lyric had handled dinner and babysat Henry all evening. Alan was right—she really was a decent person. And tonight, she'd been a lifesaver. Teddy could've liked her under other circumstances.

She drove past the barn, quiet now, as if nothing had happened. Tomorrow she'd have to tell Julia about Fancy. She was dreading it already.

The house was dark and still. Teddy came in through the laundry room. As she removed her boots and peeled off her socks, Jabba the Mutt trotted up, wagging his tail and blinking drowsily. She petted him, scooped kibble into his bowl, and crossed into the family room.

It was dimly lit and empty except for Alan, who was slumped in the recliner, clutching a tumbler of amber liquid. He was watching some home-renovation show on TV with the sound muted. A bottle of Jim Beam stood on the side table. Teddy was surprised.

Alan enjoyed a beer now and then, but he wasn't a heavy drinker. That bottle of bourbon had been in the kitchen cupboard since last Christmas.

She paused in the doorway. He was plainly upset—but she didn't have the energy for one of his *poor me* moods. Right now, she just wanted to check on Julia—and Henry, too, if he was still awake. Then maybe she could get some sleep.

She started for the hallway, but stopped when Alan spoke.

"Made it home, huh?" His words were a little slurred. He didn't take his eyes off the screen. The light from the television flickered on his face.

"Finally." Teddy hesitated, shifting her weight, then sat on the edge of the sofa. There was something in his voice—a raw strain she hadn't heard before. This wasn't just sulking. Her irritation softened. "After you and Julia left, things got a little messy." She told him about Raina's fall and trip to the hospital. "I couldn't just leave in the middle of all that."

Alan raised his glass in a *here's to you* gesture and took a drink, still without looking at her. "Always something, huh? Too bad about Raina. Hope she's all right."

"Me too." Teddy hesitated. "Are you?"

Alan swirled his glass. "Been a day."

Teddy waited, but he didn't elaborate. She started to rise. "Guess I better go talk to Julia. I'm dreading it."

"Julia's asleep."

"Oh. Really?" She sat back down, suddenly uneasy. "I figured she'd be pretty keyed up."

"I gave her some melatonin." Alan drained his tumbler.

"Okaaay," Teddy said slowly. "Was it hard to keep her from going out to see Fancy?"

For the first time, Alan's eyes left the TV screen. He grabbed the bottle and refilled his glass. "I told her about Fancy."

Teddy stared. "Are you kidding me? Why would you do that?"

The question acted as a trigger. Alan slammed down the bottle, sloshing bourbon onto the table. "You said you'd be home in a few minutes. It's been two hours." He waved at the clock. "What was I supposed to do? Julia had a terrible shock tonight—she wasn't gonna settle till she saw that horse. You would've known that if you'd been here."

"Dammit, Alan, I needed to be the one to tell her—I could've made her understand." Teddy pressed her fingers to her eyes. "You always do this—you make sure you get to play the good guy. Now I'm the wicked witch who killed her horse."

"Keep it down—you'll wake up the kids." Alan wiped the spill with his sleeve. "If you were so set on telling her, you should've been here."

"A kid died tonight, Alan. I was working."

"Bullshit—you're not on the municipal payroll. I made a judgment call, all right? Somebody had to. Believe me, telling her was the only way to keep her out of the barn."

"No it wasn't. You're just terrified of saying no to the kids. You're not their buddy, Alan. You're their dad. Start acting like it."

Alan laughed sourly. "That's pretty rich, coming from you."

"What's that supposed to mean?"

Alan's eyes closed, and he let his head fall back against the chair. "I'm tired, Ted. Tired of watching you get obsessed with some investigation. You're like a hound on a scent. Nothing else matters. Somebody's got to hold this family together while you're off chasing ghosts."

"Cheer up, then—I'm being taken off the case. Raina doesn't want me."

Alan opened his eyes. "What about now that she's hurt?"

Teddy hesitated. "Depends how bad it is, I guess. It'll be Wally's call."

"This affects me and the kids, too. Don't we get a vote?"

"You lost your vote when you filed for divorce. I listened to you gripe about my career for nineteen years. I'm done."

"If you'd listened, we wouldn't be divorced. Did it ever occur to you to actually think about what I was saying—to take it seriously, I mean?"

"Jesus, Alan, I did take it seriously. I quit the force. Not because of your whining. I could see for myself the toll it was taking."

"Give me a break. You didn't quit for us. You quit because the job turned against you. You were being investigated for shooting Terrence—"

Teddy stood. "At least get your facts straight. I was cleared before I quit. You talk like you're Dad of the Year, but you work longer hours than I do—in the summertime, anyway."

"My job's never been an obsession." Alan drained his glass again and set it down. "Kids don't parent themselves, Ted. Lyric's been picking up the ball because you've dropped it. You're their mother. Doesn't that embarrass you?"

"You're their father. Does it embarrass *you*?" Teddy inhaled and let out her breath slowly through pursed lips. She felt suddenly exhausted. "Alan, it's been a horrible day. You're drunk. I'm wet and filthy. I can't do this tonight. I can't. I'm going to check on the kids." She moved toward the hallway door.

"Sure. Run off, as usual."

Teddy knew she should keep walking, but she stopped in the doorway and turned.

"You do it all the time—to me, to that therapist," Alan went on. "Whenever someone tells you something you don't want to hear. You're just like your mother—only you disappear without leaving town. No wonder Julia's looking for love with some ranch hand she met at the rodeo."

Teddy stared at him. Her face was suddenly hot. This was marriage, she thought. Nobody told you the truth going in. You promised for better or for worse, not realizing *worse* meant letting someone into your soul so they could case it for weaknesses like they were planning a heist. They ought to put that in the marriage vows.

Before she could respond, she heard a soft noise behind her. She spun around. Had one of the kids been standing there, listening? The hallway was empty—thank God.

"Is that Henry?" Alan had gotten up and was weaving unsteadily across the family room.

"I'll check on him. You stink worse than my dad," Teddy said.

She made her way down the darkened corridor to Henry's room. He was asleep with an *Aquaman* comic book on his chest. Teddy picked it up and laid it on the nightstand. He murmured something about sharks and rolled onto his side. She waited, then kissed his forehead and turned away.

Across the hall, Julia was curled in her bed in a loose hedgehog position. She'd fallen asleep clutching Hoppity the stuffed kangaroo. Her auburn hair lay fanned across her cheek. Teddy stood watching for a moment before kissing the top of her head and tiptoeing out.

In her own bedroom, she stripped off her clothes and took a long shower. Her criminology textbook sat on the chair next to her bed. She needed to plan tomorrow's class but couldn't face it tonight. She set her alarm and crawled under the blankets. She was asleep within minutes.

Teddy woke with a start from an unpleasant dream in which she was stumbling down a dank, windowless stairwell with a bunch of rusty keys, frantically searching for something she'd lost.

She lay blinking at the ceiling as the memory dissolved, leaving an unsettling residue of vague anxiety.

Finally, she sat up and checked the time. Six thirty. The strip of sky between the curtains was dark. A noise had roused her—the garage door, maybe?

She got up, pulled on a pair of jeans, grabbed her phone, and stepped into the hall. Julia's door was ajar. Her bed was empty. Teddy hurried to the laundry room and peered into the garage. Someone had raised the roll-up door. She grabbed a jacket off the hook and thrust her bare feet into a pair of muck boots, then went outside.

The air was chilly and damp. Across the field, a sliver of light glowed beneath the barn doors. Teddy hurried along the muddy footpath and went inside.

The barn was warm and filled with the earthy smells of animals and straw. In Fancy's stall, Julia sat hunched on an upturned feed bucket beside the mare's body. She wore Alan's barn coat over her sweatshirt and leggings, the sleeves shoved back on her bare arms. Her chin rested on her knuckles.

Teddy hesitated at the stall door. "I'm so sorry, Jules. I had no choice."

Julia shifted on the bucket. "I know. Dad explained."

"Mad at me?"

Julia shook her head. Her face was half hidden by a curtain of hair. "I should've been here for her, Mom."

Teddy stepped inside, grabbed another bucket, and sat down. "You were always here for her."

"Not when it counted most."

A string of tired expressions crowded into Teddy's mind. *There's nothing you could've done. She knew you loved her. It wasn't your fault.*

She'd used them herself, standing in strangers' doorways with a badge and bad news. She'd heard them, too, as a kid—after her mother left. They never helped. They only deepened the isolation and silence that followed grief, cold as a front rolling in after a storm.

At least I'm here, Teddy thought. She wasn't her mother, no matter what Alan said. His words last night had hit home, as he'd known they would. How long had he been saving that one? The shiv in the back. The kill shot. He'd been drunk, but not too drunk to know what he was doing.

She watched Julia, who was combing Fancy's mane with her fingers. Teddy wished she'd thought to cover the mare's body with a blanket.

She reached out, rubbing Julia's back, and waited. Teddy wasn't worried about outlasting her. Milton's favorite punishment had been locking his kids in the closet. She'd spent hours alone in the dark—a whole day and night, once. The San Angelo shrink had called it the root of her claustrophobia. But it had taught her something useful—how to keep quiet and wait. A skill that had served her well—as a cop and as a mother.

"Am I going to school today, Mom?" Julia asked after several minutes.

"Do you want to?"

Julia hesitated, then nodded. "It'll get my mind off things."

"The police need to talk to you first. You can go after that, if you feel up to it."

Julia sat up straighter, her eyes clouded with worry. "I already told you everything last night."

"You found Cody's body, Jules. They'll want to hear it from you—why you went to the Wallow, what you know about his movements yesterday, who his friends were. That kind of thing."

Julia stiffened. She picked at a cuticle. "I don't know any of that, Mom. We were just friends from the rodeo. I didn't know him that well."

Teddy leaned in. "Come on, Jules. You said you talked to him yesterday. What happened?"

Julia kept her eyes on her hands. "He called when I was at work. He said he was walking on the road. Then, while we were talking, he saw someone he knew. He said he'd call me back."

"And?"

"And nothing. I never heard from him again."

Teddy let the quiet settle.

"Then how'd you know to go to the Wallow?"

"I didn't." Julia fidgeted with the stud in her ear. "I was antsy, so I rode my bike on the creek path. I saw someone in the water."

Teddy looked at her. "Jules, I know it's been a hard couple days. But you need to be straight with the police. You might as well start with me."

"I'm telling the truth."

Teddy sat back. Sometimes it was better to let people talk themselves into a corner. "You really expect people to believe you just happened to end up at the Wallow the same night Cody did?"

"You always do this—go all *cop mode* and pick everything apart. Can't you just be on my side, for once? Like a normal mom?"

"Jules, stop—just stop." Teddy leaned in, resting her hands on her daughter's knees. "I know you and Cody were more than friends. The police pulled his phone data. They've got your texts—Raina showed me."

Julia blanched, then flushed, staring at the floor.

Teddy watched her. As a mother, she wanted to back off—but she couldn't.

"I'm trying to help. But I need the truth."

Julia didn't look up. She mumbled something and waved a pair of flies off Fancy's muzzle.

"What was that?" Teddy asked.

Julia lifted her head. Her eyes were glassy. "I don't know what happened to Cody. I was looking for him—that's why I left the shop. He said he was coming by Petal Pushers, but he never showed. So I went out. I was scared he might—" She broke off, twisting her hands in her lap. "I don't know how he ended up in the Wallow, I swear."

Teddy kept her voice steady. "Okay. Tell me what you do know. It'll help when you talk to the police."

Julia sniffled and nodded. She wiped her nose on her sleeve, then picked up a piece of straw, winding it around her finger. The story came out tangled in places—rambling, circling back—but Teddy let her talk without interrupting. Ramirez might not like her taking a statement ahead of the official interview; but it seemed smarter to get it now, while Julia was still raw. Later, she might forget things—or start leaving details out.

When Julia finished, Teddy patted her knee. "That makes a lot more sense than what you said earlier. Why'd you lie?"

Julia's mouth tightened. "I was trying to avoid all this." She made a weary, sweeping gesture.

"All what?"

"This—the questions. Our story turning into public property. It's mine—mine and Cody's. It's all I have left. Once the cops start picking it apart, it turns into something else. Something ugly."

She was right, Teddy knew. No point promising otherwise.

"Remember why they're doing it, Jules. Digging through facts is how they find the truth."

Julia's face crumpled.

"The truth is somebody killed him—the person he saw on the road." She dropped her head into her hands. "Oh, God, he's gone. He's gone—and there's nothing anyone can do."

Teddy said nothing. She slid her own feed bucket closer, wrapped her arms around her daughter, and let her cry.

Chapter 23

After Julia's tears subsided and she was hiccupping softly into the crook of her arm, Teddy patted her back. "Jules, I have to ask—was Cody into anything risky? Drugs, or—"

Julia looked up, wiping her eyes on her sleeve. "He didn't even drink, Mom." Her grief had shifted, hardening into something sharper.

"Did he have enemies?"

"He didn't like Chase Loudermilk, but I wouldn't call them enemies. He just thought Chase didn't appreciate what he had. Cody acted tough, but it was all camouflage."

Teddy thought back to the station interview—how Cody's expression had softened when he showed them the charm bracelet and talked about the girl he'd met at the rodeo. *A really nice girl*, he'd said. What could a kid like that have done to get himself murdered? An orphaned ranch hand—hardly more than a boy. To most people, a nobody.

"He wasn't some dumb hick, you know," Julia said, pulling apart a bit of straw. "He wanted to be a graphic artist—illustrate comic books. He was smart." She swallowed. "And he knew how to listen. *Really* listen."

Teddy studied her daughter's face. Listening was a gift. But in the wrong context, it could get you killed.

“Did Cody ever mention hearing something he wasn’t supposed to?”

Julia’s breath snagged with a faint, scratchy hiss, like a needle lifted from vinyl. “What do you mean?”

“Could he have overheard Chase—or somebody else—talking about something illegal?”

Julia hunched her shoulders, rubbing her thumbs against her leggings—an old tell. She didn’t like the question.

Neither did Teddy—though it had to be asked. If Cody had been killed for something he knew . . . and if the killer knew Julia had been close to him—she might be next.

No. Teddy shut down the thought, even as a cold bloom of nausea unfurled inside her. Dwelling on *what-ifs* never helped. There was no clarity down that path—only noise and static.

Besides, pushing Julia on the point would just make her double down.

Teddy decided to change the subject. “What about Stan Loudermilk? Did Cody ever talk about him?”

Julia exhaled, and her shoulders relaxed. “Constantly. Cody idolized the guy. He said it was because Stan took him in when no one else would—but I think it ran deeper.”

“How so?”

Julia stared past her, chewing the inside of her cheek.

“Cody’s dad died when he was little. I think he needed a man to look up to, and Stan was the nearest one handy.” Her expression clouded. “I’m not sure he’s such a great guy, though.”

“Why not?”

“Just things Cody said. Stan had a temper. Could be pretty rough on people sometimes.”

“Physically?”

Julia shifted. “I—I don’t think so.”

“Was he rough on Cody?”

"Mostly on Chase. Cody thought he deserved it. But maybe Chase wouldn't have screwed up so much if Stan had gone easier on him."

Teddy thought of Stan at his anvil, sweating and red-faced, hammering like he could beat something into submission. Grief, maybe. Or guilt.

"That's interesting."

She was about to ask another question when her phone buzzed. She checked the caller ID and stepped into the breezeway.

"Good, you're awake," Ramirez said when she answered. He sounded steady, but his words came a beat slower than usual.

"How's Raina?" Teddy asked. "Hear anything?"

"Anthony called. They were in the ER half the night. Her leg's broke bad. They had to put her under to reset it. Splinted for now. Can't cast it till the swelling goes down."

"Damn. Poor Raina."

"Timing's crap. Bragg's out for the foreseeable, and we got at least one homicide on our hands—probably two."

"What happens now—with the investigation, I mean?"

"Just talked to Art. He'll send somebody up later today, if he can."

Art Linacre had been sheriff of Tom Green County for twenty-five years. He stood for reelection every four, but usually ran unopposed.

"Who's he sending?" Teddy asked a little nervously. She'd worked with plenty of sheriff's investigators in the past—some competent; some excellent. Some she'd rather avoid.

"Don't know. Art says they're stretched thin with that triple homicide at the reservoir. Which reminds me—heard back from the Rangers. Their deep-water team's almost finished up down there. Then they'll head our way—maybe this afternoon."

"Chase's phone's been down there for days—if it's there at all."

"One hurdle at a time, Drummond. Want to observe?"

Teddy shivered, thinking of the silo—the stench of mildew, the black water.

"The sheriff's investigator might not want me there."

"Whoever Art sends is gonna need local help getting up to speed—someone who knows the area, the people."

"Speaking of which—Stan turn up yet?"

"That's one piece of good news. Inez called. Stan came home and tumbled into bed about half an hour ago."

"Where's he been all night?"

"Your guess is as good as mine. He's drunk as hell. Wouldn't talk."

"Does he have an alibi for last night, five to eight?"

"Won't know till he sobers up. Maybe by tonight, if we're lucky."

"What about Julia? I was going to bring her in this morning. Should I wait for the sheriff's guy?"

"We can't cool our heels. We'll record her now—sheriff's guy can follow up later."

"Who interviews her?"

"I will. Have her here by eight thirty."

Teddy checked the time. Seven forty. Not much breathing room.

"I'll try."

She hung up and returned to Fancy's stall.

Julia was waiting in the doorway. "What's going on?"

Teddy explained. "Raina's home on pain meds. But Chief Ramirez is easy to talk to."

"He's an old man. I don't want to tell him about me and Cody."

Teddy slipped an arm around her waist. "He'll understand. He's got kids."

"Kids? They're nearly as old as you."

Teddy let it pass. "Just tell him what you told me." She gave her a quick squeeze. "Come on, let's go."

Julia hesitated, looking down at Fancy.

"I want to be here when you bury her."

"That's not a great idea, Jules. It won't be like Jane."

Calamity Jane—the old terrier who used to sleep on Julia's bed—had been laid to rest last year with full honors: wildflowers, a shoebox casket, and a printout of a poem Julia had found at school.

Burying a horse, on the other hand, was about as tender and respectful a process as installing a septic tank. It would take chains, heavy equipment. They'd have to use the backhoe to dig a pit in the north pasture—their unofficial graveyard for anything bigger than a dog. And getting Fancy into the ground would require the front loader. Farm animals had died before, of course; but Teddy had always arranged to bury them while the kids were at school. They understood about death. But Teddy tried to spare them the worst of it.

"I'm not a baby, Mom," Julia said. "Promise you won't do it without me."

"Sweetie—"

"Promise."

Teddy tipped her head back, staring at the ceiling. "How about this—we'll get her into the ground, but we'll wait to cover her till you're there." She paused. "That's not being disloyal, you know. It's protecting your memories of her."

Julia wavered, chewing her lip. "Yeah, okay."

"Good. Now hurry or we'll be late."

The sun was rising over the eastern mesas when they left the barn, fog pooling along the creek south of Little Branch Road. Signs of the storm were everywhere. Broken branches littered the ground, and the big sycamore behind the house had been stripped of its remaining leaves—plunged from autumn into winter overnight.

Teddy and Julia walked back to the house in silence.

Henry was dressed and at the kitchen table, picking at a bowl of soupy oatmeal, while Alan, in shorts and a t-shirt, poured coffee into his Stanley thermos. Alan smiled at Julia but avoided Teddy's eyes. She couldn't tell if he was still angry—or just embarrassed. She decided she didn't care.

"Hungry, Jules?" he asked, screwing the lid on the thermos.

Julia shook her head and slipped through the kitchen without speaking.

Teddy ruffled Henry's hair.

"Sorry we didn't get to play your game last night, bud."

He took a sip of juice.

"That's okay. Lyric made an omelet. She let me crack the eggs."

Teddy managed a smile.

"That sounds fun. If you're finished eating, go brush your teeth and get your backpack."

Henry pushed the bowl away and slid off his chair.

When he was gone, Teddy poured a cup of coffee and started toward the door.

"Ted, wait," Alan said.

She turned without enthusiasm. "Yeah?"

His face went pink. "Look, sorry about last night. Some of the stuff I said—" He rubbed the back of his neck and tried again. "I was drunk, frustrated. But I shouldn't have unloaded on you like that."

Teddy looked at him and said nothing.

He waited. "Anyway, I was an asshole. I'm sorry."

He met her eyes. The apology wasn't perfect, but it was decent—humble, without excuses or blame-shifting. And Teddy knew what came next. He was waiting for her to say her part. To share responsibility and offer absolution. To finish the script. That's how the life-cycle of a domestic fight was supposed to play out.

But this time, the reciprocal apology caught in her throat.

You're just like your mother—only you disappear without leaving town.

She could still hear his words. Still feel them sliding home—cold and certain, like a knife between the ribs. She wasn't sure she could forgive him for saying it.

Because he knew.

Alan knew she'd spent her whole life trying not to be her mother. It had been her single guiding principle—to be someone who stayed, who was present when it counted.

And for what?

Somehow, she was still the villain in everyone's book.

Teddy felt suddenly exhausted. Divorce might end a marriage, but it couldn't kill the familiar arguments. Once those got well established, they lingered, settling into the walls like old smoke.

"Don't worry about it, Alan," she said wearily. Then, after a beat, forced herself to add, "I could've handled it better, too."

It sounded thin. Grudging. Even to her own ears. But she left it there. It was the best she could do.

She turned to go.

"I'll take care of the kids' transportation for the rest of the week. Meals, too," he called after her. A peace offering.

"Great. Thanks."

Teddy didn't stop. She left the room before he could say anything else.

Ramirez was waiting by the rear entrance when Teddy and Julia arrived at the station. A faint odor of alcohol clung to him, partly masked by Listerine.

Teddy walked with them to the interview room.

Julia looked scared. Teddy squeezed her hand. "You'll be fine. Don't worry."

Ramirez ushered Julia inside. "She's underage, Ted. You can sit in, if you want."

Teddy reached out and pulled the door closed. "I'll watch on video," she whispered. "Ask her if Cody ever talked about overhearing anything suspicious."

"From who?"

"From anyone. She was evasive about that with me."

Maybe Ramirez could get Julia to talk. She was hiding something—maybe to protect Cody. Or maybe she just didn't want to tell her mother. But in a situation like this, secrets could be lethal.

Teddy went to the Chief's office and booted up the computer. She pulled up the CCTV feed and chewed her thumbnail as she watched.

The interview was disappointing. Julia stuck to her story and offered nothing more, even when Ramirez pushed her. She was prepared for the questions this time. Her responses were more polished, her evasions smoother. But she was still concealing something.

Teddy pictured Cody's face—white and slack in the water, that livid mark across his throat. Julia might not know anything definite. But that wouldn't matter to the person who'd killed him.

As the interview was concluding, Teddy heard a rustle and looked up.

Caleb Brendall stood in the doorway, the usual white lollipop stick jutting from his mouth. "Where's the Chief?"

"Interview room. He'll be out soon."

"That guy Matthew's on the phone—the one Bragg wanted to talk to. What should I do?"

Teddy considered. "Call Raina at home. If she's up to it, she'll want to handle it herself. If she's not, put it through here—I'll take it."

Brendall shifted the lollipop to the other cheek. "Right-oh!"

Teddy waited, tracing the edge of the desk with her forefinger. But the phone stayed silent. What kind of pain meds had Raina been prescribed? If she was talking to the mysterious Matthew, Teddy hoped she was clear-headed.

She glanced at the computer screen. Ramirez and Julia were on their feet now, heading for the door. Teddy got up and went down the hall.

"Take her home, Drummond. She did good." Ramirez patted Julia's shoulder. His voice was cheerful, but his eyes held disappointment.

Teddy and Julia walked to the pickup in silence. The sky was a clear blue, but the air was still damp, moisture rising like smoke from the line of scrubby hackberry trees behind the station.

Once in the truck, Julia dropped against the seat. "Don't ask, Mom. I can't talk about it anymore."

"I watched on camera."

Teddy looked at her daughter, fighting the instinct to question, to press. She didn't have much to go on when it came to mothering. But she knew Julia.

She latched her seatbelt and started the truck. "It's nine fifty. Still want to go to school?"

"Better than being home alone."

"You must be starved. I'll buy you a breakfast burrito first."

A half-hour later, she dropped off Julia, then sat in the high school parking lot, her hand on the gear shift. She pulled out her phone and texted Shane: *Can U + Frankie dig hole 4 horse in N. pasture?*

She let the phone fall into the console and dropped her forehead to the steering wheel. Her book bag sat in the cargo space behind the passenger seat, solid and inescapable. Three hours till class. If she went in now, she'd have time—time to think about how to address the monstrous elephant in the room. The empty desk by the window. The student roster, shorter now by one.

She sat up, rolled her shoulders, and grabbed her phone again.

Up 4 a visit? Lot 2 tell U, she texted.

The thumbs-up emoji came back before she had time to put the phone away.

Teddy shifted into first gear and let out the clutch.

Chapter 24

Teddy could feel her heart rate rise as she turned onto Billings Drive. The dark blue house near the end of the block had once been as familiar to her as her own. Now it seemed misaligned, somehow—both recognizable and strange—like a landmark only noticed from one direction.

It felt like a violation to pull into the driveway. She parked beneath a sycamore across the street. The Braggs' yard looked the same—pruned hedges, cracked walkway. For some reason, the sameness was more unsettling than radical change would've been.

A black gravel bike leaned against the porch rail. Teddy climbed the steps and reached for the doorbell, then paused. What exactly was the etiquette for visiting the woman whose son you'd shot? Should she have brought some kind of get-well-soon gift? A plant? A casserole? She was struck suddenly by the strangeness of the situation. Hallmark didn't make a card for this.

Teddy had always known where she stood with Raina—both when they were friends, and when they weren't. But now she felt disoriented, like the compass points had shifted and the map no longer matched the terrain.

As she reached for the bell, the door swung open and Mark McKissick stopped short. He wore cycling gear and was carrying a helmet.

He smiled. "I was just leaving. Didn't hear you knock."

"I hadn't." Teddy shifted aside to let him pass. "Do the Braggs go to Calvary Baptist now?"

"No. But Calvin's girlfriend comes to our teen devo. She messaged me last night—said Raina got hurt, and somebody drowned at the Wallow. Then Inez called and told me it was Cody Puckett." His mouth tightened. "Hard to believe. I just saw him yesterday." He clipped the helmet strap under his chin. "I'm heading out to check on Stan and Inez now. Thought I'd swing by here first—see how Detective Bragg's holding up."

"You saw Cody yesterday? Where?" Teddy's voice came out sharper than she meant.

McKissick blinked. "At the ranch. There was a blowup after y'all left. Inez kicked him out." He frowned, the crease deepening above his nose. "I tried calling him last night, but it went straight to voicemail. I was worried." He hesitated. "How did he wind up in the Wallow? Was—was it suicide?"

Teddy sidestepped the question. "What time did you leave the ranch?"

McKissick glanced off toward the street. "Four fifteen; four twenty, maybe."

"You didn't see Cody again after that?"

"No. Why?" He pulled a pair of cycling gloves from his back pocket.

"He was walking on Route 137 about the time you'd have been riding home."

McKissick frowned. "137's a long road."

"He was going north, you were going south. Hard to miss."

His face tightened. He lifted his hands, let them fall. "Maybe someone picked him up."

Teddy thought of her father's security video—the dark pickup with the dented fender. The man in the white Stetson riding shotgun.

"Maybe," she said. "Were you on 137 all the way into town?"

McKissick smacked his palm lightly against his helmet. "No, I cut through Hal Grobiner's orchard. Took the alley behind Kenmare to the church. I live just past it."

"All right. Thanks."

McKissick tugged on a glove, then paused. "Listen—I know it's an active case. But—" He hesitated, tapping the second glove against his palm. "I work with teenagers. You know how it is. One suicide can lead to more. My offices have been full since the news about Chase. And now this." He met her eyes. "If there's anything I could say tonight at the devo . . . I mean, if Cody drowned by accident—"

"That hasn't been determined," Teddy said. "It's the ME's job."

"I'm sure you've got an opinion."

Teddy studied him. He was watching her closely—too closely, maybe—but his face showed only concern. He wasn't wrong. Suicide could spread like wildfire among kids. If she were in his shoes, she knew she'd be asking, too. But Chase hadn't killed himself, and neither had Cody.

"Sorry. Like you said, the investigation's ongoing."

McKissick's face fell. "Sure. I get it." He glanced away, then back. "It's—I lost a brother years ago. I know what that kind of loneliness feels like. I just want to help." He met her eyes. "Teenagers seem so lost these days, you know? Always have been, I guess. But social media makes it worse. One dumb mistake can follow them forever now. No wonder the suicide rate keeps climbing."

"That's true." Teddy thought of Julia's photos. Had Cody shared them with anyone? Would Julia spend the rest of her life wondering when they'd resurface?

"You can't give me anything that might help me out with these kids?" McKissick asked.

"They need empathy most. You don't need me for that."

McKissick nodded. "You're right. It's easy to get hung up on what to say, when sometimes saying nothing's best." He pulled on the second glove, stooped to flick a broken sprig of vegetation from his bike's gears, and spun the pedals to check the clearance. "I better get going. Long ride out to the Rocking L."

Teddy watched him pedal to the end of the block. She was reaching for the bell when a soft rapping caught her attention. Raina was at the front window, waving her in.

Teddy opened the door. For a moment, the motion felt so natural it threw her. She caught herself almost calling out, *Hey, how's it going?* The instinct left her unsteady, as if she'd stepped into an alternate version of her own life—the version that should have been.

The place hadn't changed much. A new rug in the entry. The torchière moved to the other side of the hall. Small alterations, but they stood out.

She turned through the archway into the living room. Raina, in sweats and a t-shirt, sat in an armchair by the window, her injured leg propped on an ottoman. Crutches lay on the floor beside her. Ninja, the old black cat, was on her lap, watching Teddy with cool green eyes.

Teddy sat on the sofa and glanced around. The TV was newer, but the furniture looked older—more cat-shredded than she remembered. On the mantel, a battery candle flickered beside a framed copy of Terrence's funeral program. A blue ribbon hung from one corner; he'd won it at the barrel-racing regionals the year before he died. She and Raina had gone to Abilene for that. Teddy had screamed herself hoarse.

She looked away. Raina was watching her. A coffee mug and an orange pill bottle sat on the table beside her chair.

Teddy said the first thing that came to mind. "Are you in a lot of pain?"

"I've got two broken bones. What d'you think?" Raina snapped.

Heat flushed Teddy's neck. She wanted to say, *I told you not to go under that tree*. But she didn't.

A clumsy silence followed. Raina glared at the carpet, then burst out, "God, I am so angry right now. Two kids dead, and I'm stuck here."

Her voice cracked on "kids"—as if something deeper than anger had caught in her throat. Something older. Teddy tried to meet her eyes, but Raina kept hers down.

"What happens with the case?" Raina asked. "Ramirez wouldn't give me a straight answer—told me to get some rest and not worry my pretty little head. *Jesus*, he can be a real prick." She looked up. "I guess he called the sheriff?"

Teddy nodded. "I doubt Linacre will send his A team, though. They're stretched thin in San Angelo right now."

"Fantastic." Raina threw her head back and stared at the ceiling. Her uninjured leg bounced restlessly. "Ramirez wants you to help bring the sheriff's guy up to speed?"

"Maybe for a day or two."

Teddy braced for an angry comeback, but Raina only nodded. "Good. You can keep me in the loop—unless you decide to freeze me out, too."

"Hey, I'm not. That guy Matthew called this morning. I told Brendall to refer it to you."

"And *I* told Brendall to give him my number, but he hasn't called." Raina shifted irritably. "What were you and Saint Overstep talking about on the porch?"

"Saint Overstep?"

"McKissick gets on my nerves. I hate pop-ins. He's not even my pastor."

"I was hoping he spotted Cody Puckett on 137 yesterday. Might help us nail down the timeline."

Raina's chin rose. "Do we know yet who Cody was on the phone with?"

"Your hunch was right - It was Julia. She gave me the whole story this morning. Cody called her at Petal Pushers and told her he broke out of the police station and was on the run. Apparently, when we said we could recover his deleted texts, he panicked - scared I'd set him up for Chase's murder, or something. I don't know."

"That's ridiculous."

"Panicky people don't think straight. Julia told him to go back, but he was freaked—wanted out of town, fast."

"To go where?"

"He said something about hitchhiking to Mexico. But he didn't have anything—not even shoes. He asked Julia for money, and she said she'd help."

"She shouldn't have."

Teddy shrugged. "She's in love. All she had was twenty bucks, but she told him he could have it."

"That's where he was headed when you saw him on the Skinny's CCTV?"

"Yeah. But he called her back a few minutes later—said he'd run into someone he knew."

Raina leaned in. "Who?"

"Didn't say. Julia thought it was a guy. Whoever it was told Cody he'd loan him some cash. Cody was going home with this person to get the money, then planned to meet her back at Petal Pushers in half an hour." Teddy rubbed her cheek. "That's the last she heard. When he didn't show, she tried calling, but it went straight to voicemail. By six fifteen, she was scared."

"Scared he was in danger?"

"Scared he wasn't thinking straight. She told Ruby she had cramps and took off on her bike looking for him."

Raina pulled the ottoman closer, shifting the position of her bandaged leg. "Why the Buffalo Wallow?"

"That was just the last stop. She checked their usual hangouts—Mad Dog Bluff, Waverly Hill. The Wallow wasn't a favorite, but they'd been there a couple times."

"Was he dead when she got there?"

"It was pouring by then, and pitch-dark. She spotted him in a lightning flash. Thought he'd slipped and fallen in. She yelled, tried to find something to throw him, but she couldn't. So she called me."

"If you were on your way, why'd she jump in?"

"She was scared he'd get sucked into the culvert. She tried to haul him out, but he was heavy, and she was tired. All she could do was hang on." Teddy picked up a throw pillow, toying with the fringe. "You know the rest."

Raina, who had been leaning forward, slumped back in her chair. "Was he killed by whoever he met on the road?"

"Julia thinks so." Teddy hesitated. "Did the Chief tell you about Stan?"

"What about him?"

Before Teddy could answer, Raina's phone alarm trilled.

"Hang on, gotta take my meds. If I wait too long, it gets bad."

Raina opened the pill bottle, then glanced into the coffee cup. "Damn."

"Need some water?" Teddy asked.

Raina set the cup and bottle aside and reached for her crutches. Ninja hissed and jumped off her lap.

"Don't be stupid." Teddy stood. "You're going to hurt yourself. I'll get it."

Raina said nothing. She was struggling to hold onto the crutches and push herself up. It was painful to watch.

"For God's sake, Raina. It's just a glass of water."

Teddy snatched the cup from the table and headed for the hall.

Chapter 25

The Braggs' kitchen was almost exactly as Teddy remembered. Though the paint around the wall switch was a bit grimier now, and the football cleats by the back door were several sizes larger, the rest was unaltered—same fridge, same curtains, same electric kettle by the sink.

As she rinsed and filled Raina's coffee mug, Teddy studied a framed collage of family snapshots on the wall. One showed the Braggs on a roller-coaster at Six Flags—Anthony and Calvin in front, with Raina and Terrence behind them—all four holding up their arms and screaming as the coaster plunged down a steep drop. Another featured an eight-year-old Calvin in his Little League uniform, grinning with a bat on his shoulder.

The largest photo captured a teenage Terrence with his barrel horse at the Concho Valley Rodeo. He was leaning over Mayhem's dark, glossy neck as they raced across the arena toward the first blue barrel, a plume of red dust billowing in their wake.

Teddy turned off the faucet and stared. Terrence had boarded Mayhem at her place. She remembered the night the horse disappeared—remembered sitting here in the Braggs' kitchen, telling Terrence the search had come up empty. The next time she'd seen him had been through a rifle scope.

She wiped the bottom of the mug with a paper towel and turned away.

Opening the garbage can, she caught a sweet floral scent. A bouquet of red roses lay half buried in kitchen waste. Fairly fresh—maybe a day or two old—but wilting now from lack of water.

She pictured Raina in the station hallway the day before, blinking back tears. *Be right back—I need to make a call.*

Teddy hadn't known what to make of it then, but now she wondered. After a pause, she dropped the paper towel inside and shut the lid.

Back in the living room, Raina was resettled in her chair with her bandaged leg on the ottoman. Her eyes were squeezed shut, her hands curled into fists.

"Pain worse?" Teddy asked.

Raina opened her eyes. She took the mug and gulped down a pill. "I'm fine."

"You overdid it trying to get up." Teddy realized she was hovering and sat down. "Where's Anthony? He didn't leave you home alone today, did he?"

Anthony Bragg worked as a stenographer at the county courthouse in San Angelo. He was a charming guy, easy to like—but a little self-centered.

Raina shook her head. "He went out for a drive."

Teddy said nothing.

Raina noticed the look on her face. "It's not what you think. I told him you were coming over. He didn't want to see you."

Teddy sat very still. Raina wasn't telling the whole story. Even after years of silence, Teddy could still read her like a book. But Raina had written her out of the plot. There was no way back in.

She wanted to ask, *Y'all doing okay?* But it would only trigger some cutting remark. Did Raina have anyone to talk to now? Teddy still had Berna. But Raina had never kept much of a social circle.

Anthony's too high-maintenance for me to make friends, she used to say. *It just causes trouble.*

Teddy's bootlace had come undone, and she bent to tie it. There was no point asking, but the words slipped out anyway. "Rain, is Anth—"

Raina cut her off. "Forget it. What were you saying before, about Stan?"

Teddy sat up and sighed. "Yeah, okay."

Once someone decided you were their enemy, acceptance was the only dignified response.

She recapped Julia's impressions of Stan, and then gave a quick summary of his disappearance the night before and his sudden return home that morning.

"Have you talked to him?" Raina asked as Ninja jumped back on her lap and began licking his paw.

"Wally said wait till he sleeps off his hangover."

Raina stroked the cat's flank. "I found Marlboros at the Wallow. Stan's brand. He was smoking them yesterday at the ranch."

"Along with half the good ole boys in West Texas," Teddy murmured.

"If Stan thought Cody killed Chase, he might've hunted him down, promised him money so he could lure him to some quiet spot."

"Maybe. But the timeline's off," Teddy said. "Cody told Julia he'd be at the flower shop in half an hour. If Stan was the person he met, he would've known he couldn't go home with him and get back to town that fast."

"What if Stan said he was taking him to the bank to get the money?"

Teddy shook her head. "Cody said he was going to this person's house. I asked Julia twice."

"Assuming he told her the truth."

Teddy blinked. "Why wouldn't he?"

Raina stared down at the cat. "Men lie. Who the hell knows why?"

Teddy looked at her. "They lie for the same reasons women do—to stay out of trouble, or get something they want, or keep from hurting someone."

Raina ran her thumb down the cat's spine, and it dug its claws into her thigh. "Ow!" She shoved it off her knees. "I think they lie to avoid hassle. Other people's thoughts and feelings ruin their fun. They can't be bothered."

Teddy wasn't sure how to reply, so she let the comment go. Raina was frustrated and in pain—in the kind of mood where any response would land wrong. Safer to stick to the original subject. "If Stan picked Cody up, I guess it's possible he told him to lie to Julia—to keep his name out of it, so we'd look the other way. We don't really know enough yet to draw conclusions."

Raina picked up the mug and stared into it. "If I weren't stuck in this stupid house . . ." She shook her head and drained the last of the water. "The MO's not quite right for Stan, I suppose. He's not the ligature-strangling type—it's too cold-blooded." She looked up. "But he's connected to both our victims and has no alibi, as far as we know. And according to Julia he's borderline abusive."

"That's overstating it. She said he had a temper."

"In an airport thriller, a guy like that might be innocent. In real life, it's pretty damn suspicious."

"I'm not saying he's above suspicion," Teddy said. "But—"

She was interrupted by a shrill ringtone. Raina checked her phone screen. "It's that guy Matthew."

Teddy jumped up. "Put it on speaker." She perched on the arm of Raina's chair. "I'll record it."

As she opened the voice memo app, her own phone buzzed—Ramirez. Raina was already speaking, identifying herself and explaining the situation. Teddy's phone buzzed twice more.

"Dammit," she muttered, getting up and heading for the door.

She cut through the kitchen, answering the phone as she slipped out the back onto the brick patio. A wave of nostalgia hit her. It was impossible not to think about the long, easy evenings she and Alan used to spend here—sipping longnecks with Raina and Anthony after cookouts, while the kids shot hoops in the driveway or played badminton on the grass.

The place was dismal and neglected now. Weeds had pushed between the bricks, and the lawn chairs were layered with grime. An abandoned wasps' nest clung to the handle of the rusting grill.

"Drummond, you listening?" Ramirez snapped.

"Sorry, Chief. What was that?"

"I said the CSI report on the silo came through. I'll send a PDF."

"What's the short version?"

"Chase's gun definitely fired the fatal shot. No prints except his on it or on the note. Whoever killed him either wiped it or wore gloves."

"Not surprising. What about the bullet?"

"Winchester hollow-point."

"Winchester? You sure?"

"That's what the report says."

"His room only had Smith & Wesson cartridges."

"We'll look into it."

"That's it?" Teddy felt vaguely disappointed.

A beat of silence. "We found fingerprints—a lot of people's."

"Makes sense. Chase was giving dive lessons." Teddy waited. "Anything stand out?"

Another pause. "Frankie Aguilar's were on the sofa in the control room."

"Frankie's?" Teddy shifted the phone to her other hand.

"He ever mention knowing Chase or being down in that silo?" Ramirez's voice sounded strange. Teddy had the uncomfortable feeling he was holding something back.

"Not to me." A garbage truck rumbled up the alley behind the house, and she covered her free ear. "Why are Frankie's prints in the system? Did you take them when—the day Terrence died?"

Although she'd lowered her voice on the last question, she couldn't help glancing toward the doorway. *The day Terrence died.* How easy it was to blunt the edge of that memory with a euphemism, Teddy thought. *The day I shot Terrence.*

She'd told the story aloud last night, but the words still didn't feel like hers. Maybe that was why she avoided them—because they captured so little of the truth. No one understood what had really happened. Least of all Teddy.

What had made a kid like Terrence Bragg walk into his ex-girlfriend's house waving a loaded gun? He'd left no note, no online rant to explain himself. And if Jasmine knew why, she wasn't saying.

"No, not then," Ramirez said. "He didn't do anything. Besides, the paramedics were working on him."

"I remember."

Frankie had tried to wrestle the gun from Terrence and had taken a bullet in the process. After that, Teddy's options were limited.

She'd been cleared in the subsequent investigation. She'd followed her training—tried to keep him talking until the sheriff's SWAT team arrived. But once Terrence had shown himself to be a lethal threat, Teddy had responded the only way she could. Everyone knew it—except the Braggs. Teddy knew it, too. Most of the time. But it didn't feel true. After five and a half years, she'd decided it never would.

Damn, this place is messing with my head.

She kicked at a rusty bottle cap lodged in the weedy brickwork. Ramirez was speaking again, and she struggled to focus.

"His prints were on file from a shoplifting bust when he was a kid."

"There's a million reasons Frankie's prints might be on that sofa, Chief. Could've been there for months. Doesn't mean he killed Chase." Teddy swallowed. "You're not telling me something."

A long pause. She thought he might have hung up. Then he cleared his throat. "You're close to the Aguilars. Frankie works for Alan, right?"

"Yeah. So?"

"One of the prints is in blood, Ted."

Teddy went cold. "Blood? Whose blood?"

"We don't know. It's at the state lab, but that'll take time."

"Could be anyone's."

"Sure. But it don't look good. If it's Chase's, the DA'll charge Frankie with murder."

Teddy steadied herself against a lawn chair. What would Alan say? And Shane? Frankie was his best and oldest friend.

"What possible motive could Frankie have for killing Chase Loudermilk?" she asked, more to herself than to Ramirez.

"I don't know," he said. "But I know one thing—the sheriff's investigator's gonna go hot-footed for this."

"That's true. Maybe—"

Teddy stopped. An image rose in her mind—Frankie in his green coveralls, leaning over his sister, whispering angrily in the Skinny's office yesterday. What was it Jasmine had said? *I told you what would happen if you didn't lay off.*

Teddy hadn't thought much of it at the time—just a spat between siblings. None of her business. But now? Should she tell Ramirez? She hated to paint a bigger target on Frankie's back until she knew more.

"Frankie's a good kid, Chief. There might be a simple explanation. We should talk to him first, before the sheriff's guy gets here."

"I already sent Loomis to bring him in—I want to question him at the station, on camera. You can observe, if you want."

Teddy checked the time. "I've got class. If you could wait till after three—"

"No good. The Rangers' dive team might be here by then. I'll talk to Frankie. We can follow up later."

Teddy hung up, unsettled, and went back inside.

Raina had finished her call. "Where'd you run off to?"

Teddy sat down and filled her in. She checked her email. "Wally's sending a PDF of the crime scene report, but it hasn't come through yet."

Raina leaned back, absorbing the information. "Damn. Frankie Aguilar's fingerprint in blood?"

"Might be his own. Could've gotten a nosebleed down there."

"Were him and Chase friends?"

Teddy shrugged. "Camp buddies. Stan said they used to pal around sometimes, but not for years."

"If it is Chase's blood—why would Frankie kill him, then go touch the sofa? If his hands were bloody, why not rinse them in the launch chamber? There's a gazillion gallons of water down there."

"I was wondering the same thing," Teddy said. "What about your call? Anything there?"

Raina reached for a notepad. "The guy's name is Matt Tankersley, age thirty-seven. He's—"

A shadow passed the window, and the front door squeaked open.

Anthony appeared in the archway. He was a striking-looking man, tall and broad-shouldered, with an athlete's build and a thin, intelligent face. Raina had fallen for his easy charm and smile. But he wasn't smiling now.

"I thought you were taking a drive," Raina said.

"Couldn't circle the block forever." His voice was hard. He ignored Teddy. "I'll pull something together for lunch." He crossed the room and went into the kitchen.

Teddy stood. "I've got class soon." She nodded at the notebook. "I want to hear about that. Call me after three?"

Raina's expression was unreadable. She nodded. "You'll keep me in the loop?"

"I promise."

Chapter 26

Three p.m. Footsteps shuffled, voices murmured, and the usual after-class clatter felt strangely muted as the students filed out. Though Teddy had spent days worrying about what to say, class had gone well—better than she'd hoped.

Maybe she should always wing it, she thought, repacking her book bag at the front of the room. She seemed to teach better that way.

Not that she'd meant to show up unprepared. After leaving Raina's, she'd gone home to change and grab a quick bite. That should've left her a full hour to get to campus and throw together a lesson plan. But as she reached the driveway, something caught her eye—a metallic flash at the far end of the north pasture. She checked the time, then turned down the long dirt track. Near the tree line, she found Shane on the Bobcat, digging in the muddy red clay.

Teddy got out. A cool breeze was blowing.

Shane throttled back the motor. "Dirt's still wet—heavy as hell. Reckon it's deep enough?"

Teddy peered into the hole. "I think so. Just needs widening. I'd like to get Fancy out of the barn before the kids get home."

Shane glanced south across the pasture. "Horse is stiff. We gotta cut out the stall door. Frankie was working on it, but the cops showed up and took him." He wiped his face with his sleeve.

"What's that about? They found a joint in his pocket, but there's more to it—I could tell."

"They're interviewing a lot of people," Teddy said carefully.

Shane rummaged in a toolbox and pulled out a water bottle. "But why Frankie? Is it about Chase Loudermilk? There's rumors going around he was murdered."

He tried to sound casual, but Teddy heard the worry underneath.

"Did you and Frankie know him well?" she asked.

Shane took a drink. "Not no more. We seen him a couple times over the summer, but he ain't been around in years."

"Ever been to the missile silo on the Loudermilks' ranch?"

Shane squinted, shook his head. "Heard about it."

"What about Frankie?"

"I dunno. You'd have to ask him."

"He ever mention it?"

"Not to me." He was staring across the pasture, jiggling the water bottle in his hand. His voice had gone tight, clipped. He screwed the lid back on the bottle and gestured toward the grave. "Better get on with this."

Teddy pursed her lips. He was clearly being evasive. Was he just protecting Frankie, or was there more to it? If Shane was mixed up in something ugly—if he knew anything about Chase's death—she needed to know. Chase deserved that much.

But now wasn't the time to push. She needed to get to campus.

"See what you can do about getting Fancy in this hole. Don't cover her yet—I promised Jules we'd wait. Try to make her look . . . peaceful."

"Peaceful?"

"Like she wasn't dumped in a pit. If Alan gives you trouble, tell him to talk to me. I'll make sure he doesn't dock your pay."

Shane looked surprised. "This was Alan's idea—even before I got your text. When the cops took Frankie, Alan shut down the greenhouse and took over in the barn himself."

Teddy didn't know how to respond. "Oh. Well, that's good."

Shane reached for the throttle, but Teddy stopped him. "Hey, don't give Grandpa any more stuff you get from job sites, okay? Health Department's been after him to clean up his place."

Shane looked startled, but shrugged. "No problem."

Something in his face tripped an alarm in Teddy's mind. "Where do you get all that stuff, anyway? Not from landscaping jobs."

His eyelids flickered. "Been picking up extra work—nights and weekends. Demo jobs in San Angelo. Retail places that went under and need clearing out—that kind of thing."

His voice was casual, but Teddy could tell he was nervous. His long fingers fiddled with the control panel.

"Why the sudden need for cash?" she asked.

"Dad's appeal's coming up. He needs a better lawyer. That public defender's a joke."

Teddy held her tongue. She wanted to tell Shane not to bother. Danny wasn't in prison because of a bad lawyer but because he'd been cooking meth. He'd never be the father Shane wanted. But saying so wouldn't help. It was a lesson Shane would have to learn first-hand—as she had.

"I get it," she said finally.

Shane was watching her from the Bobcat. "Think I'm being stupid, huh?"

Teddy laid a hand on his leg. "No, hon. I've never thought that."

The barn doors were standing open as Teddy drove past it on her way back to the road. She glanced inside as she went by. Alan, in green coveralls and safety goggles, was kneeling at the stall door with a reciprocating saw.

Teddy slowed, her hand hovering near the truck's door handle. Alan was making a real effort after last night's fight, and she should try to meet him halfway. It wouldn't take much—a word, a nod. She looked at the dashboard clock and eased off the brake. Class started in forty minutes. If she went straight to campus, she'd have just enough time to get to her office and jot down a few notes.

But by the time she'd run the gauntlet of colleagues wanting updates on Chase Loudermilk, she barely had time to take off her jacket and fix her wind-blown hair before heading to the classroom.

The students seemed depressed and lethargic—working hard not to stare at the empty desk by the window. It had always been a little too small for Chase's gangly frame. Now, it seemed to take up more space than anything else in the room.

Looking at the class, Teddy decided candor was best.

"I'll be honest—I've got nothing," she said. "It's been a horrible week. I'm as shocked and sad as you are, and I haven't had the heart for school work." She picked up the textbook, then dropped it on the table. "Forget Gilchrist for today. What do y'all need to talk about?"

After some staring and shuffling, a tentative hand went up. "I heard you're helping the police," a dark-haired girl said. "Does that mean they've got doubts about what happened?"

The question functioned like the pulling of a cork. The students' pent-up grief and curiosity over Chase's death welled up in a flood of questions that occupied the rest of the hour. Teddy tried to be as open as she could without revealing anything confidential—a difficult line to walk.

"I'm not officially involved," she said, "but I've offered my help. If anyone has information—even if you think it's unimportant—let us know."

Now that class was over, she was exhausted. But it had been a good hour. She could see it in her students' faces—in the slight relaxation of their shoulders. They'd needed a way to name what they were feeling. So had she.

Teaching had always felt to Teddy like a borrowed identity, temporary and ill-fitting. She wasn't a professor—just a cop who taught. But today, something had settled into place. For once, it hadn't seemed like an act.

As she gathered up the last of her belongings, something white fluttered from beneath a folder on the table.

She picked it up—a torn scrap of notebook paper, folded in quarters. Frowning, she opened it.

CHASE GOT A PHONE CALL AT THE BOWLING ALLEY. SUNDAY 10:30 PM.

Teddy stared at the note. Any of her students could have left it—they'd all passed that front table on their way out. The handwriting told her nothing. The words were penciled in block capitals—childish and unpracticed. Not unusual these days, even for college students. Most rarely wrote anything by hand.

Someone wanted to help but didn't want to get involved. Why?

She slung her bag over her shoulder and stepped into the hallway. It was crowded with people issuing from classrooms, but she didn't see any of her own students loitering around.

She slipped the note into her back pocket and headed for the stairwell.

The catharsis she'd felt five minutes ago was already fading. If Chase had gotten a phone call that night, the caller might've been the last person to speak to him—and she needed to know who it was. She felt a prickle of unease as she descended the stairs. This case wasn't over. It was moving fast.

She thought of Julia, alone at school, still shaken from the night before. She was hiding something. But what? Could it put her at risk?

As Teddy turned the corner toward her office, her phone rang. Ramirez. The call was brief. The Rangers' dive team had arrived, and he was taking them to the silo. Did she want to observe?

"I'm on my way," she said, grabbing her purse from the back of her chair.

◆ ◆ ◆

Outside, the earlier breeze had risen to a stiff, chilly wind. Yellowed pecan leaves scudded across the parking lot, and tiny waves rippled in the puddles left by last night's storm. Teddy hurried across the asphalt, phone in hand, pulling up Raina's number as she unlocked her truck. But before she could call, her phone buzzed—Alan. Probably to say that he and Shane had gotten Fancy in the ground. She let it go to voicemail and dialed Raina instead.

The pain pill had apparently kicked in. Raina sounded relaxed, her voice low and even. But it sharpened when Teddy shared the note she'd found in class.

"This would be easy if we had Chase's phone," Raina said. "Judge won't sign a warrant for the records till the official death certificate comes through."

"I'm heading to the silo now," Teddy said. "Maybe the divers will find it."

"Even if they do, data retrieval will probably take weeks."

"Chase was bowling with the Bible study kids. McKissick gave you their names yesterday, right?"

"Yeah," Raina said, rustling paper. "Got the list here."

Teddy pulled onto the shoulder and opened the college database on her phone. "I'm sending you my class roster. Any of my students in that Bible study?"

"Hang on." A pause. "No."

"Damn." Teddy eased back onto the road.

Raina exhaled sharply. "If I weren't stuck here, I could check the bowling alley footage. Wouldn't tell us who called, but we might catch Chase's reaction."

"I'll go tonight, if I can. What about your call with Matt Tankersley? Anything helpful?"

Teddy heard more paper rustling.

"He was Chase Loudermilk's AA sponsor in Galveston. Roughneck on an offshore oil rig—says he's been out there for the past three weeks. No mobile service. Claims he didn't get my message till he got back to shore Monday night."

"Solid alibi."

"Except he's lying. I tracked down the installation manager. Crew came ashore Monday, all right. But Tankersley had a family emergency—mother sick. He left the rig last Saturday."

"You're kidding."

"I'm guessing if I talk to the mother, she'll turn out to be fine."

"Think Tankersley's our guy?"

"He's got some reason for lying."

"What else did he say? Did he know Chase fell off the wagon?"

"Claims he didn't. Says he hasn't heard from Chase in over a year. Sounded surprised Chase still had his number. He acted shocked when I told him Chase was dead—had no idea why the note would be addressed to him."

"You didn't tell him Chase was murdered?"

"If he's the killer, he already knows. I wanted to see if he'd let something slip."

Teddy said nothing, letting the pieces shift and settle. If Tankersley was the killer—

"Still there?" Raina asked.

"It's weird he didn't know Chase had been drinking again, don't you think? Assuming that's true."

"What do you mean?"

"Inez said Chase was sober for a long time. Then he had a wobble this fall. McKissick said he started going to the Bible study as a sort of AA substitute. You'd think he'd call his real sponsor—for moral support, if nothing else."

"Maybe he tried but couldn't reach him on the rig."

Teddy slowed to turn onto Route 137. "Or maybe they had a falling-out."

"Tankersley didn't mention one."

"If he's the killer, he wouldn't." Teddy passed a slow-moving tractor and merged back into the right lane. "You said he was surprised Chase still had his number? I've got numbers from people I haven't talked to in twenty years. Sounds like he expected Chase would've gotten rid of his number on purpose."

Over the phone, Raina snorted. "The guy's a liar—we can't take anything he says at face value. I called Galveston PD—they're going to track him down and bring him in for questioning."

"Perfect. Keep me posted."

The highway crested a slight rise, and through the window Teddy could see the blue-gray outline of Deadhorse Mesa in the middle distance.

"I'm at the ranch now," she said. "Call you later."

The yellow police tape that had blocked the east gate on Monday now lay fluttering in the grass. On the other side of the fence, a cluster of black Angus cows and six-month-old calves grazed placidly.

Teddy slowed as she crossed the cattle guard. The animals looked up, jaws working. When she tapped the accelerator, they turned and trotted off toward the trees. She watched them go, then drove on.

Chapter 27

Teddy stopped her truck beside the concrete cap that roofed the missile silo. Ramirez's gold Suburban was parked in the switchgrass nearby, next to a white Dodge Durango she didn't recognize.

Out here on open ranchland, away from the shelter of buildings and large trees, the wind was stronger. Tumbleweeds sailed over the scrub to collect in shaggy heaps at the foot of the mesa. Teddy got out and reached for the spare fleece she kept under the driver's seat. Pulling it on, she started toward the access port.

The steel door and outer grille were propped open by a cinderblock, and the entrance gaped like the black mouth of a cave. She hesitated, then returned to the truck and rummaged in the glovebox. When she found her flashlight, she switched it on and cupped her hand over the lens. A pale, watery glow reflected off her palm. After hours at the Wallow last night, the batteries were nearly dead. Annoyed, she tossed it onto the seat and slammed the truck door.

Approaching the entrance for the second time, she was sweating in spite of the wind, thinking of the massive chasm below, with its echoing passageways and cold, dripping tunnels.

Chase had stood here Sunday night. In the dark, it would've been worse. Why had he come? What was he hoping to find?

She should've asked him more questions at their last meeting. Something had clearly been wrong—his change in demeanor, the slipping grades, talk of transfer. Now, in the rearview, the signs lined up neat as fenceposts. But at the time, she'd been busy. And he was an adult. If he'd wanted to share, he would have. She told herself that. But did she believe it? Or was it just a story she clung to because it let her off the hook?

If she'd done things differently, would the outcome have been the same? She'd been asking herself that for five years about Terrence. Now she'd be asking it about Chase. But maybe the question itself was a kind of vanity. Whatever either of them had been going through, one thing was certain: it hadn't been about her.

Before she could muster the nerve to enter the access port, a dark shape emerged, breathing hard and carrying a Maglite.

Teddy's shoulders relaxed. "Am I glad to see you."

Ramirez studied her face. "Why? Something happen?"

"Just dreading going in there."

"That's why I came out. Stick close. We'll take it slow."

Teddy nodded, then gestured toward the Durango. "That the Rangers' SUV?"

"They're on the platform, setting up. Ready?"

"No. But more time won't help." She followed Ramirez through the doorway.

Practice mindfulness—that had been the therapist's advice for dealing with claustrophobia. *Let your thoughts float past like clouds.* It had taken effort for Teddy not to roll her eyes at the idea. But she had to admit the techniques helped—at least a little.

She trailed her palm along the stairwell wall, trying to focus on the rough, cold surface. But it only reminded her of the tons of concrete and rebar above, below, all around. She could feel the weight of it pressing in, squeezing the air from her lungs.

Below her, Ramirez was silhouetted against the Maglite's beam—a dark, man-shaped void. Teddy thought suddenly of her classroom, and of the empty seat by the window—an emptiness that had brooded there all through class. She'd caught her students stealing glances, leaning toward it as if that side of the room held some gravitational pull. Odd how vacancy could feel more palpable than its opposite.

What had Chase felt, making his way down this stairwell for the last time? Was it just another Sunday night—a quick dive before the school week began? Or had he known he was walking to his death? Had he touched this same concrete, knowing it would be his tomb?

Teddy jerked her fingers away. Her skin was damp—from sweat or condensation. Maybe both. She wiped her hand on her fleece and fixed her eyes on the outline of Ramirez's shoulders. Morbid imaginings were useless, except as fuel for inquiry. Chase had been here. Now he was gone. There were questions. Someone out there knew the answers. That was all the mindfulness she needed.

The work lights blazed from the launch control room as they passed. The Chief went by without a glance, but Teddy looked in. The card table was cluttered with empty equipment cases, and jeans and t-shirts were draped over folding chairs. The divers had evidently used this room as a staging area.

Her eyes landed on the orange plaid sofa. One of the wooden arms had been cut away—the one with Frankie's bloody print, no doubt. Had Ramirez interviewed him yet? She wanted to ask, but not now. She needed to see his face.

Beyond the control room, the passages and stairwells grew narrower and steeper. Teddy was relieved when they finally reached the utility tunnel leading to the central launch chamber.

She hurried forward. Emerging onto the metal balcony, she leaned over the railing. Below, the black water lay as flat and still as a disc of polished marble. On the dive platform, two figures in wetsuits knelt by air tanks, attaching hoses and checking regulators. A third—a stocky man in khakis, boots, and a white Oxford—was setting up some piece of electronics on a folding table.

Teddy followed the Chief down the swaying accordion stairs. The divers were focused on their prep work and didn't look up. Ramirez crossed the planking and introduced Teddy to the man in khakis. Lieutenant Pete Barrera was in his fifties, with coarse, gray-flecked hair and a pale scar above his left eyebrow that stood out against his tanned, leathery skin. He had the look of an outdoorsman, out of place in the dark, echoing pit.

But if the silo bothered him, he didn't show it. He nodded and gave Teddy a cool, appraising look—the kind that made her wonder if he'd read her file.

"I'll be monitoring the dive from up here," he said, turning back to the apparatus on the table and adjusting something on the control panel.

Teddy stepped closer. The device resembled a chunky black laptop, with buttons and dials across the base and a display screen inside the lid.

"What is that?" she asked.

"Video display unit and recorder. The divers'll film the whole thing." Barrera gestured toward a bright yellow object on the platform. It was shaped like a cartoonish gun, with a barrel the size of a two-liter bottle and a camera lens at one end. A thick cord extended from the grip and lay coiled beside it. "We can watch the dive in real time, and you'll have the recording to review—or use in court, if it comes to that."

Teddy eyed the cord. "It's powered from up here? That cable long enough?"

"Should be. It's a hundred and fifty feet." Barrera looked at Ramirez. "Water's one-forty, right?"

The Chief nodded.

"What about snags?" Teddy asked. "God only knows what's down there."

"*I* know what's down there," Ramirez said. "A few hazards on the wall, but it's open water out here, till you hit bottom. Some debris on the floor—leftover HVAC stuff the Air Force junked when it stripped the place. A cable could get tangled down there, all right."

"We'll be careful," a woman's voice said. "We're used to working around shipwrecks and things."

Teddy turned. The divers, now with air tanks, had come up while the others were talking. Their masks were pushed up on their foreheads. Both were young—late twenties, Teddy guessed—but it was hard to tell with the neoprene hoods.

Barrera introduced them as Jane Grant and Mitchell Kendrick.

"Ready to go?" he asked. "Shot-line in place?"

Kendrick nodded and gestured to a red buoy floating a few feet off the platform. In the clear water, Teddy saw a yellow rope trailing into the depths.

"Let's drop another one by the wall," Barrera said. "It'll be dark as all get-out down there—redundancy's our friend."

Grant slipped out of her air tanks and lifted a second coil of rope from an equipment case. Attaching one end to another buoy and the other to a chunky metal weight, she carried it to the inflatable dinghy.

"I'll row for you," Teddy said.

She held the dinghy steady while Grant climbed in, then followed, untying the mooring line from the cinderblock that held it. She picked up the oar and paddled to the concrete wall.

Grant dropped the weight; the rope hissed over the rubber gunnel as it uncoiled. Teddy watched the yellow line vanish into the dark. After several seconds, the buoy jerked free and bobbed on the surface, just off the wall.

"That'll work," Grant said.

"What's it for?"

"Orientation. You'd be surprised how easy it is to get turned around down there."

Grant seemed to find the idea exciting, and Teddy wasn't sure if she was fearless or just young.

"You like doing this?"

"Love it," Grant said. "This'll be my first time in a missile silo. Counts as a deep-water dive, night dive, and confined-space dive." She ticked them off on her fingers. "The diver's hat trick. I'm stoked."

Teddy paddled the dinghy to the platform and tied it to the cinderblock as Kendrick hoisted Grant's air tanks back onto her shoulders. The two divers sat on the platform's edge, pulled on fins, adjusted masks and regulators, and slipped into the water.

Barrera handed the yellow camera to Grant, and the divers swam to the nearest buoy. Kendrick looked at Grant; she gave a thumbs up.

"Ready?" Barrera called.

Both nodded, checked their dive computers, and disappeared below the surface.

Barrera and Ramirez turned to the video monitor, but Teddy lingered at the platform's edge, gazing into the mirrored depths. The divers, in their black wetsuits, vanished quickly—but for a long time she could still see the flicker of yellow fins, undulating slowly. Then those, too, were gone, and only the faint, receding discs of their dive torches remained, winking like fireflies in the dusk. Eventually, even they faded, leaving nothing but slow wreaths of white bubbles rising toward the surface.

She joined Ramirez and Barrera at the monitor in time to see Kendrick's ghostly figure descending, one hand on the yellow shot-line, as the ambient light dimmed to black. Now she understood what Grant had meant—without that line, there were no landmarks. No left, no right. Not even up or down.

Teddy's lungs burned, and she realized she'd been holding her breath. She exhaled slowly, forcing herself to relax.

It took the divers two or three minutes to reach the silo floor. When Teddy caught a glimpse of it in their flashlight beams, her heart sank. The screen filled with a tangle of debris—a rusting mass of steel beams, crumpled scaffolding, and snarled nests of wire. It looked like the wreck of a ship blown to bits in some ancient war.

"They'll never find anything," Teddy muttered.

"Never know," Barrera said.

"How long can they stay down?" Ramirez asked.

"Fifty minutes, start to finish. But decompression takes time. The longer they're at depth, the slower the ascent."

They watched as the divers crawled across the debris field. Teddy found herself counting the minutes, squinting at the screen. No sign of Chase's phone. No laptop. Just wreckage.

Two people weren't enough—not for this. The place was too big, too chaotic. It would take a full team, and multiple dives, to search it properly.

When Kendrick's shadowy figure reached the wall, Teddy saw him stop beside the second shot-line—the one she'd helped drop. He checked his dive computer, then turned to the camera, flashing a light and pointing upward.

Grant's hand, huge and bone-white, appeared at the edge of the frame with an *okay* signal.

"Dammit," Teddy groaned.

Barrera straightened, stretching his back. "Sorry, folks. Gave it our best shot. The rest'll be boring—unless you like staring at concrete."

Teddy looked at the screen and saw what he meant. Grant had reached the second line, and the divers were ascending slowly. Nothing was visible but streaky gray concrete, broken by glimpses of yellow rope. Every few minutes, they paused, floating motionless to decompress.

As the light on the screen began to brighten, the divers passed a section of ductwork bracketed to the wall. Teddy caught a flicker of steel grating and a flash of white.

She stepped forward. "Wait—what was that?"

The men had drifted away from the monitor, but now they crowded back.

"There was something on that grate," Teddy said. "They just passed it."

"The phone?" Ramirez asked.

"I don't think so. I didn't get a good look. But something." She turned to Barrera. "Can you signal them to go back?"

Barrera checked his watch. "I'll try."

He grabbed an underwater flashlight from an equipment box and dropped onto his stomach at the edge of the platform. Plunging one arm into the water, he switched the light to strobe mode to get the divers' attention, then aimed the beam toward the wall.

Kendrick kept rising, but Grant hesitated, then dropped back to the grating.

Teddy leaned in. "There. See?"

Ramirez bent over her shoulder. "What is that?"

A lumpy white object sat on the grating. When Grant's hand closed over it, they could see it was about the size of a baseball.

Something splashed behind them. Kendrick had surfaced. Barrera helped him onto the platform.

Kendrick peeled off his regulator and mask. "Couldn't stop. My tanks are too low."

A few moments later, Grant appeared. She set the white object on the platform before climbing out.

"Anyone have gloves?" Teddy asked.

"Won't have prints or DNA on it. No telling how long it's been down there." Ramirez picked it up. "It's a rock, but it ain't from around here. Only red rocks in these parts."

He ran a thumb over a set of parallel indentations on one side.

"Tool marks," Barrera said. "Chisel, maybe."

Ramirez grunted and handed the stone to Teddy. "What do you make of it, Drummond?"

Teddy examined it beneath the work lamp. Something on the stone's surface caught the light—a silver disc, no wider than a pencil.

"What in the world?" she murmured.

"It sticks up a little, doesn't it?" Grant asked. "Or is that an optical illusion?"

Teddy squinted, running her thumbnail over the disc. "You might be right. Wish I had my reading glasses." She handed it to the diver. "Your eyes are younger than mine."

"Something's embedded," Grant said.

"A bullet?" Kendrick asked.

"Too small."

Ramirez leaned in. "Anyone got tweezers? Or pliers?"

Barrera pulled a Leatherman from his pocket and handed it to Grant. She fumbled briefly, then got a grip. A small stainless-steel cylinder, about two inches long, slid cleanly out of the rock.

Grant held it up with the pliers. Ramirez reached for it.

"Don't touch it, Chief," Teddy said. "It's been protected. Might have prints."

Kendrick pulled an evidence bag from his dive belt and handed it to Grant, who dropped the cylinder inside.

Everyone took a turn examining it.

"I think it opens at one end," Barrera said. "But the lab should handle that."

Kendrick held the bag to the light. "Looks like a toothpick case."

Grant shook her head. "There's a loop, like it's made to wear on a chain."

Teddy inspected the hole where the cylinder had been. "This was drilled with a masonry bit. Somebody went to some trouble. Wonder why?"

Ramirez ran his hand over the back of his head. "If the state lab finds prints, maybe you can ask."

"If they're in IAFIS," Teddy said, but she was wondering, *What if the prints belong to Chase—or Cody*?

Teddy and Ramirez helped carry the gear back to the launch control room, then returned to the surface while the Rangers changed and packed up. As she emerged from the access port, Teddy's phone beeped—two missed calls from Alan.

She shoved it back into her pocket. He'd said he had things covered. Whatever it was, he could handle it.

A piebald longhorn was grazing on a patch of bluestem near the truck's tailgate. It barely glanced at them, but Teddy kept her distance, stopping with the Chief at his Suburban.

"How soon will the state lab get back to us about that rock?" she asked, eyeing the steer.

Ramirez leaned against the fender. "You know how it goes with interagency stuff."

Teddy sighed. "Yeah, but time's against us. We need facts."

"Well, here's one—Morley Taggert called. Confirmed Cody didn't hang himself. Not that we had much doubt."

"How can they tell?"

"Ligature mark goes all the way around. Taggert says it wouldn't in a suicide." He scratched his chin. "I hope Stan's got a damn good story about where he was last night."

"Any update on the sheriff's guy?"

"Bad news there. Linacre called me on the way out—can't send anyone till morning. They got that triple homicide they're dealing with."

"We've got a double," Teddy said.

"We got two homicides. Don't know for sure they're related."

"Come on, Chief. Two guys from the same ranch killed two days apart?"

Ramirez shrugged. "Well, Art's up for reelection next year. More voters in San Angelo than in Stone Creek."

"Whatever. Who he's sending?"

"Whoever's least useful at the reservoir, I reckon."

"Great."

"No point fussin' about what you can't change."

The steer scratched its flank with the tip of a four-foot horn, then lowered its head and began grazing slowly in their direction.

"How'd the interview go with Frankie?" Teddy asked, following Ramirez around the Suburban to keep it between them and the longhorn.

Ramirez clucked his tongue. "Looked me dead in the eye and swore on his mother's grave he was never in the silo. Accused me of planting that fingerprint. Couldn't say where he was Sunday night. Or last night, either. So I arrested him. He's in the holding cell."

"Are you charging him?"

"DA'll want to wait till we know whose blood it is. We'll hold him forty-eight hours—hope something else turns up or he starts talking." Ramirez paused. "Why don't you have a crack at him? You're a friendly face."

There was a thump and a metallic screech. The Suburban rocked. The steer was straining to get at a clump of grass under the front axle.

"That thing better not puncture my tire, dammit," Ramirez muttered. "You could sling a hammock between them horns." He wrenched open the passenger door, grabbed his Stetson, and moved around the vehicle, shouting and waving his hat.

The steer raised its head, chewing, then ambled away, swishing its tail. Teddy's phone buzzed. Alan again.

After a few seconds, it stopped, and a text appeared: *ANSWER THE PHONE, DAMMIT! IS JULIA WITH YOU????*

Chapter 28

Teddy jumped in her truck and turned the key as she hit redial. Alan answered on the first ring. His voice was strained. Julia was missing. The school had called when she hadn't shown up for ninth period. She wasn't on the high school campus, and she wasn't answering her phone.

"I've checked all her usual spots," Alan said. "I'm supposed to get Henry from football in five minutes. Where the hell are you?" He hesitated. "You don't think she's . . . done something? Hurt herself? She's pretty broken up about that boy."

A cold weight settled in Teddy's stomach. She gripped the wheel, forcing steadiness into her voice. "Jules wouldn't do that. She's skipped class before."

That was true—she had. Especially when she was upset. She'd looked strained and unsteady after her interview with the Chief.

I shouldn't have let her go to school, Teddy thought.

Julia didn't need to be wandering alone—not now, with a killer on the loose. If Cody had been silenced, the person who'd done it might be wondering how much his girlfriend knew. And Julia knew more than she was letting on.

"Try not to worry, Alan," Teddy said. "You get Henry. I'll find Jules. I'll call the second I do."

She hung up and tried Julia. Voicemail. She cursed and tossed the phone in the cup holder.

Teddy sped along the rutted track, kicking up a plume of brick-red dust. She didn't slow until she crossed the cattle guard and turned south onto Route 137.

Eight miles from town, her phone buzzed. Bertie Loomis sounded a little embarrassed.

"We got a call from Jasmine Aguilar—your daughter's over at the Skinny's. Jasmine says she's blocking the door and interfering with customers. I'm heading there now."

"On my way. Be there in five." Teddy hung up and floored the accelerator.

As she crested a low rise, her father's house came into view. Shane's Dodge was just turning into the drive. As Teddy flew by, her nephew got out and lifted a large case of Miller Lite from the truck bed. He hadn't seen her.

"Seriously, Shane?" Teddy muttered.

He knew better than to bring beer to an alcoholic. She'd told him before, but clearly they were due for another talk.

A small crowd had formed at the Skinny's by the time Teddy arrived. Half a dozen customers milled outside the store, some plainly annoyed they couldn't go in; others filming with their phones, eager for drama.

Two squad cars idled in the fire lane. Teddy parked near the lot's exit and leapt out, pushing through the crowd. Harley-Wayne Fiske was keeping onlookers back while Julia, spreadeagled against the store wall, was being patted down and cuffed by Bertie Loomis.

A hot pressure bloomed behind Teddy's breastbone. She fought the instinct to charge in and pull Julia away. The mother in her bristled, but her training won out.

Bertie, a plump, pleasant-faced young woman, gave Teddy an embarrassed shrug. "Sorry, Ted. I told her to go quietly, but she refused."

Bertie spun Julia around. Her auburn hair was mussed, her face flushed and furious.

She opened her mouth, but Teddy stopped her with a look. "We'll talk later."

Bertie put Julia in the back of the squad car and turned to the onlookers. "Show's over, folks. The Skinny's is closed for the next half-hour, at least. Harley-Wayne, don't let anyone inside." She looked at Teddy. "I'm gonna talk to Jasmine. Wanna come?"

Teddy glanced at the squad car. Through the tinted window, she saw Julia hunched forward with her head down, as if braced for a collision. She looked very small. Why had she come here? Maybe Jasmine could shed some light.

"Yeah, okay," she said.

Inside, the store was cool and quiet. A rack near the entrance had been overturned. Candy bars and bags of chips littered the floor. Someone had stepped on a bag of Cheetos. Bright orange crumbs were smeared across the tile, and footprints of carrot-colored dust trailed toward the back.

They followed them and found Jasmine Aguilar pacing the rear aisle in front of the glass-fronted coolers. Dark streaks of mascara stained her cheeks. She looked scared.

"The situation's resolved," Bertie said gently. "Can you tell us what happened?"

Jasmine cleared her throat. "I—I don't really know. Julia showed up and just went off on me. I asked her to leave, but she kept screaming that she wouldn't go till I told her the truth about Frankie."

"What'd she mean by that?" Loomis asked.

"I have no idea. There's nothing to tell." Jasmine let out a high, nervous sound—part laugh and part groan. "She kept saying 'you know what I'm talking about—don't effing lie to me.' But I don't know anything about it." She looked at Teddy. "I didn't want to call the cops, Mrs. D—but she started throwing stuff."

"It's okay," Teddy said. "Have Mel send me the bill."

"I need to get this place cleaned up." Jasmine's voice shook.

"We'll be out of your hair soon." Bertie studied her thoughtfully. "You don't know anything about what, exactly?"

Jasmine stared. "What?"

"You said 'there's nothing to tell.' Then you said you don't know anything about it."

Jasmine fidgeted with the hem of her smock. She looked at Teddy, then away—like a skittish horse about to bolt. "I don't know anything about anything."

Bertie's mouth tightened. She pulled out a notepad and pencil. "Give us a minute, will ya, Ted?"

Teddy nodded and stepped outside, thinking that Bertie Loomis was a cut above the average uniform.

The lot had cleared, and Fiske was waving off vehicles trying to turn in. Teddy peered through the rear window of Loomis's squad car. Julia sat with her head on her knees, arms hugging her shins.

Teddy itched to open the door, hug her, ask what she was thinking. But Julia in this mood was a powder keg—anything could set her off. Besides, this was Loomis's scene to manage.

Instead, Teddy leaned against the ice machine and waited. After a few minutes, Bertie emerged, tucking away her notepad. "I think Jasmine knows more than she's saying."

"Me too." Teddy glanced at the squad car. "What now?"

“I called Mel Thornton, told him there’s no real damage. He’s not pressing charges, and neither is Jasmine. You can take Julia home.”

“Thanks, Loomis.”

Bertie opened the car door, helped Julia out, and unlocked the cuffs.

“I know what you’re gonna say, Mom, so don’t bother,” Julia muttered, rubbing her wrists. “Can we just go?”

“I’d watch that tone, if I were you,” Teddy said. “Go wait in the truck.”

Julia’s backpack lay near the ice machine. She slung it over her shoulder and stalked away.

Teddy let out a breath and turned to Bertie, who grinned.

“Kids, huh?”

“You have no idea. Thanks for calling me.”

“You bet.”

The wind had died, and the sun was sinking toward the horizon as Teddy climbed into the truck. “Well?”

Julia played with the strap on her bag and gazed sullenly out the window. “Well, what?”

“I’m not playing, Jules. What’s going on?”

Julia hunched her shoulders and said nothing. A grackle, blue-black and iridescent, landed on the hood. It cocked its head and stared at them with yellow-rimmed eyes, then snatched a dead moth from under the wipers and flew off.

Teddy tried again. “Why’d you leave school early?”

“I was tired. Didn’t feel like staying.”

Teddy hit the steering wheel with the heel of her hand, making Julia jump.

“Don’t bullshit me, Jules—I’m sick of it. You’ve been lying, sneaking around, sexting with a secret boyfriend. Now you’re getting arrested for assault? Don't you think your dad and me have enough to worry about?"

Julia stared at her, cold and unreadable. Then she opened the door, climbed out, and walked away toward the alley.

"For God's sake," Teddy muttered, flinging her door open.

She caught up with Julia by the dumpster. "Where do you think you're going?"

"Leave me alone. I'm walking home."

"No you're not." Teddy grabbed her arm and spun her around. "Jules—stop. I'm going to find out the truth. You might as well give me your version before I hear a worse one from someone else."

Julia pulled away. "Why're you grilling me? You're not even a cop anymore."

"Tell me what happened—I need to know."

Julia kicked an empty Lone Star bottle across the asphalt. Then she pulled out Teddy's old phone—the one she'd been using since hers drowned.

She opened a social media app. "See for yourself."

Teddy took it and scrolled through the comments. "God," she muttered. "What muck."

"That's just Insta. They're all like that," Julia said bitterly. "Everyone's saying Cody shot Chase Loudermilk, then killed himself out of guilt. Somehow word got out I was at the Wallow last night—Kenny Nagle probably blabbed. People think I know more than I'm saying." She turned to Teddy, fists clenched at her sides. "Is it true, Mom? Was Chase really murdered?"

Teddy sighed. Of course word had leaked—she'd known it would, once Ramirez told Stan Loudermilk.

"The ME hasn't issued a death certificate yet," she said carefully. "But unofficially? Yeah. It looks that way."

"How did he—"

Teddy held up her hand. "That's all I can say for now, Jules."

Julia took back the phone and stared at her. "Well, whatever." She looked away. "With everyone shit-talking like that, I couldn't sit in school—I had to do something."

"Why bother Jasmine?"

"Shane texted me they arrested Frankie this morning. Frankie's involved, Mom—he knows what happened to Chase. I'm sure of it. And he tells Jasmine everything. I asked her politely, but she got all weird, told me to leave or she'd call 911. I kind of lost it." Julia's voice was flat and steady, but her eyes were glassy with tears.

"Jules, you're lucky nobody's pressing charges," Teddy said.

"She's hiding something," Julia said stubbornly. "Cody didn't kill Chase. And Cody didn't kill himself. Somebody murdered him."

"If that's true, it's all the more reason not to go running off alone. It could be dangerous, Jules. Did you ever think of that?"

Julia was watching a line of red ants trailing toward a greasy pizza box next to the dumpster. She mumbled something Teddy didn't catch.

"What'd you say?"

Julia looked up. "I said *somebody's* got to figure out what happened to Cody."

"What's that supposed to mean?"

"I'm not stupid, Mom. Chief Ramirez was tanked last night. I could still smell it on him this morning. And now Raina Bragg's got a broken leg, so she's out. Who else is there?"

Teddy lifted and dropped her hands. "First of all, Raina's not out—she's working from home. And second, what the hell do you think I've been doing for the last two days?"

"You're focused on Chase, not Cody. I could tell by the questions you asked me this morning." Her voice cracked. "I know how it works. Chase is a rancher's son. Cody's a nobody. I'm the only one who really cared about—"

"That's not true, and you know it." Teddy's voice was quiet now. "Come on, let's go home."

She slipped her arm through Julia's, and they walked back to the truck.

Julia opened the glovebox and pulled out a crumpled Sonic napkin. "Cody mattered, Mom. He was a human being." She wiped her eyes.

"Jules, I know that." Teddy slipped the key into the ignition, but didn't turn it. She hesitated. "Listen—if I tell you something that's absolutely inside knowledge, will you promise to keep it to yourself? Seriously—don't even tell Shane or your dad."

Julia lowered the napkin and stared. She nodded.

Teddy sighed. "You're right—Cody was murdered. The ME confirmed it today. I'm not sure how long I'll be on the case, though. The sheriff's office is taking over soon. So if you know anything, now's the time to tell me."

Julia turned the napkin in her fingers. Teddy watched her for a moment. *Best to let her sit with it.* She started the engine.

A slow-moving hay truck trundled by, and Teddy let it pass before turning onto the highway, heading south.

They drove home in silence. As they merged west onto Little Branch Road, the sinking sun blazed into their eyes, lighting up every smudge and mote of dust on the windshield.

Teddy squinted and lowered the visor. Five minutes later, she turned into the drive, passed the barn, and stopped in front of the garage. She killed the engine.

The sudden silence rang in her ears.

Julia gazed across the north pasture. Near the tree line, the Bobcat sat beside a pile of red earth.

"Is that for Fancy?" Julia whispered.

Teddy nodded. "Everything's ready." She laid a hand on her shoulder. "Jules . . . why'd you say Frankie's involved in what happened to Chase?"

Julia flinched but didn't answer.

"Is it because he was arrested? Or do you know something I don't?"

Julia kept her eyes on the gravesite. Seconds passed. A dog barked in the distance.

"Cody told me," she whispered.

The words were so quiet Teddy barely heard them. "Told you what?"

Julia wiped her eyes with her knuckles. "He—he said he was in the barn one day—"

"At the Rocking L?"

Julia nodded. "Cleaning the stalls. He heard whispering. He went around the corner and saw Chase pacing under the overhang where the four-wheelers are parked. He was on the phone, angry but trying to keep his voice low. Cody thought it was weird, so he listened." She fidgeted with the buckle of the seatbelt. "He recorded it."

"Why?"

"I don't know. Maybe he wanted proof Chase was up to something. He sent it to me on Facebook Messenger."

"Do you still have it?"

"He made me promise not to share it."

"Jules, we have Cody's phone—we're recovering the metadata. We'll find it eventually. But you could save us some time."

Julia scrolled through her phone, then handed it over. "Here." She hit play and turned up the volume.

Teddy leaned in. Beneath a wash of white noise, she heard a faint voice she thought was Chase's.

"Leave me alone, Frankie—you didn't see nothing. You can tell the cops whatever you want. I told you I'm out."

The recording stopped. Teddy replayed it. Then again. Four times in all.

"*You didn't see nothing?* What does that mean?"

"Cody didn't know."

"When was this?"

"Few weeks ago."

"What did he think was going on? Did he have a theory?"

Julia exhaled. "He thought it might be about drugs. Chase and Frankie both got into weed in high school—doing it and selling it. Shane, too. Especially that year after Grayson died. They were all at the quarry when it happened. It messed them up. That's why Chase's dad shipped him off to military school."

Teddy ran her thumb along the curve of the steering wheel. "Did Cody tell Stan and Inez about this recording? You said he was jealous of Chase. Be weird if he passed up a chance to get him into trouble."

Julia flushed. "Cody wasn't like that, Mom."

"Why didn't you tell me about this in the barn this morning?"

"I don't know—I needed to think. I felt bad breaking my promise, now that Cody's . . ." She swallowed. "Besides, I've kinda gotten out of the habit of telling you things. You're so pissed off all the time."

Teddy let the comment pass. "Is that everything?"

"I think so," Julia said. "I know Frankie's involved, Mom. I'm sure of it. I was going crazy at school. I had to do something."

Teddy studied her daughter's face. "Okay, Jules. But you have to promise me you'll let the authorities handle this."

"I want to help—I want to do it for Cody."

"I get it. But you'll only make things harder and put yourself at risk. We'll get to the truth. I promise. Now go on inside and help Dad with dinner."

"You're not coming?"

At the thought of food, Teddy's stomach growled. Had she eaten lunch? She couldn't remember. "I'll grab something later. Send me that audio file—I'm going to look into it. I'll be home in an hour or so. We'll have Fancy's funeral then."

"It's almost dark."

"We've got lanterns. It needs to happen tonight."

Julia blinked, then reached for the door handle. "Can you ask Berna to come? She gave me Fancy, remember?"

Teddy smiled. "I remember. Sure, I'll ask her."

Chapter 29

The sky had darkened to a deep indigo, and bats were swooping above the hackberry trees behind the police station as Teddy parked in the rear lot and hurried inside. Behind the front desk, Caleb Brendall was eating a barbecue sandwich out of a greasy wrapper.

"Is the Chief in?" Teddy asked.

"Nah, he took those divers over to the Crispy Cat." Brendall wiped his mouth with a paper napkin. "Anything I can help with?"

Teddy shook her head. "I need to talk to Frankie Aguilar. I won't be long." She started around the desk.

"Chief told me not to let anyone back there."

"Come on, Brendall, it was his idea. He told me to have a crack at him."

Brendall rubbed his forehead, leaving a streak of red sauce above one eyebrow. "I dunno, Ted." He reached for the desk phone. "Lemme call."

"You're going to interrupt him while he's eating catfish and hushpuppies with the Rangers to ask a question you already know the answer to?" Teddy shrugged. "Be my guest."

Brendall put down the receiver. "Okay. But he stays in his cell. After yesterday, I ain't putting nobody in the interview room without the Chief's say-so."

"Deal." Teddy slapped the counter. "Thanks, Caleb."

"And if I get chewed out," Brendall called after her, "you're going straight under the bus."

Teddy bought a Dr Pepper and a Snickers from the squad room vending machines, then headed down the hall, turned at the booking desk, and pushed through a heavy door marked "Detention—Security Cameras in Use."

At the back of the former hardware store's stockroom were two prefabricated holding cells—freestanding eight-foot-square steel boxes fronted with welded wire mesh. Inside the first, Frankie Aguilar sat on the edge of the bed, bouncing his knees. When he saw Teddy, he jumped up and laced his fingers through the mesh.

Frankie was twenty-five—just two years younger than Shane. He had a man's frame, stocky and muscular from landscaping work; but his face was still boyish, scored with angry acne.

"Mrs. D—thank God. I thought they forgot about me."

"Hey, Frankie. You okay?"

"Do I look okay? That drunk-ass police chief has me arrested, and nobody'll tell me nothin'."

"Have they fed you? I brought you a snack." Teddy pushed the soda and candy bar through the hatch. "Chief Ramirez said he talked to you. He didn't explain why you're here?"

"He thinks I killed Chase Loudermilk, but he wouldn't say why. Kept asking when was the last time I was inside Deadhorse silo and where was I Sunday night—stinking of vodka the whole time. Then he arrests me 'cause they found a joint in my pocket. One effin' joint." He popped the Dr Pepper tab and took a long drink.

"And you said—?"

Frankie wiped his mouth with the back of his hand. "Told him the truth—I never been in that silo. I barely knew Chase—not since we was kids. Why would I kill him?"

Teddy tried another tack. "All they care about is who killed Chase. If you were doing drugs in that silo—even selling—they'll overlook it, under the circumstances. But you've got to tell the truth."

"I'm telling you—I never been in that silo."

"Frankie, come on. They've got your fingerprint in there—in blood. They're testing it now. If it's Chase's—"

"If that's there, someone planted it," Frankie said stubbornly. "Look, Mrs. D, I wouldn't lie to you—you saved my life. I'll take a lie detector. Whatever you want."

Teddy studied his face. She had interviewed hundreds of people—first as a cop, then as a detective. Frankie seemed sincere. She wanted to believe him. And yet . . . *People lie, forensics don't.* That was a foundational mantra of police work.

"Okay, Frankie," she said finally.

"You believe me?"

"I want to. But some things don't add up."

"Like what?"

Teddy glanced uneasily at the CCTV camera above her head.

"A couple weeks before Chase died, he was overheard talking to you on the phone. It sounded suspicious. The call got recorded."

She pulled out her phone and played the audio file she'd gotten from Julia.

Frankie listened, and his face changed. "How'd you know he's talking to me?"

"He says your name. Clear as day."

"It wasn't me."

"You're the only Frankie I know around here. 'Leave me alone, Frankie—you didn't see nothing. You can tell the cops whatever you want. I told you I'm out.' What's he talking about?"

"How should I know? Who gave you this?"

Teddy ignored the question. "You said you barely knew Chase. But that call sounds personal. Were you threatening blackmail?"

Frankie stared, his expression wary and confused. He said nothing.

"Where were you Sunday night? Did you go into the silo with Chase?"

"No! I was home, with Jasmine and Dad. Ask 'em—they'll tell ya."

"You said you'd never lie to me."

Frankie's eyelid twitched. "I want a lawyer."

"Come on, Frankie—where were you Sunday night?"

He snatched up the candy bar and retreated to the bed. "I want a lawyer."

As she turned to leave, Teddy glanced again at the camera's dark eye. Ramirez wouldn't be happy when he saw the footage. She'd played a hunch, and it had backfired. But not entirely. Frankie was lying—but not about everything. She didn't think he'd killed Chase. And his denial about the silo felt genuine. But that overheard phone call—that had struck a nerve.

Maybe after a night in lockup, he'd be ready to talk.

Outside the station, the wind had died away. The air smelled of woodsmoke. A scrawny gray cat was perched on the hood of Teddy's truck. She expected it to flee, but as she approached, it mewed and leapt off the truck to rub against her ankles.

She bent to pet it. "Hungry, huh? Sorry, little guy. I've got nothing. Go find a mouse."

At the jingle of her keys, it darted into the shadows. Teddy unlocked the truck and checked her phone. Ten past seven. A missed call from Raina. She leaned against the truck door and hit redial.

Raina sounded tired and edgy. "I hate being stuck here. What's happening? How'd it go with the divers?"

Teddy told her about the strange white rock they'd found in the silo, and then hesitated.

"You're not telling me something," Raina said. "I'm still lead detective, in case you've forgotten."

"Okay, okay." Teddy told her about the audio file from Julia and her talk with Frankie. "Wally's going to be pissed. Maybe I shouldn't have confronted Frankie like that."

She braced for a rebuke, but Raina said, "You took a shot. You had a better chance of getting the truth out of him than anyone." A pause. "What are you doing now?"

"Heading to the vet clinic. Julia wants me to invite Berna to Fancy's funeral."

"Got time for a pit stop on the way?"

"What do you mean?"

"Couple hours ago, I started thinking—whoever left that note in your classroom was at the bowling alley Sunday night. If it wasn't a Bible study kid, maybe it was a worker. I called over there and got a list of employees."

"And—?"

"David Griffith. He's in your class. He was working concessions that night."

Teddy was surprised. David Griffith. A nice kid, but clumsy, unsure of himself—not particularly quick-witted. Destined to be the kind of cop who'd spend his career directing traffic and filing paperwork no one read. She wouldn't have guessed he'd have the nerve to slip her that note.

"Is he working tonight?" Teddy asked.

"He's not. Do you know where he lives?"

"No, but I can find out. I'll—" Teddy stopped and turned, lowering the phone. She stared into the darkness beneath the hackberry trees. Something rustled in the bushes that edged the alley. Maybe the gray cat.

No sound now, except Raina's voice, tinny and faint: "What is it? What's going on?"

Teddy raised the phone. "I heard something," she said quietly. "There was a cat earlier, so it might've been—"

Crack. A twig snapped in the brush.

"Raina, I'll call you later," Teddy whispered, jerking open the truck door.

Behind the wheel, she started the engine and turned so the headlights lit the alley. Nothing but tree trunks and scrubby brush.

As she reached into the console for her pistol, something moved. A pair of green eyes glittered through a gap in the undergrowth—a small, masked face. A raccoon, probably scrounging in the dumpsters.

Teddy's throat burned. She'd been holding her breath. She exhaled and put the truck in gear.

At the Colonel Priddy Avenue light, she pulled up the college database on her phone. Two addresses for David Griffith: one in Sterling City—likely his parents' place—and one local. She needed to get home soon, but this wouldn't take long.

When the light changed, she headed north.

David's address turned out to be a shabby pink-stucco duplex three blocks from campus. The place was dark. Teddy picked her way through the weedy yard and knocked. A small dog yapped inside, but no one answered.

Disappointed, she returned to her truck and checked the time. A text from Alan: *Ready 4 funeral. Where R U?*

Gimme 1 hr, she wrote back.

The bowling alley sat a block from campus, between a coffee shop and a laundromat. Teddy pushed through the doors and wrinkled her nose at the mingled scents of stale popcorn, floor wax, and disinfectant.

Weeknights were slow. An elderly couple was bowling with their grandkids, but all the other lanes sat empty, and a worker in gray coveralls was buffing them with a machine.

At the shoe rental kiosk, a teenage boy directed her to a small office behind the arcade, where she found the assistant manager—a thin, fair-haired college girl with a name tag identifying her as "Patrice."

Patrice hesitated when Teddy asked for the security footage. She told her to come back when the manager was on site. But when Teddy offered to have the police chief call the manager directly, the girl relented.

"I want to see the feed from Sunday night," Teddy said.

After a five-minute search, they found what she was looking for—grainy black-and-white footage from three nights earlier. The place had been packed with a weekend crowd. Eventually, Teddy spotted Chase Loudermilk bowling with the Bible study group. He looked relaxed, happy. More than once, he glanced up at the wall.

"What's he looking at?" she asked.

"There's a clock on that side of the room," Patrice said.

Chase had been watching the time. That tracked. Stan Loudermilk had said Chase promised to be home by one a.m. The time stamp read 10:13 p.m. Chase looked sober. He was drinking from a paper cup, not a beer bottle.

Teddy squinted. "Fast-forward, will you?"

Patrice nodded and punched some keys. The image blurred and sped up.

"Stop," Teddy said.

Chase had stood and was walking toward the concession stand. The camera was mounted behind the register. A plump, light-haired worker stepped up to take his order. The worker's back was to the camera, but Teddy could tell it was David Griffith.

Chase said something to him and they chatted for a minute. Then suddenly, Chase held up a finger and stepped away from the counter, fishing in his pocket. He pulled out his phone, listened, and glanced at the wall clock. The footage was fuzzy, his expression unclear, but from his posture and the tilt of his head, Teddy had the impression he was surprised—not upset.

He spoke briefly, put away his phone, and waved to David to indicate he'd changed his mind about ordering.

He walked quickly back to his friends, grabbed his backpack, said something to the group, and left camera range through a side door.

"What's through there?" Teddy demanded.

"Parking lot," Patrice said.

"Any cameras?"

"I wish. It's dark out there—creeps me out when I have to close."

After learning David Griffith wouldn't be working again until Friday night, Teddy thanked Patrice and left the office. She crossed the sticky carpet to the side door.

The lot outside was poorly maintained, and a row of scraggy saplings had sprung up along one side of the pitted asphalt.

Teddy spotted a camera on the wall of the laundromat next door and went inside. The manager was on site, overseeing repairs to a dryer. Teddy knew him—he was the father of one of Henry's classmates. He let her view the footage without hesitation.

But it was disappointing. It showed Chase exiting the bowling alley at 10:39 p.m., going directly to his truck, and driving off. The saplings obscured the view of the road, but Teddy thought he turned west—toward home.

She climbed into her truck, frustrated and confused. Who had called Chase that night? Was it his killer?

The footage raised new questions but offered few answers.

Had David Griffith overheard the call? Teddy considered messaging him, then thought better of it. He'd gone out of his way to leave an anonymous note. He clearly didn't want to get involved. If she contacted him, he might clam up—or disappear. Better to catch him off guard.

◆ ◆ ◆

Leaving the bowling alley, Teddy braked at the McCutchen Road stop sign and waited while two college-aged women in shorts and tank tops jogged across the intersection, ponytails swinging in unison. She glanced up the cross street, then at the dashboard clock. She flipped on her signal and turned north.

The Concho Valley Animal Clinic—a boxy, blond-brick building that had once housed a saddle-maker's shop—sat a half mile northeast of town on a two-lane farm-to-market road flanked by pasture and scrub. At this hour, it was usually dark. But tonight the lights were on, though the customer lot was empty.

Teddy parked beside Berna's van and got out. Through the front window, she saw vet tech Amber Brendall—Caleb Brendall's wife—sweeping the lobby floor.

Teddy knocked on the glass. "Hey, Amber, Berna still around?" she asked as the tech unlocked the door.

Amber, eight months pregnant, leaned on the broom handle and nodded, rubbing her lower back. "She's finishing some paperwork. Go on through."

Teddy passed the rack of prescription pet food and followed a narrow hallway to Berna's office. Berna was at her desk, peering through her readers at a computer screen.

Teddy rapped on the doorframe. "Nearly done?"

"Hey, Ted, give me a couple minutes," Berna said without looking up.

Teddy watched her friend peck at the keyboard with two fingers, then let her eyes wander. The office was cramped and messy, though Teddy suspected Berna knew exactly where everything was. File folders and printouts covered every surface, fluttering in the chilly breeze that ruffled the curtains. Teddy shivered. Berna had always been an outdoorsy person and had a habit of keeping her windows open at all times of the year. Bits of veterinary bric-a-brac—treat dispensers, bottles of disinfectant, plastic anatomical models—had been pressed into service as paperweights.

Beside the window stood an avocado-green refrigerator with a sign on the door: "MEDICAL SPECIMENS ONLY."

Closer to Teddy stood a metal file cabinet, its sides thick with takeout menus, greeting cards, and family photos. Some had been there a long time—Teddy spotted a menu from a pizza place that had gone out of business three years ago.

Next to it was a Thanksgiving photograph taken inside Berna's house—Grayson, twelve or thirteen, clowning for the camera at the dining room table. His tongue was hanging out and he clutched his knife and fork, watching Mark McKissick carve the turkey. Both wore paper Pilgrim hats. Mark was laughing at the photographer—presumably Berna.

The room had gone quiet. Teddy turned. Berna had swiveled away from the computer and was sitting with her long legs crossed, hands in the pockets of her lab coat. The ridges of her knuckles showed through the thin fabric. Her silvery dreadlocks were slightly frazzled. She looked tired.

"When I dream about Grayson, he always looks sad," she said quietly. "I keep that to remind myself we did have happy times—especially after John died and Mark came along. Grayson was struggling in middle school. Not easy, being biracial around here. Mark was so kind. He knows what it feels like to be an outsider. Grayson adored him."

"Seems like it was mutual," Teddy said, tapping the photo.

Berna nodded. "Mark was as broken up as I was after Grayson's accident. They were almost like brothers—except for skin color." She smiled.

"Is that why you still hang out with Mark?"

"It's a comfort. Being around him gives me a glimpse of what Grayson might've been like, if he'd grown up."

"Sounds like torture. If I lost one of my kids, I couldn't stand looking at anything that reminded me of them—pictures included. I'd want to burn it all."

A coyote yipped and wailed in the distance. Something rustled outside.

"Damned armadillos—place is overrun." Berna got up and closed the window, then returned to her seat. "You think you'd burn your photos, but you'd regret it. It's easy to rewrite history, if you're not careful."

"What do you mean?"

"Oh, you know. The mind plays tricks after someone dies. You start thinking in generalities. Pretty soon, you don't know if the person you remember is anything like how they really were. Pictures help you hold onto the truth, at least a little."

"Is that why you've still got all your pictures of John, too?"

Berna nodded. "He was a bad husband and father, but he was a human being." The corner of her mouth twitched. "God remembers every sparrow that falls. Who am I to forget?" She paused. "It's so easy to edit people into caricatures."

She pushed a wheeled stool toward Teddy, who dropped onto it with a sigh.

"That's true."

Chase had only been dead three days. But when she thought of him now, she pictured a skinny kid at a desk by the window, hunched over a sketchpad, dark-blond hair falling across his face. Had he ever actually sat like that? Maybe once or twice. Yet the image had already become a kind of mental shorthand—on its way to displacing the real person.

How much worse would it be to lose a family member that way—to feel them slipping into static impressions, fossilized by memory?

Teddy felt suddenly depressed. She groped for something to say, but Berna saved her the trouble.

"You look like hell, Ted. You okay?"

"I'm remembering why I retired from police work. That Puckett kid—"

"The boy who died at the Wallow?"

"Yeah."

Berna studied her. "He didn't drown, did he?"

Teddy rolled her shoulders like she was trying to shuck off an invisible weight. "No."

"I'm glad you're working the case. Must be hard, though. After everything."

"It's not just that. Turns out Cody Puckett was Julia's secret boyfriend."

"Oh, Lord. Poor kid. How is she?"

"Falling apart. Losing Fancy was hard enough."

"Was she upset with us for putting her down?"

"She understood. But yeah—it was rough." Teddy rubbed her temples. "That's actually why I'm here. We're burying Fancy tonight. Julia's hoping you'll come."

"What time?"

Teddy glanced at the wall clock. "Forty minutes?"

"Think she'd mind me showing up like this?" Berna waved a hand over her dark slacks, thick with short, ginger-colored hairs. "Had a battle of wills this afternoon."

Teddy smiled tiredly. "Losing your touch?"

Berna brushed at her leg with the back of her hand. "You try giving an enema to a fractious barn cat."

Before Teddy could answer, she heard a sound behind her.

Berna, facing the door, looked up. "Speaking of which—look what the cat dragged in."

Chapter 30

Teddy swiveled on her stool. Rick Castillo stood in the doorway, looking exhausted and bedraggled. His coarse dark hair and bony face were caked with dirt and the front of his coveralls slick with drying blood. He stank of manure.

When he saw Teddy, he stepped back, pulled out a blue bandana, and ran it roughly over his face.

"What happened to you?" Berna asked.

"Obstetrical mishap."

"Obstetrical? Thought you were looking at Steffke's lame steer."

Rick lowered the bandana. His face was still muddy except for pale circles around his eyes.

"I was. Then Steffke wanted me to check on a heifer that'd been calving since this morning. When she saw me coming, she bolted. We cornered her in a mud wallow at the bottom of the pasture and got her tied to Sid's UTV. When I pulled the calf, I slipped. Damn thing landed on top of me." He gestured at his coveralls.

Berna smiled. "Well, pull up a chair, take a load off."

Rick glanced at Teddy.

"Don't mind me. I'm about to leave," she said.

Rick hesitated, rubbing his thumb against his temple. "Think I'll grab a shower." He stuffed the bandana in his pocket and headed down the hall.

Teddy watched him go, feeling oddly let down, though she couldn't say why. She looked at Berna. "He seem jumpy to you?"

Berna took off her glasses and chewed thoughtfully on one of the temple tips. "For a detective, you sure can be clueless."

"What's that supposed to mean?"

Berna polished her lenses on the hem of her lab coat. "Nothing."

Teddy rose and shoved the stool under the counter. "I better go."

"Door's locked—I'll walk you out." Berna stood, her knees popping. "Ugh. All my joints are shot. Sucks getting old, Ted."

"Beats the alternative."

"Most days."

They made their way to the darkened lobby. Amber Brendall was gone. Berna unlocked the front door, and Teddy followed her down the steps and across the empty lot.

Teddy took out her keys and opened the truck door. "See you soon?"

"I'll be there. Forty minutes, right?"

Teddy glanced at the clock. "Well, thirty now."

"Wouldn't miss it," Berna said.

Teddy drove southwest toward Colonel Priddy Avenue, but at Old Homestead Road she turned on impulse, following it to Route 137. The Skinny's sat across the intersection. Other than a lone car in the lot and a farmer topping off the diesel transfer tank in his pickup, the place was quiet.

She sat in the truck for a moment, gripping the wheel as she watched the entrance, wrestling with herself. Then she got out and went inside.

The store looked undisturbed. The Cheetos had been swept up and the tile floor mopped. Jasmine Aguilar stood behind the counter, ringing up the purchases of a woman Teddy recognized as the high school guidance counselor. Not eager to discuss Julia, Teddy grabbed a basket and ducked down an aisle.

She picked up a few cans of mandarin oranges, then—as an afterthought—a bottle of Pedialyte and a package of ibuprofen.

She waited until the guidance counselor left, then approached the register.

"How are you doing, Jasmine?"

Jasmine shrugged. "Okay." She rang up the items in silence.

"Look, Jasmine—"

"I can't tell you anything about Frankie, Mrs. D."

"I'm not here about that. I wanted to check on you. I'm sorry about today. Julia was out of line." Teddy glanced around. The store was empty. "But since you bring it up—I tried to talk to Frankie tonight. He asked for a lawyer. That's not a smart move."

Jasmine picked up the Pedialyte and held it to her chest. "Mrs. D, I can't—"

"Talk to him, Jazz. Tell him he's not doing himself any favors."

Jasmine stiffened. "You didn't come to check on me." She rang up the Pedialyte, her lacquered nails clicking sharply on the register.

"I don't want to upset you," Teddy said. "Just think about it, all right?"

Jasmine's face was tight; she seemed to be fighting tears. She bagged the purchases without a word.

Teddy paid and left, feeling a little guilty. Probably a stupid move. But it had been worth a shot.

◆ ◆ ◆

Back in her truck, she checked the time. She was only a couple of miles from her father's place. She hesitated, then turned north.

Milton's porch lights were off, and the house was dark except for a faint glimmer through the kitchen blinds. Shane's truck was gone. Teddy grabbed her flashlight from the glovebox, then remembered the batteries were nearly dead. She turned on her phone's flashlight app and carried the groceries inside.

"Dad?"

She picked her way through the piles of junk to the kitchen. No one there. Eight empty Miller Lite cans sat on the table. The room stank of urine, and a puddle glistened under Milton's usual chair.

"Dammit, Shane," Teddy muttered, setting down the groceries.

She found a rag and mopped up the mess, then went down the hall to her father's squalid little bedroom.

The ceiling light was on, as well as the bedside lamp. More cans littered the bed. On the floor beside it lay a pair of damp trousers and yellowed briefs. Milton was sprawled on his back on the bare mattress, naked from the waist down and snoring softly.

"For God's sake." Teddy backed into the hall.

She crossed to the bathroom and groped for the beaded pull-chain. The overhead light clicked on. Grabbing a towel off the floor, she returned and covered her father with it.

She stood staring at him, torn between disgust and something else—grief, mingled with a terrible pity. And beneath both, the bright, hard edge of an anger rooted in helplessness. Not that it mattered what she felt. As far as Milton was concerned, it never had.

Her eyes traveled to the wet clothes by the bed. If Shane was dumb enough to bring over a case of beer, he could clean them up, or they could molder where they were. Teddy was done. That was what she told herself, anyway.

She went back to the bathroom. There was no soap or clean towel, but she rinsed her hands and wiped them on her jeans, then grabbed the pull-chain to turn off the light. The little bell on the end had broken off. In its place, someone had wired on a small pendant—a two-inch strip of burnished brass, the width of a tongue depressor, with a hole at each end. Something was etched on one side.

Teddy squinted at it, running her thumb over the symbol. She recognized the design. But what was this thing, exactly? It looked familiar, but for a moment she couldn't place it. Then the memory slid into place. What was it doing here?

She thought of a few possible answers, none of them good. Blood whooshed in her ears. It wasn't a smoking gun, exactly—but it was evidence. A line of inquiry she didn't want to follow.

You have a tendency to run, the San Angelo shrink had often said—as if it were settled fact that this was a flaw, that truth was always desirable. In Teddy's experience, some stones were better left unturned—unless you were prepared to deal with whatever slithered out.

She wanted to throw the brass strip away—or leave it where it was. Raina would never know. No one would. It could hang on this chain till Doomsday, or till Milton died and the Health Department bulldozed the house.

She stood there a while, thinking. Then she undid the twist of wire and shoved the brass strip into her pocket. She turned off the bathroom light and left the house.

Her dashboard clock read 8:38 p.m. when she reached home. Alan's pickup sat in front of the garage beside Lyric's yellow Beetle. Shane's truck was parked in the grass by the porch. But there was no sign of Berna's van.

Teddy killed the engine and made her way through the laundry room, pausing to greet Jabba the Mutt, whose tail thumped loudly against the washer. In the kitchen, Lyric was spooning leftover lasagna into a plastic container. Alan sat at the table, working on a spreadsheet.

He looked up as she came through the door. "About time."

"I said give me an hour. It's been an hour and eight minutes." Teddy's stomach growled, and she grabbed a piece of garlic bread from a basket on the counter. "Where are the kids?"

Alan nodded toward the dining room. "Finishing homework."

Teddy found Julia at the table, staring blankly at a row of math equations on her laptop. She touched her daughter's shoulder.

Julia jumped and looked up. Her eyes were red, her nose pink and raw.

"You're late." She didn't sound surprised.

Teddy thought of Milton, sprawled naked on the bed. Letting down the next generation seemed to be an inherited trait.

She ran a hand over Julia's hair, smoothing it off her shoulder.

"I know, sweets. I'm sorry." She exhaled. "Where's Shane?"

"At the grave. Keeping off the coyotes. They've been howling since sunset." Julia hesitated. "Is Berna coming?"

"Yeah." Teddy squinted at the laptop clock, then checked her phone. No missed texts. "She'll be here."

"Call her," Alan said from the doorway. "Henry'll be up late enough as it is."

Teddy popped the last bite of bread in her mouth and went into the family room. Henry lay on the couch, playing a video game with his hoodie pulled up.

Teddy sat on the arm of the sofa and rested her hand on his hood as she dialed Berna. "Aren't you hot with this on, bud?"

"No."

She held the phone to her cheek. "How was school today?"

He shrugged. "I dunno."

"How was football practice?"

The ringtone buzzed in her ear.

Henry shrugged again.

"Finished your homework?"

"Yup."

The call went to voicemail. Teddy hung up, then texted: *Gotta start. Meet us in N. pasture.*

She stuffed her phone in her pocket. Julia had followed her into the family room.

"Anything?"

Teddy shook her head. "Let's give her five minutes." She patted Henry's arm. "Turn off the game and get your boots on, bud."

She went to her room and changed from teaching clothes into jeans and a sweatshirt. When she returned, the others were in the garage, pulling on jackets and boots. Berna wasn't there. Teddy checked her phone.

Julia handed her a flashlight. "Still nothing?"

"No."

"I really wanted her here."

"Maybe she got an emergency call," Lyric said.

A series of sharp yips and a long, plaintive howl floated across the fields—followed by the crack of a rifle.

Alan zipped up his jacket. "We better go."

They took four-wheelers from the shed and rode across the muddy pasture to the gravesite. Shane was standing on the Bobcat, his .22 in one hand and a Maglite in the other. Coyotes wailed from somewhere in the trees.

"Those sound close," Teddy said.

"There's a whole pack." Shane jumped down and laid the rifle on the tractor's seat. "Getting bold. Came right up on me a while ago. Let's make it quick."

Teddy looked around. Julia stood shivering at the edge of the grave. Her flashlight beam trembled over Fancy's still form. Shane had covered the body with an old U-Haul blanket. Teddy was grateful—and a little surprised. He wasn't usually that thoughtful.

She put an arm around Julia. "Want to say a few words?"

Julia's teeth were chattering. "Will you?"

Teddy pulled her closer. The flashlight shook in Julia's hand.

Once everyone had gathered, Teddy stumbled through a halting eulogy, then nodded to Shane. He handed her the rifle and climbed onto the Bobcat.

Henry was fighting tears. "I don't want to watch this part."

"Me either," Julia said.

Teddy turned to Alan. "Take them back. I'll stay and keep the coyotes off."

After they left, Teddy watched her nephew shovel red earth into the grave, tamp it down, and drag a couple fallen logs over the top. Once or twice, she thought she saw glowing green eyes in the tree line—but when she aimed the light, they vanished.

Shane killed the engine and climbed down. "I ain't driving the Bobcat back in the dark. Can I ride with you?"

"Sure," Teddy said. "But we need to talk."

"Am I in trouble?"

"I don't know."

A volley of howls cut through the stillness. Teddy felt the hairs on her neck rise.

Shane took off his hat and scratched his head. "Let's get away from here, at least."

Teddy switched off her flashlight. The rifle stock felt cold in her hands. The moon was rising, huge and orange, behind the eastern bluffs. The air was clear and sharp. There would be frost by morning.

She climbed onto the four-wheeler and laid the rifle across her knees.

"Want me to hold that?" Shane asked.

"I got it." Teddy started the engine. "Climb on."

Chapter 31

Halfway across the pasture, Teddy braked and killed the engine. Silence settled around them. Shane climbed down, stretching his arms and stomping his feet to warm them.

"Been freezing my ass off out here for hours, Aunt Teddy. Can't we talk in the house?"

She dismounted and leaned the rifle against the four-wheeler. "It's better here."

"For curing hams, maybe," Shane muttered. His face was hidden in shadow.

Teddy stepped left, and he turned to face her, moonlight catching his features.

"Listen, Shane. I need the truth."

"About what?"

"Frankie's in serious trouble. Did you know that?"

Shane cupped his hands and blew on them. "He only had one joint. They can't call that intent."

"I'm not talking about weed. I mean murder. He was overheard threatening Chase on the phone a couple weeks before he died."

Shane's hands dropped. "Says who?"

"There's a recording. But that's not the worst of it. Police can place him in the silo—with blood on him."

Shane stood still. "What?"

"Right now, Frankie's denying everything. But that won't hold."

"There's gotta be some mistake. Frankie's no killer."

"I don't think so, either," she said.

Teddy pictured Frankie at the station, his voice urgent and earnest through the jail bars: *I wouldn't lie to you—you saved my life. I'll take a lie detector. Whatever you want.* In her experience, the guilty didn't beg to be polygraphed.

"Problem is, there's a new investigator coming tomorrow—and I doubt he'll see it that way. He'll be thrilled to have a strong suspect." Teddy stepped closer. "Shane, there's a killer out there. If you can alibi Frankie for the night Chase died, now's the time."

"What makes you think I can alibi him?"

"Y'all have been best friends since high school."

"Did you ask Jasmine?"

"I'm asking you."

Shane kicked at a tuft of grass. "I don't know nothin'."

Teddy stepped closer. "Don't lie to me. I know what you and Frankie were doing Sunday night."

Shane's head jerked up. "Sunday? I was with Grandpa."

"You were stealing horses."

"What the fuck?"

"When that new vet was here Monday, he mentioned Sid Steffke had one taken out of his pasture Sunday night. That's not a one-man job."

"And you reckon me and Frankie did it? Come on."

"It's no good, Shane." Teddy pulled the brass strip from her pocket and held it up.

"What the hell's that?"

"I found it in Grandpa's bathroom." She gave it to her nephew, who angled it into the moonlight.

"Never seen this before." He stared across the pasture, weighing the brass strip in his palm and running his forefinger along its edge, like a stone he meant to skip across a pond.

He looked so much like her brother Danny in that moment that Teddy's stomach clenched. Same stubborn jaw. Same denials when cornered.

She snatched the metal piece out of his hand. "I know Grandpa got this from you—he hasn't left that dump of his in years. You and me are the only people who visit. This is stamped with the Rocking L logo. I saw some just like it in the Loudermilk barn yesterday. It's on all their halters and bridles. Stan mentioned they had a horse stolen off the ranch a few months back."

Shane pulled down his hat brim, and his face slipped back into shadow. "I helped Stan ride fences last spring. Told you I been doing odd jobs to make a little extra. He gave me a box of junk he didn't want no more. Mighta been a busted halter in there."

Teddy shook her head. "This is hand-crafted. Stan probably made it himself. Even if he was throwing out a broken halter, he would've kept the brass—it's expensive."

Shane said nothing. Teddy waited. She couldn't see his face, but she could hear his ragged breathing. White puffs of vapor rose from beneath his hat brim, then vanished.

"They might charge Frankie with murder, hon," she said gently. "Are you going to let that happen?"

"They can't prove it if he didn't do it."

"Shane."

His shoulders dropped. He shoved his fists into his pockets. "This between us?"

Teddy hesitated, then shook her head. "You know I can't promise that."

He spat in the dirt. "Then I got nothin' to say."

He turned toward the four-wheeler, but Teddy stepped in front of him.

"Shane, use your head. Frankie's not going to let himself go down for murder. When push comes to shove, he'll tell us what he was doing Sunday. When he caves, he'll implicate you. He'll have no choice. You might as well get out in front."

Shane swallowed noisily. "I ain't a snitch."

Teddy laid a hand on his sleeve. "Horses have been disappearing around here for years. Has it been you and Frankie all along?"

Beneath the fabric, she felt his muscles tighten. She gave his arm a small shake. "Stealing horses is a third-degree felony in Texas. Why would you get Frankie involved in this? He looks up to you."

Shane jerked away. "Hey, Frankie got *me* into it."

"What?"

He stared at her for a moment, then stepped around and headed for the four-wheeler. She followed and grabbed the rifle. In one smooth movement, she opened the action and unloaded it.

Shane threw up his arms. "Think I'm gonna shoot ya now? Christ, Aunt Teddy."

She pocketed the cartridges. "I think you're scared. Talk to me."

He dropped sideways onto the four-wheeler's seat and stared at the horizon. The moon had effaced the dimmer stars, but Jupiter and the Pleiades shone fitfully through, rising together over the tree line.

"Sure you wanna hear this?" he said. "You ain't gonna like it."

Teddy shivered. "I'm listening."

Shane pulled out a pack of Camels and shook one out. He offered it to Teddy, but she declined.

"Started in high school, couple months after Grayson died." He put the pack away and produced a lighter.

"Why then?"

Shane cupped the flame with one hand and lit the cigarette. For a few seconds, Teddy saw his narrow face, pinched and drawn in the flickering light. He looked suddenly very young.

"That's when Frankie's folks were in that wreck," he said. "His mom got killed. His dad couldn't work. His grandma was sick.

Jasmine was just in middle school. It all fell on Frankie to pay the bills."

"I get it. But stealing horses? He couldn't unload them around here."

The tip of Shane's cigarette flared in the dark. "Frankie's uncle knows a guy in Sheffield who's got connections to a slaughterhouse in Mexico," he said finally, the words coming out with the smoke. "No paperwork, no questions. We can make more in one night stealing horses than we earn in a week landscaping. We just have to haul them to Big Lake. The uncle takes it from there."

"Oh, no."

"Said you wouldn't like it."

Teddy listened as Shane narrated the story in a low, flat voice. Some of the specialists Frankie's dad had needed wouldn't take his insurance. Frankie had been fifteen, then. He couldn't make enough working part-time at the Dollar Store. It was either horses or drugs.

"Thing is, you need at least two guys," Shane said. "And Frankie ain't much of a horseman. He asked me, but I said no. So he strongarmed Chase into it."

"Strongarmed how?"

Shane tapped the ash off his cigarette. "I dunno. Frankie had something on Chase. Never said what."

The arrangement hadn't lasted, Shane said. Chase was spiraling after Grayson's death. Drinking too much. Stan sent him to military school after Christmas. Then Frankie came asking again—and this time, Shane agreed.

"Why? You were living with us back then—you didn't have a lot of expenses."

Shane flicked the butt into the dirt and ground it out with his boot. "Dad was getting beat up in prison. Needed money for protection."

"You could've asked us."

"I knew how you felt about Dad. Besides, you were pregnant with Henry, having those blood-pressure problems. And now, what with Dad's parole hearing coming up—"

"For God's sake, Shane, horse rustling's no joke. You can get up to ten years."

"Dad—"

"He's using you. He's my brother—I've known him longer than you have. You've gotta cut ties before you end up sharing a cell."

Shane was quiet. "You say that like it's easy."

Teddy opened her mouth, then shut it. An image flashed in her mind—Milton passed out on his urine-soaked mattress.

She rubbed her forehead with the back of her thumb. "Yeah, I know."

"I did stop—for a while. Frankie, too. After what went down with Terrence, we decided we were done." Shane brushed some ash off the four-wheeler's gas tank. "Then Frankie's old man needed another operation. And Dad's first appeal was coming up."

Lately, it had gotten riskier. Ranchers were getting seriously pissed off—teaming up, setting night watches, laying traps. Ready to shoot first and ask questions later.

"Me and Frankie weren't fast enough, with just the two of us. So when Chase came back last year, Frankie wanted him in. Chase was a great horseman—good as me. With him, we'd have two to rope, one to drive.

"Frankie tried using the same leverage, but Chase wasn't having it. Said if Frankie didn't back off, he'd go to the cops."

"When was this?" Teddy asked.

"Last winter. Couple months after he got home."

"That recording I mentioned—it's not from last winter. It's from last month."

"Yeah, I know." Shane pushed himself off the seat and rubbed his hands for warmth. "Back in August, Frankie wanted to steal a horse from the Rocking L—to pressure Chase. But it backfired. Chase stalled a few weeks, then said he was transferring, moving away. Told Frankie to go fuck himself. That must've been the call you heard."

Teddy's phone started ringing. She ignored it. "And now Chase is dead."

"Frankie didn't do it. He was with me Sunday night—like you said. We took that horse from Steffke's. Broke-down nag. Did Steffke a favor, if you ask me."

"That's no excuse," Teddy snapped. "What time were you there?"

"We had to meet Frankie's uncle in Big Lake—didn't get home till two."

The ringing stopped. From the tree line, the woodwind call of a great horned owl floated across the pasture—five low, hollow notes trailing into silence. Then an answering call—a mated pair, checking on each other. Or maybe rivals squaring off. No way to know.

Teddy stared at Shane in the moonlight. She didn't know if she wanted to hug him or arrest him. Neither would fix anything.

"You gonna tell Ramirez?" he asked.

Teddy shivered. Her feet were numb. "I don't know. I need to think." She checked her phone. Missed call—from Rick Castillo. She hesitated. But no. It could wait.

As she pocketed the phone, it chimed with an incoming text.

Berna's hurt bad. Vet Clinic.

The words hit like a jolt—electric and raw.

Teddy shoved the phone in her pocket and slung the rifle over her shoulder. "C'mon, we have to go."

◆ ◆ ◆

Red-and-blue lights pulsed on the horizon as Teddy raced up the road toward the Concho Valley Animal Clinic. Two patrol cars blocked the entrance. Bertie Loomis and Ryan Ortega were stringing police tape around the parking lot. Only two vehicles were there—Berna's van, and Rick Castillo's dusty blue pickup.

Castillo, now cleaned up and wearing jeans and a plaid flannel shirt, was pacing by the mailbox. When he saw Teddy's truck, he ran toward her. By the time she'd unbuckled her seatbelt, he was at her window.

She jumped out and slammed the door. Her hands ached from gripping the wheel. "Where's Berna?"

Rick was breathing hard. "Ambulance just left. She's unconscious, but she's alive."

For a second, Teddy couldn't move. Her limbs felt heavy, her vision strangely bright at the edges. "What the hell happened?"

Rick shook his head. "I got out of the shower and no one was around. Figured Berna went home. When I came out to my truck a few minutes later, she was on the ground by the van. I thought she was dead."

"Was it a heart attack?"

"I don't know."

Bertie had tossed her roll of tape to Ortega and was heading over.

When she reached the truck, she dusted off her hands. "Give us a minute, Mr. Castillo."

He stared at her, then moved away.

A thread of suspicion unspooled in Teddy's mind. She didn't want to pull at it.

Bertie lowered her voice. "Berna was strangled. No sign of the ligature."

"Oh God." Teddy felt sick. She leaned against the truck. "Is she gonna make it?"

"Paramedics said fifty-fifty. They took her to San Angelo."

Teddy closed her eyes, but the glow of the cruiser's lightbar still pulsed behind her lids.

She opened them again. "Did you call the Chief?"

"Tried. No answer." Bertie licked her lips. "I phoned Raina. She told me to contact you, then the sheriff's office. To save time, I had that guy call you"—she nodded at Castillo—"while I called the sheriff."

"Let me guess—they're slammed with that triple, but they'll send someone in the morning?"

Bertie gave a humorless smile. "Yep. Told me to tape off the area till the crime scene techs can get here."

Teddy nodded, then ducked under the police tape and headed across the lot.

Bertie followed. "Watch your step."

"I know." Teddy approached Berna's van and looked around. "Where was she?"

"There—by the driver's door. Wouldn't you say, Ryan?"

Ortega had finished taping off the lot and stood nearby, winding the loose end of the caution tape into the spool.

He nodded. "Face down."

"Ortega was first on the scene," Bertie explained. "After Castillo, I mean."

"Was Berna wearing her lab coat?" Teddy asked.

Ortega looked startled. "Yeah."

Bertie shone her flashlight in Teddy's face. "Why?"

Teddy squinted. "I stopped in earlier—left around eight. She was wearing it when she followed me out to say goodbye. We were standing right here." She waved at the ground. "Must've been attacked just after I left."

"Think someone was watching?" Ortega asked.

"Had to be." Teddy rubbed her arms to shake off the chill. "Earlier tonight, I thought I was being followed. Might've been nothing."

She knelt and examined the ground.

Bertie joined her, panning the flashlight over the gravel. "No clear shoe treads. Just a mess of scuff marks."

"She fought back," Teddy murmured. She was getting up when something caught her eye. "Loomis, give me your Maglite."

Elbows on the gravel, Teddy shone the light beneath the front tire.

"What is that?" Ortega asked. "Scrap of paper?"

"I don't know."

Teddy inched closer, then suddenly scrambled backward, bumping her head on the running board. "Ow!" She stood up. "It's a cigarette. Looks fresh. 'Marlboro' stamped above the filter, plain as day. Better get some shots, Loomis."

Bertie snapped a few photos, then stood, sucking her teeth. "Should we leave it for the crime scene guys?"

"I'd say bag it. Might blow away."

Bertie nodded, staring down at the cigarette. "There was blood under Berna's nails." She glanced back. Castillo was watching from behind the tape. She lowered her voice. "Should I ask him for a cheek swab?"

"Who, the new vet?"

"You always check the first person on the scene, don't ya? He had means and opportunity."

Teddy felt a twinge of reluctance. Bertie was right—it was standard procedure. Still . . . "Berna gave him a job. Why would he—"

"The Chief says *why* never gets you anywhere. We should rule him out if we can, right?"

Teddy nodded slowly, but Bertie was already heading for Castillo. Teddy and Ortega followed.

"Can I see your hands?" Bertie asked.

Castillo's eyebrows rose. He looked at Teddy. "What's going on?"

"It's routine," she said.

He held out his hands. Bertie bent over them with the flashlight, examining his knuckles and nails closely.

"Okay. Other side."

Rick hesitated, then turned them over. His calloused palms were scored with deep, red indentations.

"What are those?" Bertie shone the light directly in his face.

"I pulled a calf tonight. Used chains. Didn't have my gloves."

"I can vouch for that," Teddy said. "I was here when he told Berna about it."

Bertie turned the light on her. "Did you see these marks then?"

Teddy tried to remember. "Can't say," she admitted finally.

Bertie turned back to Rick. "Mind coming inside with us for a minute, Mr. Castillo?"

He scratched his cheek. "Why?"

"It's just routine," Teddy said for the second time. She wasn't sure if she meant to reassure him or herself.

They walked to the clinic entrance, and Bertie tried the door. "Got the key?"

Rick glanced at Teddy. She nodded.

He hesitated, and Bertie cleared her throat. "We can do this at the station if you want."

"Do *what*?"

Teddy laid a hand on his arm. "Rick, we just need to rule you out so we can focus on finding who hurt Berna."

He blinked, then reached into his pocket and handed her the key.

She unlocked the door and they went inside.

"Ortega, you stay out here and guard the scene," Bertie said.

The lobby was dark. Castillo stood silhouetted in the dim red glow of the exit sign.

Bertie flipped the light switch, and they all squinted in the sudden glare.

"You want to check me for scratches, is that it?" Castillo asked.

"That's the idea," Bertie said. "Mind taking off your shirt?"

Rick looked uneasy, but he grabbed his collar and tugged the plaid shirt over his head.

They stared. A red-purple bruise stretched like a bandolier across his chest.

Rick touched it gingerly. "When I pulled that calf at Steffke's, it fell on top of me."

"He mentioned that to Berna, too," Teddy said, but her mind was racing.

Bertie snapped a photo. "A *calf* did that?"

"Sucker weighed a hundred pounds—ask Sid."

"Hold out your arms, please."

He held them out, then turned so they could check his back. There were no other marks.

"Would you come in tomorrow for a polygraph? Maybe give a DNA sample?" Bertie's voice was friendly, but she was watching him through narrowed eyes.

Castillo's face was unreadable. "No problem. We done?"

Teddy handed him his shirt, and she and Bertie stepped outside. Ortega was standing by his squad car.

"You buy his story?" Bertie asked.

Teddy glanced through the clinic window. Rick was tucking in his shirt. His thick black hair was mussed. He stared back at her, eyes dark with a sort of guarded, weary disappointment.

Teddy turned away. "Yeah, I do. His story tracks. He mentioned that calf hours ago. He was covered in blood and mud, too. We can check with Steffke to confirm."

The clinic light flicked off. Rick emerged, locked the door, and pocketed the key.

"Am I free to go?" He sounded tired.

Bertie nodded. "Live nearby? I can't let you move your truck yet. Part of the crime scene."

"I'll give him a lift," Teddy said. She wanted a moment with him, to explain—or at least to try. She looked at Rick. "You're still in Berna's guesthouse, right?"

"It's only a mile," he said. "I'll walk."

Chapter 32

The next morning, Teddy woke before her alarm. She went to the window and pushed aside the curtain. It was still dark, though faint gray streaks glimmered on the eastern horizon. Even through the glass, she could hear the gobbling clatter of sandhill cranes flying high overhead, migrating to their winter grounds further south.

The house was still. She dressed hurriedly in jeans and a fleece pullover, grabbed her purse, phone, and keys, and slipped out the laundry room door.

Crossing the garage, she tapped on the door of the guest room. Voices murmured inside, and Alan appeared in his t-shirt and boxers.

He looked sleepy and annoyed. Pillowcase lines creased the left side of his face. The nightstand lamp glowed behind him, and Teddy glimpsed Lyric on the bed, her long blonde hair fanned across the pillow.

Alan stepped into the cold garage and shut the door. "What do you want, Ted? It's early."

"I've gotta go. Wanted to make sure you can cover drop-offs and pick-ups for the kids."

"I told you I would." He yawned and ran a hand through his thinning hair. "What the hell happened last night? Where'd you go after the funeral?"

Teddy apologized and explained, though she omitted the conversation with Shane.

"Oh my God—Berna? Is she—?"

"I don't know. I'm headed to the hospital now. Might be late getting back."

Alan's brow furrowed. "Berna's tough—she'll pull through." He was trying to sound certain, but his eyes told a different story. "Don't stress about the kids. I got it covered."

At least he wasn't being a jerk about it, Teddy thought. That counted for a lot.

He turned to go, but she stopped him. She hated to break their fragile truce—but he needed to know.

"Berna's the third attack this week. Whoever's doing this is out of control. I'm worried about Julia."

Alan's pink face went white. "Why?"

"She was Cody Puckett's girlfriend. This killer might think she knows something. I warned her, but I'm not sure she listened. That's why I wanted to make sure she doesn't ride her bike to school."

She watched his expression shift, emotions moving like cloud shadows across a landscape.

"Should I keep her home—make her come to the greenhouse with me?" he asked finally.

"She's got exams in a couple weeks. She'll be fine at school, as long as she stays there and waits for you to pick her up. But she can't run off again. It's dangerous."

"I'll talk to her."

"Thanks."

Alan laid a hand on the doorknob. "Good luck, Ted. Watch out for yourself."

"Thanks," she said again, and realized she meant it.

The Concho Valley lay still and quiet beneath a pale autumn sky as Teddy sped south through the rolling scrubland. Vultures warmed their wings on utility poles. Deer grazing the mown strip beside the asphalt startled and bounded into the mesquite as she passed.

Except for a couple of cattle trucks, Highway 208 was empty. But the streets of San Angelo were already filling with rush-hour traffic by the time Teddy reached the hospital. It was eight fifteen by the dashboard clock when she parked in the visitors' lot and hurried through the automatic doors.

The vestibule was quiet, nearly empty. A few bleary-eyed customers cradled hot beverages inside the little coffee shop off the lobby. A middle-aged woman sat at an information kiosk near a bank of elevators, scrolling through her phone.

As Teddy approached, she heard a soft *ding.* One of the elevator doors slid open, and a tall, slender man stepped out, dressed in khakis and a yellow Oxford. A "Clergy" badge was pinned to his chest. Mark McKissick, looking strange without his bike gear. He stopped when he saw her.

He looked like he hadn't slept. His hair was mussed, his unshaven face pale and drawn. He walked over and surprised Teddy with a hug.

She tried to swallow. "Is Berna—?"

McKissick stepped back. "She's unconscious. Stable, but still critical."

"You saw her?"

He shook his head. "No visitors except immediate family in the ICU."

"She doesn't have any."

McKissick dragged both hands down his face. "She's family to me, but that doesn't count, I guess."

"Where's the ICU?"

"There's no point. They won't let you in."

"I'm going to try."

She moved past him. He turned and fell into step beside her. "I'll take you."

They rode the elevator in silence. McKissick led her past a nurses' station and down a wide corridor to a waiting area. One wall was lined with windows overlooking the ICU—a bleak, sterile room crammed with equipment and beds. Only half appeared occupied. Scanning the space, Teddy caught a glimpse of silvery dreadlocks behind a partially drawn curtain, under which a pair of blue cuffs and white athletic shoes were moving.

She fought the urge to knock on the glass.

Berna—tough, smart, devout. Universally liked. Why would anyone want to hurt her? Unless someone thought she knew something.

Teddy stepped back and studied the door marked "Authorized Personnel Only," then turned and headed up the hall.

McKissick hurried after her. "What are you doing?"

Teddy didn't answer.

At the nurses' station, a stocky man in scrubs was squinting at a computer screen through thick-rimmed glasses.

Teddy cleared her throat. "I need to speak to someone about Berna Robles."

The man pushed the glasses onto his forehead. "Are you family?"

"I'm a friend. A private investigator."

"Sorry, I can't release information or let you in to see her."

Teddy waved that off. "Fine. That's good. You shouldn't let anyone in—*anyone*. You need an armed guard on that door." She gestured toward the ICU.

The man sat back. "Who'd you say you were?"

Teddy showed her ID. "Retired detective. Assisting the Stone Creek force."

"I'll have to get—"

"Look, someone tried to murder her last night. There's no keycard access into the ICU—not even cameras in the waiting room. You're vulnerable. If you can't authorize a guard, point me to someone who can."

The man's forehead wrinkled. His hand hovered uncertainly over the desk phone.

"I'll get the sheriff's office to confirm," Teddy said. "In the meantime, posting a guard can't hurt. You might save a life."

He hesitated, then picked up the phone.

Teddy paced the hall until the security guard appeared—a stolid, slow-moving man in his sixties. She glanced at his utility belt. At least he had a gun. She gave him her phone number and a brief overview of the situation.

"If anyone tries to get in, call me or the sheriff's office," she said. "Berna Robles has no family. If someone says they're a relative, they're lying."

She summoned McKissick, who was staring glumly through the window into the ICU, and they walked up the hall in silence. While they waited for the elevator, Teddy studied the pastor's reflection in the steel door. He looked worse than he had in the lobby. His eyes were bloodshot, his face almost gray.

"You all right?" she asked as the doors opened and they stepped inside.

McKissick pushed the button. "Didn't sleep much."

"Because of Berna? When did you hear?"

"Our church secretary's got a police scanner. She texted me last night. I wanted to head for the clinic right then, but I figured I'd just be in the way." He shut his eyes briefly, then looked at her. "Any idea who did this?"

"It's still early," Teddy said. "We're pursuing several leads."

McKissick started to say something, then thought better of it. He leaned back, fighting a yawn.

The elevator stopped, and the doors slid open.

"You hanging around?" Teddy asked.

McKissick pushed away from the wall. "Can't. Thursday's my counseling day. Full slate."

"You shouldn't drive when you're this tired." Teddy knew what could happen when drivers dozed off—she'd seen the unrecognizable heaps of mangled metal and flesh. "Let's get some coffee, first. My treat."

McKissick smiled faintly. "Thanks."

They crossed the lobby to the coffee shop and ordered, then sat at one of the bistro tables roped off from the central vestibule. Teddy took the seat facing the main entrance so she could keep an eye on who was coming and going.

Mark popped the lid off his cup, added a pack of powdered creamer, and sat staring into the dark liquid.

He looked so wretched that Teddy set her own cup down. "Sure you're okay?"

"Not really." His voice was hoarse. "Berna, of all people. If there was ever a person who was good—truly good. Gruff on the outside, but underneath—" His voice cracked.

"Yeah, she is," Teddy said.

They sat in silence.

After a while, McKissick cleared his throat. "When I moved here after seminary, I didn't know a soul," he said quietly. "It was hard. Lonely. Everyone expects a pastor to minister to them, you know? But nobody thinks about what it's like for us. Rural communities don't accept new people easily. Without Berna and Grayson, I might've thrown in the towel."

"You mean a lot to her, too. She was telling me last night."

McKissick picked up the plastic cup lid and turned it in his fingers. "Why did this have to happen? Whatever was going on with Chase and that poor Puckett kid—it should never have touched Berna. Never. Feels like God took a nap and the universe slipped off the rails." He stared at the lid, then crushed it in his fist. "It's wrong to be angry. I should set an example. But honestly, I don't think I can go through this again."

"Go through what—losing someone?"

"Not just someone." McKissick pulled out his phone, thumbed through photos, and handed it to her.

A young woman's head and shoulders filled the screen—slim and pretty, in a neon blue dress. She had blonde hair feathered in a mid-eighties style and was smiling up at something out of frame. The image was somewhat pixelated, a copy of a snapshot that had been blown up and cropped.

Teddy looked up.

"My mother," McKissick said.

"She's beautiful."

He took the phone back and stared at it. "She died when I was little. Overdose. My grandmother did her best. But really, Berna's the one who's been like a mother to me—these last few years, anyway." He swallowed and rubbed his eyes.

"Don't talk like she's dead," Teddy said. "She'll be okay."

McKissick sat back. "God, I'm so sorry. Here I am, acting like this is about me." He put away the phone. "All this is bringing up feelings I wasn't prepared for."

"No worries. I asked."

"Thanks." He gave a wan smile. "What about you? How're you holding up?"

Teddy pressed her hands around the warm cup and pictured Berna at the barn Monday night, cradling one of the newborn kittens, holding a stethoscope to its tiny ribcage as it paddled and mewled.

Her vision swam. She shook off the memory. "I'm good. Just want to catch this bastard."

They said goodbye a few minutes later, and Teddy was crossing the parking lot when her phone rang.

It was Ramirez, and he was in a bad mood.

He answered her "Hey, Chief" with a gruff "Where the hell are you?"

Annoyed, Teddy explained. "Didn't Loomis tell you—?"

"Course she did." His tone softened a little. "How's Berna?"

"Critical. I'm worried about her safety. When the sheriff's investigator gets there, see if he'll request a twenty-four-hour guard on the ICU."

"He's here, now—I'll ask him. He's not happy, by the way. We need to talk to you. ASAP."

"I'll be at the station in thirty."

"Meet us at the vet clinic. Crime scene guys are en route."

Teddy stuffed her phone in her pocket and yanked open the truck door.

It was nearly ten a.m. when she arrived at the Concho Valley Animal Clinic. Police tape still ringed the parking lot. Someone had taped a sign to the door: "Closed Thursday," with a number to call Rick Castillo in case of emergency.

The crime scene technicians hadn't arrived yet. The rookie who'd guarded the scene overnight was still in his cruiser on the shoulder of the road, hunched over his phone. A white SUV blocked the clinic drive. On the door, the words "Tom Green County Sheriff" hovered above a star badge.

Teddy pulled in behind the cruiser and climbed out. A deafening clamor hit her ears—the shrill, whistling shrieks of thousands of grackles perched in the cottonwoods along the property line. She slammed her truck door hard, and the trees erupted with an explosion of beating wings.

Two men were crouched beside Berna's van, their backs to her. One was Ramirez. Ducking under the tape, Teddy crossed the lot, her boots crunching on the gravel. They heard her coming and got up stiffly.

The Chief looked terrible. His face was the color of putty, and his eyes were bloodshot. The man beside him wore a sheriff's department uniform. He was in his fifties, broad and florid, with a fleshy nose and a gray combover—the embodiment of the Southern deputy stereotype. He was even chewing a toothpick. Teddy recognized him instantly.

Wade Rummler.

Now a detective in Art Linacre's office, he'd been a Ranger five years ago, part of the team that reviewed the Terrence Bragg shooting—the only one who believed Teddy's actions had been unjustified. She'd found him lazy, smug, and sexist, more interested in closing cases than in solving them. Ramirez had been right—Linacre had sent his most useless investigator.

Teddy exhaled through her teeth. "Hey, Chief."

She gave Rummler a neutral nod. He scowled and folded his arms.

Ramirez shook a few Tic Tacs into his mouth. "Thanks for coming. We needed a word—sooner the better."

Teddy thought she could guess why. "What about?"

Rummler took out the toothpick. "What *about*?"

Ramirez cut in. "Wade and me tried to interview Frankie Aguilar this morning, but he's lawyered up. Brendall said you talked to him last night."

"You asked me to."

"I asked you to establish a rapport, not shut him down. We watched the footage."

Teddy squared her shoulders. "I took a gamble—thought I could get him to open up. For what it's worth, I think some of his story's true."

"Which part?"

"He swears he's never been in the silo. I don't think he's lying."

Rummler stepped closer. "The kid left fingerprints down there."

"On a sofa—not a wall or railing. They could've gotten there any time."

"One's in blood, for Chrissakes."

"We don't know whose yet."

"Nine times outta ten—" Rummler started, but Teddy cut him off.

"Frankie couldn't explain the prints, but I thought he was shooting straight. He offered to take a polygraph."

"Well, now he wants a lawyer, so a polygraph's off the table. Thank you very much. If you'd—"

"Hang on, Wade," Ramirez said. "What about that recorded phone call, Ted? How come I have to find out about it from the CCTV footage?"

"I didn't know about it myself till last night." Teddy explained the history of the audio file. "I went to the station to tell you, but Brendall said you were out with the Rangers. So I thought I'd try my luck with Frankie."

"Yeah, okay." Ramirez rubbed his jaw with the heel of his hand. "Frankie denies that was him on the call. You believe him?"

"No, he's lying there. When I pushed, that's when he lawyered up. But I don't think he killed Chase."

"Are you trying to protect him because he works for your husband, or are you really that stupid?" Rummler snapped. "He was blackmailing Chase. He's heard making threats over the phone, then Chase is murdered. He's got no alibi for Sunday night, and his bloody fingerprint's in the silo. If it walks like a duck and swims like a duck, you don't need it to quack 'The Yellow Rose of Texas' to know it's a goddamn duck."

Teddy ran the zipper of her fleece up and down, weighing her options. Frankie did have an alibi for Sunday—but she wasn't prepared to share it. Not yet.

"Use your head, Rummler. Frankie was in custody last night. If he's the killer, who attacked Berna?"

Even as she said it, the question echoed back at her. Could it have been Shane? He and Frankie were partners, after all—at least in horse rustling. But why would he target Berna?

He'd been in the pasture when it happened, standing guard over Fancy's remains. Hadn't he? No one was with him. He could've slipped away for an hour. But if he had, the coyotes would've torn the corpse apart.

Teddy suddenly remembered the blanket draped carefully over the mare. She'd assumed Shane had done it out of kindness. Now she wasn't sure.

She shoved the thought aside. Rummler was still talking—loud and angry. Of course Frankie hadn't attacked Berna himself. He'd obviously had an accomplice, and Rummler thought he knew who.

"Who?" Teddy asked, nervous.

"None of your business." Rummler jabbed the toothpick toward her. "You're not a detective anymore." He looked at Ramirez. "If you want my help, keep her away from this case."

He clamped the toothpick between his teeth and walked off toward his SUV.

Teddy and Ramirez watched him go.

"Who's he think the accomplice is, Chief?" she asked once Rummler was out of earshot.

Ramirez slipped a hand under her elbow and guided her to the rear of Berna's van.

He leaned against the spare tire. "Loomis says y'all found a Marlboro cigarette out here last night. Then there's the pack Bragg picked up at the Wallow. Rummler asked if I know anyone who smokes 'em."

"You mentioned Stan?"

Ramirez rubbed the back of his neck. "No point lying. He's gonna find out. I can't look like I'm covering for my brother-in-law. With Stan having no alibi for Tuesday night, Rummler got excited."

"But Stan's got an alibi for last night, doesn't he?"

Ramirez shook his head.

"He wasn't home with Inez?"

"She says he spent most of yesterday in bed, shaking off Tuesday's hangover. Then last night, he couldn't sleep, so he went out riding after supper and didn't come in till dawn, the big idiot."

"For the love of—"

"I know. He ain't doing himself any favors. Rummler's been here two hours, and he already thinks Stan and Frankie were both involved."

"How does *that* work?"

"He reckons Frankie killed Chase in the silo. But Stan thought Cody did it, so he strangled the kid and dumped him at the Wallow."

"And Berna? I suppose Stan attacked her, too?"

Ramirez spread his hands in a *beats me* gesture. "Rummler's still finessing his theory. Wants me to take him out to the Rocking L this afternoon, see what we can get out of Stan."

"What do you want from me?"

"That depends." Ramirez ran his thumb along the ridges of the spare tire. "Think Rummler might be right?"

"If he is, it'll be by sheer accident."

"But you think it's possible Stan's part of this?"

"Anything's possible. You've got to follow the evidence—can't get stuck on a theory."

Ramirez stared at her. "Good. That's what I wanted to hear." He straightened and brushed at a tire smudge on his shirt. "Rummler's gonna hare off after this Stan-and-Frankie notion. If they did it, fine. They deserve to pay. But I want to be sure. Keep working the case—quietly. I'll keep you posted on our end."

Teddy walked to her truck, grumbling under her breath. As if the case weren't complicated enough, now the Chief expected her to tiptoe around Wade freaking Rummler? It had been Ramirez's idea to call in the sheriff's office in the first place—and now he wanted her to protect the case from the consequences.

"Why am I always cleaning up other people's messes?" she muttered, opening the truck door.

She could refuse. Let Rummler botch it. But Chase and Cody deserved better. So did Berna.

She slid behind the wheel and stared across the road at a herd of black Angus grazing in the pasture. She had no idea what to do next.

What would Raina say? Wouldn't hurt to ask.

Teddy reached for her phone. She had a missed call from Raina, followed by a text*: Come over when u get this. I've got news.*

On my way, Teddy typed, then buckled her seatbelt and started the truck.

Chapter 33

Teddy had been nervous the day before as she'd approached the Braggs' house, but today, as she parked at the curb and hurried up the walk, she was too preoccupied with the case to think of anything else.

She trotted up the steps and knocked. No answer. She peered through the front room window. Raina's chair was empty. A coffee cup sat on the side table by the bottle of pain pills. The ottoman was pushed aside.

Teddy knocked again, then tried the knob. The door swung open.

"Hello!" she called. "Raina?"

A muffled shout came from deeper in the house. She stepped inside and called again.

"Back here—I need help. Dammit!"

Teddy hurried past the kitchen and around the corner. Raina was on the floor, propped against the wall outside the little half bath. One crutch lay beside her; the other had fallen into the bathroom.

Teddy rushed over. "What happened?"

Raina glared up at her. "What do you think? I had to pee."

"Where's Anthony? You shouldn't be alone."

"He was driving me crazy. I sent him to work. Help me up."

Teddy got behind her, pulled her to her feet, and retrieved the crutch.

"Should we call the doctor?"

"I'm fine."

Teddy eyed the splint on Raina's ankle. "What if you dislocated it or something?"

"I said I'm fine."

Teddy followed her nervously to the living room. Raina dropped into the armchair.

Teddy pushed the ottoman closer and laid the crutches on the floor. "Can I get you anything? Do you need—"

"Stop hovering. Just sit."

"All right, all right." Teddy moved to the sofa.

Raina opened the bottle and swallowed a pill.

"Hurts, huh?"

Raina grimaced and leaned back. "It'll ease up soon."

"How often are you supposed to take those?"

"Every four to six. I've been trying to stretch it to eight, but—"

"It's only been two days. Maybe you should follow the doctor's advice."

"I don't like taking meds. I want to control what I feel." Raina shifted restlessly. "I'm losing my mind sitting here. But you wouldn't know anything about that. You still get to be out there, working the case."

Teddy looked at her—flushed, exhausted, pissed off. At least anger was honest. Raina still had the right to her feelings. Teddy had forfeited hers the day she pulled the trigger. That's how it worked. Shoot someone's son, and you don't get to be angry anymore. Or defensive. Or sad. Only sorry—quietly, endlessly sorry.

She cleared her throat. "You just have to sit tight till the swelling goes down. Once you get the real cast, it'll be easier."

Raina waved away the subject. "What's going on? Is the sheriff's guy here yet?"

Teddy brought her up to speed. Raina knew about the attack on Berna, but she listened to Teddy's account with interest.

"Berna gets along with everybody," she said when Teddy finished. "Why would someone try to kill her?"

"It must've happened right after I drove off. Whoever did it was watching us—and listening."

"Maybe she said something that spooked him—made him think she could ID him. What were y'all talking about?"

"Just chatting, really. Nothing about the case."

"And the only evidence you found was that cigarette?"

Teddy nodded. "Not a butt. It was fresh out of the pack." She met Raina's eyes. "And that parking lot's gravel—noisy to walk on. Nobody could've snuck up on her. Whoever it was, she knew them."

"Smart to put her under guard," Raina said. "If someone tries to get to her at the hospital, we'll have footage and witnesses. Rummler wouldn't have thought of it. That guy's a joke." She caught Teddy's look. "What? You figured I'd be a fan of his because he wanted to put you in jail?"

Hearing the words said aloud was shocking. "Well . . . yeah."

Raina looked away. "You shouldn't have shot Terrence. But I never thought you showed 'callous indifference to life.'"

Teddy didn't know what to say. It wasn't forgiveness, but it was more than she'd ever gotten before—more than she'd expected. She wasn't sure she could have said as much, if their positions were reversed.

Her gaze drifted to the window. The sky had clouded over. Dry sycamore leaves scudded along the street, and high in the air, a tiny bird was fighting the wind, beating its wings and getting nowhere.

"Gonna be a dust storm if this keeps up," Teddy murmured. She looked back at Raina. "What's your news? You said you had something."

Raina nodded and dug in the chair cushions for her notebook. "Matt Tankersley."

"Chase's AA sponsor? Did Galveston PD find him?"

"Not yet. But I had Brendall run his name. He's got a record."

"For what?"

"Arrested twice for assault. Went to prison the second time."

"When?"

"Two thousand six. He was eighteen."

"Clean since then?"

"Yeah, but get this—his ex-wife tried to get a restraining order against him last year. Claimed he was abusive. They've got a couple kids, and she's trying to get his parental rights revoked. Judge didn't buy it. Denied the order. But Tankersley never mentioned any of it when I talked to him. I'd call that a red flag."

"Sure—if we were investigating his ex's murder."

"I'm not finished." Raina flipped a page. "I wanted to talk to Chase's former fiancée, get her take. So I called Inez for the number." She ran a finger down the margin till she found the line she was looking for. "Ashlyn Davis." She looked up. "Guess who she's dating now?"

"You're kidding."

"Nope. She swears Tankersley and her were just friends till after the breakup. Chase introduced them. The three of them used to hang out. But when things with Chase went sideways, Tankersley was her shoulder to cry on. Strictly platonic, at first, she says. But Chase blamed Matt for coming between them. Wrecked their friendship. That's when Chase left Galveston and moved back here."

Teddy picked up a throw pillow, absently fingering the tassel. "I can see why Chase might want to kill Tankersley. But what's Tankersley's motive?"

Raina dropped the notebook in her lap. "I don't know. But he lied to his boss, and he lied to me. Maybe he thought Chase was still a threat to his relationship, somehow."

"That's an idea." Teddy tossed the pillow aside and leaned in. "What about this—maybe Chase gave that charm bracelet to Ashlyn, trying to win her back. The sketch we found in his room—maybe he was planning to send that next, as a follow-up gift. If Tankersley found out, he'd be pissed."

"But Cody found the bracelet in the silo."

"Right. So maybe Tankersley took it from Ashlyn and drove here to confront Chase. Calls him Sunday night at the bowling alley, says he wants to talk. They meet in the silo. Tankersley throws the bracelet in his face, says 'You're never getting her back,' and shoots him." Teddy stopped. "Except Chase was shot with his own gun."

"Maybe he brought it for protection," Raina said. "Tankersley could've grabbed it."

"What about the suicide note?"

"He could've forced Chase to write it at gunpoint."

"But would he let Chase address it to *him*?" Teddy flopped back against the sofa. "The pieces don't fit."

"No, they don't. And that sketch had a thank-you card with it. Not exactly romantic." Raina rested her chin on her hand. Her eyes were heavy. "Ashlyn swears she never had a charm bracelet. Maybe she's lying, but—"

"Maybe. Maybe," Teddy said, restless now. "Everything's a *maybe*. Till we find hard evidence, we're making up fairy tales."

She tilted her head back and stared at the ceiling. Something brushed her calf. The Braggs' black cat rubbed against her jeans, then leapt onto her lap, purring and kneading her thigh.

Teddy stroked its back. "Wouldn't hurt to ask Ashlyn if Chase ever tried to reconnect."

"I did," Raina said. "She denied it. But she could've been protecting Tankersley."

"Even if he killed Chase, what would he have against Cody and Berna? He's a stranger here. No way he lurked around town all week without somebody noticing."

"Once Galveston PD talks to him, maybe we'll have more to go on." Raina yawned.

"Meds kicking in?" Teddy asked. "Want me to leave?"

"No." Raina sat up straighter, adjusting the pillow behind her back. "Forget Tankersley for now. What about Frankie Aguilar? Why'd he lawyer up?"

"He didn't kill anyone, Raina."

"He's got no alibi for Sunday night."

"Well, he—" Teddy hesitated, staring down at the cat, now asleep with one paw curled over its nose. "He might have an alibi. He wouldn't say."

Raina was watching her. "What about Jasmine? She might know where he was—or why he's lying about the silo."

Teddy shifted. The cat stirred. It jumped down, stretched and yawned, then padded away.

"I tried talking to her. Went by the Skinny's last night."

Raina kicked away the ottoman and grabbed the arms of her chair, pulling herself upright. "Jasmine might owe you—but she owes me more. If I'm there, she'll talk."

She struggled to stand. Teddy jumped up and grabbed her arm.

"What the hell are you doing? You're supposed to be resting."

Raina balanced on her good leg. "I want to look Jasmine in the eye. Hand me my crutches."

"Raina, stop—this is crazy. You already fell once today."

Raina turned, opened a drawer in the side table, and pulled out her service pistol.

"Shut up, Ted. I am not gonna sit here with my leg in the air while Wade Rummler botches this case."

◆ ◆ ◆

It took time to track down Jasmine Aguilar. After helping Raina to the truck, Teddy drove to the Skinny's.

"I'll see if she'll come out here to talk," she told Raina, and hurried inside.

At the register was a gangly college kid with an infected-looking Roadrunner tattoo on his wrist. It was Jasmine's day off, he said—she'd mentioned looking for a second job. Teddy thanked him and left.

They checked the feed store, Goodwill, and Sonic—all three with *Help Wanted* signs in the window. No one had seen Jasmine Aguilar.

At the traffic light on Colonel Priddy, they debated their options.

"What do you want to do?" Teddy asked.

Raina fidgeted with her seatbelt. "Let's go to her house."

"You sure? I can go by myself if—"

"I'm not going home."

"Okay." Teddy swallowed. "But I have to tell you something first. You won't like it." The light turned green. She crossed the intersection, pulled into the Jiffy Lube lot, and engaged the parking brake. "Frankie does have an alibi for Sunday night."

Raina turned. "You been holding out on me?"

"I didn't know till last night." Teddy kept her eyes on the dash. "He was with Shane. They were stealing a horse."

Raina stared. "What?"

"They've been doing it for years. It's Frankie's operation, but Shane helps. Chase Loudermilk did, too, back in high school."

Teddy glanced over. Raina's face had gone rigid.

"Why didn't you tell me at the house?"

"I needed to think it through. I knew it would hit you hard—because of Mayhem."

Teddy forced the words out. Each one felt like a betrayal—of Raina, of Shane, of the uneasy middle ground she was trying to hold. But Raina deserved the truth.

"Oh my God." Raina's face changed. "Those bastards."

"Shane wasn't involved that time," Teddy said. "He was serving thirty days for a DUI when Mayhem was taken."

"Frankie works for Alan—why would he raid your place?"

"Good question. I plan to ask him."

"What'd they do with the horses?"

"Don't ask."

"Tell me."

Teddy met her eyes. "Trust me, Raina. You do not want to know."

Raina's jaw clenched. The fine muscles around her eyes twitched. She gave a small, tight nod and looked away.

"Sure you're up for this?" Teddy asked after a moment. "We'll have to be tactful. We need Jasmine's help."

"I'm not going to lose it, Ted."

"I'd lose it, if I were you."

"I don't need your sympathy. Just drive."

Teddy pursed her lips, then nodded and let out the clutch.

The Aguilars lived in a neighborhood that had seen better days. Small frame houses lined Boxhill Drive—some neat and carefully tended, others neglected. A few were already strung with Christmas lights. Others still had faded skeleton cut-outs hanging on the doors.

The Aguilars' house bore no decorations at all. It had been well-kept the last time Teddy had seen it, but now the paint was peeling and a blue tarp covered part of the roof. For a brief, disorienting moment, she wondered if she'd pulled up to the wrong place. Then she spotted the weathered work van on cinderblocks in the driveway. "Aguilar's Heating and Cooling" was stenciled on the door. A late-model silver Honda sat behind it.

Teddy killed the engine. Then froze. She'd parked almost exactly where her squad car had stood that hot June day five years ago.

The memories boiled up—vivid and inescapable. The rifle grip, slick in her palm. The blood thudding in her ears. Terrence's voice on the phone, teetering between fury and panic.

"Just stall. Keep him talking," the Chief had said. The Hostage Negotiation Team was on its way from San Angelo. Teddy knew Terrence. He trusted her. Maybe she could calm him down.

Terrence was a cop's kid, the therapist had insisted later. He'd known what would happen if he fired that gun. He'd forced Teddy's hand.

But the therapist hadn't changed Terrence's diapers, babysat him, taught him to ride. She wasn't the one who'd had to sit across from his parents and explain why their son was dead.

After five years, Teddy knew she could spin justifications forever. No amount of therapy, or journaling, or late-night self-talk could stop the nightmares, or silence that inner accusatory voice.

After a moment's hesitation, she restarted the truck and let it roll a few yards further down the curb.

Raina said nothing. Her eyes were fixed on the house. Half a decade had passed, but the right front window was still broken. Someone had boarded it up with a rough-cut piece of plywood, but it stood out like a scar—raw and unfaded. Had it been left as a memorial, Teddy wondered, or were some breaks just too costly to mend?

"You can wait out here, if you want," Teddy said.

Raina unbuckled her seatbelt. "Get the crutches. Let's go."

Chapter 34

Despite the cool breeze, Teddy was sweating, and a high-pitched hum vibrated in her ears as they crossed the street and walked up the drive. She glanced inside the silver Honda as they passed: a rosary hung from the rearview mirror, and a black suit coat was folded neatly on the back seat. She knew Frankie and Jasmine's father had been in poor health for years. Had his condition worsened?

"Let me do the talking, okay? Wait here," Teddy said, climbing the steps.

She knocked, waited, knocked again.

A man's voice shouted inside. Moments later, the door opened. Jasmine stood there, looking strange without her Skinny's uniform. She was wearing an oversized Dallas Mavericks t-shirt and glasses instead of her usual contacts. A TV blared somewhere behind her.

"Hi, Mrs. D. What—" Jasmine spotted Raina and inhaled sharply. She looked both embarrassed and afraid. "Why'd you bring *her* here?"

"She's working this case. I know it's awkward, but we need to talk." Teddy nodded toward the Honda. "You have company?"

"Just my cousin," Jasmine said. "This isn't a good time."

Inside, the man's voice rose again—followed by another, low and steady.

Jasmine turned and called back, "It's okay, Dad—I'm handling it." Then, to Teddy: "Frankie told us not to talk to anyone."

She started to shut the door, but Teddy put a foot across the threshold. "It's urgent, Jasmine. The sheriff's investigator's in town. He thinks Frankie's guilty—he said so this morning. If you care about your brother, for God's sake talk to us."

Something clattered behind her. Teddy turned. Raina, her face rigid, was struggling up the steps. The crutches thudded against the wood.

Teddy grabbed her arm and helped her onto the porch. "What are you doing?"

Raina didn't answer. She was sweating with the pain and staring hard at Jasmine, who had closed the door to a crack.

"Don't you dare shut that door," Raina snapped. "Talking to me is the least—"

Teddy gave her arm a warning squeeze. "Not helpful."

"Frankie never killed nobody," Jasmine whispered.

Suddenly, the door swung open. A tall man in a clerical collar stepped into view. He was in his early thirties though already balding, which made him seem older. Dark, deep-set eyes and a long, straight nose gave him a serious, ascetic look.

He took in the scene. "Everything all right, Jazz?"

"Yeah, it's fine. They're just going."

"We're not going anywhere," Raina snapped. "We'll stand here all day."

The man looked at Jasmine. "What's going on? Should I—?" He reached for his phone.

"We're not here to cause trouble," Teddy put in quickly.

Jasmine sighed. "They want to talk about Frankie."

"We want to help him," Teddy said. "We don't think he killed Chase."

Jasmine chewed her thumbnail. She glanced from them to the man. "What do you think?"

"Your dad's not feeling well," he said gently. "He shouldn't be upset."

Jasmine turned back to Teddy. "You really think you can help Frankie?"

"I don't know," Teddy admitted. "Depends what you can tell us."

Jasmine hesitated, then opened the door.

"Sure about this, Jazz?" the man asked quietly.

"Frankie's not a murderer," she said.

Teddy and Raina exchanged a look and followed her inside.

Jasmine gestured toward the priest. "This is my cousin, Father Alex Tomlin—from Carlsbad. Our grandma died last year. He's been helping sort through her things."

Teddy nodded politely and glanced around. Five years ago, the place had been homey and inviting. Now, it was almost bare. Family photos still lined the walls, but the furniture was gone, leaving pale indentations in the carpet. A crucifix hung above a dark patch of wall where a television had been.

Only a folding card table remained. On it sat a half-finished puzzle, thick with dust.

Teddy looked at Raina. She was leaning on her crutches, staring under the table at an ugly throw rug laid at a strange angle. Teddy wondered if the stains were still visible beneath it. She looked away.

A man shouted from the back of the house.

Jasmine flinched. "Alex, can you check on Dad?"

"Sure," he said, moving away.

Jasmine turned to Teddy and Raina. "We don't use this room anymore. We can talk outside—it'll be quieter."

Just as well, Teddy thought. This wasn't a room to linger in. It was a place people avoided—even in their minds. Too many ghosts. It was difficult for her to be here. For Raina, it had to be torture.

Teddy slipped a hand beneath Raina's arm to help steady her as they followed Jasmine down a short hall. Passing an open bedroom door, Teddy glanced inside. The space had been turned into a makeshift den, crammed with furniture. A middle-aged man in slippers and a bathrobe sat in a recliner by the window, watching an infomercial at full volume. An aluminum walker stood beside his chair.

Father Alex was kneeling next to him, speaking in a low, soothing voice.

Teddy hadn't seen Rod Aguilar in years. His face, once strong and well-defined, was slack and pale, his chin shaded with stubble. He stared as they passed. His pupils were huge, and Teddy wondered what medications he was taking.

She nodded hello, unsure if he recognized her. He lifted a shaky hand, then looked away.

Jasmine led them through the kitchen and out into the garage, opening the roll-up door for better light. The concrete slab was strewn with dead leaves and crowded with lumpy black trash bags and stacks of cardboard boxes. A workbench stood along the back wall, piled with more boxes, some taped shut, others open. The blue work van in the driveway blocked their view of the street.

"Excuse the mess," Jasmine said. "My grandma was a packrat. When we sold her house, we had to bring everything here."

There was no place to sit. Raina propped herself against a barrel of garden tools, and Teddy stood close by, in case she needed help.

Jasmine leaned on the workbench, twisting her fingers.

"What do y'all need from me?"

Raina shifted but said nothing. Teddy admired her restraint. She knew what Raina most wanted to ask—the same question she'd screamed at Jasmine five years ago, beside the coffin, in front of two hundred mourners. Jasmine had fled the church that day without answering, and in all the police interviews that followed, she'd remained maddeningly vague. She didn't know why Terrence had shown up that day with a gun. She figured he was upset about their breakup. An inadequate response—but maybe there was no answer. Maybe Terrence himself hadn't known.

Teddy cleared her throat.

"If we're going to help Frankie, we need to know everything, Jazz. Everything."

Jasmine threw up her hands.

"He didn't kill anyone. What else is there?"

Teddy and Raina exchanged a look. Teddy took out her phone and opened the voice memo app.

She kept her eyes on Jasmine as they listened to the recording—Chase's voice ghostly through the static: "Leave me alone, Frankie—you didn't see nothing. You can tell the cops whatever you want. I told you I'm out."

Jasmine's eyes went wide. "Where'd you get that?"

"Never mind," Raina said. "What was Frankie threatening to tell the cops?"

Jasmine edged toward the kitchen door. "I—I don't know."

Teddy stepped in her way.

"Jasmine, I know you want to protect your brother, but we can't sit on this. It's evidence. We'll have to turn it over to the sheriff's guy. But if we understand what it's about—"

"I have no idea, Mrs. D. I swear." Jasmine had picked up a glass scraper from the workbench and was turning it in her hands. "I knew Frankie had something on Chase—he has for a long time. If he didn't, Chase never would've—"

She froze and shot a guilty glance at Raina.

"Never would've what? Helped Frankie steal horses?" Raina said.

Jasmine stared at the scraper, chafing it against her thumb. "How'd you find out?"

Raina's phone rang. She silenced it. "We're investigators."

Jasmine squared her shoulders and tossed the scraper on the workbench. "You think Frankie's a bad person? You didn't have to watch your dad lying there in pain, practically paralyzed—knowing there's an operation that could help if only the fucking insurance would approve it. Everything fell apart after the accident. Mom was gone, Dad couldn't work, our grandma was sick. I was just a kid. It all fell on Frankie. He did what he had to do."

Raina pushed away from the post and swung forward on her crutches. "Even if stealing was the only solution—which it wasn't, by the way—there are hundreds of horses in Tom Green County. Thousands. Frankie didn't have to target Terrence's." Her voice was thick. She was fighting tears. "He didn't have to take my son's. He could've—" She stopped. Her face changed. She stared at Jasmine. "Oh my God."

"What? What is it?" Teddy asked.

But Raina didn't answer. "Terrence knew, didn't he? He knew Frankie took Mayhem. That's why he snapped. He didn't come here to confront you—he came for your brother."

Jasmine didn't deny it. She stood hugging herself, her eyes fixed on a drift of dead leaves.

Teddy's mind raced. Raina was pale, leaning heavily on her crutches, as if she might collapse.

Teddy edged toward her. "Maybe this isn't the best time—"

But Raina cut her off. "How did Terrence find out, Jasmine?" Her voice was low and cold.

Jasmine's nails dug into her arms. She shook her head.

Raina moved closer. "You told him, didn't you? Wanted to rub his nose in it."

Jasmine looked up, her eyes glassy and pink. "I was pissed off when he dumped me. If I'd known what he would do . . ." She shook her head. Tears slid down her cheeks. "It's no good saying I'm sorry. But I am. I'm so sorry."

Raina had gone gray. She swayed, and the crutches wobbled.

Teddy lunged. Jasmine, closer, reached to steady her, but Raina jerked away.

The motion sent her stumbling backward. Teddy caught her around the waist. One crutch clattered to the floor.

Jasmine picked it up and held it out.

Teddy gave it back to Raina.

"Come on," Teddy said. "Let's get you to the truck."

Raina was shaking. She let Teddy steer her toward the driveway. But as they left the garage, she stopped and turned.

"Horse rustling's a felony in Texas, Jasmine. Your brother might not be a murderer, but I'll do everything in my power to put him in prison for as long as possible."

Teddy got her to the pickup and settled her in the passenger seat.

"Rest here," she said. "I'll be right back."

She returned to the carport. Jasmine was still standing by the workbench, staring at the ground.

She looked up as Teddy approached and wiped her eyes with the back of her hand. "What do you want now?"

Teddy leaned against a tall tool chest beside a pile of boxes. The metal was cold against her back. She thought of Terrence—remembered hunkering behind her cruiser, watching him through the Aguilars' front window as he waved the pistol, sobbing. Through the rifle scope, she'd seen the tears on his cheeks, his mouth moving silently, screaming at Jasmine and Frankie, who were pressed against the wall, white with terror. She could still feel the warm curve of the trigger beneath her finger. The phone against her ear, ringing to voicemail again and again. The tightness in her chest as she held her breath, willing him to put the gun down.

She swallowed. "I want the whole truth."

"You have it."

Teddy shook her head. "No, not quite. You said you told Terrence about Mayhem—but you did more than that, didn't you?"

A flicker of alarm crossed Jasmine's face. "What do you mean?"

"There were several horses in my pasture that night. But only one was taken."

Jasmine licked her lips but didn't speak.

"Horse theft's a two-person job," Teddy said. "And Frankie only ever worked with Chase and Shane. Chase was overseas then. Shane was in jail." She paused. "You helped, didn't you? It was your idea."

Jasmine didn't answer.

Teddy slapped the side of the tool chest. The sound reverberated loudly in the enclosed space.

Jasmine flinched. Teddy's ears rang.

"Tell me."

Jasmine stared at the ground, then slowly nodded.

"At first, Frankie said no. Said Shane would kill him if he stole from your place." She looked up. "I—I threatened him. Told him I'd turn him in unless he did what I wanted. Frankie drove. I got Mayhem in the trailer. It wasn't hard," she added sadly. "I brought sugar cubes, and he came right over. Terrence used to let me ride him, so he trusted me."

Teddy felt tears rising. She pinched the bridge of her nose.

"I had to kill that boy, Jasmine—I had to kill Terrence to save you. Do you understand what that means—how many lives that's destroyed?"

Jasmine's face was in her hands. Teddy wanted to grab her, shake her, scream. But what would that solve? Terrence was dead. Chase and Cody were dead. Berna lay in a coma. And someone out there still had to be stopped.

This was all connected. It had to be.

And Frankie was the link. Frankie, who'd blackmailed Chase. Frankie, who'd lied to her. Who'd lawyered up. Maybe he hadn't pulled the trigger—but he knew something.

Teddy's head throbbed. She rubbed her temples and glanced at the pile of boxes beside her. The top one was open, revealing a disorganized jumble of old clothes, bits of knitting, loose photos. A framed snapshot caught her eye—an elderly woman reading to a toddler in pink pajamas and a boy in a Transformers t-shirt.

The Aguilars, in happier times.

She stared at it blankly for a few seconds—then froze.

She snatched up the picture and turned it toward Jasmine. "Where was this taken?"

Jasmine looked up, sniffling. "Wh-what?"

Teddy pointed. "That's your grandmother, right?"

Jasmine nodded.

"At her house?"

Another nod.

Teddy tapped the photo. "And that belonged to her? What happened to it?"

"We sold it—on Craigslist."

"Who bought it?"

Jasmine bit her lip. "I wasn't here—Alex was. He told me what happened."

"Something happened? What do you mean?"

Jasmine hesitated. It took time—some backtracking, some coaxing—but eventually, the story came out. As she listened, Teddy stared at the photo. It seemed to grow heavier in her hand.

"You won't use this against Frankie, will you?" Jasmine said when she finished. "It wasn't all his fault. You can ask Alex, if you don't believe me."

Teddy tucked the photo under her arm. "You didn't get Frankie in more trouble," she said. "You may have just saved him—from murder charges, anyway."

Chapter 35

As Teddy jogged toward the truck, she saw through the window that Raina was on the phone. She didn't look happy. The wind was picking up, hissing along the street. Teddy climbed into the driver's seat and smoothed back her hair.

When Raina hung up, she said, "Bad news. That—"

She broke off as Teddy thrust the photograph at her.

Raina stared. "Is this—?"

Teddy nodded, scrolling through her phone. Finally, she found the image she wanted.

"This is the couch from the silo control room. Look."

She angled the screen toward Raina. The sofa in Teddy's photo was rattier and more worn than the one in the frame, but unmistakable: same wooden arms, same ugly orange plaid.

Raina looked up. "I don't get it."

"It was the grandmother's couch. The Aguilars sold it."

"So what? If the blood from that print turns out to be Chase's—"

"It is."

"What?"

"It's Chase's blood, all right. But Frankie didn't kill him. I just got the story from Jasmine. Chase bought the couch online a few months ago. Jasmine and Frankie were both at work when he came by to pick it up. He didn't realize whose house it was or who he bought it from. Father Alex was here—he helped Chase load it. But Frankie showed up while they were tying it down. There's bad blood between them. Frankie didn't want Chase to have it, tried to yank it off the truck. Frankie took a couple swings at Chase, till Alex pulled him off and said the deal was done. Some of Chase's blood must've gotten on Frankie's hands in the scuffle."

Raina was looking a little blank. "So Frankie—?"

"Frankie's got a priest to back his story. The blood from that print proves nothing."

Raina shifted her injured leg and winced. "We already knew Frankie didn't kill Chase. He was with Shane that night. And anyway, it makes no sense—why commit murder to cover up stealing? Not that people always think straight when they're panicked."

"Frankie knows something, though. Whatever dirt he had on Chase—maybe the killer knew about it, too. We need to find out what it was. And that print was our only leverage." Teddy tossed her phone on the dash. "Barring new evidence, the Chief'll have to let Frankie go. We're back to square one."

"We're further back than that," Raina said grimly. "I just got off the phone with Galveston PD."

"They found Matt Tankersley?"

"Yep. Not our guy. He was in family court in Houston at eight a.m. Monday—custody hearing. Alibi checks out."

"He could've killed Chase at midnight and made it back to Houston by eight. It'd be tight, but it's doable."

Raina shook her head. "Security footage puts him at the Friendswood Walmart with his mother Sunday."

"What time?"

"Seven p.m. Timeline doesn't work, Ted."

Teddy gripped the wheel and watched her knuckles go white. "Then why make up that stupid story about his mom being sick?"

Raina shrugged. "His ex is accusing him of child abuse. He didn't want work to find out the real reason he left the rig."

"But the note—Chase addressed it to him."

"Maybe there's some other Matt we don't know about yet."

Teddy's phone buzzed, the vibration sending it skittering across the dash and onto the floor. She groped between her feet, then jumped out and ducked under the steering wheel, fishing it from behind the clutch.

She shut the door and leaned against the fender. "Julia—are you all right?"

A noisy gust of wind drowned out her daughter's reply.

Teddy stuck a finger in her ear. "I can't hear you, Jules. Where are you?"

The wind dropped, and Julia's reply came through, her voice faint and peevish. "In the bathroom."

"What bathroom?" Teddy checked the time. "It's sixth period, isn't it? Why aren't you in biology?"

"I heard you've been taken off the case."

A sharp *beep* sounded in Teddy's ear. Call waiting. She glanced at the screen. Ramirez. He could wait.

She declined the call. "Heard where?"

"It's all over the school. Everyone's saying the sheriff's office is taking over. Is that true?"

The wind whipped her hair into her eyes, and Teddy brushed it back with a quick, frustrated motion. Word was bound to spread. This was the biggest case ever to hit Stone Creek. People in town were scared—especially now, after Berna's attack. Teddy knew what was being said—that Chase and Cody must have gotten into something bad, and it had caught up with them. After all, everyone knew the Loudermilks had shipped Chase off to military school to straighten him out. And Cody was the orphaned son of an addict.

But Berna was different. A woman in her sixties, established, valuable. A pillar of the community. If Berna had been targeted, anyone could be next.

Teddy's eyes burned. She rubbed them with her knuckles. "Yeah, it's true. I told you last night this was coming."

Julia exhaled noisily into the phone. "You promised you'd get to the truth, Mom. And now you're just gonna quit?"

Teddy felt a flash of defensive irritation. "Nobody's quitting. I'm—"

"Stop! I don't want to hear it."

A second beep told Teddy that Ramirez had left a voicemail—a long one. She wondered if something had happened.

"Hear what?"

"All the crappy excuses about chain of command and how it's out of your hands and blah blah blah." Julia sounded close to tears. "I knew you'd do this—you did it with therapy, and your career, and with Dad, and Fancy, and now this. You're always saying how much you hated your mom for leaving, but at least she had the guts to actually do something about her shitty life. You never fight for anything—you just give up. It's pathetic."

Teddy squeezed her eyes shut. "Oh, for God's sake, Julia—you are a kid. A *kid*. Do you get that? If you really want Cody's murder solved, stay out of it. Is that so hard? I'm doing the best I can."

For a moment, there was silence. Then a click. The line went dead.

She turned. Raina was watching her in the visor mirror. Teddy saw her lips move as she mouthed: "*What?*"

Teddy hesitated, then shook her head.

A few years ago, she would've climbed back into the truck and vented her parenting frustrations. Raina had a way of putting things in perspective—of finding the humor in moments like this. She wondered what the old Raina would've said. Something snarky and irreverent and exactly right. That was what she missed most about their friendship—Raina could always make things better.

Teddy leaned against the tailgate, feeling the cool metal through her fleece. Then she remembered Ramirez's voicemail.

She pulled out her phone and listened, then climbed back into the cab.

"What was that about? Are—" Raina began.

"Nothing. You've got to hear this."

Teddy hit play, and Ramirez's voice crackled through the speaker. The state lab had opened the steel cylinder from the chunk of white rock the divers had found in the Deadhorse silo. It held a powdery substance. They were running tests, but results would take a while. Rummler thought it was unrelated to Chase's murder. But Ramirez thought Teddy should know.

The message ended.

Teddy and Raina looked at each other.

"Powder?" Raina said. "Drugs, maybe?"

Teddy dropped her phone in the cup holder. "No point guessing. Too many unknowns."

Raina half turned in her seat and grimaced in pain. "We're out of leads. What now?"

"I'm not sure."

They sat in silence, watching the sycamore leaves flying down the street. The wind was rising. The sky had turned a bleak, muddy brown. Teddy could feel grit between her teeth, and a thin scrim of dust already coated the dash.

She thought of home. Alan would be having a rough time—this was impossible landscaping weather. And in the barn, the animals would be restless. During the last big windstorm, Sebastian, the blind donkey, had kicked through his stall door and sliced his leg to the bone. It had taken Berna over an hour to stitch up the layers of muscle and skin. If something like that happened today, she'd have to get a hold of Rick Castillo—who was probably still pissed about being searched last night. She couldn't call Berna in the ICU.

Berna. What did that—? Something stirred. A memory, there and gone again, like breath on cold glass.

Why had Berna been attacked? The killer was panicking, getting sloppy. Chase's death had been meticulously planned—a premeditated assassination, organized and cautious. Chase had been the primary target, Teddy felt sure. Cody's murder seemed like an afterthought in comparison—an attempt to tie up loose ends. It was rash and impulsive, but still careful. The killer had kept his head.

But the attack on Berna—that was the anomaly. It had been brutal. Messy. Ineffective. Why? What had triggered it? And why had the killer failed? If Teddy could only—

She sensed an idea lying just beyond reach. She struggled to glimpse it, but it remained stubbornly submerged. Her mind was letting her down, playing tricks.

Playing tricks.

There it was again—that sensation of something on the tip of her tongue. What had Berna said last night? Something about the mind playing tricks. About how memories could become static. You had to fight that, she'd said. You had to make an effort to remember people as they really were—the good and the bad.

They'd been talking about photographs. About why Berna kept so many—even the painful ones. You couldn't allow your mind to edit people into a single dimension. You couldn't look away.

Something teased at the edge of thought, so close Teddy could almost touch it.

"Well, we can't sit here all day," Raina said, breaking the silence. "Let's try to track down that student of yours—David Griffith."

"Later." Teddy turned the key. "First, I want to take a look at Berna's place."

◆ ◆ ◆

Berna's house—a brick structure nestled in a grove of trees a mile past the vet clinic—looked like it always did. The blinds were open, and the neat window boxes brimmed with gold chrysanthemums as Teddy steered up the dusty drive. Behind the house, she glimpsed the single-wide trailer that doubled as the guest quarters, and beyond it, the sloping roof of the pole barn.

The barn. A hot flicker of guilt. With Berna in the hospital, had anyone checked on her goats and chickens? And what about Dottie, her elderly Great Dane? Had she been locked inside for over a day?

Teddy was pulling up under the big sycamore by the porch when Raina said sharply, "Who's that?"

Teddy looked. A dark-haired man in green coveralls had emerged from the barn, fighting the wind as he carried a five-gallon bucket toward the paddock. A dog the size and color of a small donkey trailed behind him, her head bobbing.

Dottie. Teddy exhaled, relieved.

She cut the engine. "Rick Castillo. New vet."

"The guy who found Berna last night?"

"Yeah. He called 911." Teddy unfastened her seatbelt. "Seems on the level—but he had some bruises."

They exchanged a look.

"Consistent with trying to kill someone?" Raina asked.

"Also consistent with pulling a hundred-pound calf out of an eight-hundred-pound heifer. That's his story. Shouldn't be hard to confirm."

Teddy got out of the cab and retrieved the crutches. Castillo had spotted them. He waved. A gust of wind caught his hat, and he set down the bucket to chase it.

He caught up to them on the porch. Teddy introduced him to Raina. "Nice of you to check on Berna's animals," she added.

Castillo shrugged. "Least I can do. She's letting me stay in her trailer till I find a place."

"You're not at the clinic today?" Raina asked.

"It's a crime scene. I'm on call if anyone needs me." He looked at Teddy. "Any word on Berna? I called, but the hospital wouldn't tell me nothin'."

"She's still critical, but stable," Teddy said, flipping through her keys.

Rick smacked his fist into his palm. "Pisses me off how close I was. I could've caught the bastard."

Teddy found Berna's house key and unlocked the door. Dottie lurched forward, whining.

Rick grabbed her collar. "Stay, girl."

A new thought occurred to Teddy. "How'd you get Dottie out? You've got a key, too?"

"Nah. Jimmied a window. Didn't want Berna coming home to a dead dog."

"Any signs of disturbance inside?" Raina asked.

Castillo scratched his cheek. "Just some dog crap by the door."

Teddy pocketed the keys. "When was this? Last night?"

"Around four a.m. Howling woke me up. I was so upset when I got home I forgot she was in here." He rubbed the dog's floppy ears. "If there's nothing else, I should get back to work."

They watched him cross the lawn, then went inside.

The house was dim and quiet. The only sounds were the ticking of the mantel clock and the faint, whistling rattle of wind in the flue. The odor of lemon-scented ammonia hung in the air, fighting with the lingering stench of excrement. The doormat was missing, and a bottle of Lysol sat on the entryway table.

Teddy looked at Raina. She was pale, and her fingers were white on the crutch grips.

"Pain getting bad?"

Raina shook her head—a stiff, irritated movement. "No worse than at home. What are we looking for?"

"Honestly, I'm not sure." Teddy scanned the living room. "I think the killer was tailing me last night. He must've heard me and Berna talking. I—" Her eyes fell on the wall of family photos above the sofa—some of John, a few of Berna, most of Grayson. In the center was a framed copy of Grayson's funeral program.

There it was again, that sense of an idea just out of reach.

"I thought it might help to look around."

Raina was thumbing through a small pile of unopened mail. "Not much to go on."

"Let's do a walk-through. See what turns up."

Raina nodded and swung herself forward. Her crutch caught the edge of the living room rug. Teddy grabbed her arm.

"You need to rest. You've been overdoing it."

To Teddy's surprise, Raina didn't argue. She let Teddy help her onto the sofa. Teddy pulled the coffee table closer and shoved aside a stack of photo albums. A tall wicker basket of throw pillows and crocheted lap blankets stood next to the couch.

Teddy grabbed a pillow and laid it on the table. "Put your foot up."

"I'll help search. Just give me a minute."

"You're going to break another bone if you're not careful. Wait here." She picked up the crutches. "I'm taking these so you don't do anything stupid."

Teddy expected a fight, but Raina only nodded and said nothing.

Teddy went to the kitchen. Though Berna usually ate a full breakfast and left the house before dawn, the room was pristine. Teddy wasn't surprised. Great Dane owners knew better than to leave food or dirty dishes out. Everything looked untouched.

She propped the crutches against the fridge and headed down the hallway toward the bedrooms. In contrast with her clinic office, Berna's home was immaculate, furnished in the kind of mass-produced modern style popular in the middle of the last century. Teddy always teased her that her house looked like the set of a 1950s sitcom. She hoped this one had a happy ending.

She stepped into the master bedroom. It was as tidy as the rest of the place, though the bedspread was slightly rucked up, and short gray hairs covered the white chenille. Dottie had either been napping on forbidden ground or searching for her missing owner.

The walls were bare except for a single neat row of framed photographs opposite the bed—Grayson's school portraits, arranged in order from kindergarten through ninth grade. The row was off-center. Berna had left space for the last three high school photos that should've hung there.

Something stirred again in Teddy's mind. Grayson had been a stocky, serious-eyed boy with a habit of keeping his chin tucked and his mouth taut. In the first few portraits, he wore a look she'd seen in her own early photographs—the look of a child braced for something painful. By the third grade, the guarded watchfulness had started to lift. That was the year his father died.

John Robles had been a hard man—controlling and jealous. Berna had met him shortly after moving to Stone Creek. He was from Oklahoma, an accountant at the John Deere plant. They were both new to town, both lonely, and neither deterred by the local prejudice against interracial couples.

He'd seemed kind. But after Grayson was born, John's true nature emerged. He'd been passed over for promotion twice, and he was envious of the way Berna's veterinary practice had taken off. He never crossed the line into physical abuse—as far as Teddy knew. But he took out his frustrations in a string of petty cruelties and infidelities that left his wife and son perpetually on edge. Berna had been planning to leave him when a sudden heart attack at forty solved the problem. His death was a shock—to her and to Grayson—but also a relief.

Teddy gazed into Grayson's five-year-old face—the dark, sad eyes. The uncertain grin showing two neat rows of baby teeth. The photographer had probably told him to smile, and this wobbly effort was the best he could manage. So different from the goofy, grinning middle-schooler hamming it up for the camera with Mark McKissick in the snapshot from Berna's office.

Teddy moved to the head of the bed and turned to stare at the portraits.

Grayson had been gone ten years. Yet this was Berna's view from her pillow every night and every morning. Why did she torture herself like that? Why not at least center the frames? Their asymmetry must be a constant, aching reminder of what she'd lost—a heavy emptiness, hollowed by the shape of a life that should have been.

Teddy felt it once more—that elusive thought, just out of reach.

God remembers every sparrow that falls. Who am I to forget? Berna had said last night.

Every sparrow that falls. A Bible verse. The kind calligraphed on condolence cards and cross-stitched on throw pillows sold on Etsy.

A memory slid smoothly into place, like a key in a freshly oiled lock.

With a sudden, sharp exclamation, Teddy turned and rushed out of the room.

Chapter 36

In the living room, Teddy found Raina with her splinted leg propped on the coffee table. She had one of Berna's photo albums open on her lap and was staring down at it with a puzzled frown.

She glanced up as Teddy approached. "Find anything?"

"Not yet." Teddy crossed the room to the wicker basket and began digging through it with short, impatient movements.

Raina turned back to the album and flipped another page. "Why does she have all these pictures of John? Keeping Grayson's makes sense—but her slimeball husband's been dead fifteen years."

"Berna's funny about saving photos." Teddy pulled out a throw pillow, checked both sides, and dropped it. "Says she doesn't want the real John to disappear."

"Why not? You'd think she'd be glad to forget the bastard." Raina turned another page. "She's even got pictures from before she met him—with other women, for God's sake. Look."

She held up the album. Teddy glanced over. A tall, broad-shouldered teenager with wavy brown hair stared back at her. Teddy recognized him immediately. Even in high school, John Robles had had the same cocky, petulant smile. He was dressed in a red-and-gold football uniform, his helmet under one arm, the other slung casually around a girl gazing up at him with adoring eyes.

"Homecoming photo." Teddy resumed digging, tugging a knitted blanket from the basket.

"You can tell the guy was a jerk even then," Raina said. She watched Teddy for a moment. "What are you doing?"

"Looking for something." Teddy pulled out another pillow.

"I can see that. Looking for what?"

"Berna used to have this cushion with writing on it." Teddy was bent over the basket, her voice muffled. "Lena Hadley made it for her, I think—after Grayson died." She tossed aside another blanket and straightened, frowning at the mess.

"Why do you need it?"

"Something Berna said last night. Been bugging me all day." Teddy dropped down on the sofa beside Raina. "Where is the damn thing?"

Raina tossed the album onto the coffee table, still open. "What now?"

"I don't know." Teddy dropped her head back and stared at the ceiling fan, watching its slow, hypnotic spin. A thought hovered just out of reach—shapeless and insistent.

"Let's go find your student," Raina said. "See if he overheard any of Chase's phone call in the bowling alley."

Teddy exhaled. "Yeah. Okay."

Raina scratched under her splint. "Where are my crutches?"

"Kitchen. I'll get them."

When Teddy returned a moment later, Raina's foot was off the coffee table. She was sitting up, holding the pillow she'd used to elevate her leg.

"This what you were looking for?"

Blue needlepoint letters ran across the cushion's front—"Matthew 10.29: *God knows every sparrow that falls*." Above the words, a cross-stitched bird hovered in mid-air, its small brown wings outspread.

Teddy sat down and took the pillow, resting it on her knees. She stared at it, then read the verse aloud.

"What is it?" Raina asked.

Teddy pulled out her phone and began scrolling fast. "Crap, where is it?"

"What?"

"That note you found by Chase's body. Do you have the photo?"

Raina pulled it up and handed her the phone. Teddy zoomed in.

"That's it. Last night, Berna mentioned the sparrow that falls. I knew it reminded me of something."

She dropped Raina's phone in her lap and began typing rapidly on her own.

"What are you talking about?" Raina asked.

Teddy didn't answer. She hit "search." As the results began to load, her screen lit up with a call—Shane. She sent it to voicemail and kept scrolling. A moment later, she found the site she wanted and tapped on the link.

As she began to read, a text popped up: *CALL ME ASAP.*

She stared at it for a second. Probably something about her dad. Whatever it was, it could wait.

She read quickly, then handed the phone to Raina, who stared at the screen.

"Another Bible verse?"

"*Look.*" Teddy held the phones side by side.

Raina frowned. "I don't get it."

"There never was a *Matthew*—Chase didn't sign this."

"It's his handwriting."

"But that's not his signature. Inez was right—people don't ask for help in suicide notes. We've been looking at it wrong. We kept asking how the killer made him write it. We should've been asking—" Teddy stopped.

She was looking at Berna's photo album, still open on the coffee table. She hadn't really paid attention before, but now she stared at the forty-year-old snapshot—two teenagers with their whole lives ahead of them. John Robles in his football uniform, his arm around a pretty blonde girl in a sleeveless blue dress. In her right hand, a bouquet of bronze chrysanthemums. Something glinted in the sunlight.

Teddy pulled the album onto her knees. "Oh my God."

Her thoughts reeled. A pattern was forming, its pieces clicking into place. She ran through the last few days, replayed conversations, expressions. Testing the theory. Did the timeline work? Yes, maybe. But how to prove it?

She peeled the photograph from beneath the plastic page cover.

"Come on," she said. "We've got to go. I know who the killer is—I'll explain on the way."

◆ ◆ ◆

Back outside, Teddy scanned the property. No sign of Rick Castillo. His blue pickup was gone. She helped Raina into the truck, then climbed behind the wheel, already dialing.

The call went through to a computerized menu and routed her to the office she wanted. Voicemail. Teddy hung up, cursing, and threw the gearshift into reverse.

As they pulled onto the road, Raina said, "Where are we going? You gonna tell me what the hell's going on?"

Teddy floored the accelerator, fastening her seatbelt with one hand. "That photo of John Robles—it all fits."

She launched into a breathless explanation, her words clipped by adrenaline. Wind buffeted the truck, and she gripped the steering wheel, wrestling to stay in the lane. By the time they reached Colonel Priddy Avenue, she'd finished.

Raina was quiet for a beat. "Jesus. Are you sure?" She sounded shaken. "Even if that's true, it doesn't prove murder. It's all circumstantial."

"Forget proof," Teddy said, turning right toward town. "When people panic, they do crazy things. We have to stop this before anyone else gets hurt."

They sped along an empty stretch of road beside a field of winter wheat, the wind ruffling its surface like ripples on a pale green lake. Up ahead, the culvert over the Buffalo Wallow came into view. Something lay near the shoulder—metallic and out of place.

Teddy slammed on the brakes.

The truck fishtailed and stopped.

Raina leaned forward. "Is that—?"

But Teddy was already out of the truck, running.

A bicycle lay on its side. The handlebars were twisted, one pedal half buried in gravel. A thin layer of red dust coated the frame.

Teddy reached for her phone—and swore. She'd left it in the truck.

She crossed the road and shaded her eyes, squinting into the blowing dust as she scanned the water. The Wallow was empty. She called out, but the wind swallowed her voice.

She grabbed the bike and ran it back to the truck, heaving it into the bed beside Raina's crutches before jumping into the cab.

"It's Julia's," she said, snatching her phone and hitting speed dial. "No sign of her."

She listened as the phone rang, then went to voicemail.

"Alan, call me—Julia's missing again."

Harsh, but no time to soften it. Where the hell was he? Most likely at a job site, his phone tossed in the glovebox—as usual.

Why hadn't the school called? She glanced at the clock. Julia's lunch hour. They probably hadn't yet noticed she was gone. She hadn't ridden her bike to school; she must have walked home to get it. But why?

"She wouldn't just leave her bike," Raina said.

"Unless someone took her."

Teddy's phone rang—Shane again. She answered mid-ring and said, "Whatever Grandpa did, it can wait. Have you heard from Julia?"

She listened as Shane rattled off an explanation in a voice shaky with suppressed panic. By the time he finished, Teddy's skin had gone clammy. Her shirt clung to her back.

"What is it?" Raina asked.

"Shane's at the greenhouse. Julia showed up there on foot maybe half an hour ago. She asked for the pistol he keeps in his truck." Teddy pushed back her hair. Her hand shook. "She told him I'd given up on the case. Said she was going to take care of it herself—that she knew where to start."

"He just let her go?"

"He was the only one working—he had customers. He didn't give her the gun, but he couldn't follow her. He's been trying to call me and Alan ever since."

Raina shifted, wincing with pain. "She told him she knew where to start? What does that mean? Why would she come to the Wallow?"

A gust of wind shook the truck. Teddy stared at the road ahead—empty, dead straight, dissolving into the brown murk.

"She was Cody's girlfriend. She's been questioned by police. Maybe she was lured here."

Raina met her eyes. "You think the killer's tying up loose ends." It wasn't a question. "Where would they go?"

Teddy tried to swallow. A knot of fear was rising in her throat. Normally, she was steady in a crisis. Alan was the one who fell apart. But now her mind felt heavy, sluggish—her thoughts sodden with panic.

She gripped the wheel but didn't move. Her pulse was hammering. She could feel it in her teeth. She couldn't breathe, couldn't make her body respond.

"Ted—what are you thinking?"

"I don't know, I don't know . . ." Silver motes wheeled in front of Teddy's eyes. She was going to pass out.

Raina reached over to touch her arm but hesitated, settling instead on the console between them. "Okay," she said. "Let's think it through. Sounds like Julia had a plan. Maybe the killer met her here—took her somewhere."

"But where?" Teddy looked around wildly. "There's so much land . . . so many places to hide a—" She stopped. She couldn't think it, couldn't say it.

"Julia's a smart girl. She wouldn't let someone just take her," Raina said.

"What are you talking about? Smart girls get taken all the time—you know that."

"She's got her phone, right? Maybe she—" Raina broke off, watching Teddy's face. "What? What is it?"

"Her phone." Teddy blinked at Raina, then down at the screen in her hand. The phone.

Her fingers fumbled, stiff with fear, as she searched for the app. There. There it was.

"What are you doing?"

"Julia's phone got drowned in the Wallow Tuesday," Teddy said. "I gave her my old one. But after that stunt she pulled, I installed this."

She tapped the screen and angled it toward Raina.

"FindMyKids?"

They both leaned in.

"There it is—north of town." Raina said. "Looks like it's off-road."

But Teddy had already tossed her phone in Raina's lap and thrown the truck into gear. "I know where they are. Let's go."

The wind howled over the scrubland, hurling tumbleweeds through the air as Teddy sped across the cattle guard and onto the Loudermilk Ranch. The sky had darkened to an umber gloom. Behind a smothering veil of dust, the pale disc of the sun was sinking toward the Callahan Divide. Teddy switched on her headlights.

The dirt track was rougher than she remembered. Beside her, Raina grunted at every jolt. Now that they were off the blacktop, the windshield quickly caked with a rust-colored film. Teddy hit the washer fluid. When she switched on the wipers, red rivulets streaked the glass like blood.

She was relieved when they reached the old military service road—cracked and weedy, but paved. Just as she was starting to wonder if she'd missed the silo, a dark smudge took shape in the haze. She slowed. A dozen yards later, the access port came into view.

The metal door was propped open. An empty vehicle stood nearby.

"Where are they?" Raina asked. "There's no service in the silo. They've got to be topside."

Teddy scanned the area. Something glinted in the dust near the concrete pad. She cut the engine and got out.

Julia's phone lay face down in the gravel. Teddy picked it up. The case was cracked, the screen streaked with red dust. Her fingertips tingled, then went numb. She carried it back to the truck.

"It's Julia's," she said, leaning in and tossing it on the dash. "I think she dropped it on purpose. I'm going in."

"You should wait for backup. They're on their way," Raina said.

"I'm not waiting."

Teddy popped the glovebox. She pulled out her flashlight and, after a second's hesitation, her revolver.

Raina eyed her. "You can't shoot down there. Bullet would ricochet all over the place."

"A gun's persuasive—even if you don't fire."

"I'm coming, too. Get my crutches."

"You're too slow. Besides, there's a thousand concrete stairs. Want to break your other leg?"

Teddy checked the cylinder, then shoved the revolver into the pocket of her fleece.

Anger and frustration played across Raina's face—resolving into resignation. She slammed her fist against the door and slumped back.

"What about your claustrophobia?"

"I've been down there twice this week. I'll be fine." Teddy reached for the handle. "You've got your service pistol. Stay here. If something happens to me, the killer might—"

"Nobody's gonna escape," Raina said.

Teddy nodded and jumped out.

She crossed to the access port and hesitated, then forced herself over the threshold.

A blast of cold air struck her like a slap—fusty, reeking of mold. She shivered and pulled out her flashlight. When she clicked it on, it cast a feeble yellow glow, weaker than a child's nightlight. It barely illuminated her boots.

"You've got to be kidding me," she muttered, frustrated with herself. She'd been meaning to change the batteries for two days. A stupid lapse—the kind that got people killed.

Tossing the flashlight aside, Teddy took out her phone and opened the flashlight app.

A sharp white beam sliced through the dark, throwing long, distorted shadows up the walls. But the space swallowed the light almost instantly. Beyond a few steps, the stairwell vanished into blackness.

Outside the access port, the wind shrieked. Teddy checked the phone's battery. Fifteen percent. She hesitated—but there was no help for it.

She took a breath, squared her shoulders, and stepped into the dark.

She'd thought she might be better prepared this time. But without proper light and other people to distract her, the silo felt more terrifying than before. Her senses had sharpened to a painful edge.

The deeper she went, the more keenly she felt the burden of earth above her—the vast, immovable silence pressing down. She moved in a shrinking bubble of light. The sound of the wind had vanished. Her own breath roared in her ears. Thin air currents whispered like ghosts through invisible ventilation shafts above her head.

Where was Julia? Somewhere down here in the dark—afraid. Teddy wanted to call out. But the silence felt absolute, like breath held by the earth itself. Her voice might shatter it—might bring the whole place down. A slow, soft implosion into nothing.

By the time she reached the little vestibule outside the launch control room, she was shaking. Her fingers had gone numb—from cold or nerves, or both.

The work lights inside the room were off. As she passed the open doorway, she shivered with something primal, a pressure in the air that made her skin hum.

She stepped quickly aside and swung her phone toward the black opening.

"Hello?" Her voice scraped out in a hoarse croak. "Anyone there?"

She waited. The silence pulsed. Then a soft sound, like an intake of breath. Or was it just the movement of air in the passage?

"Julia?" she whispered. "Are you there?"

Nothing answered but her own echo, thin and distant.

That didn't mean the place was unoccupied. Julia might be in there, bound and gagged. Teddy couldn't risk missing her in the dark—or giving someone the chance to circle behind her. She had to clear the room.

She reached for her gun and stepped inside.

After a minute's fumbling, she located the work light and groped for the switch. White light flooded the room, blinding her. She tensed for an attack, but nothing happened.

When her eyes adjusted, she saw that the room was empty.

Chase had only been dead four days, but already the place had an abandoned feel. The card table and the folding chairs had been shoved aside, and someone had begun half-heartedly packing up the equipment. Partially filled cardboard boxes dotted the room.

Teddy rifled through them. Batteries in every size—but no flashlights.

She felt an unreasonable surge of misplaced annoyance at Chase, followed by a twinge of guilt. It wasn't his fault she'd tossed her flashlight. Rookie mistake.

She considered grabbing batteries, running back upstairs, retrieving the flashlight. She checked her phone—nine percent. She did the math in her head. The smart move would be to go back.

But no. Reascending that dark, whispering stairwell would cost her fifteen minutes she didn't have.

She ducked out of the room and turned left, heading deeper into the silo.

On her previous trips, she'd followed Ramirez and hadn't paid much attention to where she was going. Now, she was surprised to find that the way wasn't as clear-cut as she thought. She passed several unmarked steel doors that branched off what appeared to be the main passage—doors she didn't remember. Most were closed, but a few stood ajar, opening onto equipment rooms and other, narrower corridors and stairwells.

With each door she passed, fresh doubt gripped her. Julia could be behind any of them—injured, afraid. Should she turn aside? Search every tunnel?

Her gut said no. The killer would return to the main missile chamber—where it all began.

But what if she was wrong? Had she already passed the one door that mattered?

Second-guessing wouldn't help. She didn't have time—or battery—to search this place right. All she could do was keep going.

The air grew colder, damper. Teddy's sense of being watched intensified with each step. After fifteen minutes of slow descent down narrow stairwells and along rust-streaked corridors, she was shaking with cold. Surely it hadn't taken this long to reach the water before.

She was about to turn back when the stairs leveled out beneath her. A small lobby opened ahead, dimly lit by her screen. A sign hung on the wall: "DANGER: AUTHORIZED PERSONNEL ONLY," just above the black mouth of a corrugated metal tunnel.

Finally—something familiar.

At that moment, her phone died.

For a few seconds, Teddy was plunged into a darkness so profound that she could almost feel it brushing against her skin. She held her hand in front of her face—nothing. Not even a dim silhouette.

Panic bloomed. Her mouth went dry, her pulse drumming in her throat. She closed her eyes and took a few slow breaths.

The tunnel lay straight ahead—she knew that much. It led to the main missile chamber. She dropped the dead phone in her pocket and took a step, waving her hands in front of her like a blindfolded child.

After a few paces, her fingertips brushed cold concrete. She edged forward, groping her way, until the texture shifted and she felt the smooth ridges of corrugated steel beneath her palms.

She advanced cautiously, shuffling, her hand skimming the wall, until she sensed a change in the air. A faint glow shimmered in the darkness ahead.

She stopped. Was it an illusion?

But as she moved forward, the glow sharpened. Pale light was spilling through the tunnel's far end.

Teddy took another step—then froze.

From the open space beyond came the sounds of water lapping against concrete, the intermittent *plink* of condensation falling from a great height. And then—beneath it all—a voice reverberating in the vast, hollow space, familiar and terrifying.

"You don't have to do this. I won't tell."

Julia.

Chapter 37

Teddy's jaw tightened. Her teeth ached with the pressure. She steadied herself against the wall and slipped her hand into the pocket of her fleece. The gun was there, solid and reassuring. She drew it and inched forward.

A gust of icy air struck her face. She emerged from the entry shaft into the cavernous missile chamber and stood on the metal balcony, hidden in shadow. The concrete walls of the silo loomed around her, towering into the darkness.

Thirty feet below, the water lay like a disc of black glass, polished and hard.

The dive platform floated on its surface. A single halogen work lamp lit it like an empty stage in a darkened theater.

Not quite empty.

Julia stood in the center, shoulders hunched, hugging herself and shivering. Her plaid skirt and navy sweater were rumpled. Her windblown hair glowed dull chestnut-red in the light. She was turning slowly, like the fixed leg of a compass, to face the man pacing in a circle around her.

Red dust streaked his clothes. He moved erratically, one hand tugging at his dark hair. In the other, something flashed—a large hunting knife. He was mumbling, eyes down, not looking at Julia.

But she was watching him.

It was Mark McKissick.

The balcony seemed to shift beneath Teddy's feet. Time skewed and slipped sideways to the day of Henry's accident. She was back in the imaging suite, watching through glass as his small body slid into the bore of the MRI scanner. She'd been there and not there—present but powerless, like a ghost.

She felt the same way now.

A thread of cold sweat traced her ribs. Her fingers tightened on the gun.

"You don't have to do this," Julia said again. "You can still walk away. Nobody knows."

McKissick stopped pacing. "You know. Berna knows. It's over. The best I can hope for is a little time . . ."

"I can give you that," Julia said quickly. "Mexico's not far. I won't tell my mom till tomorrow, I swear. Berna can't talk. Just leave me here and go."

He didn't seem to hear. He began moving again, his steps jerky and uneven. His face was slick with sweat or tears. He'd shed his jacket and rolled up his sleeves, as if bracing for something messy and unpleasant. The jacket lay crumpled near the dive ladder.

"This is all wrong," he muttered. "It wasn't supposed to go like this." He slashed the air with the knife, sweeping it in a broad arc that passed too close to Julia's face. She flinched and stepped back.

Teddy held her breath and gripped the railing with her free hand.

"How was it supposed to go?" Julia asked.

McKissick stopped. His knife hand dipped. "It was about justice—making sure Chase got what he deserved. Doing to him what he should've done to himself a long time ago."

Julia's fingers dug into her arms. "I don't get it."

"No, you wouldn't," he said bitterly. "Imagine facing the person who wrecked your life—knowing you're supposed to forgive. Knowing they walked free while your world stayed broken."

"I don't have to imagine." Julia's voice wavered. "I loved Cody. You promised to help him, and you killed him."

McKissick flinched. The knife dangled at his side. "That's different. I didn't plan to kill him. I took him home to give him money, so he could get across the border." His gaze drifted toward the water, unfocused. "But then he saw something."

"Saw what?"

"A photograph that gave me away." McKissick was breathing hard, the knife hand twitching in a jittery, aimless rhythm. "He looked at me—and I could tell. He knew. I had no choice."

Julia shook her head. "That's bullshit. You did have a choice. You always did." She stepped closer, and the light caught her face. "You still do."

He stared at her, blinking.

On the balcony, a muscle spasmed in Teddy's right arm. She rested the gun on the rail and bent down, sighting along the barrel.

She had a clean shot. But Julia was so close. Raina was right—a bullet could ricochet in this place—go anywhere.

Below, the silence held. Teddy's heart wasn't pounding anymore. It had gone quiet, waiting.

McKissick began to pace again, the knife now reversed in his fist—the blade jutting down, ready to strike.

"What are you talking about? There's no choice." His voice was low and tight. He stabbed the air, fending off the thought.

"You're a pastor," Julia said. "You know the choices. Right or wrong. Good or evil."

He shook his head, not looking at her. "It's not that simple. You'll understand that in a few years."

"You're only saying that to make yourself feel better—like this is some big spiritual mystery. But any preschooler would get it. You had to choose between saving Cody or yourself, and you chose yourself." Her voice cut sharper. "Cody was a person—he had a life. You took all that away because you wouldn't man up and pay for what you did. How is that justice?"

Something caught in Teddy's throat—panic or pride, she couldn't tell. *Don't push him, Julia,* she thought. But even through the fear, a quieter part of herself stood back, watching. Where had this kid come from—this child speaking with a woman's voice? Scared but steady. Holding her ground.

McKissick stopped by the work light.

"It's not that simple," he said again. "What's the right choice now? What am I supposed to do with you?"

"Kinda late to be asking that, don't you think?" Julia said. "You lured me to the Wallow to kill me. Why didn't you? Why'd you bring me here?"

He hesitated. "After you do something terrible, your mind plays tricks. You get paranoid. I heard the police questioned you, and I thought—" He shook his head, the knife tapping softly against the work light's metal stand. "But when I saw you at the Wallow, I lost my nerve . . ." He trailed off, and when he spoke again, his voice was quiet, dreamlike. "This has to end."

He seized the tripod and angled the light downward. The beam swept the platform, settling on a dark, ragged stain a few feet from where the inflatable dinghy lay moored.

"Blood cries out. It has to be answered for. But it was a mistake. I hope Chase forgives me. I just wanted the universe to make sense. I wanted my brother's life to mean something." His voice caught. "What do I do now?"

Crouched behind the balcony railing, Teddy held still, not daring to shift her weight.

McKissick looked and sounded like a man on the brink—swaying toward the edge, flirting with a fall. He gripped the knife, his knuckles bloodless.

He turned slowly to Julia. The light shone obliquely on his face, shadows pooling in the eye sockets, beneath the cheekbones.

"I can't go to prison. I can't. There's only one way out. But I'm afraid. Eternity—how am I supposed to face that now?" He looked down at the knife, as if surprised to find it still in his hand. "I don't want to hurt anyone. But what else is there?"

He took a step toward her—halting, uncertain—as if the thought had moved his body before his mind had decided to follow.

Julia's chin lifted. She squared her shoulders. "For God's sakes, if you're gonna kill me, just do it and get it over with. Don't make me listen while you talk yourself into it."

McKissick paused, nodded, took another step.

Teddy moved without thinking. She rose and raised the gun in one fluid motion, but the barrel struck the metal railing, the sound reverberating through the silo like a gong.

Both Julia and McKissick started and turned. For one suspended second, his eyes locked on Teddy's. He teetered on the balls of his feet, not sure what to do or where to go.

Then he spun around and lunged toward the edge of the platform.

By the time Teddy reached the top of the stairs, he was already yanking at the dinghy's mooring line.

"Stop!" she shouted.

But McKissick didn't look back. He shoved off hard and dropped into the boat. The dinghy rocked wildly, then drifted into the dark.

Teddy rushed down the swaying staircase. Julia, so steady before, had folded onto the platform, arms wrapped around her knees, face buried in the crook of her arm.

Teddy dropped beside her. "Are you hurt?"

Julia looked up, shaking and pale with shock. "N-no."

Teddy let out a long breath and kissed her hair. Then she stood, moved to the work light, and swept it across the water.

The dinghy floated near the center of the silo, its polyurethane sides white against the water's inky surface. McKissick sat on the bench, motionless. The paddle lay across his lap, pinned in place by his forearms. His hands hung loosely between his knees, out of sight.

She couldn't see the knife.

"Come back to the platform, Mark," she called. "You can't sit out there forever."

He said nothing.

"Don't make this harder than it has to be. There's no way out."

He murmured something she couldn't catch.

"What?"

"That's not true."

His voice was faint, edged with a weary finality that Teddy didn't like. Something was wrong. He was too still.

"Where's the knife, Mark? Did you drop it?"

He raised his head. His face was pale, eyes shadowed and dull. He looked exhausted.

"Show me your hands," Teddy said.

For a moment, he didn't move. Then, elbows on knees, he slowly raised his forearms.

Teddy sucked in a breath. "Oh God. What did you do?"

Blood dripped steadily from a gash on his left wrist. His right hand held the knife.

"You need medical attention, Mark."

She turned to Julia, who had gotten to her feet and was standing beside her, arms rigid and teeth chattering.

"There's probably a first-aid kit in the launch control room. Go, Jules—hurry."

Julia didn't move. "He doesn't deserve help."

"Don't let him choose how this ends." Teddy stopped. "Dammit—we don't have a flashlight."

Julia's expression didn't change. But, after a beat, she said, "He's got one."

She picked up McKissick's jacket, felt the pockets, and pulled out a keychain flashlight no bigger than a roll of Lifesavers. It looked absurdly inadequate for the job, but she ran up the stairs without hesitation and vanished into the tunnel.

Teddy turned back. McKissick was staring at his arm. He licked his lips. "I flinched. Missed the big vein. It'll take a while." His eyes closed.

He'd only been out there a few minutes, but already he seemed close to collapse. It wasn't just blood loss. The adrenaline was gone, and hopelessness was settling over him like a fog.

"Mark, listen," she said. "That cut might be shallow, but you could go into shock. If you pass out, it might be a long time before we can reach you. Do you understand? I need you to row closer."

McKissick didn't answer or open his eyes.

Teddy stepped to the platform's edge, squinting at the dinghy. Twenty, maybe twenty-five feet. Could she swim it? The water would be freezing. She'd cramp immediately, and hypothermia would start to set in. She couldn't take her gun. She'd be helpless in the water with an armed murderer above her. A tactically untenable situation.

Her mind raced. Backup was coming. If she could stall—keep him conscious . . .

"Mark, you're getting weaker. Come back to the platform."

"Doesn't matter anymore," he murmured.

Teddy cupped a hand behind her ear. "I can't hear you." What could she say to reach him? Was there any bargaining chip—anything left to offer? "Don't you want to explain what happened, Mark? Face God with a clear conscience?"

He raised his head. His eyes fluttered open. "Confess?"

Teddy nodded. "There's still time. You need to say it, and I want to understand. Come closer—please—so we can talk."

He glanced over the side of the boat. "I won't let you arrest me. I want to die in water, like my brother."

"I won't arrest you. Just come closer—so we don't have to shout."

McKissick hesitated and looked over his shoulder at the balcony. Seeing no one, he laid the knife on the bench and picked up the paddle.

Moving as if underwater, he brought the dinghy to within six feet of the platform. He was sweating heavily, his movements slack and clumsy.

Teddy scanned the boat. A puddle of blood the size of a dinner plate had formed between his feet. Not a fatal amount—yet. But the bleeding hadn't slowed.

She slipped off her fleece and tossed it into the dinghy. "Wrap your wrist, Mark—it'll buy you time."

He didn't move. "There's time enough."

Teddy waited. He was quiet. Then—

"I thought I was so careful. How'd you figure it out?" There was a dull curiosity in his voice.

His teeth were chattering now. The puddle of blood was growing, spreading around his feet.

"Bunch of little things, really," Teddy said. "Chase's head wound, for starters. He was shot through the teeth. Suicides don't do that. And the ammo in the gun wasn't his. There was the fresh mistletoe in his truck bed. Then that note—with the Bible citation:

'Matthew, chapter twelve.' The unforgivable sin. You tore the word 'chapter' in half, so it looked like Chase's signature." She paused. "But I didn't connect any of it to you till today."

"Was it the charm bracelet?"

Teddy nodded. "I saw a photo at Berna's—her late husband, back in high school. The girl he's with is wearing that bracelet. She was your mother, wasn't she? I recognized her from the picture you showed me at the hospital. If that bracelet was hers, who else but you could've dropped it?"

McKissick let out a long sigh that might have been relief, or disappointment, or both. "Ah. My own mother gives me away. It's like a Greek tragedy." He picked up the knife, turning it in his hand. "I know that picture. I've got the original. My mother must've sent John a copy. I never knew that."

"John Robles was your father?"

McKissick nodded slowly. "I never met him. Didn't even know his name till after he died. He gave her that bracelet. It was all she had from him—other than me."

"Cody found it by Chase's body."

"It was always in my pocket. I didn't realize I'd dropped it till the next day."

"We found a sketch of it in Chase's room—wrapped as a gift. Was it for you?"

A flicker of pain crossed his face. "Must've been. I wouldn't take his money. He said he'd find some other way to thank me."

"Thank you for what?"

"Counseling him. He saw the photo in my office. Asked who she was."

"Then why?" Teddy asked. "You were helping him. Why would you kill him?"

McKissick ran his thumb along the bleeding gash on his wrist.

"Chase wasn't what he seemed." He gestured toward the black water. "Everything's like that. Land. People. The past. Scratch the surface, and there's always something darker below. We all pretend not to know it's there—a weird kind of shared delusion. But nothing stays buried forever. Sooner or later, it erupts. And no one ever sees it coming." He looked up. "You know what that's like, don't you?"

Teddy ignored the question. "Police are on their way, Mark. Just tell me what happened."

He said nothing, staring into the water. His face glistened with sweat, but he was shivering.

Teddy was conscious of the steady, snare-drum beat of the blood falling from his wrist, pinging off the floor of the dinghy. She glanced at the balcony. What was taking Julia so long? Maybe there wasn't a first-aid kit. Maybe she'd taken a wrong turn, gotten lost in the maze of corridors.

Teddy took a breath. The air felt cold and thin. "Mark, the bleeding's worse. You need to wrap that wrist—or come over here and let me do it."

"Forget it." He raised his knife hand, rubbing his eyes with the back of his wrist. "I want to explain. But I don't know where to start."

Teddy glanced at the balcony again.

"Start from the beginning."

"In the beginning . . ." McKissick's voice had gone soft and distant. "It started with a mistake. Funny how just one can ripple out and wreck so many lives. Ever notice that? Two kids from Oklahoma fool around one night nearly forty years ago—and Agamemnon's dead."

Teddy blinked. "Agamemnon?"

He gave a faint, almost embarrassed smile. "It's from a poem. About consequences, among other things. Grayson's gone. And

Chase. Cody Puckett. Maybe Berna, too." He swayed a little, as if struggling to follow his own thoughts. "So many points where history could've shifted. One tiny change, that's all it would've taken . . ." He lifted a pale hand, then let it fall. "But maybe we were always going to end up here."

Teddy fought back a surge of impatience. "Let's stick to facts."

McKissick nodded. "John Robles knocked up my mother, then dumped her and left—there's a fact. Just a high school fling for him. I wonder if he ever thought of us at all."

He paused to cough—dry, hoarse—and then went on.

It hadn't been easy, growing up fatherless in the shadow of his mother's overdose. He'd felt abandoned. Alone. His grandmother had done her best, but she was struggling, too.

"All I needed was someone to care," he said. "Every kid needs that. It's why I became a pastor."

He was in seminary when his grandmother died. While cleaning out her house, he found a box of his mother's things in the attic.

A diary. A charm bracelet. A photo of her with a boy in a football jersey.

"That diary's how I found out his name," McKissick said. "He went to U of O on a scholarship. When she told him she was pregnant, he ghosted her—as the kids say."

McKissick had tracked down John Robles on Facebook. Dead. Too late to ask questions, to make anything right.

But he'd left behind a widow. And a son.

Mark looked up at Teddy. His hair was wet with sweat and plastered to his forehead. His mouth made sticky, smacking noises when he spoke.

"For the first time, I wasn't just somebody's mistake. I had a brother. Flesh and blood. Do you understand what that meant?"

"Is that why you came to Stone Creek?" Teddy asked.

He nodded. "Right after seminary. I wanted to be near Grayson. Get to know him." His voice rasped, the words catching like sand in his throat. "I'm so thirsty. Do you have anything to drink?"

"You're sitting on a few million gallons of fresh groundwater."

McKissick stared as the idea registered, then leaned over the dinghy's side and scooped handfuls of cold water into his mouth.

He sat up and wiped his face with his shirt. His lips were tinged blue. Shock was setting in. Organ failure and unconsciousness wouldn't be far behind.

"Better?" Teddy asked.

He nodded. "Water's a weird thing—symbolic of life and death."

"Stay focused. Grayson—how old was he when you came here?"

"Twelve." McKissick's voice was thick. "Tough age for a boy with no dad. Believe me, I know. He needed a role model. Berna let me in, made me part of the family."

"Did you tell them who you were?"

He shook his head.

"Why not?"

He stared at his arm, caught a drop of blood, rolled it between his fingers.

"Didn't want them to think I'd been stalking them. Longer I waited, the harder it got."

"So Berna still doesn't know you're her stepson?"

McKissick looked up, his eyes glassy—pupils large. "What's the point of telling her now?"

He was fading. The knife had slipped from his grasp. He sagged against the gunnel, and his eyes closed.

Teddy glanced toward the balcony, uneasy. Still no Julia.

She turned back to McKissick. "Mark. Stay with me." She clapped sharply.

He opened his eyes. "I think I fell asleep."

"You have to keep talking. You were telling me about Grayson."

With an effort, he dipped his hand over the side again, splashing his face. "I only had three years with him. Happiest of my life."

The memory seemed to steady him. He straightened a little and continued.

Grayson had died in what the police called a freak accident. The flooded quarry was off-limits to kids at Camp Wildwood.

"Counselors drilled it into them with safety talks and horror stories, but you know teenagers—they always think they're immortal." McKissick's hand tightened on his knees, and he added in a whisper: "I couldn't believe it. I felt cursed. Every family member I'd ever had was gone. Just—*poof*." He tried to snap his fingers but couldn't make them work.

"I'm surprised you stuck around," Teddy said. "I'd want to get as far away as I could."

"I wasn't lying this morning. Berna's been like a mother to me. We got each other through it." He swallowed thickly. "Anyway, I love it here. There's something about West Texas—I don't know. Feels like home."

His eyes drifted shut.

"Mark."

He stirred.

"Tell me what happened after."

He nodded, the movement slow and heavy. "Work helped. Took my mind off things. I threw myself into ministry. Took the college chaplain job. Set up the campus Bible study."

"Students started coming to you for counseling?"

"Yeah. I'm not really trained—just a couple basic courses in seminary. But I cared. I listened. That goes a long way." He paused, rubbing his eyes with the heels of his hands. When he dropped them, his voice was lower. "Then a few weeks ago, Chase showed up for the study. Quiet kid, a little sad. Didn't say much at first.

But after the second meeting, he handed me a note—said he was in trouble. Scared he'd committed an unforgivable sin."

McKissick's head bobbed. He went still.

"Mark, wake up!" Teddy clanged her gun against the work light's metal tripod.

He jolted, flinging out an arm. It struck the paddle, which spun, clattered, and shot out of the boat. He made a weak grab for it, but it hit the water with a splash and skated across the surface, drifting to a stop fifteen feet away.

He eyed it dully, as if struggling with a math problem he couldn't quite solve.

"If you're thinking of swimming for it, don't," Teddy said. "Here."

She pulled up the yellow mooring line tied to the cinderblock near her feet and tossed it toward him. The loose end landed in the dinghy with a wet slap, sending up a spray of blood.

"Tie that to the D-ring. I'll pull you in."

McKissick gazed dumbly at the rope but didn't move.

Teddy needed to keep him talking. "Chase thought he'd committed some unforgivable sin?" she prompted. "What'd you make of that?"

"I knew he'd been in the military. Thought maybe something happened during deployment that was haunting him. He didn't want to meet on campus—afraid other kids would see him. So we met at my home office."

His voice was almost inaudible. Teddy leaned in.

"At our third session, he gave me a paper bag with a pistol inside. Unloaded. Asked if I'd keep it a while. He'd been having suicidal thoughts. Said he'd done something terrible years ago, and he couldn't live with the guilt. He coped with alcohol for a long time."

He paused, struggling for breath.

"Couple years ago, Chase got sober and came home. Thought it'd be good for him—a fresh start."

McKissick looked up at Teddy, hollow-eyed. "Instead, everything crumbled. He and his dad were fighting. Someone was leaning on him, pushing him to do something illegal. He was drowning again. But he was too scared to tell anyone. Thought he'd go to prison because of this unforgivable sin."

McKissick swallowed hard and grimaced. "I told him the only unforgivable sin is the one you never confess. That he'd never be free till he faced it. But for over a month . . . he couldn't do it. I was at my wits' end.

"Then about three weeks ago, Chase came into the office. His dad had given him an ultimatum, and he'd decided to transfer schools—get far away. He wanted his gun back.

"That worried me." McKissick said. "He seemed determined. Calmer. Almost peaceful. Less depressed. But you can't outrun the past. It doesn't work. I was afraid of what he might do. So I made a deal with him."

He paused. His hands dangled loosely over his knees.

"What kind of deal?"

"We played cards. I've got a fishbowl of index cards in my office. They say things like *Something that makes me sad* or *What I fear most.* Prompts to help people open up. I told Chase if he'd draw a card and do whatever it said, I'd give him his gun and send him off with my blessing. I just wanted to keep him talking."

A flicker of memory surfaced—the pink index card, fluttering from a textbook.

"*One true thing*," Teddy said.

"You found it?"

"In his backpack."

"I looked," McKissick whispered. "Must've missed it."

"That's what made him confess?"

"He just needed a little push." McKissick pressed his lips together. "Turns out, he was right, though. What he did was unforgivable."

Chapter 38

McKissick stopped speaking and swayed on the dinghy's bench. In the work lamp's harsh glow, his skin was mottled a sickly blue-white, slick with sweat.

"You should drink some more, Mark. Keep your blood pressure up," Teddy said.

She expected him to ignore her, but he nodded and leaned over the dinghy's side. Blood from his wrist ran in a thin rivulet down the gunnel and dripped into the water as he drank.

A shift in the air drew Teddy's attention—a faint stir, the animal sense of being watched.

She turned. Julia stood on the balcony, breathing hard. Her face was flushed. She held up a small green case and pointed from herself to the platform.

Teddy glanced back at the boat. McKissick had finished drinking and was struggling to sit upright. She wasn't sure how he'd react when he saw Julia—but she couldn't worry about that now.

She nodded and waved Julia forward, then turned back to McKissick.

He was sitting up, drying his face with his shirt. He looked steadier. The water had helped. But the amount of blood on the dinghy floor told her he didn't have long.

Teddy shivered. "Well, Mark? You said it yourself—the unconfessed sin can't be forgiven. What did Chase tell you that made you think he deserved to die?"

McKissick closed his eyes and exhaled. His breath smoked in the frigid air.

"Yes, all right," he said. "It'll be a relief to say it."

A long, metallic creak echoed through the silo. Teddy looked up.

Julia stood frozen on the third step, eyes wide.

McKissick twisted on the bench and saw her. "No!" His voice was surprisingly strong.

Julia didn't move. "Sorry, Mom."

"Hurry with that kit," Teddy called. "He's bleeding out."

McKissick's gaze snapped back to her. "If she takes one more step, you won't get another word out of me. I won't be treated, and I won't be arrested."

Teddy hesitated, arguing with herself. Chase, Cody, and Berna deserved justice. McKissick should have to face an earthly judge—in addition to whatever waited for him on the other side.

On the other hand, even with the kit, there might not be much she could do. She wasn't a medic, and he'd lost a lot of blood.

But he was still a human being, wasn't he? Whatever he'd done, she owed him a duty of care. The kit might have a space blanket, hard candies—something to keep him going until help arrived.

And yet . . . if someone was truly determined to escape their life, you couldn't stop them. No matter what you gave or offered, they slipped through your hands. She'd learned that lesson repeatedly—with her mother, with Curtis, with Alan.

She couldn't bring in the boat without McKissick's cooperation. If he was set on dying, she should at least get the truth.

Teddy drew a breath. "Okay, Mark, you win. She'll stay where she is."

McKissick nodded—barely. His shoulders slumped, spent from the effort of protest.

Teddy looked to Julia. Her expression didn't change, but a faint crease had formed between her brows, and her mouth was set. Teddy wasn't sure if she would obey. But after a moment, she turned and climbed slowly back to the balcony, the kit still in her hand.

Teddy watched her go, then turned back to McKissick.

"All right, Mark. Tell me what happened with Chase."

Chase sat on the overstuffed sofa in McKissick's home office, tracing the edges of the pink index card with his fingers. McKissick waited. The young man's dark-blond hair hung down, hiding his eyes. The scent of woodsmoke drifted through the open window. On the wall, the clock ticked loudly.

"I killed someone," Chase whispered finally.

McKissick's heart was pounding. He sent up a silent prayer for guidance. "In combat?"

Chase shook his head. "Ten years ago. I was fifteen."

His voice was low and halting as he told the story. Every year, he used to go to Camp Wildwood, down in the Hill Country, with other kids from the area. He and a few other boys had snuck out of their cabins one night to go swimming.

"There was a limestone quarry full of groundwater a mile from the camp. The counselors used to take us canoeing and swimming there. But the cliffs were strictly off-limits. They were around thirty feet high, and some of the high school guys liked sneaking out at night to go cliff jumping. But it was dumb. There were submerged boulders, especially near the edge. You had to get a running start to clear them. If you jumped from the wrong spot, or didn't get out far enough . . ." He shook his head.

"I'm scared of heights, so I always made excuses not to go." He looked up, and for a moment his expression lightened. "That's what I love about scuba diving. You can float over these really deep places, look straight down into canyons, even—but you can't fall. It's like flying."

The smile faded, and he continued. The other guys he hung around with used to give him a hard time every year because he wouldn't dive. They were all from Stone Creek—Frankie Aguilar, Shane Spivey, and Grayson Robles. Chase didn't live in town, and he was homeschooled, so he was always the odd man out. They let him tag along, but he never quite fit in.

"That summer, though, I wasn't hanging out with them as much," Chase said. "I had a huge crush on this girl—the camp director's daughter, Mandy Wescott. She had this long red hair. Really gorgeous."

He smiled faintly. "Mandy could've gone out with anyone, but she was fooling around with me. Nothing serious—just making out. Kids' stuff. She said we had to keep it quiet because her folks would freak. She wasn't supposed to date till she turned sixteen. I thought I was seriously in love."

He looked down at the index card again. "The other guys wanted to go cliff jumping all week. But it was really windy. Too dangerous. That Friday, though, it was calm. They were pumped. At mess hall, they started bragging in front of the girls. The girls were calling them idiots, but they were acting all impressed—you know how girls do. Frankie and Shane were playing it up, making it sound even crazier than it was. Mandy asked if I was going. So of course I said yes."

He swallowed, then went on.

"Around two a.m., we snuck out of our cabins. There was a full moon—plenty of light. The cliffs looked huge. Bigger than I remembered. The guys were amping each other up, daring each other. Frankie and Shane were teasing me, saying if I didn't jump they'd tell the whole camp." Chase fidgeted with the card, folding it in half, then opening it again and holding it in front of him with both hands, like a prayer book.

"They jumped right away. I could hear them down in the water, horsing around. But Grayson knew I was scared. He stayed back with me. He was a sweet guy. Just trying to help."

Chase squeezed his eyes shut and blew out a breath.

"We were standing a few feet from the edge, looking down. The moon glinted off the ripples, like they were tipped in silver. So pretty. I remember thinking how much I'd like to sketch it. But jumping scared the shit out of me.

"I told Grayson I changed my mind. I asked him to go back to camp with me. He said he couldn't. He'd been making out with this girl all week, and she said she'd go to third base with him if he jumped. I asked who, but he wouldn't say. She didn't want it getting around. She'd been seeing some other guy—some loser she was planning to dump. That's when I got a bad feeling. I asked him flat-out if it was Mandy. And from the look on his face, I knew.

"We got in a fight—one of those stupid high school fights that nine times out of ten blows over in a couple days. Grayson swore he didn't know I was the other guy. He actually apologized—meant it, too. But I was raw. All the emotions—all that fear building all day.

"I said, 'If you're really sorry, forget the damn jump. Let's both go back.'"

Chase dropped the notecard and pressed his hands to his temples, like his head hurt. "If he'd just said 'okay,' none of it would've happened. All he had to do was say 'okay.'"

The room was quiet. A dog barked in the distance.

McKissick cleared his throat. "Grayson refused?"

Chase opened his eyes. "Not really. He just . . . hesitated. That's all it took." He clenched his fists and ground them against his knees. "Everything's a blur, after that. Grayson was standing with his back to the cliff. I ran up, and I just—" Chase put up his hands, palms out, and mimed a push. "He went over backward. The look on his face—I dream about it every night, unless I'm drunk."

He stared at his hands. "I wasn't thinking about hurting him. I wasn't thinking anything. I'm not even sure I knew he was that close to the edge. Or maybe I've just told myself that till I believe it."

The office was silent. Even the clock seemed to have stopped. McKissick's throat ached. His heart pounded so loudly he was sure Chase could hear it. Still, he kept his expression steady and nodded for Chase to go on.

It had been dark under the trees, he said. He and Grayson had been alone on the clifftop. When the cops asked, he told them Grayson slipped while looking over the edge.

Nobody questioned that. A boy had died at the quarry in a similar way back in the seventies. Chase thought he was in the clear.

Then, a couple months later, Frankie came to him. His dad was injured, and they needed money. He wanted Chase to help him steal horses.

Chase told him forget it.

But Frankie said: *Is that how you're gonna play this? I ain't a guy you want to piss off.*

"That's when he told me." Chase's voice was flat now. "Frankie saw Grayson fall that night. Knew he fell backward. Knew I lied to the police—and he guessed why. He's held it over me, ever since. That's why I stayed away so long. After all this time, I hoped he'd let it go. Let me move on."

Chase looked up, dull-eyed. "But nothing's ever going to change for me in Stone Creek. I need out."

McKissick stopped speaking. His face was in his hands.

"Is that when you decided to kill him, Mark?" Teddy asked.

He raised his head. "Of course not—I'm not a monster. I was in shock. Two minutes earlier, all I wanted was to help this kid. Then I find out he killed my brother. I didn't know what to think."

He couldn't remember what he'd said next—something about forgiveness. The blessing of confession.

"I think I even prayed with him," he said. "Scary how easy it is to default to training. Like muscle memory."

When Chase left his office, he seemed better. Lighter. But McKissick felt like he'd been hit by a train.

His first instinct, once the initial shock wore off, was to call the police. Confidentiality didn't apply when someone confessed to a serious crime. Chase had even signed a waiver saying he understood that.

Maybe the push hadn't been premeditated—but Grayson deserved justice. The truth needed to come out.

"What changed your mind?" Teddy asked.

McKissick's hands were trembling. He stared down at the knife lying in the blood at his feet.

"Wally Ramirez is Chase's uncle. I figured he'd find some way to sweep it under the rug. And there was Berna. She's said a thousand times how grateful she is that Grayson's death was an accident."

Teddy nodded. She knew that was true. Grayson had grown up afraid of his father's temper. Berna took comfort knowing he hadn't been scared when he died—at least not of a human being. She clung to the idea that there was no villain in this tragedy. It was just one of those terrible things that happened in a random universe.

And yet . . .

"You staged Chase's suicide to spare Berna's *feelings*?"

"I know how it sounds. But I had his gun. I had his note. All I needed were the bullets. It felt like fate—God allowing me to be the instrument of vengeance."

McKissick called Chase at the bowling alley Sunday night. Chase had been offering to show him the missile silo. Was now a good time?

He was proud of that place. He didn't take much convincing.

"I told him I was out on my bike. He picked me up on 137," McKissick said. "We were lying on our backs, right where you're standing—staring up at those bomb doors. Talking about life. His hopes and dreams. He never saw it coming. I had his gun in my pocket. I pulled it out and said, 'This is for my brother.' And that was it."

Afterward, McKissick threw Chase's phone and laptop in the water so police wouldn't find their texts. Then he rode home. He must've broken off the piece of mistletoe with his bike when he lifted it out of Chase's truck.

"It was dark. I didn't see it." He let out a raspy breath. "No such thing as a perfect crime."

"Or a perfect investigation," Teddy said. "I watched you pull a twig out of your gears on Raina's porch the other day. But I didn't connect the dots. Without that bracelet, I never would've."

"If you hadn't, someone else would. Sooner or later, justice comes for us all."

McKissick stopped. Telling his story seemed to have drained the last of his strength. His head bobbed. The silo was quiet. Teddy could hear the soft lap of water against the platform.

"I'm so tired. I need to sleep, now," he murmured.

He slumped sideways onto the dinghy's floor, leaning against the gunnel and closing his eyes. He was sitting in a lake of his own blood. It wicked up his jeans and shirttail like black mold. The tie-off rope, dark with blood, lay near his left hand, the knife near his right.

"You can't sleep yet, Mark," Teddy said. "Tell me about Cody and Berna. Then you can rest."

His eyelids fluttered. He held her gaze for a moment, then nodded.

In a halting monotone, he resumed. Teddy listened, setting aside her own outrage, committing the narrative to memory. McKissick was right—it was scary how easy it was to default to training.

She kept one eye on Julia, wondering how much of the story she was picking up. There was no shielding her now. She'd never be able to unhear words like these.

When he finished, McKissick fell silent. His eyes were closed.

"You went to the hospital this morning to finish Berna off, didn't you, Mark?" Teddy asked.

He had stopped shivering. Sweat was pouring down his face. He ran a hand across his forehead, leaving long, bloody streaks.

"I couldn't get to her. I'm glad, now. Guilt's worse than grief." He paused, breathing heavily. "I never meant things to go this far. What kind of God lets me kill and doesn't lift a finger to stop it? He stopped Balaam. He stopped Saul on the road to Damascus. Where was my divine intervention?"

"Maybe you didn't get one because you already knew what was right."

"You know what terrifies me most? I still feel Him everywhere." McKissick's eyes drifted around the silo—over the walls, the water, up to the steel bomb doors concealed in shadow. "There's this psalm I used to love—'Where can I go to flee from Your presence? Even darkness is not dark to You.'"

He met Teddy's eyes. "I always took that as a comfort. Now I think it was a warning."

A metallic thump echoed above, followed by a scrape—rubber on steel. Something dragging.

McKissick inhaled sharply and froze, staring up at the balcony.

Teddy followed his gaze.

Raina stood at the mouth of the tunnel, flushed and winded, swaying on her crutches. She took one unsteady step and pitched forward.

"Julia, get her!" Teddy shouted. "She's gonna fall!"

Julia darted over, caught Raina's arm, steadied her at the rail.

"Raina, what are you doing?" Teddy said.

Raina gripped the railing, breathing fast. "I couldn't sit up there any longer. I thought maybe you got ambushed." Her eyes swept the scene below—McKissick, the dinghy, the blood. "What the hell's going on?"

"He's bleeding out. I can't get to him—he won't tie off."

"The crutches, Mom," Julia said. "You could hook the boat—pull it in."

She turned. Raina had already slipped free of one and was handing it to her.

Behind Teddy, a sharp intake of breath.

McKissick had pushed himself upright and was fumbling for the knife. "Stay away!" he gasped.

"Mark—don't," Teddy said. "Listen to me—"

They locked eyes. He shook his head.

From above, footsteps rattled on the stairs.

McKissick raised the knife—but instead of turning it on himself, he jabbed at the inflated gunnel. His hand slipped. The blade skittered sideways, slicing across his palm. He grunted, but didn't let go.

Clutching the handle with both hands, he set the point against the polyurethane and, with a surge of adrenaline, threw his weight forward—driving the blade down.

With a loud *whoosh*, the side of the dinghy nearest to the platform buckled, collapsing like a paper cup. Water rushed in, mixing with blood.

"No!" Teddy shouted.

She didn't think. The dinghy was six feet out. She backed up, ran, jumped—landing half in, half out of the boat. Her legs and feet felt instantly scalded. It took a second to register the pain as cold.

Her boots dragged her down. She scrabbled for a grip, trying not to panic.

The knife was gone. McKissick's hands were empty. He flailed as the dinghy collapsed beneath him. Teddy had trained as a lifeguard in high school. But now, just keeping herself afloat was a battle.

Behind her, Julia's voice was frantic. "Mom—grab this!"

She was at the platform's edge, reaching with the crutch. But it was too far.

Julia flung it aside and picked up the anchor line without stopping to untie it from the cinderblock. "Get the rope!"

The loose end was floating near Teddy. She slipped it over her shoulder and reached for McKissick. He struggled—but he was spent. She rolled him onto his back, looped the rope under his arms, and tied it off in a hasty knot between his shoulder blades.

Then she kicked back, pulling them both off the sinking boat. The weight of her boots and soaked clothes dragged her under.

"I've got you," Julia yelled. "Hold on!"

She was hauling them in, hand over hand.

When McKissick realized what was happening, he twisted, grabbed the rope, and, with a final burst of strength, yanked it hard. Julia stumbled forward, dropping it and windmilling her arms to keep from falling in.

The cinderblock flew off the platform and plunged into the water with a heavy splash.

A moment later, McKissick was torn from Teddy's grip—dragged under by the weight of the sinking block and the rope still knotted around him. She watched him vanish beneath the churning surface.

Teddy dove.

Her arms shot out, groping blindly. Nothing but water. Then—something brushed against her fingertips. She grabbed.

It was firm and cold, like the flesh of a fish. She realized her eyes were shut. She opened them.

She was being dragged downward, head first. The light above faded. Pressure built in her ears and lungs.

In her hand, something pale and white—McKissick's wrist. A red haze seeped between her fingers. Below her, his hair floated like sea moss. The yellow rope trailed past his feet, still tied to the cinderblock, now vanished into the dark below.

A sharp pain stabbed Teddy's ears. She tried to kick toward the surface. The glow of the work lamp had shrunk to a pinprick. She hung suspended in icy blackness. Only the pressure in her skull and the closing darkness told her she was still sinking.

Her chest burned, the breath tightening, rising.

She looked up. Something flashed in the water above—like silver light glancing off distant glass. Her head reeled, and fiery dots swam across her vision. The silver thing seemed just overhead, but when she reached for it, she realized it was far away—at the surface, receding fast.

She kicked, struggling to rise, but the silver object kept shrinking.

Teddy looked down. She was still clutching McKissick's arm. He was looking up at her now. In the fading light, his white face was fixed and rigid with terror.

The weight of the cinderblock had already dragged the rope down to his waist. He was clutching it with his free hand, like a man holding up loose trousers.

He only had to let go. He'd be free. They both would.

"Drop it, drop it," Teddy mouthed.

McKissick stared back. If he understood, he gave no sign.

Teddy looked up again. The light had shrunk even more—collapsing inward like a dying star. The wreckage of the dinghy hovered far above, dark as a storm cloud against the shimmering surface.

Her chest spasmed. The pressure in her ears was unbearable.

She looked back down. A curtain of bubbles poured from McKissick's mouth.

Teddy had no choice. If she didn't let go, she would die.

With an enormous effort, she forced her fingers open. McKissick slipped from her grasp.

His white face was still upturned. As he felt her release him, his mouth rounded into an astonished O. She met his shocked eyes and watched as he slipped away, vanishing into darkness.

Nothing remained but a thin ribbon of bubbles rising from the deep.

Teddy looked up. The silver object was still there—but now it seemed fathoms above her. With the last of her strength, she kicked off her boots and clawed toward the surface. Her lungs were bursting. The water felt like quicksand.

But she was rising. The light was growing, spreading. The silver object seemed to be coming at her, like a spear thrown in slow motion. As she drew closer, she saw it clearly. The aluminum crutch.

She reached out. Her fingers brushed metal. She grabbed it. For a second, it gave—then steadied, pulling her upward. The light grew. Finally, her head broke the surface, and she was gasping air in ragged sobs.

Someone was shouting. "Mom! Mom! Hang on—don't let go!"

Her body bumped against something solid, and hands grabbed her wrists. Julia was trying to pull her up, but Teddy was too heavy.

Then came shouting. Men's voices. The rattle of feet on metal stairs. More hands, large and warm, hauling her out.

Her limbs felt like lead as she collapsed onto the platform. Someone covered her with a crinkly emergency blanket. There were shouts, echoes. Lights in her eyes.

"Put her on her side," someone ordered.

Teddy was rolled over. She vomited water, and then the light was shrinking again, and the voices faded to a muffled hum. She closed her eyes.

And as she slipped into unconsciousness, she saw Mark McKissick's white, terrified face sliding into the abyss.

Chapter 39

It was one of those warm, humid December days that happen frequently in West Texas. Through the laundry room door, Bing Crosby was crooning about a white Christmas as Teddy stood in the open garage, struggling with the clamps on the family ping-pong table. She wrestled the thin green net into place, then stood up, gasping for air.

Three weeks had passed since she'd been pulled from the waters of Deadhorse Missile Silo. Her lungs still weren't right. She'd aspirated water, then developed pneumonia. But all things considered, it could've been worse.

She whistled for Jabba the Mutt, who was snoring under the table. He scrambled out and followed her inside. The music grew louder—the Temptations now, singing "Silent Night." Next up would probably be "Grandma Got Run Over by a Reindeer," or maybe something by Ariana Grande. The holiday soundtrack was a Grand Compromise—a confused mishmash of everyone's favorites, Lyric's included.

The last thing Teddy had ever imagined for post-divorce life was having to negotiate a Spotify playlist with her ex-husband's fiancée. But it was a small price to pay for domestic harmony.

Lyric was in the kitchen, humming along tunelessly as she pulled something from the oven.

“What’s that?” Teddy asked, washing her hands.

“Pineapple upside-down cake—my grandma’s recipe.” Lyric beamed as she set the pan on the cooling rack. “Baking puts me in a Christmas mood.”

Teddy dried her hands and pulled out her keys. “Smells amazing.”

“Are you going to Berna’s?” Lyric took off her oven mitts, unconsciously straightening her new diamond ring. “I made her a pound cake.” She handed Teddy a foil-wrapped brick.

“That’s really thoughtful. Thanks.”

Teddy found Alan, Julia, and Henry in the family room. Alan was wrestling with a tangled strand of lights while the kids lounged at either end of the sofa, watching some low-budget Hallmark movie.

Henry wasn’t hiding beneath his hoodie, for once. The swelling from his last surgery had finally subsided, and with it, some of his self-consciousness.

Teddy tousled his hair. “Ping-pong table’s ready, bud.”

“Yes!” He jumped up and slid into a pair of camo-colored Crocs. “Play with me?”

“After dinner. But Julia will play now. Right, Jules?”

Julia rolled her eyes but clicked off the TV without protest and followed her brother out of the room. Her gait was steady and slow, the childish exuberance gone.

She’d been quieter since the silo—less irritable, her sharp edges softened into something more yielding. But a muted sadness had settled over her, like ash after a wildfire. She was easier to parent now—a relief in some ways. But Teddy couldn’t help missing the girl who flared hot, even when caution might’ve served her better. That fire hadn’t gone out, she knew. It was folding inward, being tempered by grief into something steadier, more controlled. Teddy remembered the feeling—how her own early pain had hardened into something that held. But the crucible left scars. That, too, was part of growing up. Still, it hurt to watch.

Teddy sighed and looked at Alan, who dropped the lights and picked up the longneck by his chair. "Where are you going? Thought you were helping with this tree."

"You're lights. The kids and me are ornaments. That's the deal. I won't be long."

"I'll walk you out."

He followed her across the lawn to her truck.

She opened the door and tossed the pound cake onto the passenger seat. "That's quite the rock you gave Lyric."

"I'm trying to do things right this time, Ted."

"Good. I'm glad." She smiled. "Y'all set a date?"

"Lyric wants to finish school first."

"Then why the rush with the ring? Staking your claim before she starts rubbing shoulders with all those cute young Future Chiropractors of America?"

Alan blushed. "Is that so wrong?"

Teddy laughed, then started coughing. She used her inhaler as she slid behind the wheel. "I'm gonna sit with Berna a while. Maybe check on Dad. Shane's arrest really got to him."

"Inviting him for Christmas?"

"Not this year. I need a break." She stuck the key in the ignition. "But I feel guilty."

"Hey. You give your dad way more than he deserves. You always have."

Teddy blinked, then started the truck. "Thanks, Alan."

She stopped at the Skinny's for a six-pack of Lone Star. When she got to Berna's, she pulled a small, wrapped object from the console, then grabbed the beer and cake.

She found Berna on the back patio, watching the sun drop toward the barn's peaked roofline. A knitted throw lay across her shoulders despite the warm weather, and Dottie the Great Dane was snoring at her feet.

Berna looked thinner, the bones in her face more pronounced. Faint bruising still shadowed her throat. She'd been home three days. The attack had caused nerve damage, and after her hospital stay, she'd spent ten days in inpatient rehab.

Teddy stooped to hug her. "How you doing, lady?"

"Tired of sitting around." Berna's voice rasped now, like a four-pack-a-day smoker. The cartilage in her neck had been crushed. "But I'm glad to be here."

"Amen, sister." Teddy dropped into a rocker, uncapped a Lone Star, and handed it over.

"I'm not supposed to drink yet."

"Me, neither. I won't tell your doctor if you won't tell mine." They clinked bottles. "Merry Christmas."

Teddy took a sip, then waved her beer in a loose gesture that took in the pastures, paddock, and barn. "Place looks great. Hope you're not overdoing it."

"It's all Rick. He's been pulling double-duty here, plus carrying the full clinic load. Made an amazing casserole last night—says he'll do his grandmother's Christmas tamales if I promise to take it easy."

"Maybe he's flirting." Teddy grinned.

Berna snorted and rubbed Dottie's belly with her foot. "I'm not who he's after."

Teddy let that go, and they sipped their beers in silence. The sun had turned a deep golden-red and was nearly gone behind the barn when Berna pulled the blanket tighter around her shoulders.

"Any change in the silo situation?"

"No," Teddy said slowly. "The body may be down there a while. The case is closed, and Mark's got no family to kick up a fuss. The Rangers' divers are tied up with some investigation in the Gulf. Said they'd come after New Year's."

Berna took a drink. "I loved Mark like a son."

"He loved you, too."

"Funny way of showing it." Berna squinted toward the sunset, watching a jet carve a glowing contrail across the sky. "Tell me what happened down there, Ted. I'm ready."

"You sure? Once it's in your brain . . ."

"I'm a big girl. I want to know."

Teddy stared at her longneck, turning it in her hand. "Okay. But stop me if it gets too much."

In a low, steady voice, she told her what McKissick had done—and why.

She paused. "Sorry, Berna. I know it meant a lot to you for Grayson's death to be accidental."

"Better a hard truth than a comfortable lie," Berna said. She let out a long breath. "Mark wanted revenge for his brother. It's wrong, but I get it. Killing that poor Puckett boy, though? Trying to kill me . . ." Her hand drifted to her throat.

"Mark was in panic mode by then. A wild animal in a trap, snapping at everything."

"That's no excuse."

"No. But once you've killed someone, it gets easier, I think. Becomes an option. The Loudermilks told him Cody knew something and was talking to police. Mark was terrified.

"On his way home that afternoon, he ran into Cody on Route 137. Divine intervention, he thought. Cody spilled everything. He was scared we'd charge him with Chase's murder. He was heading for Mexico with nothing but the clothes on his back. Mark didn't want him talking to us again. He was afraid Cody had seen something else—some missing piece he didn't even know he had."

"That's why he killed him?"

Teddy shook her head. "He took him home, meaning to give him clothes and money. But at the house, Cody saw that photo of

John with Mark's mother—the same one in your album. He spotted the charm bracelet, put two and two together. Mark panicked."

Berna gave a sharp, derisive snort. "Strangling someone's not like squeezing a trigger. Takes five minutes, sometimes more. That's a long time to think about what you're doing. And then to dump that poor boy like trash—"

"He meant to stage it as another suicide," Teddy said. "But then that storm hit. He had a corpse in the house. Roads were washing out. Tornado warnings everywhere. He freaked—threw the body in his hatchback and started driving."

Teddy's bottle was slick with condensation. She dried it against her jeans. "He got the idea to dump Cody in the Wallow, hoping the flood would suck him through the culvert and down to the Concho. He planted a pack of Stan's Marlboros to throw us off."

"Mark didn't stop at the Skinny's to buy smokes in the middle of that storm," Berna said. "Doesn't that prove premeditation?"

"More like serendipity. Before Chase died, Stan was trying to quit. He was gonna throw out his cigarettes—but you know Inez. Wastefulness is a sin. She gave them to Mark."

"Was he supposed to hand 'em out for Sunday School prizes?"

Teddy's chuckle turned into a cough. "He didn't know what to do with them. That's why they were still in his car."

Cody's murder had been an amateur job—sloppy, rushed. But it had forced Ramirez to call in the sheriff's investigator. And Rummler had jumped to all the wrong conclusions.

"If Mark had stopped there, he might've gotten away with everything," Teddy said. "But he couldn't leave well enough alone."

Cody had told him he was seeing Julia. McKissick started worrying. She was the daughter of one of the detectives. What did she know? What did her mother know? The questions were eating him alive.

"When Inez told him I'd been down in the silo for hours with the Rangers, he got even more rattled. Then the church secretary heard on her police scanner that Julia was causing a scene at the Skinny's and I was on my way. Mark couldn't wait for the other shoe to drop. He had to know what was happening.

"He rode over, but we were already gone. So he went to the station. No particular plan—just hoping to learn something useful. Being a pastor gets you into a lot of places without raising suspicion.

"He got there as I was leaving. I'd just interviewed Frankie. Mark followed me to the bowling alley, which convinced him I was onto him." Teddy sighed. "That was his state of mind when he followed me to your clinic."

Berna took a long breath but said nothing.

"Your window was open," Teddy said. "Mark was eavesdropping. He heard you tell me how close he was to Grayson—how they were like brothers."

"That's why he attacked me?"

"He thought you knew his secret. He was in fight-or-flight mode, out of control." Teddy took a long drink. "No stranger could've snuck up on you in that gravel lot. I knew it had to be someone you felt safe with. We briefly suspected Rick. But Mark never crossed my mind."

"Wonder why he didn't stay to finish the job."

"Like you said—takes time to strangle someone. Cody was just some kid to him. But Mark loved you."

Dottie sat up and laid her chin on Berna's knee. Berna scratched her ears.

"I might've died if Rick hadn't found me."

"Or if the ICU in San Angelo was a little more lax," Teddy added. "Mark's whole world was crumbling. You might have woken up and remembered who attacked you. Julia might know something. He couldn't get to you—so he went after her. He sent her an anonymous text. Told her to meet him at the Wallow."

Teddy's neck prickled. She shivered.

Berna stirred. "He was going to kill her, too?"

"That was the plan."

"Why didn't he?"

"Conscience, I guess. Couldn't work himself up to it," Teddy said. "But he couldn't let her go, either. So he took her to the silo—where it all started. Buying time. Maybe he thought it'd be easier to kill her in a place he'd killed before. Or maybe he just wanted to go back to where he lost himself, and let the end find him there."

Berna was quiet for a moment. "How'd they get in?"

"The Chief forgot to lock up after the Rangers' dive, believe it or not."

"Simple as that?"

"Simple as that."

Teddy looked over. Tears were rolling down Berna's face. She made no effort to wipe them away.

"I'm so sorry," Teddy said. "I know it feels like losing another son. I tried to save him. I tried."

Chapter 40

The silence hung in the air between them, broken at last by the rasping bark of a gray fox in the field beyond the barn.

Eventually, Berna sniffled and wiped her cheeks. "Oh, stop it, Ted." She reached over and gave Teddy's arm a brisk squeeze. "If you'd saved Mark, I'd have to see him in court. He might've changed his story. The whole thing could've dragged out for years. This way, I can feel angry and sad—and I can let him go." She shrugged. "Besides, I could've lost you, too. You nearly drowned."

"I would have, if it weren't for Jules. And Raina, with her crutches."

"Think things'll be better between you two now?"

Teddy thought back to their last conversation. After recovering from pneumonia, she'd gone by Raina's house. Raina was in her armchair, leg propped on the ottoman. She was unusually quiet. The hard edge of her anger had dissolved, replaced with a mild melancholy that somehow felt worse.

They'd talked for a few minutes about the case. As Teddy stood to go, she'd ventured, "Maybe I could come by tomorrow, take you out for a shake? You must be going stir-crazy."

Raina had stared out the window. Finally, she shook her head. "I can't do it. I understand why you shot Terrence, Ted. And I forgive you—I really do. But I can't be your friend. It's just too hard."

Now Teddy leaned back in Berna's rocker. The sun was gone, the barn a black silhouette against the evening sky. From the trees, a mockingbird started to sing.

"Things are better with Raina," she said finally. "But they'll never be the same."

Berna shifted. Her chair creaked. "Some things can't be fixed. Doesn't mean you did anything wrong."

They fell silent, watching the evening stars prick to life one by one against a deep cobalt sky.

Teddy drained her beer and checked the time. "Better get back. I promised Henry I'd play ping-pong—and then he's got his heart set on a Monopoly marathon." She made a face.

Berna laughed. "Fast-track to childhood trauma. Grayson loved that game, but it always ended in tears."

"No kidding." Teddy stood. "I almost forgot—I have something for you."

She reached into her pocket and pulled out an object the size of a baseball, swaddled in a tea towel. She handed it to Berna, who unwrapped it. In the light from the window, she stared at the white stone in her hand, puzzled.

"Mark threw that in the silo after he killed Chase," Teddy said. "A tribute, I guess. The divers found it. It's limestone from the quarry where Grayson died. There's a vial of his ashes inside—the one you gave Mark. I asked the Rangers if we could get it back. It belongs here with you, not sitting in the State Crime Lab."

A small sob escaped Berna's throat. She covered her mouth with one hand, nodding but saying nothing.

Teddy nodded back and rested a hand on her thin shoulder. "See you tomorrow," she said.

◆ ◆ ◆

The sky was black and spangled with stars by the time Teddy turned into her own gravel drive. Through the open garage door, she could see Julia, Henry, Lyric, and Alan playing an erratic game of doubles ping-pong while the dogs ran in circles, barking and chasing missed balls.

As she neared the barn, she wondered if the kids had remembered to feed the animals. She parked beneath the flickering pole light and killed the engine.

Inside, all was well. The stalls had been passably cleaned and the mangers filled. Goats, pigs, and donkey were bedded down for the night.

She was about to switch off the lights and close the barn door when a pair of bright beams swept across the lawn. A vehicle turned into the drive—a blue Ford F-150, dusty and mud-caked.

Teddy's mouth went dry. She smoothed her hair.

The sound of the engine died, and Rick Castillo jumped out. He wore army-green coveralls, torn at the knees and neatly patched. They were streaked with mud and manure.

Teddy hadn't seen him since the investigation ended, but she'd been thinking about him—more than she cared to admit.

He grabbed a straw Stetson from the dashboard and put it on, then took it off again, fidgeting with the brim as he approached.

"Hey," he said.

It was too dark to see his face clearly, but he seemed nervous.

"Hey."

"How you doing? Heard you were sick."

"Better, thanks."

"That's good." Rick cleared his throat. "Thought about stopping by a few times, but figured you'd probably be . . . I don't know." He hunched his shoulders and went quiet, nudging the toe of his boot against the ground. The silence gathered weight.

"That's okay. What's up?" Teddy asked finally.

Rick licked his lips. "Want to show you something."

He put the hat back on and turned. Teddy followed him to the rear of his pickup. He opened the tailgate.

A thick layer of straw covered the truck bed. On it lay a sorrel-colored foal. It was tiny, emaciated—dull-eyed and matted with grass awns. Its forelegs extended stiffly in front of its body; they seemed bent at unnatural angles.

Teddy looked at Rick. "What's this?"

"Jacky Tozier called me out. Colt was born a couple weeks back with contracted tendons. Happens sometimes. That's why it's such a little runt of a thing. Can't walk, can't stand up to nurse. Knuckles over on its fetlocks when it tries." He gently turned one of the colt's forelegs into the light. "See? All tore up."

A large open wound covered the joint just above the hoof.

Teddy stooped for a closer look and caught the strong, sour-sweet odor of infection. She held out her hand. The foal nuzzled her palm, then latched onto her fingers and suckled with surprising vigor.

"Poor thing's starved," she said.

"Miracle he's alive. Little guy's a fighter. Jacky wanted me to put him down. I asked if I could have him." Rick shuffled and cleared his throat. "I thought—I wondered if your daughter . . . I mean, sometimes all it takes is a little TLC—" He stopped when he saw Teddy's face. "Maybe it was a dumb idea."

"No, it wasn't. But . . ." She hesitated. "What are his chances? Realistically, I mean. Julia just lost Fancy. I don't want her to get attached and then lose him, too."

"I got a daughter. I get it." Rick ran a hand over the back of his neck. "I won't lie—it's a gamble," he said finally. "But I reckon the odds are pretty good. I can help you make braces, and there's meds that'll loosen the tendons. But the main thing's physical therapy."

He hunched his shoulders. "Be a lot of work. Those wounds'll need cleaning and wrapping every couple days. She'd have to bottle-feed him, massage his legs, do exercises. But I can show her how."

From the open garage came laughter and gleeful screams, punctuated by a dog's manic bark. The ping-pong game was wrapping up.

"Mom, are you coming?" Henry yelled. "Hurry up so we can eat and play Monopoly!"

"Give me a couple minutes," Teddy called back.

She looked at Rick.

"I'll wait here if you want to ask her," he said.

Teddy was surprised to feel tears stinging her eyes. "I don't need to ask. Pull up to the barn—help me get him inside."

Rick's shoulders relaxed. In the semi-darkness, his teeth flashed white in his grime-streaked face.

When they had the little colt bedded down in Fancy's stall, Rick treated and wrapped its wounded fetlocks and gave it a couple shots, then rattled off a string of complicated instructions.

"I'll never remember all that," Teddy said as they walked back to his truck.

Rick was fidgeting. He seemed unsure what to do with his hands. "I can come by tomorrow and go over it again, or write it out in an email, if that's easier. Or, uh—" He paused, suddenly noticing a blotch of mud on his sleeve and scraping at it with his thumbnail as if grateful for a reason not to meet her eyes. "Or I could maybe tell you again over dinner, sometime. I mean—if that would help."

Teddy was caught off guard. She tried to read his expression, but his face was lost in shadow.

She glanced toward the house. Alan and Lyric had gone inside. Henry was playing tug-of-war with Jabba, while Julia crawled under the ping-pong table, gathering stray balls into a paper bag.

Teddy turned back to Rick. "Don't email. Come by tomorrow, if you can. Julia'll want to hear this for herself." A beat. "But—" she added, a little nervously, "I wouldn't mind dinner. After the holidays, maybe."

Rick pushed up the brim of his Stetson and gave her a quick, tentative smile—there and then gone. "Yeah? After the holidays. Great." He brushed bits of straw off the tailgate, then shut it. "See you tomorrow." He climbed into his pickup.

The truck roared to life. Teddy watched it go, her eyes on the taillights until they winked and vanished over the hill.

A cool, dry breeze drifted from the north, carrying the scents of woodsmoke and sage. Teddy shivered.

Time to go in.

She switched off the pole light and stood for a moment, watching the winter stars glitter above the tree line. Somewhere in the pasture, a killdeer was crying its name—a high, lonely wail that floated over the stubbled fields.

Across the lawn, the Christmas tree lights twinkled in the window, warm against the night. Teddy waited until her eyes adjusted. Then, with the familiar darkness settling behind her, she walked slowly up the tree-lined path toward home.

To my many dear friends and to my family—thank you for your emotional support, insight, and belief in me.

Finally, I want to thank my daughter, Emily, who helps me in many practical ways, and whose companionship, wisdom, and courage continue to inspire me.

ACKNOWLEDGEMENTS

From first draft to final page, this book came together with the support and guidance of people I'm incredibly fortunate to thank here.

Once again, I owe a heartfelt thank-you to my agent, Marilia Savvides, for her steadfast support and dedication at every stage of the process. I'm also thankful to my editors, Vic Haslam and Hannah Shaw at Thomas & Mercer, and to editor Laura Gerrard, whose perceptive guidance during revisions made the book stronger.

I'm especially grateful to my writing group—Al Haley, Dr. Debbie J. Williams, Dr. Steven T. Moore, and Dr. Shelly Sanders—for their chapter-by-chapter feedback, encouragement, and friendship over many, many years.

Special thanks to Joyce Haley, whose suggestion to include a missile silo added a key layer to the story; and to Arlene Kasselman at Seven and One Books in Abilene for her support of West Texas writers.

For their practical advice and logistical support, I'm thankful to Dr. Steven T. Moore, Dr. Greg Straughn, Dr. Cole Bennett, and Dr. Rachael Milligan. I'm also indebted to retired Houston Detective Bob Delony for generously sharing his expertise over coffee.

ABOUT THE AUTHOR

Photo © 2023 by Matt Maxwell

Sherry Rankin grew up in New Jersey and has taught creative writing and literature in West Texas since 1997. After winning the Crime Writers' Association's Debut Dagger award and being shortlisted for the Daniel Goldsmith First Novel Prize in 2017 (for an as-yet-unpublished novel), she went on to be shortlisted in the Margery Allingham Short Mystery Competition in 2019.

Sherry has a daughter in New Mexico and enjoys gardening and walking her dogs.

The Dark Below is her second novel; her first, *The Killing Plains*, was published in 2025.

Follow the Author on Amazon

If you enjoyed this book, follow Sherry Rankin on Amazon to be notified when the author releases a new book!

To do this, please follow these instructions:

Desktop:

1) Search for the author's name on Amazon or in the Amazon App.
2) Click on the author's name to arrive on their Amazon page.
3) Click the "Follow" button.

Mobile and Tablet:

1) Search for the author's name on Amazon or in the Amazon App.
2) Click on one of the author's books.
3) Click on the author's name to arrive on their Amazon page.
4) Click the "Follow" button.

Kindle eReader and Kindle App:

If you enjoyed this book on a Kindle eReader or in the Kindle App, you will find the author "Follow" button after the last page.